SON O...

"A good ... ...ical fantasy."
—*Science Fiction Chronicle*

"A veritable *Braveheart* buffet for the Scottish fan.
The plot is energetic and the characters likeable.
The details of everyday life are excellent."
—*KLIATT*

"A stand-out novel."
—*The Historical Novels Review*

**Don't miss the second volume in the thrilling
Summons of the Sword series . . .**

OUTLAW SWORD

And coming in July 2003, in trade paperback . . .

SWORD OF KING JAMES

Both available from Ace Books

SON OF
THE SWORD

J. ARDIAN LEE

ACE BOOKS, NEW YORK

SON OF THE SWORD

An Ace Book / published by arrangement with
the author

PRINTING HISTORY
Ace trade paperback edition / July 2001
Ace mass-market edition / February 2003

Copyright © 2001 by Julianne Lee.
Cover art by Paul Robinson.
Cover design by Judy Murello.

Visit our website at
www.penguinputnam.com
Check out the ACE Science Fiction & Fantasy newsletter!

ISBN: 0-441-01050-4

ACE®
Ace Books are published by The Berkley Publishing Group,
a division of Penguin Putnam Inc.,
375 Hudson Street, New York, New York 10014.
ACE and the "A" design
are trademarks belonging to Penguin Putnam Inc.

PRINTED IN THE UNITED STATES OF AMERICA

10 9 8 7 6 5 4 3 2 1

For
Alan Ross Bedford, Sr.,
my first and best role model

ACKNOWLEDGMENTS

Thank you to the following, for all your support, moral and otherwise: Jersey Conspirators Keith DeCandido, Marina Frants, Laura Anne Gilman, Sue Stiefel, Donna Dietrich, Ashley McConnell, Doris Egan, Cleindori, Karen Jones, and Margie Maggiulli; swordmaster F. Braun McAsh; fight consultants Rev. HyeonSik Hong, Sam Alden, Cecily M. McMahan, and Aaron Anderson; Ernie O'Dell and the Green River Writers of Louisville, Kentucky; Gaelic language instructor John Ross; the sweet and helpful ladies of the Ft. William, Scotland, Public Library; native guides Gail Montrose and Duncan MacFarlane of Glenfinnan, Scotland; High Hallack Research Library, Murfreesboro, Tennessee; Teri McLaren; Susan Bowmer; Trisha Mundy; Diana Diaz; Sue Wolven; Jenni Bohn; Candy Gaskin; Dale Lee; and especially Ginjer Buchanan, editor extraordinaire.

PROLOGUE

The aristocratic voice of the red-coated English Captain droned as he read the order of eviction, words snapping one after another in his hurry to say them. His precise enunciation never faltered. Sinann Eire watched from the cover of high branches in a nearby tree, as aghast as those whose belongings were being loaded into the wooden cart.

Ending in a perfunctory monotone, the Englishman then refolded the document and stuffed it into his coat pocket. He sat straight as a ramrod and spurred his light sorrel gelding to the other side of the cart, riding as if he had been born in the saddle. More Redcoats, each with a musket slung over his back and a sword at his side, scurried to and fro, methodical as ants. It was a misty day, and though patches of blue sky were visible, there were showers along the southern ridge and low clouds hugged granite crags that jutted on either side of the tiny glen.

A black and white sheepdog barked and danced around the yard at a safe distance while young Alasdair, the father of the displaced family, railed under his breath in venomous Gaelic against the English monsters. His wife, Sarah, urged him to be still. She herded their three small children into a cluster behind her and took the youngest onto her hip, but though she tried to draw her husband away from the soldiers, he shook her off. Her voice went shrill with desperation. Sinann, too, could see blood in Alasdair's eye and knew the wife had no hope of calming her husband. The faerie longed to fly down there, but if she let anyone see her it would only make matters worse, witch-hunts being what they were. In her rage she jumped and shook the branch that held her weight. Nobody below noticed the tree rustling in a nonexistent breeze.

One dragoon, carrying a long bundle, ducked out of the door of the low, thatched peat house. Alasdair gasped and swore, his already ruddy cheeks darkening to feverish red. He made a move to intervene, but Sarah held him back, her fingers digging deep into his arm. In the soldier's hands, wrapped in a ragged old Great Kilt, was the ancient claymore sword handed down through five generations of fathers and sons. Alasdair's eyes followed the dirty and crumbling *feileadh mór,* from which protruded the two-handed grip decorated in Celtic knot design and straight double quillons, as the dragoon offered the gigantic sword to his superior.

"Lookit what I found, buried in a corner."

The Captain grunted. "In the cart." He gazed about, satisfied with the find. "There's one less sword to kill our men." He said it as if he'd single-handedly saved untold English lives.

The dragoon set the weapon in with the other household goods: wooden bowls, linen clothes and sheets, iron pots and utensils, sacks of wheat and oats, wool, flax, a plow, a harness, a sickle, stools, a wooden table, bedding, and the small family Bible in the English of King James I.

Sinann was the only one who saw the look of hopelessness cross the Scot's face at sight of the Bible, and she understood he had decided to die rather than watch the English take everything. She emitted a long, loud cry of despair, which nobody heard for she'd hidden the sound of herself from the mortals, as well as sight of her. Tears sprung to her eyes, as she remembered her dear Donnchadh, who had died horribly not so long ago at the hands of this very *Sassunach.*

Alasdair shook himself loose from his wife, lunged at the Captain, and caught the blood-red coat in his fists. The officer's hat flew from his head and landed on the sod behind.

He cried out and kicked at his assailant. The Scot, his nose bloodied, kept hold and tried to pull the Englishman from his horse. The animal whickered and backed away, but the young man followed. The officer kicked again, swore, then called to his men.

"Get the bloody bastard off!"

The nearest dragoon, lips pressed together, hauled back with the butt of his musket and knocked Alasdair sideways. Sarah screamed and set the baby down with his brothers. The children cried, more at their mother's terror than any real understanding of what was happening. Undaunted, the Scot pursued the retreating horse and attempted another hold on the officer, who hauled back in the saddle as far as he could and kicked again so Alasdair stumbled. He hit the dirt with a grunt. As he tried to rise and renew his assault, the dragoon turned his musket and fired.

The back of his head was blown off by the force of the ball, bloody bits strewn over the dooryard. Still Alasdair stood for the briefest moment, his chin on his chest, until he dropped to his knees, then all the way to the ground so his face thudded on the sod. A pool of dark blood quickly stained the ground and soaked into the turf. Sarah shrieked in terror.

The horse danced, skittish at the excitement and noise. The officer reined away with a hard yank at the bit and circled from the corpse to bring the steed under control. A look of disgust crumpled the well-bred lines of his face, and he looked away as the woman ran to her dead husband. The children were all screaming now, like hysterical tin whistles, taking little steps this way and that as if unsure whether to approach their dead father and grieving mother. Tears streamed down Sinann's face.

"Sorry, sah." The soldier who had fired stared at the body and spoke as if he'd had to shoot a mad dog.

The officer sniffed and brushed a piece of pink skull from his coat. "Oh, well. Nothing for it, I suppose. Can't expect sense from them." His clear, brown eyes narrowed at the cacophonous brood. He addressed his men.

"Hurry this along. Before their relatives come swarming and we have to shoot our way out of this wretched place."

"Aye, sah." The soldiers hurried at the loading, having their orders.

Sinann's fists clenched and unclenched. Oh, how she wished to curse them all! How she would love to wave her hand and bring them bad luck and death as she had done many times in the far distant past! She waved her hand, but only succeeded in popping two buttons on the Captain's coat. They went ignored. If only her powers weren't failing. She leaned her face against the trunk of the tree in which she sat, and fought the tears. If only her people weren't so powerless! If only Donnchadh . . . she sobbed, her heart broken. *If only.*

She sighed and watched the loading of the cart, then the lighting of the house as a torch was thrown onto the thatching. Quickly, the dried straw caught, and flames licked from thatching to peat walls. Fire grew and consumed, and grew stronger. The remnants of the family watched their home burn, until the roof tree collapsed in a rain of sparks and the fire slowly died into blackness and glowing red embers.

Having seen their task accomplished, the soldiers mounted their horses and the order was given to ride out with the herd of cattle. The cart with two goats tied to it brought up the rear, pulled by a single mare and driven by a soldier who perched on the front rail. The claymore, bundled in faded, rust-colored tartan, stuck out of the rear of the possessions like a captured flag.

Sinann's heart galvanized and she hiccuped through her tears. Her voice became low and dangerous, roughened as it was by her crying and anger.

"I think not, laddies."

She leapt from the tree and spread her white wings to swoop down on the cart. She hovered for a moment over the hilt of the claymore, gathering her strength, then grabbed it by the quillons and pulled.

It didn't budge. She muttered some very bad language, even for faeries, flew to catch up with the moving cart, and grabbed it again. This time it loosened from the other goods. One more yank, and the sword flew free. Taken by surprise, Sinann almost dropped it. But she was determined not to let the English have this weapon, so she held on and kept it airborne. The dragoons rode onward, unaware of the theft to their rear. She swooped and wobbled, then steadied herself over the road. Each hand held a quillon, and she carried it back to the destroyed house.

Sarah and the children had fled to safety, most likely the *Tigh* in Glen Ciorram below, and it would be a bit of a walk over steep terrain to the castle on the loch. The corpse lay where it had died, to be buried by the clan when the men could be summoned.

Sinann rose into the air. The large claymore pulled at her arms and tried to slip from her fingers. She was scarcely four and a half feet tall, thin and not strong. But something had to be done. The killing had to end. Tears returned, and she blinked them back. Yes, something had to be done about these English, and if she was powerless to stop them and her people were powerless, she still had to do whatever she could. She let go of the sword, then hovered and watched it fall to earth to stick in the sod below.

She settled to sit cross-legged on the ground, gasping to catch her breath. The sword stood over her, a silhouette against the now-purple sky. One or two stars had made an appearance. After a short rest, she stood, nearly as tall as the sword, and squeezed her eyes shut to cast the spell in the old tongue:

> *"Ancient sword of my people, the life within you brings life to those who belong to this land. Bring me a hero, a Cuchulain, to save from tyranny the sons and daughters of this land. Let a Matheson lay hands on you and become that hero. By the powers of earth, moon, and sun, by the powers of air, fire, and water, the will of the great art be done."*

Sinann then stood back as the sword glowed for a moment. It shimmered in the gathering gloom, with a promise of power the faerie hadn't felt in ever so long. Her heart swelled with hope.

She turned as the pounding gait of a galloping horse came from up the road, and her moment was shattered. The English officer rode up, blond queue flying, and reined his horse to a skidding stop as he searched the ground. Sinann stood still

as she willed him to go away, but his knees urged the horse
farther on, until he found what he was looking for: his hat.

Quickly he leapt to the ground, snatched up the hat, and
slapped it against his breeches to remove some dirt. Then he
set it on his head and remounted.

Sinann breathed with relief. He would leave.

But, just as he was about to spur his horse after his troops,
he spotted the sword stuck in the dooryard sod. He uttered
a disgusted noise, then guided his horse to the sword, nearly
overunning Sinann as he did so. With one hand he reached
down and pulled the claymore from the ground, held it with
the long blade away from himself and the horse, and galloped
away to his men.

The faerie sagged to the ground, her wings drooping, and
laid her face in her hands.

Moments passed. Mere moments, she was sure, though it
could have been longer. It could even have been much
longer. The sun was almost gone, though it was not quite
dark. But a glow came to the air above the spot in the dirt
where the sword had been. Warmth gathered. Sinann looked
up, hardly able to believe her eyes. The light grew bright,
until it began to take shape. It was a man. A tall man, wearing
kilt and sark. Then, as the glow died, the form became solid.
Braw and bonnie, he was, real and breathing.

Sinann's heart soared, and she fluttered into the air, eye
level to him.

He looked around, his eyes wide. Sinann examined him
closely, for he couldn't see her unless she willed it. He swallowed hard and blinked, then shook back a shaggy lock of
dark hair long enough to tie in a queue but too short to
bother. His eyes were blue, though his skin was the darkest
she'd ever seen with the exception of the southern races from
over the sea. But he wasn't a Moor, nor even a Roman. He
was a Scot, all right; she could see it in the line of his brow
and the light of his blue eyes.

The man squeezed those eyes shut, and when he opened
them didn't seem any more pleased with the view than before. He turned, looked, and turned again. Then he spoke,
and Sinann's heart clutched with alarm. His words were English.

"Holy moley," he muttered to himself. "What just happened?"

CHAPTER 1

Dylan Matheson drifted to consciousness with a morning laziness rare for him. A smile formed on his face for no reason that came to mind. He floated in a half-dream of sun-soaked water. Wetness and heat. Ah, yes, reality formed around him, even more pleasant than the dream he abandoned, and he took a deep breath to wake up. Ginny would be there very soon, and today was the Games.

It was a glorious morning, and the rising sun reflecting from the white walls of his bedroom made him blink. He slid from the bed, and went to the sash window to raise it by smacking the heel of his hand upward against the frame. It creaked and made cracking, rattling noises, groaned in the slides, and shuddered up high enough for Dylan to lean out.

He rested his elbows on the sill to gaze across the lake where the sun peeked over the trees. The Main Street causeway a block to his left was backed up with vans, sport utility vehicles, and station wagons filled with soccer moms taking their children to the city fields up Drake's Creek. Soccer was a Saturday ritual in this upper–middle-class suburb. He knew his mother had loved the mornings she'd spent cheering him on and visiting with other women. They may or may not have been friends, but at least they'd all had something in common, with sons nearly the same age. Dylan suspected his mother missed his childhood more than he did—which was not at all.

He took deep breaths of the fall air, which today was devoid of the humidity that all his life had made Tennessee summers so evil, and the lack of which made Tennessee falls so fine. This last day of September promised sparkling weather for the Highland Games at Moss Wright Park.

His attention was caught by the curling paint on the outer sill, which he flicked off with his fingers. He owned this building and would have to paint it himself, a job he dreaded. Though it was on the wrong side of the creek from the fashionable neighborhood where his parents lived, and was situated between a thrift shop and a run-down apartment building half a block off Main Street, he knew he had the better deal than the more affluent folks across the water. From his bedroom window he enjoyed a spectacular view of rambling mansions, exquisitely groomed lawns, and lush trees that just now were turning amazing shades of red, orange, coral, purple, and yellow. The high-rent neighborhood yonder, though, had a panoramic view of . . . his place. Rickety wooden stairs zagged down the otherwise blank rear wall of his building, giving exterior access to the apartment where he lived over his place of business. For foliage, other than the grass along his section of shore, there was only a lilac bush and a young willow tree under which he kept a rowboat stored upside-down on blocks. This town had an ordinance against parking RVs in yards, but around here boats were privileged and his qualified, no matter how ugly.

He stretched and yawned, then scrubbed his scalp with his fingers to wake up. It was a quick trip to relieve his aching bladder in the tiny bathroom off the bedroom, and on the way out he reached to the shelf behind the door and snagged a towel, which he threw over his shoulder. Then he headed for the balcony living area overlooking the dojo. Another yawn took him, and he had to shake it off.

The kitchen was tucked into a corner of the upstairs by the back door, and he stopped for an apple from the fridge. The phone rang, and he picked up the wall unit as he bit into the apple. Around a large chunk of fruit, he said, "Hwwow."

"Dylan."

"Mom." He moved the mouthpiece away from his face and chewed quickly to avoid a lecture on phone etiquette.

"How are you, sweetie?"

There had been a time when her endearments had irked him to the bone, but he'd long since outgrown that sort of impatience. He swallowed. "I'm fine."

"And that nice little girl you're dating? Ginny?"

"She's fine, too." He sucked a little on a small chunk of apple left in his mouth.

"How are things going between you two? Has she moved in yet?" Mom, being a former hippie who not only had attended Woodstock but claimed her son had been conceived there, had always assumed that living together came before marriage. Nevertheless, she had never shaken her roots and so assumed that marriage was the inevitable consequence of moving in. It puzzled him that cohabitation was such a necessary first step in her view, and he had no intention of marrying soon in any case, no matter how "nice" or "little" Ginny was.

Impatience crept up on him now, and he stifled a groan. "No, she hasn't moved in, Mom."

There was a knock on the back door, and he moved the cheap cotton curtains to peek out the window over the sink. Speak of the devil, it was Ginny. She leaned against the railing, waiting for him to answer the door. Time to get off the subject of her moving in. *Now.*

Brightly, he said, "So, Mom, what's on your mind this lovely morning?" He rested the phone on his shoulder, tied the towel around his waist, and went to let Ginny in. She gave him a quick kiss, then went to sit on the low wall of the balcony, fifteen feet above the dojo floor behind her. *Uh uh.* He frowned and shook his head, so she sighed, gave him a pouty lip, and moved to safety on the arm of the sofa. He couldn't help but smile. He loved that pouty lip, and checked the wall clock to see if there might be time to dally some before leaving for the Games.

She wasn't dressed for the festival, wearing jeans and T-shirt instead of the period costume he'd expected, and he

wondered why but couldn't dwell on it as his mother continued, "Wednesday is your father's birthday."

He knew that. Though he'd forgotten, somewhere in the
back of his brain the information had lurked. His voice went
a little sarcastic, despite an effort to control it.

"Yeah. Family get-together?" *Please say no.*

"Of course." There was a pause. Dylan couldn't think of
a response. He looked over at Ginny and wished she could
give him an excuse to hurry off the phone. Mom said, "I
think if you two would just talk. . . ."

Temper surged and his restraint broke. "He doesn't talk.
He grunts. And he drinks. Then when I go home he smacks
you around for fun."

"That won't happen again. I made him promise."

"He's promised before. Mom—"

"No, really. He's serious this time. We've been to coun-
seling—"

"*Both* of you?" His jaw clenched. They'd had this argument before.

She hesitated, and he knew the answer was that *she'd*
gone but Dad had not. She said, "It's so hard for him, Dylan.
You don't know the pressures he's under."

He snorted. "What I know is that he's put my mother in
the hospital twice. What I know is he's a worthless bastard
who should—"

"Dylan Robert Matheson!"

Dylan bit his lower lip and took a deep breath. There was
a long silence as he struggled to bring his temper under control, then he said, "I'm sorry, Mom. I shouldn't have said
that. But the fact remains that if you don't get out of there
he's going to kill you one day."

There was another long silence. His voice softened as he
said, "You know it's true."

Mom still wouldn't reply. Finally, Dylan said, "Okay,
Mom, I'll come see y'all on Wednesday."

His mother sounded relieved, as if this solved everything.
"Oh, good. I hate to see you two feuding."

"I'm sorry, Mom." Dylan's glorious day was on the skids,
and the sun was barely up. "I'll see you Wednesday."

When he hung up, he had to take a moment to clear his

head and center himself. He went to give Ginny a proper greeting, but she seemed reluctant to take it any further than a kiss. She backed off quickly and held his hands away from her.

Huh. But he let it go. This day was not shaping up well at all. He forced himself to relax enough to head down the creaky stairs along the far wall to the wooden dojo floor. "Come sit with me while I work out." If she didn't want to go back to bed with him, he needed to proceed with his morning routine.

Ginny stayed where she was. Dylan shrugged it off though it put him out. She sometimes liked to make the point that she wasn't required to take orders from him, even over a simple request. He knew she would come down eventually, if only just to talk to him. She was easily bored and couldn't stand her own company for any length of time.

Bluish morning light filtered between the white vertical blinds on the storefront windows. He left the lights off, preferring the cool calm of semidarkness.

The poise on the old, loose-jointed physician's scale in front of the mirrored wall clattered over its notches and claimed 184 today, up an entire pound since he'd last weighed. He pinched the tight skin over his belly and decided the new weight must be muscle, from the increased workouts in preparation for the Games. Much new business could be had from people watching the sword demonstrations, so he needed to be fast, sharp, and trim.

The apple core landed in the trash can under the practice swords, next to the rack of wooden quarterstaffs. Across the room, high on the wall, hung an ancient, glass-fronted display case where he kept his collection of period broadswords. Most were replicas, for originals in good shape tended to be far beyond his price range, but even the replicas were expensive enough and nice examples of metal craft.

He picked out a staff from the rack. The dark one was the straightest, and its finish was smooth with age and use. He went to the center of the floor, set the staff down, and began to stretch. Feet apart, he bent at the waist, back level, and slowly bounced then touched the floor. Again. Slowly, never jerking, he concentrated on his breathing as he repeated until the muscles began to loosen. Then the same thing, feet together.

His muscles sang as the blood rushed to them. Goose bumps rose, and his skin tingled. For fifteen minutes he worked and warmed all the muscle groups. He was awake now, and eager for his workout. Done stretching, he put his feet together and straightened, one vertebrae at a time. Then he took a deep breath and let it out slowly.

Ginny's fingers dug into his ribs from behind, but he was too relaxed to give the desired startled jump. He did, however, say "Ow."

She giggled, then straddled the bench press nearby. Her fingers fiddled with her sunglasses, opening and closing the temple pieces, then twirling them.

"You're not dressed," he accused, meaning the costume.

"Neither are you." Her gaze went to his crotch, where a bulge was forming under his towel. It fled in a hurry, leaving Dylan annoyed at her and at himself.

He frowned. Something bad was up. He could smell it.

She then continued, "How can you do that karate stuff—"

"Kung fu."

She sighed. "That kung fu stuff, with no clothes on?" The sunglasses clacked open. Closed. Open.

"Why do I need clothes?" He picked up the staff and began his formal exercise.

"Doesn't it, like, feel funny?"

An eyebrow crinkled at her. "No. If I let it feel funny, then I'm not doing it right." Ginny was cute, adorable, witty, and a blast in bed, but completely oblivious to the martial arts and sword fighting by which he made his living as a teacher.

He concentrated on the form. *Step, block, step, thrust, turn . . .* He said, "Besides, today I represent Clan Matheson in the Games. I've got to wear a kilt, and I'm going to wear it in the traditional manner: no drawers."

"You're going to do karate—"

"Kung fu."

"Yeah, that . . . in a *kilt?*"

Step, block, retreat, retreat, block, turn . . . "No." His breathing was getting heavier and it was hard to talk now.

"Swords. It's a sword fighting demonstration, all choreographed. Real broadswords, not foils. Bigtime dangerous if you don't pay close attention to what you're doing." Ronnie, Dylan's assistant, would wear breeches in the demonstration because they both felt he would be more comfortable in pants, and therefore at less risk for making a mistake.

"Ah." Ginny was silent for a moment as she watched him. *Clack, clack.* Open. closed. *Lunge, lunge, turn, block* . . . Then she spoke. "Dylan . . ."

He really didn't like that tone, and knew he was going to hate what came next. "Yes?"

Clack, clack. "I can't see you anymore."

Whoa. That brought Dylan to a standstill, like a sock in the gut. He hated this a lot more than he'd thought. He stood, his breathing already heavy and becoming heavier. He tucked the quarterstaff behind his right arm and gazed at the floor a few feet ahead—not at her. Though he knew he didn't want to hear the answer, he had to ask, "Why?"

"Well, you see . . ."

He hoped she wasn't going to drag this out. "It's okay. Just say it."

"Um, well, I've been seeing Peter."

Aw, jeez. "Who?" It was a struggle to keep his voice level.

"Peter Donaldson. You know him, I think."

Yeah. Peter had been three years behind him in high school, and attended the Tuesday night fencing class taught by Ronnie. Peter was a nice guy, a poor but earnest swordsman, paid his fees in a timely manner, and just then Dylan wished to throttle the bastard. However, he held his temper.

"*Seeing* him?" Dylan didn't *even* want to know what that meant. "How long?"

"About a month. You know, Dyl, I think it's really cool you're not upset about this."

He finally looked at her, appalled. But she wasn't looking at him. Instead she'd given up on the sunglasses and was picking at her fingernails. She held them out to the dim light from the front windows. He supposed she'd know how he felt if he began shouting. His voice was still level as he said, "Why?"

She thought long about that before answering, then said,

"You're awfully wrapped up in those swords and things."

"It's my business. It's how I make my living. If I ignore it, I go under."

"Nobody's asking you to ignore it. But . . ." She looked around at the display cases, and her gaze rested on the Matheson crest hung by the office door. "Dylan, with you it's always *Scottish* this and *Scotland* that. It's like you don't even know you're an American."

That stung. "Excuse me for having an ethnic identity."

"But just how Scottish can your family be after three hundred years? Surely you don't believe your entire ancestry originated in Scotland. You're even part Cherokee. That's what your mom says, anyway."

He stood hipshot and leaned on his staff. "My maternal grandmother's great-great-great-grandfather was a Cherokee. That makes me 1/128th Indian, which means nothing except that I tan real easy. If I ever tried to call myself an Indian I'd get laughed off the reservation. I wouldn't even know about the Cherokee ancestor, except my mother went looking for Indian ancestry back when she was a hippie and thought it would be cool to be part of a fashionable minority."

He shifted his weight, and continued in a tense voice. "A couple of the names I've found in my tree come from France, one from Germany, and one from England, but for the most part my ancestry is Scottish and some Irish. Wearing a kilt is, for me, no different from an African American wearing a caftan, an Italian American guy eating a cannoli, or a Latino speaking bad Spanish, regardless of how long ago, or not long ago, their ancestors became Americans." His eyes narrowed and anger bloomed in his gut that he had to explain this at all, but he continued.

"Having said all that, bottom line, Ginny, my name is Matheson. That's who I am, and it's Scottish. I don't know about you, but I kind of like having a cultural heritage that goes back millennia rather than centuries. American culture didn't spring into existence like magic when Europeans set foot in the New World."

She considered that for a moment, but continued, "Most guys I know wouldn't be caught dead in a skirt."

"*Kilt.*"

"But they look like skirts! They look . . . funny."

He looked at her, wondering if he really knew this woman at all. She was in her mid-twenties, but just then she sounded like a teenager. Worse than that, a *backwoods* teenager. How in the world had he made it through six months with her and not known this? He had to clear his throat to find his voice, but found he had nothing to say.

She finally looked up at him, saw his eyes, and suddenly it was time to leave. "Uh, listen, Dylan, I gotta go."

"Yes, you do."

She picked up her purse. "I'll let myself out." He said nothing by way of reply, so she told him goodbye and let herself out the glass front door. The panic bar clattered, and the plate windows shook. Then she was gone. The door slowly closed, then clanked shut behind her.

Dylan stood in his dojo and struggled to keep the anger down. His gut twisted. It had been so easy for her. Ginny and Donaldson? For a *month*, and he'd had no clue. *A month*!

Rage won. He spun with the quarterstaff, windmilled it twice over his head, and flung it blind. It sailed across the dojo and crashed through the window of his office.

Glass flew everywhere. The tinkling of falling shards was like accusation, and his anger at Ginny dissipated in self-reproach for the cost of that huge window.

"Damn," he muttered. "I'm an idiot."

CHAPTER 2

Shelter #3 at Moss Wright Park was where the administration tables had been set up for the Fifth Annual Middle Tennessee Clan Society Highland Games. Almost the entire park was filled with people of Scottish ancestry from all over the state, most in plaid of one sort or another. Some of those plaids were established setts of real clans, some fanciful, some in modern style, and others part of a traditional costume.

Dylan pulled his sword from the back of his Jeep, hung the leather baldric across his chest, then slipped the scabbarded sword through the frog and secured it at his side. He headed on to check in, along with a scattering of others who wore brightly colored MacNotice-me tartan. Dylan didn't particularly care for the modern colors that didn't exist back when kilts were daily dress in Scotland. Day-Glo oranges and electric blues stood out from the crowd, mixed in with the more authentic greens, browns, and rust-reds. His was the Matheson sett of red with a fine mesh of black, dark blue, and dark green against it.

The enticing smell of food booths wafted past, and though he'd just eaten breakfast, he looked forward to lunch. None of the competitions and demonstrations had begun yet, but clusters of men were forming up yonder on the fields, and some men in kilts were setting up equipment. Painted lines defined fields for tossing cabers, exhibition sparring with swords, and other traditional pastimes. A set of bagpipes warming up in the distance sounded in short spurts of intermittent song that drifted among the rustling trees.

A squeal of delight came from somewhere nearby, and the corners of his mouth turned up. *The Girls* were here, though he was never sure this was a good thing. He'd expected the teenage trio and, though on any other day he would as soon they'd stayed home, today his torn ego welcomed a visit from the wide-eyed gaggle.

Cay, Silvia, and Kym were all Saturday morning kung fu students—not a one of them over seventeen—who had less interest in martial arts than they did in the teacher they all thought was *just totally adorable*. Well, maybe Kym had a genuine interest in the study.

Dylan got a kick out of the attention, and often wished he'd had that effect on teenage girls a decade before when he himself had been a teenager. The girls were sometimes amusing and sometimes a pain in the ass, but today he guessed it'd be a blessing to let them salve his ego. He smiled his best *cute teacher* smile as the threesome ran up to greet him.

"Hey, Mr. Dylan!" cried Cay. She wore a plaid skirt that was a uniform from private school and a red poet's shirt she must have thought looked period. The other two girls wore jeans and tank tops. Their bra straps were visible, and it made him feel old that he didn't understand this fashion quirk.

"Hey, yourself." He adjusted the baldric on his shoulder as he walked. They followed like pilot fish. "Y'all been practicing real hard?"

They assured him they exercised their martial arts skills every day, like good little ninjas. "Which sword did you bring this time?" Kym peered at the scabbard as if to see through to the blade.

"A new one. Well, a new-old one. It's a Scottish broadsword replica made in Toledo. Spain, I mean."

Silvia giggled. "Hey, Dylan, show us your sword!"

He suppressed a smile and ignored the obvious entendre as he paused to draw the sword. The girls oohed dutifully over the shiny blade and steel basket hilt. "It's a replica after one from the middle of the eighteenth century. See, there, they even engraved the blade with Jacobite mottoes."

"What's a Jacobite?"

Dylan opened his mouth to speak, then closed it. Dang, how could he explain centuries of Scottish history to a teenager who barely knew where Scotland was and likely wasn't interested anyway? He said, "They fought for Scottish independence from England." Sort of.

Kym said, "Like the American Revolution, right?"

He considered that. "Yeah, I reckon. Only they lost."

Her face fell. "Drag."

Dylan chuckled, and imagined the Jacobites' reaction to the defeat must have been a mite stronger. He scabbarded the sword and continued walking.

The girls followed. Cay said, "You've got great knees. What's under that kilt?"

His eyes narrowed at her. "Never you mind."

"Oh, come on!"

"No."

Now they *had* to see what was under the kilt. "Oh, Dylan! Please! Please, please, please!" they chorused. Cay giggled like a maniac, and Silvia jumped up and down.

With a heavy sigh, he reached for his hem. The three stood back, wide-eyed and breathless that he was actually going to do it. He stifled a grin, then rucked the red plaid wool up to his hip.

They laughed. Tucked into the kilt was his linen shirt, and the tail of it was almost as long as the kilt itself. It covered all, like a slip, nearly to his knees.

He let down the tartan. "Happy?"

"No," said Cay with a big, sunny smile.

He chuckled and started off again. They followed.

"Think this thing's got enough cloth?" Cay tugged at the plaid thrown forward over his left shoulder, slung around the right side of his waist, and then across his back and up over the shoulder again. The end was secured with a large steel brooch bearing the Matheson crest of a hand, wielding a sword, emerging from a crown. Engraved along the outer circle of the brooch was the motto: *Fac et spera*. Do and hope.

"Don't pull, it's all of one piece. The kilt and the plaid." She pulled again. "It sure is soft."

"I said, let go. It's soft because it's real Highland wool." She poked at his belt. "Really?"

He dodged. "Really. It's an authentic *feileadh mór*. An old-style Great Kilt. To put it on, I have to spread it out on the ground, lie down on it, then belt it on. Leave it alone— you'll pull it crooked. . . ." She pulled on it, and he warned, "I'm fixing to smack your hand, girl." Finally, just as they reached the admin tables, she listened and quit fooling with his belt.

Some of the folks there whom he'd met at other games, and others just from around town, greeted him and he waved back. There were lots of unfamiliar faces as well, all eager to experience the culture of their ancestors. Dylan took a deep breath as his soul eased with the pleasure of the day, and wondered if this was how it had felt at a real gathering of the clans, where greeting old friends and making new ones was as important as the games themselves.

Cody Marshall caught his attention in the midst of the milling people, and he gave her a cheerful smile as she wended her way toward him with Raymond, her husband, in tow. Dylan had known Cody all his life, but not the husband; the man always seemed a mite vacant. *Weenie* was the word that popped into Dylan's mind. His hair looked like it was made of polyester, long in front and graying just enough to give it a sheen of plastic fibers. But Cody loved the guy to pieces, so who was he to criticize?

Cody was in a seventeenth-century plaid overdress and bodice, her shiny red hair plaited and pinned under a white linen kerchief folded into a three-cornered *corrachd trichearnach*. But Raymond wore denim cutoffs and a T-shirt that declared him a Titans fan. Dylan said to Cody, "Well, if it isn't the Scottish Maiden!"

She laughed. "You think I don't know what that means, but I do. You think I want to cut off your head?"

"I'll just bet."

She said, "But I wouldn't, because you're the one who taught me how."

He gave her an air kiss and murmured, *"Ciamar a tha thu?"*

"I'm fine," Cody replied to his query, which was the only Gaelic she knew. "Yourself? Where's Ginny?" She looked around.

Dylan's gut clenched, and he shrugged a shoulder. "History."

Cody gave him a *bless your heart* smile of sympathy and said in a low voice, "You'll forgive me if I fall down dead from *Not Surprised.*" Dylan peered at her, wondering what she knew, but she shrugged. "I had a feeling." Then she put her hand on his arm and changed the subject. "Oh! I just saw the most fabulous claymore! A real one!"

Dylan's interest perked. "No kidding? How old?"

"Centuries. At least four hundred years. Maybe five."

Dylan looked around at the milling crowds and display tables, hoping to spot the sword. "Fantastic! I've got to—"

Raymond interrupted. "Something I've been wondering about. Isn't Matheson an English name?"

"It's not." Dylan almost slipped into a Scottish accent at the thought of how his ancestors would have reacted to such an accusation.

Raymond smiled. "But the *son* part—"

"The clan's traditional homelands were in the western Highlands. Matheson is only English in that it's an Anglicization of *MacMhathain*, which, I'm told, means *son of the heroes.* Or *son of the bears*, which in the traditional iconography means more or less the same thing."

Raymond's eyebrows went up, which Dylan found annoying. The man said, "I keep forgetting how well read you are on this stuff."

Dylan shrugged and looked around for an excuse to leave, but found none, so he replied, "I got curious when I was a kid and found out I was named for a famous member of Clan Matheson. My grandfather used to tell this story all the time before he died. He didn't know exactly when the guy lived, but there was a Matheson, name of Black Dylan, who was a highwayman. Used to rip people off all over Scotland, but they still thought he was some sort of hero. Dad thought of the name because of the color of my hair, and Mom liked it because she was a huge Bob Dylan fan at the time. So I'm named after a guy who was probably hung for lifting cattle, or robbing coaches, or something. Which, I expect, is more than you ever wanted to know." He offered Marshall his social smile, with teeth.

Raymond said, without a sign of sarcasm, "For someone who lives in the past the way you do, it must be hell to live in the twentieth century."

Cody chirped, "Twenty-*first* century."

Raymond smiled at her. "No, hon, not for another three months when the calendar turns 2001." His voice went to a conspiratorial stage whisper. "That's why the movie wasn't called *2000: A Space Odyssey*."

There was a brief silence as Dylan and Cody stared at Raymond. "Anyway," Dylan said, "come on, Cody, show me that clay—"

"Dylan Matheson?" It was the admin guy with a form in his hand. "I need you to fill this out. Insurance. We need it if you're going to take that there sword out of its scabbard." He wore a green-and-black military-style kilt with a matching waistcoat and plaid. His hair was decidedly non-period, neatly trimmed for a twentieth-century office job.

Dylan sighed and went to do paperwork, and Cody wandered off with her husband to enjoy the rest of the festival. Dylan figured he'd hook back up with them later.

The broadsword exhibitions weren't until the afternoon. Ronnie would arrive after covering the Saturday morning classes at the dojo, so Dylan and the girls hung out for the morning and watched the more brawny types throw telephone-pole-looking cabers, stones, and whatnot. Dylan was well built, but some of those men were like mountains. Several wore their hair long, and on the field at their competitions reminded him of Klingons in drag. He himself was built more like a quarterback than an ox, and he liked his swords just fine. He didn't much see the point in hurling logs, a sport Cay called "chunking the pole," which struck Dylan as so funny he chuckled periodically for the rest of the morning.

The girls followed him around the entire morning, and along the way the group picked up another couple of students, Steve and Jeff, who were also in a Saturday morning class. The day was beginning to feel like a field trip, and he wondered if there was anyone left for Ronnie to teach. They caught up with Cody and her husband in time for lunch.

The food booths offered meat pasties and sausage rolls, scones and bannocks, turnip greens cooked in ham (though Dylan wasn't sure if that was a concession to the Tennessee crowd or a Scottish thing that had become a Southern thing by emigration), tarts, fish and chips, shortbread, American beer, and imported English ale. The kids ate hot dogs and drank Coke, though Dylan was able to talk Kym into trying a bite of mincemeat pasty. Haggis was available, but not even Dylan wanted to eat boiled sheep guts, no matter how traditional.

Ronnie arrived just in time to eat with them, and the group squeezed onto one cement picnic table. The breeze was gentle and the trees threw dappled shade over them. A cluster of marching pipers passed, and Cody grimaced. "You know, I like bagpipes, but I swear, if I hear 'Scotland the Brave' one more time, I'm going to run, screaming, into the next county. I'm beginning to feel like I'm trapped in a men's cologne commercial."

Dylan *hee-heed* into his lunch. "Well, watch out. Their other song is 'Amazing Grace.' "

Cody rolled her eyes, then chattered about how wonderful all the men looked in their kilts. She ragged Ronnie a little about not wearing one, and he declared them uncomfortable.

She nodded and said, "I bet for guys that wool and linen under there must get pretty rough. Probably a lot easier for Dylan to wear those things, seeing as how he's not been circumcised." She took a big bite out of her pasty.

The table fell silent. Dylan's ears warmed, and he began picking flakes from the pastry of his meat pie. Raymond stared hard at his wife. The students sneaked looks at Dylan's reddening face.

Cody looked around the table, swallowed the bite she'd taken, and said, "What?" Then she laughed. "Oh, for crying in a bucket of bolts! We were four years old! We played

Show Me Yours I'll Show You Mine in the bushes behind his garage. I haven't seen it since. Relax, you guys."

The girls giggled helplessly, snorting through their noses. Dylan sighed. Raymond said to Cody, "And did you reciprocate?"

She rolled her eyes again. "Of course, I did. I'm not a welcher."

Dylan cleared his throat and said, "Anyway, I find my kilt comfortable enough, thank you all for your concern."

The girls collapsed onto the table in paroxysms of laughter.

The broadsword exhibitions were after lunch. Dylan gave an instructional talk to a fair-sized cluster of onlookers about the techniques of broadsword fighting. He demonstrated some in slow, careful motions, then trounced Ronnie in a carefully staged and rehearsed duel, complete with dialogue. Dylan played the Jacobite hero defending his homeland, and Ronnie was hissed and booed by the crowd as the Lowland fop, waving a lace handkerchief in his free hand. It was nearly impossible to keep a straight face while shouting at each other, "You scoundrel!" and "Filthy *Sassunach*!" At the end Ronnie gave a less-than-convincing, staggering, reeling death that had Dylan smothering a smile as he scabbarded his sword.

"You ham," he said as he helped his assistant off the grass. Ronnie just laughed and bowed to the crowd.

After his own bow and the crowd's applause, Dylan took his entourage on a tour of the sword display tables. He was pleased to show his martial arts students a wider variety of European weapons than his own collection. He pointed out the differences between the English and Scottish broadswords (in general, fancy vs. affordable), then discussed how to tell those from a rapier and a rapier from a smallsword, explaining the century-long evolution from broadswords that cut to smallswords that could only stab. Then they came upon the claymore Cody had seen.

Dylan uttered a small moan at sight of it, and reached out to touch the glass cover of its case. It was a real claymore from the fifteenth or sixteenth century, maybe even earlier, not the later basket-hilt claybeg.

He'd never seen one up close that wasn't a replica, and he ached to hold it in his hands. The straight quillons that slanted toward the blade had no finials and were sharp, and the grip had an intricate, interwoven Celtic pattern so graceful as to entrance the eye. It was a monster weapon, able to cleave a man's head in half to the shoulders, not meant for stabbing so much as for hacking pieces from an opponent. It had a two-handed grip, which was required to control and balance the long blade. Oh, how he longed to try it out!

The owner of the sword, a Yankee named Bedford, declined to allow it. "Can't," he said. "It's a family heirloom. My great-great-great . . ." He paused for a moment, counting on his fingers, "great . . . well, one of my ancestors was in the English army back during the reign of Queen Anne, and he captured it somewhere in Scotland. Up until about ten years ago, it hung in the house where my grandfather grew up, in London. When his brother died, my grandfather asked my cousins for the sword for me."

"It belongs in a museum." Dylan couldn't take his hands off the case, as if by pure will he could feel the weapon beneath the glass.

"Maybe when I die. Unless one of my kids wants it." He had an odd way of speaking. Precisely, but with utter ease and a vocal tone that was almost lazy. He was the most casual, composed Yankee Dylan had ever seen.

"How did you get it out of the country, it being an antiquity and all?"

Bedford grinned and slipped into a passable English accent. "Smuggled it up me arse."

Dylan and his entourage laughed, then Dylan looked the man in the eye and said, "I really want to hold this sword. What'll you take just to let me heft it?"

The request didn't bring the laugh he'd expected, but Bedford's eyes narrowed instead. "I saw your exhibition. You're pretty good. You ever do any real sword fighting? Sparring, I mean?"

Dylan's interest perked. "Of course."

"Spar with me to first touch? Beat me, and I'll open the case for you."

"And if you win?" Dylan now assessed the guy as an

opponent. Tall, broad shoulders, broad hands, and an elegance he knew could be deceptive.

Bedford grinned. "Then I win. Hey, if we make it look like another exhibition, the insurance geeks won't have a hemorrhage."

Dylan knew he was being talked into a bit more than just a sparring match. There was a certain reckless thrill to sparring without protection, and the chance of drawing blood made the proposition as intriguing as it was dangerous. Dylan agreed to it with whole heart.

They moved to the empty exhibition field just beyond the display tables, Dylan windmilling his broadsword in a fidgety mulinette to the side as the energy built. His pulse picked up, and his muscles were alerted to the contest. He took a deep breath of the fall air, and a thrill ran down his back. A smile crept onto his face.

Bedford wielded an Italian storta, with curved quillons and knuckle guard, which he swung back and forth by way of warming up. Dylan figured it was a replica, seeing as how a real antique would be worth too much to risk in a fight. His own sword was lighter and faster, but the storta was longer, which meant a longer reach. In a real fight the storta could do more damage, but here a touch was a touch, they would be attacking with the flat of the blade, and the amount of potential damage should be irrelevant.

Hopefully. Dylan figured, though, someone was going to bleed today.

The contestants squared off and saluted each other, then went to *en garde*. Bedford's stance was haughty and assured, and relaxed in a way that seemed natural to him. In an instant, he rushed. Dylan parried, again and again in a flurry of clanging swords, until he was almost backed against the boundary line. Then he feinted, sidestepped, and attacked Bedford's flank. The attack was parried, so Dylan went high to be parried again. Bedford captured the broadsword blade with his own and threw it aside. The metal sang. Then he backed up to gain room, but Dylan pressed him.

The storta flew, and Bedford wielded it with speed astonishing for such a large blade. Dylan grinned at the challenge of a skilled opponent who was not his employee. He beat hard with his broadsword, not trying to meet Bedford's speed but throwing him off with each hard, odd-timed beat. It was working; Dylan was wearing him down. Bedford backed toward the tables, parrying fast as he went, lips pressed together. Dylan looked for openings, but Bedford gave none. Then Dylan laid off and circled.

Bedford laughed out loud and shouted. *"Fucking hillbilly!"*

Dylan refused to take the bait, so the expected attack didn't come. That threw Bedford off balance, and he was momentarily unsure of himself. He attacked in confusion. Dylan parried and lunged for a sidestroke that took Bedford at his rib cage.

"Gotcha!"

Bedford staggered sideways, though Dylan had pulled the attack, then he laughed again and shouted with heavy breaths, "Ah! A touch! A touch, I do confess it!"

Applause rose from the spectators, and the combatants both bowed to them. Then they saluted each other with swords and shook hands before walking together to the display table. Dylan scabbarded his broadsword, lifted its baldric from his shoulder, and handed scabbard and baldric off to Ronnie, who hurried to put it in its case. "Yo! Ron!" His assistant turned, and Dylan threw him his car keys. "It's locked."

"That was a right good fight," said Dylan to Bedford, still trying to catch his breath, then he saw Bedford held his side. "What, did I get you?"

Bedford shrugged. "I think you cut my shirt. Maybe a little skin. No big deal." He showed the hole in his shirt, and a thin red line that looked like a long scratch.

"Dang. Sorry about that."

Bedford shrugged again. "You win. You now have the right to molest my family's property." He winked and gave a white grin as he unlocked the case and opened the glass cover.

Dylan reached in, reverent in the presence of such an historical weapon. He slipped both hands around the hilt and lifted it from the case. For such a long sword, the weight was only a few pounds, easily wielded by two hands, and

the balance was amazing. It felt warm in his grip. Goose
bumps rose all over him, and he shivered them down as he
let the sunshine glint from the blade. But the tingling in his
hands remained. The warmth increased until he had to set
the sword back in its case. Puzzled, he stared at it and at his
still-warm hands.

"What's wrong?" Cody asked.

"Don't rightly know." The heat in his palms grew, though
they no longer held the sword. He stared at them, and the
tingling swept through him. Frowning, he tried to shake it
off, but it wouldn't go. He looked around, afraid now, almost
in pain. Everyone around him stared at him, concerned.

"Are you all right?" Cody reached for him, but he held
her off. Something was very wrong, and he didn't want her
to catch whatever it was.

His heart leapt in his chest as the world went black. He
tried to stay conscious, but focusing on faces did no good.
He reached out to them as they disappeared into swirling
nothingness.

Almost as quickly as it had disappeared, though, the world
returned. It seemed a miracle he was still standing. But when
he could see again, the mid-afternoon sun was gone and it
was cold. He blinked, but the dusk remained. The crowds
were gone. All was silent. He stood in a grassy area, but the
tables and booths were all gone as well, and the grass was
weird-looking. Sort of knobby, like a poorly woven blanket.
He turned, and turned again. Mountains! Higher mountains
than he'd seen in his life, more brown, and certainly steeper,
than any he'd seen in Tennessee! Some of the peaks disappeared into intermittent mist and jutted up to a dark purple
sky scattered with more stars than he could comprehend.

The sharp smell of wood smoke greeted him, and he
looked around to see the smoldering ruins of . . . something.
A barn, maybe? He muttered to himself, "Holy moley. What
just happened?"

Voices came from up the slope, and he looked to see
moving shapes. About four or five of them, and they were
hurrying toward him. Good. Maybe here was someone who
could answer his question.

CHAPTER 3

The men looked like stragglers from the festival, dressed in kilts and linen shirts. *Authentic* garb, he noticed as they drew closer. He was impressed that they wore their kilts as if they'd done so all their lives. He went toward them, but their attention was elsewhere.

One, a big, redneck-looking guy with blond hair and a dirty-blond beard, said something Dylan couldn't quite make out and knelt next to a dark shape on the ground. The three-quarters moon was up, but it was scant light. Two of the other men were very young, in their teens. They spoke in voices that had not yet steadied. The fourth was much older than the other three, tall and thin.

The four muttered to each other so low that Dylan couldn't catch a word except *Sassunach*. The often derogatory term that meant "Englishman" was one of the few words of Gaelic he knew. He wondered if these guys might be taking this whole festival thing just a mite too seriously. Though it was plain something extremely weird was going on, his mind still clung to the idea of the festival. Now that the sun had gone down, his goal now was to find his way back to his car and go home. That is, if he could find Ronnie to get the keys.

"Hey!" he said as he approached.

They all looked up, startled. *"Och!"* the redneck cried, and leapt over the dark shape toward Dylan. The others spoke fast and loud, a jumble of nonsense, and the big guy pulled a dirk from his belt as he ran.

Even in the moonlight, Dylan could tell this redneck wasn't fixing to shake his hand in greeting. Dylan's eyes went wide. He blocked, took the knife arm, and threw the attacker over his hip. Redneck was big, but fast for his size. As he landed, his foot went out to catch Dylan's side. The big guy hit the ground with a *whump*. At the same moment Dylan yelped from the hit to his kidney.

For a moment lights of pain flashed behind his eyes. That dirk had come in low, aimed upward at his solar plexus, where it could have slipped under his ribs and straight into his heart. The realization hit him: *This guy is trying to kill me!* Sparring was one thing. And he'd even fought in anger a few times. But the concept of truly fighting for his life had always been a theoretical one. His mind wanted to slew sideways into more acceptable thought, but he had to focus. Now. He took a deep breath and readied for the next assault.

Redneck scrambled to his feet and rushed him once more with the dirk. Dylan blocked again then grabbed the knife arm, fell back onto the ground, drove his heel into Redneck's solid gut, and heaved him over and onto his head a second time.

Now Redneck was pissed, and Dyían knew he had a wounded bear after him. The knife slashed out before the man was even on his feet. Dylan jumped back. He glanced around, hoping to see a stray weapon left behind, but there was nothing. Not even a stick or rock.

He spotted the other three spreading out to surround him, and he tried to back up to keep them all in front of him. Redneck lunged with his dirk. Dylan responded with a block, snap kick to the gut, then a high side thrust kick to the face that sent his opponent staggering back. He then turned to the other three and held up his hands. "Hey! What's going—"

With a collective roar, the three charged, and hauled him to the ground. He went down in a flurry of elbows, fists, knees, and feet, but they were too many and way too angry. They beat him until he could no longer breathe. He figured he was fixing to die, and thought stupidly he would have preferred the knife. The last thing he saw before losing consciousness was a glimpse of an angel fluttering overhead, tiny and glowing, wearing a diaphanous white dress. As he slipped into blackness he realized she had shiny, white wings. . . .

His head began throbbing long before he was conscious enough to know it was his head. Slowly he returned to the world, and groaned over the really weird dream he'd had. Something about mountains and Gaelic-speaking Scots and a knife fight. . . .

As he came to, it seemed the dream continued. The floor under his face was cold, stone tile, and the place smelled like dirt, animals, cooking food, and smoke. There were people in the room—he could hear voices—but they all spoke Gaelic. At least, he was pretty sure it was Gaelic, though it was sometimes hard to tell. He tried to make out words, but they were talking awfully fast and on top of each other. He knew too little of the language. He only succeeded in making his head hurt worse.

He stirred, and discovered his hands were bound. It was a struggle to move at all, so he lay still and looked around. Wherever he was, it was dark. Candlelight flickered off the stone walls of a fairly long room that faded into shadows at the far end. Several kilted men stood nearby in low-voiced conference. One was Redneck, who was too big to miss and from Dylan's vantage point seemed gigantic.

Dylan looked around with caution, taking care not to attract the attention of the men. Near the far wall was a low trestle table bearing a nude man. A woman wept as she cleaned him. He looked dead. Blackened blood covered his face and matted his hair. Slowly she wiped the pale skin, then rinsed the rag in a wooden bucket, wrung it out, and wiped again with care. Small snuffling noises drifted to Dylan, under the low conversation of the four men.

The floor was strewn with straw, which smelled musty and moldy in the closed space. Three Border collies lounged nearby, watching him as if they'd each been promised a piece of him if he moved. At the other end of the room, light came from a hearth set into the wall. Someone, a woman, he discerned from the silhouette, tended a small pot over a low fire. There was stone carving over the mantle, but it was too dark to see what it was.

Where on God's earth was he?

He needed to start asking questions, and heaved himself to a sitting position. The men fell silent, staring at him . . . no, *glaring*. He muttered through a lip gummy with blood, "Where am I?"

One of the teenagers, this one with a strawberry-blond mop of hair, shouted and pointed at him, and Redneck pulled out his dirk again. The older man, who resembled nothing other than the stereotypical American hillbilly—tall, thin, and raw-boned—stayed his hand. A loud and tense argument ensued between the four of them. Once more Dylan went ignored.

A small voice, like a child's, said near his head, "They think you're English."

Dylan turned, and found himself gawking at the angel. Thinking he'd died, he squeezed his eyes shut as his heart leapt to his throat. He looked again. The angel's silvery-white hair was short and hugged her face with feathered locks, through which poked pointed ears. He still had no idea what was happening, but by the look in her bright blue eyes the little thing was no angel and this place was absolutely *not* heaven. He blinked and peered at her. "Why do they think that?"

"Shhh, not so loud." She glanced at the arguing men, her thin arms crossed over her chest, "You mean, you're not?"

"No. Matheson isn't an English name."

She seemed relieved. "Then speak to them in Gaelic if you're a Matheson!" Her hands fluttered in urgency.

He shook his head then regretted it. "I don't speak Gaelic. Not enough, anyway."

Her fists rested on her hips. "Dinnae be daft. Surely you must have Gaelic."

He shook his head, gently this time. She sulked. His head throbbed, and he took inventory of his injuries. The iron taste of blood was strong in his mouth, and as he ran his tongue over his teeth he felt torn places inside his lip. Thick blood had dried on his face, and one eye was swollen not quite shut. All his bones seemed intact, but both his kidneys ached and his gut was sore. He said, "Hey. Do you think I could get an aspirin?"

"A what?" Once more her arms were crossed.

"Aspirin. For my head."

"I know not this *aspirin* garment."

"Pill. It's a pill. You've never heard of aspirin?"

"Nae. Nor pill, neither. Are you sure it's English you're speaking?"

Dylan sighed and bit back an irritated comment. Then he said, "Where am I?"

"Glen Ciorram, in an old castle that is called *Tigh a' Mhadaidh Bhàin*. House of the White Hound, to you. Domain of the local Laird, Iain Matheson, known to his friends and family as Iain Mór. His cousin, Alasdair Matheson, was just this very afternoon murdered in his dooryard before the horrified eyes of his wife and wee bairns, by an English pig and his infernal dragoons who then made off with the family's goods and gear and burnt the poor man's house to the ground."

That explained the stinking ruins he'd seen, the dead man on the table, and the dark shape on the ground. He said slowly, "And they think I had something to do with it because . . ."

"Because you speak English."

"Big deal. Half the world speaks English."

"Indeed. And so do these lads, but they generally choose not to. Particularly they would choose not to if they ever found themselves under suspicion of spying, as you are. Which you would know if you weren't a bloody *Sassunach* with nae Gaelic."

Spying? In Scotland? And how in hell did he make it all the way to *Scotland*? Dylan closed his eyes. His head hurt. His *mind* hurt. How many centuries had it been since the English had needed actual *spies* in Scotland? At least one, more like two. And here he was, five thousand miles away from where he'd been an instant before being attacked by a big Scottish thug, talking to a four-feet-tall, shimmery-white woman with wings and pointy ears. "What *are* you?"

As casual as could be, she said, "A faerie. Sinann Eire by name, maiden of the *Tuatha De Danann* and granddaughter of the sea-god Lir. I brought you here to save my people from the English."

Huh? His aching head couldn't even address the faerie issue, and focused on the last thing she said. "Scotland isn't in any danger from England. It's been part of England, more or less, since the reign of James I, officially under English rule, more or less, since 1707, and there hasn't even been a Jacobite uprising since 1745."

An odd light came into the faerie's eye, which turned Dylan's gut to ice though he wasn't sure why. She said, her voice suddenly doubtful, "Not since then? And how long would that be?"

His eyes narrowed. "You don't know?"

Her cheeks flushed, and her pale blue eyes snapped. She set her fists on her hips and leaned toward him. "Just tell me how long it's been for you since this famous 1745 rising."

"Over two hundred and fifty years, something like that."

Her face went dark, and she began muttering in Gaelic, turning in place as if looking for something to hit.

"Hey! Hey, Sinann! Faerie lady!" She ignored him. "*Hey!*"

"*What?*" She turned back to him, fists on hips.

"What's the surprise? What year is it for *you?*" A feeling of lightheadedness came as he realized what a bizarre thing he'd just said.

For a moment he thought she might not answer, but she finally said, "Today, as of sunset, is the first day of October, in the year 1713." Then, half to herself, she went back to muttering. "It took nearly three centuries for that *claidheamh mór* to find you! This is bad! This is very bad! If only that English bastard hadn't returned!"

Dylan didn't care what English bastard she meant. He gave a forced laugh. "You're funning me, I know it."

She peered at him. "*Funning?* Perhaps you think this is fun, but I dinnae think it so jolly."

The date grew large in his mind as he realized she was serious. *1713.* Not just thousands of miles, but hundreds of years. He looked around at his captors, and knew the faerie was telling the truth. All that wonderfully authentic garb looked so good because it was *genuine*. Those men wore their kilts as if they'd done so all their lives, because they had. The real danger of his situation sank in. Redneck, who had truly intended to kill him earlier, might yet succeed.

He hissed at the faerie, "Psst! Sinann! Hush!"

She paused in mid-rant. "Why?"

"They'll hear you."

"Nae. You they'll hear, but not me."

"How come?"

She hissed back, impatient with his stupidity, "Because I *like* it that way, that's why not! I do still have *some* powers left, you know!"

"Well, I'm impressed! Next time why don't you send a sword after someone from your *own* century, how about it!"

"I wouldn't want the likes of you trying to help, sure enough! Can't even keep out of trouble with your own clan!"

"I didn't ask to come here!"

"And I dinnae ask you to!"

"Then send me home!"

At that, she made a frustrated noise, snapped her fingers, and disappeared. Dylan collapsed and pressed his forehead to his knee. He was dead meat.

In the way that the human mind has of conjuring the most unlikely images while under stress, Dylan found himself dredging up a vague memory of a television cartoon he'd watched as a child. Something about a turtle and a wizard. The turtle always blundered into trouble, and at the end of every episode the wizard always got him out of it. Dylan muttered, "Help me, Mr. Wizard. . . ."

But nothing happened. No wizard waved a hand to send him back to turn-of-the-twenty-first-century Tennessee. Unwilling to just sit and wait for his fate, he decided to take action. Let Redneck either kill him or not. He took a deep breath and struggled to his feet with his hands still bound behind his back. "*Ciamar a tha sibh?*"

The men stopped arguing and looked at him. The two women also stopped what they were doing and stared. Grabbing at straws, he said to the men, "Iain Matheson?"

Redneck stepped forward, and Dylan had to swallow a

groan. "Aye." *Iain Mór*, the faerie had called him. *Big John*. A reference to his size, no doubt.

"I didn't kill your cousin."

Hillbilly said, "Oh, aye, we know that. Sarah saw it all." He nodded in the direction of the weeping woman with the dead man.

Iain roared at Hillbilly, *"Malcolm!"* There was more argument in Gaelic, then Iain returned his attention to Dylan. "Tell us who you are, or we'll kill you where you stand."

Dylan resisted the urge to take a step back, and held his ground. "My name is Dylan Robert Matheson."

"Ye *lie!*" Iain came at him again, and Dylan wasn't quite fast enough in his bindings to escape a ham-fisted sock in the gut.

He folded in half, unable to breathe for a few seconds while pain turned the world black. Slowly he recovered enough to take a shuddering breath, straightened, and looked Iain in the eye. With almost no voice he said, "It's the truth!"

"You're nae a Matheson, and I'll kill you for taking me for a fool!" He hauled back and took a swing at Dylan's face, which Dylan dodged. Then Iain pounded him in the gut once more. Dylan's throbbing head began to spin.

When he could breathe again, he said harshly, "Untie me and give me a knife, you sonofabitch, and let's see if you can take me!" Big as Iain was, Dylan figured he could beat this bumpkin in a fair fight.

Malcolm took Iain's arm and spoke sternly. The big man glared, but after that took no more swings at Dylan.

"Listen to me!" Dylan spoke as clearly as he could through his bloody lip. "Listen to the way I talk! I'm not English!" Iain paused, his hand creeping toward his dirk, and Dylan spoke faster, countrifying his suburban South drawl. "I ain't English, and you know it. I don't talk like no Englishman you've ever heard. Listen to me!"

Malcolm said, "He's right, Iain. He's nae English, nor French, neither. Listen a spell."

Dylan, encouraged, said, "I'm not English, I'm an American." He corrected himself. "I mean, I'm from the colonies." Through the pain in his skull he struggled to remember what he knew about his early American ancestors. What was the name his grandfather had told him? The name of that convict? The first of his Matheson ancestors to set foot in the New World? It had been sometime during the late seventeenth century. 1660-ish, a little over fifty years ago, according to that faerie. "My father was . . ." He took a deep breath. The name? *The name*? Oh, yeah! "Roderick Matheson."

The entire room came to attention, silent and still. He'd struck a nerve. He continued, memory clearing as he spoke, "Roderick was transported to the colony of Virginia as a young man. I was born . . ." Uh oh, now he had to lie. *He* had been born in Tennessee, which even in 1713 hadn't been much explored by white men. He decided not to stretch the credibility factor. "I was born in Virginia in . . ." some quick math here, "1683."

Iain grumbled, "You dinnae look as old as a' that. Nor much like a Matheson, to me." Dylan guessed that was a reference to his tan body and nearly black hair, a coloring combination not unheard of in Scotland. But it appeared to be rare among this family who seemed mostly light-haired: blond, red, and light brown. Without thinking, he blurted, "I worked all summer on this tan." Everyone in the room blinked at him, uncomprehending.

Yeah, there were about fifteen generations between himself and Roderick Matheson, and at best these people would probably have been third or fourth cousins even to old Roderick. The lack of physical resemblance was not a huge surprise. He prevaricated. "Well, my mother's people are all very long-lived," relative to the life expectancy in 1713, that was true, "so I'm older than I look. And I have her coloring, too." He thought it might be confusing to mention the Cherokee influence.

Malcolm said something to the men in Gaelic, and the anger began to bleed from them. They seemed to buy the story. Iain's eyes narrowed. "So what brings you here, then?"

Dylan shrugged, as if it weren't such a big deal to get on a ship and spend several months in passage to a place that wasn't his home to visit distant relatives who did not expect him or even know he existed. "I came to see my father's people."

"And did you forget to bring your gear?"

He shrugged again. "I travel light?" When that wasn't received with the intended humor, he added quickly, "I was robbed. At the docks in . . ." Dang, not knowing where Glen Ciorram was, he couldn't know where the nearest port town was. "At the docks, after I arrived. I was mug . . . uh, jumped . . . um, accosted . . ."

Malcolm grinned and said, "Now, I'm having a little trouble believing you would let yourself be robbed."

The others laughed, except Iain who still scowled. Dylan gave a dry smile, then chafed at the bindings on his wrists. "I can be outnumbered. I was, and I lost my lug . . . uh, belongings. And my . . . um . . . purse." Was that right? Did men carry purses then? The others gave no outward sign, so Dylan figured he was okay on that account.

"You've nae sporran, neither. Nor weapons. They truly made off with everything." He gestured to Dylan's shoes. "It's fortunate they left you your brogues, or what you might call them. Boots, perhaps?" The others snickered again. Dylan's shoes were rubber-soled suede, ankle-high chukka boots. They were the closest to hand-sewn brogues he'd been able to find at the mall.

Dylan tried to laugh with them, but started to black out. He went to his knees, then began to retch. He knew the signs. Concussion. Oh, joy.

There was more muttering in Gaelic among the men while Dylan's gut hitched, but at least Iain Mór no longer sounded like he was after blood.

A woman's calm voice came from behind him. She spoke to the men, then said to him in English, "They'll be taking your bindings off now for you to drink this."

He looked up at her. A trickle of sweat ran down the side of his face as Malcolm came at him with a dirk. Dylan let him cut the bindings around his wrists.

It was a relief to his shoulders to bring his arms around front, and he rubbed his wrists, still looking at the woman. She was a delight to the eye, a kind face among those who condemned and threatened. Her gleaming blonde hair fell mostly loose, with a thin braid down one side. Woven into the plait was the thinnest of white ribbons with a blue embroidered edge. Her eyes were wide and deep, deep blue, and the sympathy in them touched him at the core. She offered him a shallow wooden cup with handles, half-filled with liquid.

"Drink this. It'll ease your head."

He held the cup to his mouth and took a sip. The liquid was vile, and tasted bitter as it went down. His face screwed up with disgust, but the woman urged him with a murmur to continue drinking. At the second sip, he realized that anything tasting this bad must work or nobody would drink it. So he held his breath and downed the rest, then returned the cup and watched her walk back to the hearth. Wearing a white overdress with thin blue lines of plaid, she moved with a grace and confidence that was rare even among the athletic women he knew.

Iain Mór growled, "What might you be staring at, lad?"

Dylan's gaze went to the floor and he said nothing. He figured he'd best watch himself. The woman was probably Iain's wife. Trophy wife, more than likely, judging from her youth and beauty, and Iain's age and social status.

Malcolm said to Iain, "He'll sleep in my chamber tonight while the rest of us keep watch with Alasdair." Since he spoke English, Dylan knew he was supposed to hear and understand.

Iain's reaction was something angry in Gaelic.

Malcolm answered him in English. "Coll can stay by the door." He indicated the blond teenager, who narrowed his eyes at Dylan. Again, Dylan knew he was supposed to hear.

Iain stared at the floor a moment, considering, then looked at Malcolm and nodded. "Aye."

Malcolm said something in Gaelic to the other men, then to Dylan, "Come along." Dylan climbed to his feet to follow the length of the hall, through a heavy wooden door dotted with iron studs, into a corridor. Two of the dogs came along at his heels. "Have you people who're expecting you?" Malcolm's manner was sure and calm, as if whatever answer Dylan might give would be fine with him. The corridor was dim, lit sparsely by infrequent but large candles set in sconces along the wall. Long shadows crawled everywhere over stone turned orange by firelight. The darkness and the rock all around gave a sense of being buried alive, as if the corridor were a small cave from which there might be no escape.

It occurred to Dylan to suggest there would be a search party out after him by daybreak, but he knew he couldn't pull off that bald a lie, particularly one that would be disproved in a short matter of time. Neither could he keep the desolation from his voice as the realization hit home. *Nowhere to go.* "No," he said, "I didn't know myself I would end up here." Where was that stupid faerie, anyway?

Malcolm lifted a candle from a sconce and guided him down the corridor then up stone stairs that spiraled steeply clockwise. The dogs' claws clicked on the stone as they climbed behind the men. The walls on either side came together overhead, and it was like climbing in a tunnel. The sense of being buried was even more intense, though they were going up. There were landings, and at each landing was one door set into a small, odd-shaped alcove to the left of the steps. These areas were dark, and Malcolm's candle made wild shadows on the odd-angled walls. Dylan looked up the stairs and saw more darkness.

Malcolm said as he continued upward, "Is your family dead, then? I expect your father must be dead."

"Why do you say that?"

Malcolm glanced at him with surprise. "Sure, I dinnae ken how a man can leave his family—to pick up and leave his home. I could never bring myself to it. Not even if I had to."

"I didn't have a whole lot of choice."

Malcolm grinned. "Her Majesty has taken to transporting folk *back* to Scotland, then?"

Dylan laughed. "No. I just . . ." He plied his scrambled brain for a good lie, but nothing came. He was left with the truth. "I just . . . blacked out one afternoon, and next thing I knew I was in Scotland."

"Oh, aye," said Malcolm with a full understanding Dylan envied, "a press gang. You're lucky to have escaped. Are they looking for you, lad?"

Dylan didn't know what a press gang was. He wanted off the subject, and said simply, "No. Nobody is after me." There was a long pause while they climbed, then Dylan asked point blank, "Why aren't I dead?"

Malcolm answered without hesitation. "Roderick Matheson, who we have not seen in almost forty years, was my mother's brother and Iain, Coll, and Artair's father's brother. I was a child when I last saw him, but you have the look of him about your eyes. If not for that, you'd be in chains in the gatehouse prison tower, have nae doubt. I dinnae think we'd have kilt ye already, even were you a spy."

The voice was as matter-of-fact as ever, and gave Dylan a shudder.

They stopped at the fifth landing, and Malcolm led him into a mostly round chamber, where a large fireplace dominated the interior wall and the heavy ceiling beams disappeared into gloom above the center of the room. They were carved with a crude floral design. Dylan was surprised to see the high windows fully glazed with small panes, some colored. Glass windows in this century, in this country, usually meant wealth.

A four-poster bed stood near one of the windows. A bulky, carved wooden chair was near the hearth, and at the far end of the room were an armoire and a small set of bookshelves. At the foot of the bed stood a low table with fine, turned legs, bearing a ewer and basin of etched pewter. Castle, glass, pewter, turned wood . . . yeah; rich folks.

Malcolm waved his hand at the bed. "I'll nae be needing the bed tonight, so make yourself at home. And Gracie should be in with—"

A knock on the door interrupted. A small, graying woman entered, carrying some towels. Her face was so badly scarred as to look deformed, and Dylan guessed she was a survivor of smallpox. She smiled at him with thin lips, then went about her business, laying the towels next to the ewer, taking long glances at Dylan the entire time. Dylan looked over at Malcolm, wondering if this castle was really so short of beds that he needed to sleep in Malcolm's, or if he was up here only to be watched. They were high in one of the towers, with probably only one way out. One obvious way, in any case. Dylan guessed there would be more than just Coll posted outside the door, and others along the route to the outside.

He relaxed. That was okay with him. He had nowhere to go.

Malcolm gestured to the ewer. "You'll want to wash your face."

Dylan touched a crusty spot on his chin that had begun to itch, and went to pour water into the basin. The swelling in his eye wasn't too bad, but was tender to the touch. As he washed, a cut in his upper lip began to bleed again, and he pressed a towel to it until it stopped. Eventually the blood and dirt were gone from his face and hands. He dried himself with the towel, and found the soreness was easing.

The dogs stared at him with bright eyes, like shaggy, black and white children waiting for some attention. One was mostly white, with random black patches here and there, and the other was black with a white underside. The white one stretched out on the wooden floor. The smaller black one eyed Dylan and sniffed the air. He took a few steps forward.

Dylan reached out. The knot in his gut loosened a little as the black dog rolled onto his back to have his belly scratched. Dylan couldn't help but grin, and he obliged. "Yeah, you know a Matheson when you see one."

When he looked up, Malcolm and Gracie were both gone. He sat on the bed and pulled off his shoes, then peeled his red-and-black argyle socks from his feet and stuffed them in the shoes. Those hit the floor. Then he unpinned his plaid and unwound it from his body. He was dirty and sore, and wanted nothing more than to go home. He took the brooch from the plaid and dropped it into a shoe, then unbuckled his belt and pulled off the red-and-black wool. The clothing slipped to the floor on top of the shoes. Stripped to his shirt, he blew out the candle on the windowsill, and settled into the linen sheets spread over a straw mattress on the wooden frame.

Leaning on one elbow, Dylan stared at the fire as it dulled to embers, and wondered what he'd done to deserve this. Then he lay down to sleep in his shirt. One of the dogs sighed in the creeping darkness.

CHAPTER 4

Dylan awoke at dawn, alert at the low sound of men's voices outside the chamber door. He slipped quickly from the bed and moved toward the voices, on silent bare feet, shocked by the cold of the wood floor, shivering in his shirt. The dogs were up, tails sweeping the chill air, ready to play and offering dog-smiles for whomever was coming. Dylan eased to a position by the hearth, where he couldn't be seen unless the door was completely open. He rubbed down goose bumps in the icy blue dawn that slanted through the wavy-thick panes of the windows.

The door swung toward him, and he stepped back to balance his weight, ready for whatever. The strawberry-blond teenager entered—the one Iain Matheson had called Artair. He was thin, though not skinny or knobby-looking like Malcolm, filled with an energy that seemed to emanate in waves. Like all the other men Dylan had seen here, he wore a full beard, but his was thin, wavy rather than curly, and shiny-reddish. The color was close enough to the shade of his pink skin that it gave the appearance of a face frayed at the edges.

The older blond one, Coll, was behind him. He looked like a mindless enforcer: larger, quieter, more economical of movement. His dull, watery-blue eyes seemed to look straight through Dylan. Malcolm had said these were Iain's brothers.

Artair peered at Dylan, then at the bare knees below his shirttail. Dylan shifted his weight again in a casual attitude of unconcern, forward and hipshot. "You want something?"

Artair snorted. "I came to ask you that very thing. I expect you're hungry by now." His voice betrayed his equal unconcern about Dylan's welfare, and Dylan shrugged despite his gurgling stomach. "But you'll most likely be wanting to piss first before you eat, and you'll have noticed the lack of a chamber pot." Dylan had a vague idea of what a chamber pot was, but he wouldn't have known where to find one if he'd decided to look. He was just as happy he needn't have.

Without waiting for a reply, Artair continued, "You'll find a garderobe atop the steps. Follow the battlement around, and it's on the right where the tower meets the curtain. Once you're done, and if you can find your way back to the Great Hall, there's breakfast awaiting you. You'll hurry, or you'll be eating it cold."

Dylan thanked him, but Artair's reply was, "Wouldn't want you pissing in the corners now." He and Coll disappeared through the door without closing it. Their footfalls clattered down the stone steps and faded into the distance, and they muttered to each other in Gaelic.

Huh.

Dylan belted his kilt around himself and pinned it as he'd done yesterday. While he dressed, a cold ball settled in his gut. When he'd last put this on he'd not dreamed it would become his entire wardrobe and the one thing essential to fitting in. It was a good thing he'd not been wearing jeans yesterday.

The dark alcove outside the sleeping chamber was empty and cold. Dylan went up the steps in search of the "garderobe." If it was a place for him to pee, he figured it must at least resemble a latrine of some sort.

At the top of the steps he found a wooden door that opened onto a battlement. To his left was the peaked wooden ceiling of Malcolm's quarters, and to the right was a curved, crenelated wall with an arrow loop in each of its raised sections. The fresh air, icy in Dylan's lungs, made him gasp. A stiff breeze tossed his hair around his face. He leaned on the deep stone embrasure to look out, and found the castle was situated on an island or peninsula near the edge of a small loch. Dark blue water reflected the clouds above, and beyond it brown mountains dotted with exposed granite rose directly from the water in violent contrast to the peaceful loch. The air was so clear and the colors so crystalline that Dylan could only stand and gawk at the beauty of this gray, blue, and green landscape.

When he was able to take his eyes away from the jagged horizon, he looked down and found the castle surrounded by a ruined wall near the water's edge, torn down so completely there was nothing left but the bare indication there had once been a castle curtain around the perimeter of the land. Some swans floated near the shore, and a smile came to his face which quickly died. He'd never seen a live swan before. They were creatures of faerie tale and myth. People were transformed into swans or they brought the enchantments of the "wee folk." Faeries, which had once been the stuff of children's stories, were now hard reality for him, and he could have lived his whole life without ever having seen a swan or a faerie and been perfectly happy.

He couldn't dawdle long and his need to find that "garde-robe" pressed him onward. He found it, just past where the tower battlement met the curtain. It was a tiny room built into the wall, closed off by an extremely narrow wooden door that groaned when he shoved on it, and moved with great protest. He shouldered his way in, ducking through the small opening, then pushed it shut behind him and turned to examine the castle latrine.

Its seat was wooden, a one-holer against the outer wall. A small basket stuffed with hay sat next to the hole, and when he realized what the hay was for, he flinched. "Owww." There was a smell, but not the stink he'd expected from a centuries-old latrine. In fact it didn't even smell as bad as the average phone booth in downtown Nashville. Gray dawn slanted through the arrow loop, *and* up through the hole.

Dylan looked in and saw the ground several stories below. At the foot of the tower, directly under the hole, was a dark

mound that occupied one end of a fenced garden. The patch
was bare, but the worked ground was bordered by a small
rail fence covered with blooming white rose vines.

Idly, he wondered how many of these garderobes there
were and what the morning fallout of human waste looked
like when viewed from a distance. That struck him as funny.
The weirdness of everything around him made him want to
giggle, but he swallowed it for fear he might start laughing
and never stop.

He sighed, figured it was his turn to add to the pile below,
and reached for the hem of his kilt.

"Aye, there's a bonnie backside! Sure, I came at the right
time!"

That faerie! Dylan whirled at the voice behind him. "You!
Send me home!" He reached for her, but she rose to the
ceiling, out of reach, with a flutter of wings and a tiny laugh.

"After you've done what you came to do, lad."

He cocked his head at her. "What, pee?"

She crossed her arms. "Save my people."

"Not possible. They'll fail at Sheriffmuir, at Glen Shiel,
and finally at Culloden. Scotland will remain under British
rule and won't even get its own parliament again until almost
the end of the twentieth century. Nobody can change history."

"You can. And you will. You're the hero who will save
the Gaels from the *Sassunaich*. You're the one who can free
our people, or the sword would never have brought you here
when you laid hands on it."

His eyes narrowed, and he crossed his arms. "I guess you
must be an awfully powerful faerie to make a sword do that."

She fluttered lower and nodded. "Oh, aye! Powerful, indeed!"

"Then how come you can't save them yourself? Leave
me out of your squabbles with the English!"

Her eyes narrowed, and she settled to her feet. She aimed
a threatening finger at him. "Lad, there was a time when I
would have struck you dead for that!"

Dylan's patience wore thin, and his bladder demanded
attention, so he turned his back on Sinann and lifted his kilt

to pee through the hole into the garden below. "Right," he said.

There was a silence, and Dylan hoped Sinann had gone, but when he shook himself off, let his kilt down, and turned around, she was still there. A sullen, narrow look was in her eyes.

"You're destined."

"Then why was I born in 1970, if I'm so destined to save eighteenth-century Scotland? Huh? Who died and made you God?" He shoved past her and out the door. She followed him, past the battlement, and down the stone steps of the tower.

When she caught up with him she cried, "I was a god long before your Yahweh was anyone!"

"Don't *even* go there. Just, don't." He clattered down the flights as quickly as he could without tripping in the semi-darkness.

"I was—"

"Don't!" He stopped and turned on her. "I don't want to hear about the *Sidhe*, the goddess, or any of that New Age stuff, okay?" She crossed her arms and glared down at him from a few steps above.

"I mean, yesterday I didn't believe in faeries, and now I'm held hostage by one. Yesterday I believed in an orderly universe, and now I think I'm in hell. Yesterday I had a life," he flashed on Ginny and his stomach tightened, "and now I'm a broke stranger among people who would as soon see me dead as see me at all. People you want me to *save*? Take a reality break. You're not God nor goddess to me, you're nothing more than a little, fluttery wad of misplaced power. Get off my back, get out of my life, but first, for crying out loud, *send me home!*"

Sinann's eyes left his and focused over his shoulder. *Uh oh.* He turned to find the widow of Alasdair Matheson standing on the stairs below. Sarah held a bundle in her arms and gawked at him with wide eyes.

Dylan tried to smile at her, but knew he was not convincing anyone. He muttered to Sinann, "She can't see you, can she?"

The faerie giggled, entirely too amused. "Nae, she cannae."

He sighed, turned back to the woman and said, "Hello, uh . . . ma'am?"

She nodded to him. "*A Dhilein* . . . I have these for you." Her eyes were red-rimmed windows onto an abyss of grief, but she tried to smile with her mouth as she held out the bundle of leather and fur. "My poor Alasdair will no longer be needing them, and it's been pointed out to me that you're a kinsman and without. You should have them."

Dylan was at a loss. His voice went low for he could barely speak. "I can't take your husband's stuff . . . uh, property. It wouldn't be right."

"By the time my boys are old enough to wear them, these things will be old and stiff and of no use to anyone. It wouldn't be right for them to lie around, useless, when there's someone as can use them. Here, take them." She stepped upward and shoved the bundle into his arms, then turned, picked up her skirts, and hurried back down the steps.

The wad loosened in his arms, and a leather thong dangled to the stones. He sat on a step to examine the gifts. There were a couple of smallish pieces of sheepskin, leather straps, and a large bag made of some sort of black fur.

"That's seal skin. A sporran of seal skin is a treasure," said Sinann, in awe. "She wasn't asked to give that up, for she could have sold it. *Should* have sold it, if you ask me. I'd say she's taken a liking to ye."

Dylan snorted. "She's been a widow one day."

"And a practical woman all her life. Oh, she mourns her husband well enough. And if you approach her too soon she'll put you off for a respectable amount of time. But, mark me, she's looking to the future."

The faerie's words made Dylan's heart clench. "The future. Right." He held up one of the sheepskins, which was curved almost into a tube, wool to the inside.

"Leggings," said Sinann. "Use the thongs to strap them on."

Dylan complied, and swallowed a creepy feeling as he strapped on the skins that were shaped to a dead man's legs. But he found relief from the cold with the leather and wool

snug from ankles to knees. Almost as good as jeans. The
black sporran he hung on his belt by its thong, then stood.

"You dinnae need that brooch, you know. Sure, I dinnae
ken how you breathe with your plaid so tight.

"What do you mean?"

"Ye've wrapped it around ye like a winding sheet.
Here . . ." She leapt into the air and released the brooch from
the wool with a flick of her wrist.

"Hey!" Dylan reached and swiped at her, but she dodged
like a fly and ducked in to tug his plaid loose so it hung
down in front, draped over his shoulder. "Hey! Stop! Look
at this!" The end of the plaid now brushed his toes.

"Now let it hang some in the back . . ." Sinann swung
around him and tugged the plaid. Dylan gave up and let her
rearrange him. His eyes narrowed in irritation. "Now, see,
you then tuck the end of it in your belt." She came around
to tuck, but he waved her off and did it himself. She fluttered
back, hands on her hips. "And there you have it."

"It'll fall."

"It won't fall, if you hold yourself like a man. And if it
does, you put it right again." She twirled the brooch in her
fingers. "There's one less thing for you to keep track of."
She made like she would throw it out an arrow loop, but
Dylan snatched it from her hand and slipped it into his sporran.

"Thanks for the fashion tip." He proceeded down the
steps, wishing Sinann would send him away, but also wondering if breakfast would be cold by now.

By following the echoing sound of voices, he found the
Great Hall where he'd come conscious the night before, and
entered through the door opposite the huge hearth. The black
Border collie rose from his spot by the large main entrance
at the middle of the room and trotted over. Dylan bent to
scratch him behind the ears, then went on into the room.
Sinann followed like a bee hovering, and the collie trotted
along behind.

Long trestle tables had been set up, with many short
benches and stools beside them for people to sit on. Some
small children chased each other the length of the room while
a few women were unsuccessful in quieting them. One man

was slumped over one of the tables, snoring, and several people were sitting and eating from wooden bowls. Two other men lay curled up and snoring, one in a corner and the other beneath a bench, both wrapped in their plaids. Finally one of the women succeeded in herding the noisiest children from the room, clucking at them in hushed Gaelic.

The body of Alasdair Matheson still lay on the table against the long wall, but it was now wrapped in a white cloth. After the night-long wake, most of those present ignored the body. But there was a dull silence while they ate.

A screech sounded from across the room, and Dylan spun to see a young man wailing and jumping about like an ape, pointing at him. "*Ha shee!*" he screamed in great excitement, "*Ha shee! Ha shee!*" He wore no kilt, but only a dirty shirt and a pair of worn shoes. His face was almost completely obscured by ragged hair, but his adolescent beard and voice betrayed his youth. One of the women rose from the table to deal with the uproar.

Dylan muttered to Sinann, "What's with him?"

The faerie lit on the floor, and Dylan realized she was ducking behind him, out of sight of the raving boy. "Ignore him. He's an idiot."

"He can see you."

"And curse him for it." She watched, in full fume, as the noisy one was urged to a table to sit. He finally quieted, but kept staring at Sinann.

Dylan noted that the woman soothing the boy was the pretty one who had given him the painkilling potion the night before—Iain's trophy wife. He looked away to avoid being caught staring again. But he couldn't help a rush of pleasure that she was there, nor could he help the rising desire to gawk. He peered at Sinann instead. "How come he can see you?"

"I told you. He's an idiot. Not right in the head."

"Ah. Mentally challenged."

She snorted. "Ye have a way with euphemisms, lad, that would do an Englishman proud." Her gaze returned to the noisy one. "The others I can fool, but over the likes of him I have nae power at all."

The young man still muttered, "*Ha shee. . . .*"

"What's he saying?"

Sinann sighed. *"Tha i a' Sidhe.* He's telling everyone I'm here." To the young man she hissed, "Hush Ranald!" But her words only brought more excitement and squealing from the young man.

"They don't seem to believe him."

"They do."

"They really believe in faeries?"

"Don't you?" With her chin she pointed to the room at large. "They know I'm here, but even when I let them see me they ignore me in public lest they be accused of witchcraft. You should be discreet as well. Go, sit. Eat. You're not going home today, lad, and you'll need your strength."

He frowned at her, but obeyed and went on down the long hall to sit on one of the stools. The dog followed. Sarah came from the hearth at the far end, bearing a wooden bowl and spoon, which she gave to him. Dylan thanked her and she slipped away. The bowl was filled with a sort of gray, steaming mush. He tasted it and realized it was oatmeal. *Duh.* But the meal was of a finer texture than he'd ever seen before, sort of gummy, and it had a toasted flavor. There was no sugar or butter in it, just some milk. A little bland, but not bad. And he realized quickly, very filling.

Sinann settled on the next bench and said, "She's lovely, isn't she?"

Dylan refrained from glancing after Sarah and stared into his bowl. "Mind your own business, Tinkerbell. I'm not on the market, whether you send me home or not. So you might as well send me home. Now would be good."

"And what makes you so sure I *can* send you home?"

He turned to glare at her, then remembered himself and turned back to his oatmeal. "What? Do you mean you can't send me home?"

"I didn't say that, either. I only suggest you not be so confident in my powers. I might be able to send you back, or I might not. And that's even aside from the question of whether or not I want to."

Dylan stared hard into his bowl and struggled to hide his rising panic. She had to send him back. She *had* to let him go home. His life would be over if he were stuck here.

A not unwelcome voice came from the tower entrance, and Dylan turned to see Malcolm, who silenced Ranald with a finger to his lips before settling opposite Dylan. He peeked under the table and smiled. "I see Sigurd has attached himself to ye."

Dylan looked down at the dog, who had stationed himself at his feet. "Sigurd? Strange name for a Scottish dog."

Malcolm laughed. "Sigurd the Mighty wouldnae be pleased to hear you say that, Earl of Orkney as he once was. Besides, had Alasdair given him a true Scottish name, he couldnae call the animal without having a dozen relatives answer." His smile widened at Dylan. "Sleep well, did ye, lad?"

Dylan nodded.

"How's that parritch going down?" A bowl was set in front of Malcolm and he tried it out for himself.

"Well enough. Thank you."

Malcolm peered at him for a moment, then said, "From what you told us last night, it would seem you've reached the end of your long journey. You say you jumped ship and headed here. Why here instead of back to Virginia?"

Dylan cast about for an answer, but realized there was no good one. He made swirls in the goo at the bottom of his bowl. "I told you I jumped ship. I had to get away from the port. I came where there were relatives."

There was a long silence. Finally Malcolm said, "Tell me, did you expect to find four male cousins when you arrived?"

Dylan's eyebrow raised. Why would the gender of his nominal cousins matter? "No. I didn't expect to come here at all. Right now all I really want is to go home. I would leave today if I could." He threw a glance at Sinann.

Malcolm considered that for a moment, then relaxed and proceeded. "Passage to the colonies is dear. Unless you're game to annoy Her Majesty just enough to get yourself transported, but not enough to get yourself hung, and to take the floggings in the meantime, you'll need money."

Dylan's interest perked at this. He would need money regardless of where he might go, and as long as Sinann refused to send him home, he was stuck in the eighteenth century where broke was more than just a figurative term. "You've got work?"

Malcolm laughed. "There's always work, but especially now. It's a late harvest we're bringing in, and if we dawdle we'll lose what we cannae save before the cold comes. The board and bed will keep you alive, and if you're intent on leaving for the colonies and take care with your expenses, the cash will be sufficient in time. We've a small force of retainers attached to the *Tigh* and in this circumstance of need they're helping with the harvest. But even so, with Alasdair's death it's a race with the weather. What say you?"

Dylan glanced at Sinann, still hoping that she would wave her hand and zap him back to turn of the twenty-first-century Tennessee, but she looked away and ignored him. Then he returned his attention to Malcolm, and, without seeming too eager, he nodded slowly. "All right."

Malcolm also nodded slowly, then said, "Today being the funeral and all, and Sunday besides, there'll be nae work. But tomorrow you start in the fields." He reached under the table to his sporran and laid upon the boards something hidden in his long, bony hand, then slid it across to Dylan. "And here. Take it as a loan, but I couldnae stand to see you get your throat slit for being too close a relative and you the prodigal and all." He removed his hand to reveal a small knife in a steel scabbard. "This *sgian dubh* has saved my life more than once."

"Here?" Dylan was thoroughly confused now, but he took the knife and slipped it into the top of his right legging.

Again Malcolm laughed. "Nae, not here. I was born here. But you were not. There are some who would accept you as kin, but others who will never. And still others who would call you kin and see you dead just the same, or even because of it. Take care."

Dylan wanted to renew his pleading with Sinann but kept quiet in front of Malcolm. He fingered the knife tucked into his legging, and hoped he would never have to use it.

The funeral that day was, for Dylan, a study in ambivalence. He'd never known Alasdair, and felt no personal loss over his death, but he was also compassionate enough to understand the grief of those around him. Women wailed and carried on as if each were his widow, leaving Sarah to cry quietly into a handkerchief. The body was carried from the castle on boards that had been the top of the trestle table on which Alasdair had spent his last night above ground. The funeral party crossed a small drawbridge to the loch shore, and on down to a tiny cluster of buildings in the glen. Bagpipes wailed to the surrounding mountainsides, and Dylan's blood surged with the rise and fall of the music.

He took this opportunity to check out the lay of the land outside. The castle took up most of the tiny island it occupied, and the ruined wall he'd seen that morning looked like it had once risen straight up at the loch shore. There the water lapped at the medieval stonework, the better to keep enemy boats from landing. The castle's outer curtain was now no more than a ragged line of rubble circling the outer bailey.

The loch lay at one end of a narrow valley that ran east to west. The land along the north sloped to low wooded hills, then erupted in round granite peaks just behind. A good-sized creek tumbled from behind one of the wooded hills, and ran a crooked course across the flat of the glen, between low stone walls that meandered here and there, to the loch. Wooded areas were mostly clustered on low hills and between the higher mountains, and the trees that were no longer green had turned fall colors of either yellow or brown. The southern perimeter was tightly defined by cliffs and steep, rocky slopes where very little vegetation clung.

The tiny village of Ciorram was no more than a few houses in a loose cluster near the castle's drawbridge. They were small houses, one of peat grown over with moss and grass, and the rest of gray stone, each thatched with straw. They seemed to crouch low. Rows of mounds that looked like haystacks stood along a low stone wall. They had peaked tops, though, and on second glance didn't look much like hay. Thatched haystacks?

Fields lay in narrow strips across the valley and up the gentle northern slopes as far as they could climb and still find arable land. Some were empty, some dotted with leaning sheaves that from a distance looked like an Indian village of miniature teepees. Some on down the valley were still high and silvery with their waving crop. In the distance more houses could be seen against the slopes, and the people wandered down from the surrounding hills in clusters to join the procession. Women gathered around Sarah, and men walked without speaking as the pipes called for all to mourn the passing of Alasdair Matheson. The glen was emptied in this way, and Clan Matheson crowded into and around a small churchyard at the foot of a granite cliff, where the east end of the small glen took a turn to the north.

The crowd held back while the bearers made three circles around a spot on the ground, clockwise, before setting down the body in its winding sheet. Dylan looked around and wondered why there was no grave dug, though some shovels stood against the stone church wall. Few of the graves bore markers, but it was plain the yard was crowded with many buried within the past couple of years. There were plots of all sizes, some appallingly small, outlined as fresh grass or disturbed ground. Not far from Alasdair's intended resting spot was one fresh enough to have been dug since the last rain.

The church was small, but to Dylan's twentieth-century eye it was elaborately appointed. The peaked roof was decorated with carvings, the door was a mass of Celtic knots carved deep into the wood, and a huge, round window of intricately stained and leaded glass dominated the face of the building. Dylan had no idea when it had been built, but even in this century it looked old and worn. Nevertheless, it was the cleanest and best-kept building in the glen, even more so than the castle.

Alasdair Matheson, recent victim of the ongoing conflict with English authority, was memorialized to the accompaniment of bagpipes, wailing women, and a long, tedious speech in Latin by a tall priest wearing black robes and an ornate, white and gold stole. Dylan stood with respect near the stone wall at the yard perimeter, at the edge of the cluster of stony-faced Matheson men from the castle, and struggled not to be caught up in the pain around him. Sarah stood with her three little boys, and he dared not look at her for fear he might lose his hard-won control. The oldest of the kids couldn't have been more than five, and the youngest was barely walking. Way too young to lose their father.

Sinann showed up. She appeared before him, fluttering a couple of feet off the ground to be eye-to-eye. "A pity, isn't it?"

Dylan looked down and didn't answer.

She landed beside him and continued, her voice filled to overflowing with compassion. "Three weans without their da, and all because a Lowland pig wanted their land and could use the English courts to get it. They're killing us, lad. Sometimes in numbers, sometimes one by one. If they have their way, the Gaels will be wiped from the earth, never to be heard from again. You can stop it."

Dylan half-closed his eyes and said nothing.

Sinann fluttered into the air again and looked around. "See over there? The Laird and his Lady?"

Dylan looked with his eyes, but kept his head down. Iain Mór stood nearby, murmuring to a woman Dylan had not seen before. She was tall, handsome, of regal bearing, and closer in age to the Laird than the woman he'd thought was Iain's wife. He glanced at Sinann, then toward the cluster of women. There was the pretty, young blonde from the night before, whose tears for Alasdair were now silent but still copious.

Sinann continued, "Iain Matheson is a suspected Jacobite. It's why the Crown encourages and facilitates confiscation of his lands whenever possible. They cannae prove his sympathies, or they'd have hung him for treason by now and taken all of Glen Ciorram."

Dylan finally spoke in the lowest whisper possible, trying to look like he was praying. "I thought it was Alasdair's own land he died for."

Sinann shrugged. "It's true that many men are now buying their own land. The title was Alasdair's, but nevertheless, as a Matheson in allegiance with the Laird Iain Mór, taking his land is the same as if the land had been owned by Iain and as if Alasdair had been his tenant. Any man here would have fought and died for that very property, for they all prosper when a one of them prospers. One of them goes under, they all are hurt. One of them is murdered, each has a grievance as if it were his own brother who was killed. How can you be a Matheson and not understand that?"

Dylan thought of his relatives back home who had inherited the same sense of kinship by which were born ugly family politics and blood feuds. He didn't reply.

Sinann continued, undaunted by his reluctance. "Surely you must know of Glencoe."

He shrugged and nodded. He'd heard of the massacre, but knew little about the specifics.

The faerie enlightened him. "Just slightly more than twenty years ago the treacherous Lowland whoreson John Dalrymple, who was Scottish Secretary of State under William III, sent a regiment of king's men, made up of the equally treacherous Campbells, to partake of the hospitality of the MacDonalds of Glencoe. For a fortnight they stayed, in the depths of winter with snow on the ground and provisions growing scarce. Though the MacDonalds had previously been in bad odor with the Crown, the Laird had recently taken an oath of allegiance and the clan took the soldiers' presence as a gesture of peace. Then, in the dead of night, the regiment rose from their borrowed beds and attacked their hosts, who'd had nae warning they were to be butchered as example to those clans the English consider *lawless*. Women and children they murdered, like so many sheep. And they think *we're* the barbarians. They continue to butcher and enslave. To grind the Gael under their fine polished boots is their wish, for they dinnae think we are people."

Dylan stole a glance at Sinann from the corner of his eye and was shocked at her obvious fury. Her face was flushed, her posture tense. He couldn't reply. Even if he had an excuse to talk to himself in the midst of a funeral, he had nothing to say to her, for there was no doubt the massacre had been despicable. However, he surely didn't know what he could do about it. He was just one man.

So he kept silent and raised his eyes again for another look at the blonde. She was amazingly beautiful, though her nose was now as ruddy as her cheeks from crying. Who was she, if not Iain's wife? While everyone else's attention was riveted on the sheeted corpse, Dylan indulged himself by staring at her.

*   *   *

Having been accepted, nominally at least, as a kinsman and especially as an extra pair of working hands, Dylan was given a bunk in a barracks-sort of place over the stables, where nine other men snored and stank in racks that stood to the ceiling. The room was dank and windowless, lit only by a couple of candles set on a table in the middle of the room, and the stench of horse stalls wafted from below through the wooden flooring.

The bunk assigned to Dylan had hash marks carved all along the head rail, in a pattern he could tell was not accidental. They were not simple tallies of numbers, but he couldn't read them. There were other carvings, and a date: 1645. Old graffiti, even in this time. He slipped off his shoes and leggings, put his sporran with them at the foot of his bunk, and curled up on the straw mattress under his plaid, with Malcolm's knife in his fist. He closed his eyes to sleep and tried not to feel the cold.

The sun wasn't anywhere near rising when he was shouted awake and bade in English to get his lazy colonial ass out of bed and eat breakfast while it was still hot. He tried to move quickly, but his body shrieked with pain at the cold. It took a monstrous effort to move at all, and the shivering made him clumsy, but he forced himself to pull his belt on around his kilt and tuck it the way Sinann had told him. He'd not taken his shirt off in three days now, and it was beginning to stick to him, but bathing with no hot water in this cold was unthinkable. He figured he might as well stink like everyone else here. Piece by piece he put himself back together exactly as the day before. It was a leap from his bed to the wood floor, and when he landed he nearly collapsed onto the straw scattered about. He groaned and tried to control his shivering as he ran his fingers through his hair.

The Great Hall was relatively warm, and the parritch good and hot. By the time he'd finished eating, he was feeling more or less human and the shivering had stilled. The sky was purpling above the peaks when the men and women of the castle started on their way to a small, narrow field tucked between two hills off the valley on the far side of the village, and the chill of the air was mellowing.

Dylan learned quickly how to wield a sickle. It was pretty straightforward stuff, just another edged weapon, only this one had teeth and was used on inanimate plants instead of a moving, intelligent opponent. The crop was oats, which he and other men mowed with the curved blades then let drop to the ground. The women and children then picked it up to tie into sheaves, which they stacked in teepees. Back toward the village, Dylan could see other folk loading the sheaves into wooden carts pulled by small, shaggy horses. He discovered the thatched haystacks were actually stacks of oat sheaves, set for drying then thatched to keep out the rain.

The men around him spoke in tones that suggested they weren't happy with the work. They hacked awkwardly at the oats, as if they didn't want to appear proficient. Dylan kept his mouth shut and his attention on the job, not caring if the work was beneath him. A job was a job, as far as he was concerned, and right now nothing that paid honest money was beneath him.

Very early into the day he found himself wishing he had had an opportunity to warm up his muscles. A nice bit of light movement and stretching would have been good before starting this repetitive, jarring work.

As the sun climbed, the temperature rose to almost warm. Sweat began to appear on the men's faces and shirts, and Dylan wiped his forehead on his sleeve almost as repetitively as he swung his sickle. The others tied pieces of cloth around their heads, but Dylan owned only the clothing on his person and was pretty sure he didn't want to start tearing pieces from his only shirt. Every so often a woman made the rounds of the workers with a wooden bucket and drinking cup, from which everyone drank.

Ranald ran with the children as they loaded carts with cut oats, and squealed with delight at everything he saw. His relentless cheer and noise was an annoyance that wore on and on all morning until it was Dylan's dearest wish the boy be taken back to the castle. He wished in vain.

By noon Dylan's shoulder ached and his back felt like it might break in half. As the fall sun reached the middle of the sky, some older women brought baskets filled with bannocks cut and stuffed with meat and cheese to distribute among the workers. These bannocks, though, were triangular instead of round, crisper on the outside, and heavier on the inside than the ones he'd seen at Scottish festivals. The heavy work that morning had made him hungry enough to think they also tasted better, in spite of the burned spots.

After eating, the men and women rested a bit, chattering to each other in Gaelic and generally ignoring Dylan. That was okay with him. He was still hoping for the faerie to show up, announce her error, apologize profusely, and zap him back home. She didn't, though, and he finished his sandwich by himself.

He looked around at the flat, mowed field behind them, then rose and walked to a clear area and began to do some stretching. Then he slipped into a formal exercise. *Block, step, block, retreat.* It felt good to return to that part of him. It reminded him of who he was.

When he came to the end of the form, he bowed and shook himself off. Then he looked around and realized the chatter had stopped and everyone in the field was staring at him. Artair shouted to him, "Are ye daft, now?"

Dylan knew he was a fool to answer, but he said it anyway. "It relaxes me."

A huge grin crossed Artair's face. "Well, then, if exercise relaxes ye, I expect ye'll be sleeping well come nightfall."

The others laughed, and Dylan bowed Asian style just to piss off Artair, then turned to find his sickle. He had nothing to say, and was ready to work again even if they weren't.

Draped over his sickle where he'd left it was a piece of white linen he recognized as one of the napkins that had lined the baskets used to transport the sandwiches. He looked around for the woman who had dropped it there, but the rest of the workers were turning to the harvest again, and the baskets had been taken back to the castle.

Checking again to see who might own the napkin, he shrugged and decided to put it to use. He tore a strip from one side, folded it lengthwise, and tied it around his forehead, then lifted his hair over it to let air to his scalp. The remain-

der of the cloth he tucked into his belt. Then he went back
to work.

Sinann showed up at sunset and hovered before Dylan
with crossed arms. "Have you decided to help, or nae?"

CHAPTER 5

Dylan kept his attention on his sickle and continued whacking oats. "Bite me, Tinkerbell."

She laughed. "It's a wise laddie who is careful what he wishes for."

He glanced at her between strokes, but said nothing.

"That Sarah, I think she's taken a liking to ye. Perhaps if you're in a mood for biting—"

"Knock it off, Tink." He was beginning to feel like the city visitor in an old movie about hillbillies. "I'm not in the mood for much of anything. I'm tired, hungry, thirsty, and I want to go home. I miss my bed, I miss my television, I miss my refrigerator, I miss my . . ."

One of the other men, whose name Dylan thought he'd overheard as Robin, slapped his shoulder to get his attention. The others were wrapping up for the day. The men had all put their tools in one of the carts, and everyone was helping the children scoop up the last of the fallen oats. Dylan did likewise, and when the field was cleared of stray objects he followed the group back toward the village. Sinann followed him, sometimes walking, but flying a few feet whenever Dylan's strides left her too far behind.

"The Great Cuchulain never worried about having a bed to sleep in."

"In case you haven't noticed, I'm not Irish and I'm not a hero. I have no intention of being anyone's watchdog, and I'm not likely to burst forth with superhuman feats of strength and skill."

"You know of Cuchulain, then?"

He nodded, still with his eyes to the ground as he walked. "He killed some dog . . . belonged to this guy named Culain. So to replace the dog he worked in the animal's place for a while. That's how he ended up being called Cuchulain. *Hound of Culain*. He was a human watchdog."

"Very good. I'm pleased to know the stories haven't died even if your Gaelic has."

"It's a hobby, and those stories aren't all that easy to find. Not like Robin Hood or King Arthur."

"And what else do you know about him?"

"That he was an extremely violent man, that he killed people wholesale, and that he was finally killed in battle himself. But before he died he tied himself to a rock so he wouldn't fall to the ground."

"Of course he killed. He was a defender of his people. But he was fiercely loyal and ever true to his word. He always did what was right, no matter how the deed might hurt himself. He made good his promises, no matter if they might end in his death, and when he was buried his wife loved him so much she lay down and died right there in his grave with him. He was a great man."

Dylan gave a crooked smile. "Yeah, he sounds like a real fun guy."

He'd been following the field-workers and expected those living in the castle to return there, but instead he found them gravitating toward a large bonfire in the center of the village. It wasn't so much a community center as simply a spot equidistant from the few houses near the castle. Women Dylan recognized from the castle bustled about in preparations for supper, and some began to serve cups of drink to the men coming in from the field. The children ran and played, shouting, shrieking, and laughing, and Dylan realized he couldn't tell whose kids they were. All the adults attended to all the children, it seemed.

The men washed up in a couple of wooden buckets set

on boards placed across low stools that stood out of the way
of traffic. Dylan joined them to roll up his sleeves and rinse
some of the sweat and grime from his hands, arms, face, and
neck. Without a towel, he had to wipe himself dry with his
shirtsleeves. Then he scratched the itchy beginnings of his
beard and wished he had a razor. Someone thrust a cup
into his hands, and he smelled of it then took a taste.
Beer. Wait. . . . he tasted again. Not beer, but . . . ale? It was
smoother than beer and went down a lot faster. The foam
bubbles were smaller. He looked into the cup. Is this what
real ale tasted like? He took another drink and decided he
liked it. Hearty, almost like food, and better than beer, which
was bitter and watery by comparison.

Exhaustion overwhelmed him, and he wondered where all
this energy was coming from, for the people of Ciorram
seemed ready for a cookout. Meat was on the fire, warm
bread was passed among the workers, and everyone seemed
in a hurry to down as much ale as possible before eating
anything. The mood was not exactly festive, but Dylan could
tell it was time to relax and enjoy the evening. As the sun
set, the cold made them all gather around the fire, pulling
their plaids and coats around them. Dylan found a seat on
the ground between an old woman on a stool and some men
who shared a log. He sat on the sod cross-legged, and flashed
back to his boy scout days.

Wooden plates filled with meat and bread were passed to
the men, who chattered in low voices as they ate with their
hands and alternated swallows of meat with draughts of ale.
Dylan was too hungry to care much about utensils, and
picked up his slab just like everyone else. A cluster of bare-
foot children in plaid dresses and miniature kilts stared at
him, until he stared back, and then they ran, giggling. Tired
as he was, he couldn't help the smile that touched the corners
of his mouth.

He said to the faerie who sat next to him, also cross-
legged, "So you're Sinann Eire. Eire, meaning 'from Ireland'?" He took a bite of the beef, and was surprised at how
tender it was. He had to look at it to be sure it was beef and
not chicken.

"Aye," she replied.

He swallowed a bit too quickly, and the meat went down hard. "Don't look now, but this isn't Ireland. How did these get to be *your* people?" He took a drink of ale to wash down the beef, then another bite of meat.

She raised her chin at him. "There's nae so much difference between the Irish and the Highland Scots, you know. It's nearly a common language we speak, and the North Channel is nae so wide that a number of people couldn't cross it and cross it again with ease. In the early days, even before Kenneth MacAlpine, the first Scottish king, it was custom for Irish families to foster their sons in Alba and Scots to return the honor."

Dylan nodded. "Yeah, I know. So how come you're no longer in Ireland?"

"They think I'm dead. And they named a river after me."

"The Shannon."

"Aye, again. You're not as dense as you at first appeared, lad."

He sighed. "So, not to belabor the question . . ." One of the men nearby glanced at him, so he lowered his head and his voice, and peered into his ale cup as he continued, "But what are you doing in Scotland?"

She took a deep breath before starting in. "The story goes, and it's true what I'm telling you, Irish Druids once made a crystal fountain in the heart of the island, surrounded by seven trees that bore the fruit that contained all the knowledge of the *Tuatha De Danann*. Hazelnuts, they were, big and plump ones."

"Hazelnuts?"

"I like hazelnuts."

"You also like power, I bet."

Her mouth went crooked for a moment, then she proceeded with her story. "Well, to make a short story even shorter, I picked from one of the trees. . . ."

"Which you shouldn't have."

"How was I to know it was forbidden?"

"Tree of Knowledge, forbidden fruit . . . makes sense to me."

She frowned at him and made a disgusted noise, then continued, "*Whereupon* the fountain exploded in a monstrous gush of water and carried me off. The water from that fountain became a great river, and to this day that river flows to the sea."

"They think you drowned on the sea?"

She laughed. "Aye. Imagine me, granddaughter of the sea-god Lir, drowned! So I turned myself into a salmon, ye see, and swam north until I came to Alba—Scotland, to you. Up the Sound of Sleat I came, to Loch Alsh. There I landed, and have lived among the Mathesons since, the Scottish Gaels having so little difference from the Irish. It's the Lowland scum that—"

"So the Mathesons are sort of your pet mortals, eh?"

She frowned, and her slanted eyes narrowed to slits. "Not pets. Never pets. If ye cannae understand, question it not nevertheless. It's more than likely beyond your grasp in any case, you being an outlander and all."

Dylan grunted and fell silent, then chewed on the last of his supper.

After a silence, Sinann continued as if the talk had never quit. "It was a MacMhathain caught me in his net."

"Oh, we're still on the Escape to Alba story?"

She ignored the comment. "He caught me in his boat I was forced to turn back to myself and was nearly strangled in the net. Well, you can imagine the poor man's reaction when he saw who he'd caught. He cut his net open, but I was near death. He hurried his boat to shore, and there made a conjure over me for healing. It saved my life, such as it was. When I was recovered, I gave him a new net and thereafter watched over him and his family, his sons and grandsons for generations, and followed the MacMhathain line that came to Glen Ciorram in retreat of the Vikings."

"You've been here awhile."

"I've known many generations of Mathesons, and MacMhathains before that. I . . ."

She fell silent as one old man started up a story and the talk around the fire soon became less chatter and more listening. The others quieted, and the gray-bearded man spoke Gaelic in a voice so strong and clear it belied his age. His face almost told a story by itself, with eyes that went wide or narrowed with the emotion of the story he told, a grin that displayed a very few teeth that were blackened, and a voice that expressed joy or tears with equal intensity. He spoke in a rhythm, almost like song.

Dylan whispered to Sinann, "What's he saying?"

She sniffed and said to the air, "Oh, he wants something from me, now?"

He shut up, but she continued, unable to keep to herself what she knew, "He's telling the story of how the castle got its name."

"Don't they all know the story?"

"The adults do, but they never tire of hearing it. And to the weans it's all new. Half the joy of a story is telling it to those who havenae heard it."

"So how did the castle get its name?"

Sinann cleared her throat and proceeded. "That is easily told. There was once a Laird of this castle called Cormac Matheson, who had an enormous white dog, so big he could break a cow's leg bone in his jaws, but so gentle he could carry a lamb in his maw without a-frighting it. That dog followed the Laird everywhere, and nowhere was there a man who would harm Cormac when the dog was about, for he was a creature loyal to his master and would allow no other man to touch him nor even go near. The Laird was a wise and good man, who had the misfortune to fall in love with a neighbor lass of the MacDonell clan. But her father wouldnae let her go to the Mathesons, for a grievance even older than this story. Cormac was forced to kidnap his bride, and the two were married in the castle the very next day.

"When the MacDonells came to reclaim Cormac's bride, the Laird and his men met them, bristling with arms, on this very spot." Sinann pointed to the ground, and Dylan looked on reflex as if there would be something to see. He saw grass. She went on. "Cormac pleaded with his father-in-law to allow his young bride to stay, but MacDonell would have none of it. The two factions clashed, with claymores, dirks, and targes, and the MacDonells, being the angrier, laid waste to the men of Glen Ciorram who dinnae wish to fight at all. Every man in the glen of fighting age fell, and it was fortunate that Cormac's young brother was in fosterage at the time for there was no other heir to the lairdship and if he had fought, the Ciorram Mathesons would have ended then and there.

"The white hound also fought, with as much courage as any of the men. But when the battle was over and the Mathesons beaten, Cormac was dead, and his white dog lay at his side, his throat cut with a dirk. MacDonell reclaimed his daughter and led his men toward their home."

Dylan took some more ale and whispered, "So Cormac's little brother named the castle after the brave dog?"

"The story isnae finished, and aren't you just the impatient one. For, you see, MacDonell never made it back to his own lands. The rescue party made camp not far from here. Nobody knows exactly what happened, but sometime during that night the MacDonells were attacked by an animal of some sort, and every last soul in the camp had his throat torn from him, including Cormac's bride. They say it was the dog killed the MacDonells. And to this day, you can sometimes see the white hound guarding the gate to the castle, with blood dripping from its mouth. The young Laird had nae choice in the naming of the castle, ye see. It's what everyone hereabouts has called the place ever since."

Dylan shuddered. "Do you think the story is true?"

She peered at him sideways, "You wouldnae suggest your kinsman was a liar now, would ye, lad?"

"If it's just a story . . ."

"There's nae such thing as *just* a story."

Dylan began to wonder, and shuddered again, and when a lull came in the talk he spoke up to ask the bard, "Sir!" The side-chatter died in an instant, and Dylan had the distinct feeling his English tongue was not particularly welcome. But he continued, "Would you know the story of Roderick Matheson?"

The graybeard burst forth with his jack-o-lantern grin. "*Och, tha!* Aye, indeed I know that story well, for I was a lad at the time, don't you know! Not that there's all that much to tell, mind you."

"Will you tell us what happened?"

"Gladly." As the old man proceeded to tell the story in English, there was a low muttering in Gaelic among a couple of clusters of people. At first it seemed rude, until Dylan realized the speakers were translating the story for those whose English was not so fluent.

"During the reign of Charles II, first of the restored house of Stuart, in the Year of Our Lord sixteen hundred and sixty-six it was. Young Roderick Matheson, who at the time was but eighteen, ventured away from his home, which was *Tigh a' Mhadhaigh Bhàin*. It was his first time to go with the drovers all the way to Edinburgh, and his mother, the beautiful and fair Sìla NicAngus, ever sweet of disposition, cried and said he was far too young to go. But his father, the mighty Fearghas Matheson, thought it would be all right for his youngest child to accompany the drovers, as he himself had gone on a *creach* at barely sixteen. And so the lad went. On the day he left, he bade his mother farewell, and his father, then walked along with the cattle and the drovers." The graybeard's shoulders slumped, then he said, "And that was the last his family or anyone else living ever saw of him."

Dylan waited for the rest of the story, and it took a moment to realize the bard was finished. "That's all? That's the whole story?"

"The lad never returned from Edinburgh. Nobody ever learned why, though they searched for years and begged help from every authority. It was as if he'd vanished from the earth."

Well, hell, no wonder everyone had been so surprised to hear him utter the name. Dylan shrugged. "Shoot, even I know more about what happened than that." It was then he noticed every eye was on him and every ear perked to hear what he would say. He hesitated, then cleared his throat.

"All right, it was in the year . . ." he coughed and looked around, then proceeded with the story he'd heard from his grandfather ten years before, "the Year of Our Lord sixteen hundred and sixty-six. He, um . . . Roderick Matheson was a young man, as you said, on his first trip to Edinburgh. While he was in that city, there was a demonstra . . . uh, a *rising*. A protest. Some Covenanters, who had lost power in the Restoration of the Crown in 1660 were protesting royal preference for the Episcopal Church. Roderick, young as he was, found himself curious about the crowds and went to see what was up . . . I mean, what was happening. He somehow ended up in a fight and, well, the other guy didn't survive. Roderick was arrested and thrown in the Tolbooth, convicted of murder, and from there put on a ship bound for the New World under sentence of banishment and seven years' indenture to a Virginia plantation. By the time he'd completed his service, he'd met his future wife and had found an opportunity to obtain some land."

"And why did he nae write if he was alive?" Iain appeared personally offended by Roderick's failure to contact his family, even though Iain wasn't old enough to have known him.

Dylan shrugged. "I don't know. I never asked. Could be he didn't want his parents to know he'd committed a murder. As for his living past 1666, I'm proof that he did." Which was a fact. He wasn't Roderick's son, but he certainly was a direct descendant and wouldn't be alive if Roderick had died in Edinburgh.

"Does he yet live?" This from Malcolm, who appeared old enough to have been, maybe, ten or so at the time of the arrest.

Dylan did some quick math and calculated that in 1713 Roderick would have been sixty-five. He went with the odds and shook his head. "No, he died a few years ago."

"Have you brothers or sisters?"

Dylan shook his head again. He didn't have any, and had no idea how many children Roderick had fathered. He only knew there had been at least one son to have carried on the name, who was currently living somewhere south of the Mason–Dixon line. Dylan's knowledge wasn't complete enough to be sure just how far south and west Roderick's progeny had progressed by now.

Malcolm looked like he had more questions, but barking dogs broke the silence and everyone looked to see what had the animals so excited. What they saw made the men stand and the women fade behind them, taking with them all the children they could reach. The kids made not even a peep, but were wide-eyed with terror.

Dylan stood and turned to look, and his pulse jumped to see a cluster of Redcoats on horseback enter the circle of

light thrown by the fire. Though his specific historical knowledge of this area and this year was limited, he knew it would
be nearly a century before the presence of an English soldier
in these parts would be anything less than a deadly threat.
He waited with the rest of the Mathesons to hear what the
Captain wanted. Iain Mór stepped forward.

"Good evening," the officer greeted him with a distracted
air. Iain declined to reply. There was some muttering in
Gaelic, but the Laird hushed it, also in Gaelic. The English
officer with the blond queue and periwig went on with delicate diction in a voice that dripped breeding but conveyed
no sincerity whatsoever, "I wish to express my condolences
for the death of your cousin."

Iain finally opened his mouth. "I expect you're heartbro-
ken over it. Will that be all? It's a pity you cannae stay for
a bite of supper, Captain Bedford."

Dylan did a take at the name and his pulse jumped again,
but he kept still and quiet.

The Captain looked around at the gathering, and his face
screwed up with disgust. "Yes, a pity indeed. One thing,
though, Ciorram," he glanced at his well-armed, mounted
men, "you should be a bit more careful about your relations
with certain of your neighbors. If there is any more trouble,
any rumors of subversive talk or dealing in stolen property,
I shall be forced to more extreme measures than confiscating
land. It would behoove you all to obey the Queen's law and
the Privy Council. I say this as keeper of the peace here."
There were snorts of laughter. The Captain's jaw clenched.
"Mark me, all of you. Her Majesty desires peace, but will
not tolerate lawlessness."

Iain gave no reply. There was a long silence as the men
stared each other down. Finally Bedford sighed and ordered
his men about to ride away at a stately walk.

Once the Redcoats were out of earshot, the Scotsmen sat
back down by their fire, and mutterings in Gaelic riffled
among them. Dylan found himself as angry as they. He
looked to the trail the soldiers had taken, and knew what it
meant to live in a country occupied by a foreign power and
what it meant to hate that occupation.

CHAPTER 6

For weeks Dylan labored in Iain Matheson's fields, hating the scarcity of food, the cold, and especially hating that damned faerie. No matter how he pleaded, Sinann refused to countenance the idea of sending him home. Over and over, he told her there would be no saving the Scottish from southern oppression. One man could not change history. But she would not believe it. All there was left to do was wait for Sinann to tire of her game, and meanwhile he needed money, food, and a place to sleep. He did his job, and hoarded the coins Malcolm gave him on paydays.

He had no clue how much he was being paid, and if he had he wouldn't have known how much things cost in any case. The bits of silver didn't even seem like money to him. Small and crudely struck, some with a queen for heads and a crowned "3" on the tails side, they were more like something a woman would dangle from a charm bracelet than like cash. All Dylan could tell was that these were worth three of something, and he took the queen to be Anne, who was currently on the English throne. The ones with a "1" on the back had a male profile, but Dylan was stumped as to which king this would be. Charles? William? Certainly not James. Too early for any of the Georges. He kept the tiny cache of coins in his sporran, tied tight inside the remainder of the linen napkin to keep them from jingling.

Not all of his pay came in coins. In kind he received a new shirt of unbleached linen and a *sgian dubh* of his own that he now carried in a sheath up under his left arm. The sheath also had come to him as pay. The black iron knife was small, only about eight or nine inches total, and the blade three inches of that, but the double-edged triangular blade was very sharp. The hilt had a tiny guard at the base, which amounted to little more than a ledge but made it unusual among Scottish dirks. He wondered why anyone would put a guard on such a short blade. There was no telling what might have motivated the maker of this dirk, and it was probably that very design flaw that had put the item in circulation as payment. On the plus side, its handle was of stag horn and the deep grooves made for a steady grip. Many of the knives he'd seen lately were little more than pointed iron rods stuck in wooden handles.

Malcolm said as he handed Dylan the weapon, "It might interest you, this dirk has a history."

Dylan chuckled. "Everything in this place has a history. You can't breathe for all the history in the air around here."

That brought a smile, but Malcolm said, "Well, it's a wee bit of notoriety this blade has. The story is complicated, but I can tell you that if you were to ever see Captain Bedford without his pants . . ." Dylan crinkled his nose in distaste, and Malcolm laughed out loud. "Aye, I can't imagine the sight myself. But if you were to see it, ye'd also see above his knee a scar exactly the width of this here blade, put there by Iain's father some years ago."

"No kidding?" Dylan examined the blade as if for bloodstains, but found nothing out of the ordinary.

"Nae kidding, as ye say." He chuckled again. "I think."

Dylan was quite pleased to take this weapon in exchange for a few days' work, and returned Malcolm's knife to him.

The village raced the cold to get the harvest in, and each day the wind smelled more like snow. There was no more sweating now, and the men wound their plaids tightly around themselves for warmth. Dylan took to wearing both his shirts at once. Shaggy black cattle were brought in from high pasture to winter in the very peat huts occupied by the villagers, and the kitchen pens of the castle's inner bailey swarmed with goats, sheep, and pigs, adding their pungency to that of the horses already housed in the castle stable. More people had come down from the pastures, called *shielings*. The halls and corridors of the castle as well as the tracks of the glen bustled with more folks readying for winter. A holiday atmosphere was in the air, like Christmas at home, though it was only October.

A couple of Sundays passed, punctuating each week with one day of rest. Dylan hadn't seen Sinann in a few days, and he began to wonder where she had gotten off to. Not that it wasn't pleasant to escape her constant harassment, but he figured if she no longer wanted him to "save her people" she might give in and send him home.

He also kept an eye out for the pretty blond woman, who he learned was the Laird's daughter, Caitrionagh. He never had occasion to talk to her, and didn't dare in any case if Iain Mór's reaction to him merely looking was an indication of how he would take an actual conversation. But in the evenings Dylan stole glances from across the Great Hall where the clan often gathered for talk, clustered together on stools and benches, sometimes sitting on the trestle tables if room was scarce. Occasionally, if the gatherings were well attended, there was music and dancing, particularly if teenagers were there, and sometimes there was but a small clutch of men in heated debate with heads close together before the hearth. Caitrionagh was there often, which pleased Dylan greatly.

One morning the entire clan gathered formally in the Great Hall, in subdued expectation. The mood of the gathering tensed as people were brought before the Laird. None of them looked very happy about being there. Dylan leaned against the wall by the bailey doors. He was out of the way but could still see almost everyone. Puzzled, he mumbled to the absent faerie as if she could hear him, "Yo, Tink, what's going on here?"

She popped into view before him, a huge smile on her face as she hovered at eye level.

He blinked. "Tink. How long have you been here?"

"And who's to say I ever left? I can see it's a hard worker you are, and the picture of grace with a sickle. I was just admiring the view."

Dylan made a face. "I need a translator. What's going on?"

"Judgment."

That explained the breathless tension that filled the room. The mood in the hall was more serious than the evening gatherings, but the proceedings still weren't conducted with the formality of the courts of law to which Dylan was accustomed. Iain merely sat in a creaky wooden chair near the hearth at the kitchen end of the hall, Malcolm stood behind him, and persons in dispute took turns presenting their problems. Sinann informed Dylan that the man now standing before Iain, wearing a ragged and faded kilt and yellow shirt, was Colin Matheson, accused of stealing grazing.

Iain glared at the defendant without hearing any more than the accusation from someone who appeared to be the plaintiff. "Colin, did I nae tell you to give over that land? It isnae part of your tenancy now." Sinann translated as he spoke.

Colin was surly, obviously unhappy with having a portion of his land parceled out to someone else. "I cannae live without that land."

"And why not? Your rent was reduced accordingly. You've as much land, and of the same quality, as everyone else of your need."

"But Iain—"

"Dinnae argue with me, man! Ye've been told. Now, pay for the grazing at one Scots shilling per day, or what you can give in kind valued according to your rent payment. And if we find your cattle off your own pasture again, you'll spend time in the guardhouse. Are we clear on that?"

Colin took a long time to reply, but finally said, "Aye."

When Sinann finished translating, Dylan whispered back, "Stealing grazing?"

"Grass feeds the cattle, which feed the people. Mathesons are thick on the ground these days, and the ground they're thick on is smaller and smaller each year, as the English and the Whigs take more and more from us. The cattle have little to eat in the winter, so a few blades of grass can mean the difference between a dead cow and a live one come spring. Cattle dead of starvation can mean the difference between an expectant mother having enough to eat or not, which can mean the difference between a live birth or a still one, or a child surviving an illness or not. It's a serious thing Colin Matheson has done."

Dylan found himself agreeing.

The next case was a very young woman who seemed to be showing a pregnancy, though it was hard to tell with the style of dress being what it was in these times. The man at her elbow appeared to be her father, an older and very angry man. Dylan's suspicions were confirmed when Sinann translated that the complaint against the girl, Iseabail Wilkie, was unlawful congress. Her father, Myles Wilkie, jerked her arm, trying to get her to confess the name of the baby's father, but she stared at the stone floor and would not speak, though tears ran down her cheeks and dripped from her chin.

Sinann said, "Everyone knows who the father is." Dylan looked at her. "It's Marsaili's husband, Seóras Roy Matheson." She pointed with her chin to a thin, quiet man with dark auburn coloring, who sat against the far wall amid three children. He also stared at the stone floor, his face as white as his shirt.

Iain asked some questions, and Dylan said, "What is he saying now?"

"He wants to know if there are relatives to whom Iseabail can go." The girl began to wail and tug at her father's restraint. Great sobs shook her as she cried. Sinann continued, "He's going to banish her."

Dylan frowned, and Sinann explained with strained patience, "The Laird cannae suffer fornication to flourish in the glen. If he were to allow bastard babies to stay without support, they would soon outnumber those born legitimately, for it's far easier to make a child than to raise it. And if you want my opinion on it, a man who cannot or will not support his by-blow should also be banished along with his seed. It's a burden on the entire clan. The Laird must be firm in this, or lose the respect of every man in the glen who supports his children."

Dylan stared at the white-faced Seóras and wondered

what sort of coward would just sit there and let Iseabail be banished without saying a word. When the case was decided, he looked to Sinann, who translated, "She's off to relatives in Inverness."

"And if there were no relatives in Inverness?"

Sinann shrugged. "She would go somewhere in any case, whether it be Inverness, Glasgow, Aberdeen . . . it matters not where. The long and the short of it is that she cannae stay here, not with a fatherless baby."

Dylan peered again at the baby's father, who didn't seem any happier for being off the hook. Whatever might be going on in the man's mind, Dylan couldn't know.

That night there was some sort of celebration in the village, involving a lot of singing and dancing around a bonfire, but Dylan didn't attend. He only heard the bagpipes on the distant hill from where he lay in his bunk, trying to sleep. He was cold, dirty, and more pissed off by the day. This was an ugly place, and he wanted to go home.

By the fifth week, the harvest was in, the cattle turned out to graze on the oat stubble, and Dylan was put to work helping cut pieces of peat moss from a bog above an inlet of the lake.

The man named Robin worked with him and cut the peats with a hoe-like cutting tool. The blade was L-shaped, and with his foot he shoved the tool into the peat, sliced again, and pulled up pieces about the size of a modern building brick. Dylan packed them in large baskets astride small, shaggy horses called *garrons*, which looked to Dylan like Shetland ponies. The work went in silence, since Robin's English was as poor as Dylan's Gaelic, but the silence was companionable. Each man did his job with a minimum of fuss and, though each evening they tried to communicate on the way back to the castle to lay out the peats for drying, Dylan found out little more than Robin's last name, which was Innis, and that he was a distant cousin to Iain on his mother's side. Except for the chestnut-brown hair and slender build, he was like a Matheson in height and in the blue eyes everyone around here seemed to have.

On a hill above where they worked, a cluster of women were throwing oat corns into the air and letting the chaff float off on the wind. Dylan strained to see if Caitrionagh was with them, but had no luck.

Sunday came again, a day of rest and no church since the parish priest made the circuit only every few weeks. Though the cold was still very near, a sickly sun low in the south was out and most people were outside. Over on the mainland, near the loch shore, a cluster of boys ranging in age from barely school-age to young teens were playing soccer with a brown ball of leather. They shouted and chased each other, some in kilts and some wearing only shirts. Ranald scurried up and down the field and though he didn't play, he urged the players on with his squealing and laughter. Dylan watched them for a moment as his soul turned nostalgic for his soccer days, then went to soak up the few rays available by the south wall of the castle where the stones held the heat.

The view was of green, brown, and gray peaks reflected in the perfect silver surface of the lake, which he'd come to know was Loch Sgàthan. He leaned against the wall and sighed as his sore muscles relaxed. He'd never in his life lived in a place of such unrelenting cold, and even the scant warmth of the sun-washed stone behind him was welcome relief. He drifted, and for a while felt less like an ice pop and more like a human being. The rest of the men were inside, playing chess and backgammon. He liked backgammon, but needed the sunshine more than he needed to challenge his bunk mates in competition that would probably only get him in trouble anyway.

He dozed, and was awakened by distant singing. Women's voices drifted to him from somewhere. Down by the water, he thought. He shaded his eyes to see under the willow tree that hung over the island shore, and made out a gathering of women in pale overdresses and blouses of yellow and red, pounding laundry in large, wooden tubs. They stood in the tubs and swished the clothes with their feet, like stomping grapes. It struck him that this method looked a whole lot easier and more fun than bending over to do laundry by hand.

He got to his feet and wandered toward the women to listen. They sang what seemed to him a call and response, where one woman would sing a line and the others would answer in chorus. The rhythm of their work drove the music, and Dylan smiled as the tune reminded him of home, of oldies CD's, and a rock and roll song called "Doo Wa Diddy." His heart lifted at the memory, and he began to sing to himself. It really did fit with the rhythm of the women's singing. He went with the pleasure of it and danced a couple of steps, shook his shoulders, and tossed back his hair as he rocked out by himself, still singing. He did a Michael Jackson turn, and came face-to-face with the Laird's daughter.

Her eyes were bright with amusement, and when he turned she could no longer hold it in, but held her hand over her mouth so it snorted through her nose. Dylan's cheeks burned and he wanted to walk away, but he couldn't take his eyes off her. Now that nobody else was there to see him looking, he wanted to memorize her face for later when there would be male relatives all over the place and he wouldn't dare stare.

She went around him and headed for the water. He turned with her and said, "Are you going to do laundry?"

"Not likely," she replied as she spread her arms to indicate her lack of laundry to do. She opened her hand to show him the kitchen knife she carried. "I'm off to the willow tree. This winter we will need a good bit of bark."

"Willow bark? Why?"

"That tea I gave you for your head was made of it. The bark eases pain."

Dylan felt his now-healed skull where her father and uncles had clobbered him. "Oh, yes. Then by all means get all the willow bark you can. Don't let me stop you." She turned to go on her way, but he stopped her. "I'm Dylan Matheson, by the way."

A smile touched her lips, which made him smile in return. She said, "I know."

He spoke quickly to keep her from turning away again. "I'm sorry, I've been here awhile, but I never caught your name." It was a lie, but it was also the only line he had left.

Her smile widened to a grin. For one horrible moment he thought she would walk away, but she said, "My name is Caitrionagh Matheson. Or Caitrionagh NicIain, if you will. Iain Mór is my father. That makes you my cousin."

Dylan glanced around at the countryside. "Is there anyone within a hundred miles of here who *isn't* your cousin?"

She shook her head, serious, though he'd meant the question as a joke. "Only my parents and my uncles."

There was an awkward silence, and Dylan plundered his brain for something else to say as he found himself drawn into her eyes. She had the biggest, deepest eyes he'd ever seen. Her skin was pale, but each cheek held a splash of pink and seemed to glow from deep inside. As she turned, he blurted out, to keep her from going away, "How come those women are working on Sunday?"

Her smile this time was indulgent. "And when else are they likely to get a man's sark off his back?" Then she reached out to tug on his sleeve. "Yours could do with a bit of a wash."

Boy, could it! He shrugged and pulled the fabric away from his body. Even the new shirt tended to stick to him, and they were both so disgusting he could hardly stand them. "I don't know how to do it myself."

"And neither should you. Here, take it off and I'll give it to Seonag who washes for my father." She held out her hand for his shirt.

He hesitated. Plunked down in the midst of a century he knew only from books, he couldn't be sure that stripping to the waist in front of the Laird's daughter wouldn't get him killed. Or at least beaten again. But she waved her hand, impatient for him to comply. Maybe it was okay. So he slipped his plaid from his shoulder and removed the two shirts he wore.

The chill air gave him goose bumps as he handed over the shirts, one white and one almost beige. She took the wad of linen, and her eyes on him made him shiver once. For a long moment she stared, and he stared back, then she blinked and smiled. The spell broken, he pulled his plaid back over his shoulder and secured it in his belt again.

"Seonag will have these back to you this evening."

"How will she tell them from your father's shir . . . uh, *sarks*?"

Caitrionagh laughed. "Yours will be the ones that do not look like ship's sails."

Dylan chuckled, and watched her walk away.

Sinann's voice beside him said, "A bonnie lass, true, but not for you."

"Sez you." He turned to see the faerie also staring after Caitrionagh.

Sinann said, "You've no imagination. It's time you were taught to think outside yourself. With your head, and not with your nether regions."

Dylan sighed. "What's that supposed to mean?"

"Come, lad." She started toward the castle, but he hung back. She stopped, leapt to hover just over the ground, her voice impatient. "I said *come*. We must make the most of the time we have." Still Dylan only shifted his weight and stared, so she said, "Get over here, laddie, or I'll give ye warts on your bonnie wee nose."

That moved him. He followed her across the drawbridge to the village. "Where are we going?"

"To a private place. Nary a body goes there because they believe it's enchanted." She gave him a sly glance. "The wee folk frequent the place, don't you know."

He chuckled. "I bet they do."

It was a long walk by Dylan's standards. He hadn't walked much of anywhere since his sixteenth birthday when he'd passed his driver's test. Out the other side of the village, Sinann ducked off the main trail and followed the creek, or "burn" as he'd learned it was called here. Up the north side of the glen she took him, and around a hill dotted with white birches and wide-crowned oaks yellow for the fall, then up a narrow gorge choked with trees and bushes. Thick pines with knotted trunks and twisted branches shaded the burn as it burbled over rocks and under gnarled roots, over which Sinann and Dylan made their way along a faint trail.

Fungus ridged some trees, and huge toadstools grew in large, brown colonies that brought to mind dancing figures of women twirling their skirts. Reeds growing in the water bent with the flow and gave the streambed a furred sort of appearance. Yellow flowers were everywhere in the woods, and Dylan found it strange to find blossoms so thick in the fall. Back in Tennessee, flowers were the glory of spring and sometimes seen in summer, but in the fall back home, colors came from dead leaves. Lower among the growth were some tiny purple blossoms as well, but they were fading to brown on their green stalks.

Finally they came to the grassy flat of a short, narrow valley surrounded by steep granite peaks, where a ruins stood in mossy antiquity.

Stone walls, furred with moss that was dark in spots but shiny, velvety green in others, seemed to melt into the sod like a green and gray sand castle washed by rain. The walls had been crumbling for a long time, centuries, perhaps millennia, and the structure was now little more than a windbreak a couple of stories high. Where the door must have been was now only a tall, narrow gap in the wall. Sinann guided him through it.

"What did this used to be? Why is it here?"

"A *broch*. Tower, to you. Nobody knows how old it is, even me. But if you could fly, as I do . . . well, see for yourself."

She pointed to his feet and leapt into the air. Something seemed to grab him by the ankles and lift. He almost fell, but as his feet rose he spread them for balance and managed to keep upright. Steadily he was lifted. His heart thudded in his ears as he reached a dangerous height and kept going. "Tink," he said in a deadly warning voice. "Stop this."

"*Och*, it's harmless, lad. It's not as if I were changing you and couldn't change you back. Take a look around, see the answer to your question now that you can look out from where the top of the *broch* once was."

Dylan straightened, steadied his balance, and looked. Sinann said, "When the thing was at its full height it looked out over yonder trees, giving it a wide view of the east end of the glen, which is the only approach by land to your Laird's castle."

Dylan then understood. "It was a lookout tower. A place to garrison men and ambush anyone approaching the village along this valley . . . I mean glen. The shortcut we took is how messengers warned the castle of attack."

"Aye. You're not as thick as you appear." Dylan curled his lip at her. "Except the tower is a great deal older than the castle. There was a time when it stood on its own as a

place of shelter and yonder bolthole was a route to boats on
the loch. But that was before my time."

In the midst of the glen beyond was a long, low stone
building surrounded by tenant fields. "What's that?"

" 'Tis the barracks the *Sassunaich* built to house their
lobster-backed minions. It's wise they were, to put it out of
sight of the castle. Here they're close enough to make their
presence known, but not in the midst of things where they
might be hurt, should the villagers take a notion to remind
the soldiers they are outnumbered." Then she sighed and
said, "Also, like those who built this tower, the English know
this is the easiest approach to the glen by land."

Dylan stared hard at the barracks, as if he could wish them
away, then said, "Let me down." He dropped, and yelled in
alarm, but then slowed just above the ground and landed as
if he'd leapt from a sidewalk curb.

Once recovered, he looked around at the curved walls.
Worn stone stairs rose along the inside in a spiral that came
to an end near an upper window. A tall oak tree grew just
outside and poked through that window, its gnarled branches
twisted by the stone and grown to it then spread out across
the tower interior, throwing shade both inside and out. A
small, stone-lined hearth overgrown with grass, nothing more
than a depression about the size of a car tire in the center of
the enclosed area, was partly grassed over, and Dylan
guessed the ceiling had once vented smoke through a hole.
Some large pieces of fallen wall lay about, scattered across
the sod floor. Dylan sat on one of them, which was almost
entirely covered over with moss and lichen. The grass at his
feet was spotted with a black fungus that grew all through it
like crabgrass.

He turned to Sinann, who had settled onto that grass. "If
you can do magic, how come you need me?"

Sinann's face went dark, and he knew he'd said the completely wrong thing. For a few minutes he thought she
wouldn't answer, but she finally said, "There was a time
when I wouldn't have needed you. I wish I *dinnae* need you,
for all the help you're being." She was silent for another
minute or so, then she said, "Watch."

She waved her hand, and a goat appeared in the middle

of the enclosure. It stared around and bleated, then took a step and bleated again. Dylan said, "Okay, a goat." He reached out to let the creature sniff his hand, then retrieved it when it nibbled him with soft, exploring lips.

"Now, watch me undo what I just did." Another hand wave, and the goat collapsed onto the grass. At first it looked like the animal had simply fallen, but on second glance Dylan could see it was now a rotten carcass, stinking and fly-blown. He moved from the stone and backed away, and put his hand over his mouth and nose to keep out the stench. Sinann said, "Nothing ever goes back the way it was. Nothing done can be undone. I've lost that much of my power."

Dylan's gut tightened. "You can't send me home."

Sinann flew, then lit on a stone block to be at eye level with him. "It's time you learned a few things, lad." Another wave of her hand and the carcass became a dry skeleton. A final wave made it go away entirely.

Dylan was not in any mood for her tricks. "Like what?"

"First of all, you've got to learn Gaelic. You'll never be a true clansman until you speak the language of your people. You've also to learn the Craft. It will give you the bit of power you'll need—"

"Wait a minute. Craft . . . witchcraft?"

"Aye. If you know the power of everything around you, nae man—"

"Uh uh." Dylan waved his hands in denial. "Nope, not gonna. No witchcraft for me." He began to back away.

She flew to the steps, now above him. He turned to face her, and she said, "And why not?"

"I don't believe in it."

"It exists, whether you believe in it or nae. Since it's there, it's my opinion you should use it."

"No."

"If you're going to save my people—"

Again with the "save my people" stuff! "Get a clue, Tink! I'm not going to save anyone! The Scots can't be saved! History will call them beaten by the English, and they will become a subculture of the conquerors. There's nothing you nor I can do about it. You've taken me from my time . . . from my *life* for nothing!"

He turned and started for the exit, but she said, "Such a braw face to be covered with great, bulging warts!"

Dylan stopped and turned back. She glared at him, and he glared in return. He wanted to go home, and wanted to strangle her for bringing him here. It was a long standoff.

Finally, he said, "What is it with you? Why can't you just let destiny run its course?"

She unlocked her eyes from his and looked around at the ruined walls. After another long moment, she said in a voice much softened, "Donnchadh used to come here." Her eyes misted up, and Dylan was surprised to learn she could cry. "He loved this place. So peaceful it was, hidden away from the English and those thieving MacDonells. Oh, how he hated the English! When he fought them, he fought as bravely as any man who ever walked the Highlands. And when he died . . ." For a moment she lost her voice, but she coughed and continued, "When he died, it was with my name on his lips."

"Donnchadh was a faerie?"

She shook her head and stared at the ground. "He was a Matheson. Iain's father. But he loved me, and I loved him in return. More than anything in my long, worthless life."

"Iain and his brothers, are they—"

She raised her head, eyes flaming. "Get yer filthy mind out o' yer groin!" She stood on the stone block, on her toes, looking like she might assault him. "Love of the heart and love of the body are entirely different things and not to be mistaken for each other."

Dylan took a step back, shocked by her vehemence. "Okay, I'm sorry."

She took a moment to calm down, muttering dark things to herself about perverted mortals, then sat on the stone and went on with her tale. "Donnchadh had two mortal wives, the first of which gave him Iain and promptly died. Then he remarried, and the other had many children who died, but eventually produced Artair and Coll. But I loved him more than I can say. More than a mortal, even Donnchadh himself, could ever comprehend. I loved him in ways that only a faerie can know, with a soul thousands of years old and a knowing deeper than eternity. And now I mourn him with that soul and that knowing. He made my whole sorry life worth the living."

"How did it happen?"

She closed her eyes for a moment, then began to speak. "Donnchadh was a man people loved and feared, much like his son, Iain. He cared for his people, as his eldest son does, treated them fairly, and protected them from harm. I first revealed myself to him when he came to this *broch* asking for help. His lands had suffered drought for two seasons, and the people of the glen were dying. He came to the *broch*, desperate, hoping to find someone to help."

"And he found you?" Dylan's voice carried a touch of sarcasm, and Sinann threw him a quick frown before she continued.

"In the many centuries after the priests came, with their church buildings and their abhorrence of things natural, nobody had ever come to ask me for help. I was surprised, to say the least, to see the young Laird come asking after the *Sidhe*. He was a handsome lad, with strength and bearing as you have. His hair was the color of a new copper pot, and his eyes blue as the depths of yon loch, and as mysterious. He had an intelligence about him, and a sense of things around him he did not pass to his sons. He knew I was here, and came for help because his people would die without it."

"Did you help him?"

"Of course I did. I made it rain."

Dylan chuckled and poked at the fungus on the ground with the toe of his shoe. "Making it rain in Scotland. There's a stretch. How many drowned?"

Her eyes narrowed at him. "Nobody drowned, ye goof. It was a good harvest that year, and the clan prospered. And just because the Laird had the good sense to use help where he could get it."

"But he died."

Her face darkened again. "He was killed by that redcoated bastard with the rod up his arse and his nose in the air. Bedford was but a Lieutenant then, and newly assigned to command the independent company of dragoons garrisoned across the way. The soldiers had appropriated some cattle that had been brought north from the Trossachs, which the clan would need to butcher and salt for winter. The English took fully half the cattle in the glen, and to feed but twenty men for the winter. The English eat like pigs, and what one soldier requires in a day could feed three sturdy Scottish men."

"The Crown didn't pay for the cattle?"

"Aye, they did. But a starving village cannae eat shillings. They needed food."

"And Donnchadh died because—"

"He died because he tried to take back his property. He and his sons made a raid on the garrison to drive the cattle north."

"Not to the castle, then?"

"Dinnae be an idiot. Donnchadh certainly was not. His plan was to take the *spréidhe* into Ross-Shire and there he would have traded it for less . . . *identifiable* provisions."

"Would have? They didn't make it?"

"Nae. Bedford was waiting for them, with five other men. He let the Mathesons herd the cattle out, then opened fire. Donnchadh was cut down straightaway, but lay, dying, for a long spell. I heard the commotion from here and flew to him. Iain and Coll escaped without having been identified, but it was without the cattle and without the other men who were killed in the fray. There was nae sign of Artair, who had just shortly returned from fosterage up north. I think he wasnae on the *creach*."

Dylan's voice went low. "Donnchadh didn't die right off. You can't heal people, can you? How come?"

Her face screwed up with grief. "I sorely wish I could. I wish I could have put right the injury, and he would yet live. But even when my power was strong the healing eluded me. I cannae put straight the inner workings of a man, no matter how I try."

"So Donnchadh died."

"As he died, he called for me. The English Lieutenant made jokes. He laughed with his men at Donnchadh's 'superstition' and his 'barbaric morality'. I tried to strike him down, but succeeded only in popping the buttons from his coat."

Dylan had to stifle a laugh at the visual, and a smile did

curl Sinann's mouth. "Aye, it was a sight. They continued to fly off for several days, and kept his servant busy with a needle and thread, it's true." She grew serious again. "But it was death he deserved. The clan suffered that winter. They suffered horribly for the sake of feeding those English pigs. Children died. Donnchadh died for taking what was rightfully his, and Bedford should die a horrible, painful death. He and every other *Sassunach* that comes here to rule what is not his."

"And that's why you hate the English so much, because they killed Donnchadh?"

Fire flashed in her eyes again. "A true Scot wouldnae ask for a reason to hate the English. Our people have never been more than an infestation to them, on land they would have use of themselves. Poor as it is, they would turn us off it and have tried for centuries to do so. They have butchered children and raped young wives. Of our men, those they dinnae kill they send across the ocean." Dylan knew she hadn't seen anything yet for the numbers that would emigrate in another fifty years.

"The English must be fought, or they would see us all dead."

"But now it's personal between you and Bedford."

She sighed. "Aye, now it's personal." As if that settled everything, she looked him in the eye and said, "So let us get down to the business of learning the Craft."

"No. Not in the mood to be burned at the stake, thankyouverymuch." Witch burnings had slacked off at the beginning of this century, but Dylan knew the last execution for witchcraft wouldn't occur for another eight or nine years. He didn't want to be next. "Besides, I don't believe in it."

"Ye believe in me."

"I believe you're a pain in the ass."

Her eyes narrowed. "It's that Yahweh, isn't it? You think I'm the devil."

Dylan had to think about that. He replied, "No, I don't. I think you really are what you say you are."

"And do you think witches deserve to be burned at the stake?"

That was an easy one. "No."

"You attended Mass last Sunday, and you crossed yourself. Do you think you should be punished for being a superstitious Catholic?"

Even easier. He let go a nervous laugh. "No."

"Then why—"

"No. I said no Craft, and I mean it."

"But—"

"No."

She glared at him, then yielded the argument far too suddenly for it to be more than a temporary retreat. "All right, then, you've nothing against your ancestral language, have you? Let's start adding to the Gaelic you've learned since you came."

"I've learned nothing."

"You know more than you think, lad. Take, for instance, *tigh.*"

Dylan dug back through memory for the thing Sinann had called the castle. "House."

"Tha mi a' dol dhan tigh."

His eyes narrowed in concentration. He'd heard those words before. *A' dol* . . . going. House. "I am going to the house?"

"Aye! Very good! *Glè mhath!*"

"I don't see why I need to learn this. Almost everyone in the castle speaks English."

Sinann looked like she would say something cross, but her brow cleared instead and she said, "But just think, laddie, how pleased Herself will be when you talk to her in her native tongue."

Putting it that way shed a whole new light on the language issue. Dylan sat on the grass and listened to the translations of Gaelic words he'd been hearing all month. For hours they talked, and in spite of himself he became fascinated by the language he'd never had the patience to learn before when nobody around him spoke it.

He discovered certain aspects of it were echoed in Tennessee dialect. For centuries American southerners had been ridiculed by Yankees for conjugating the verb "to be" as "I be, you be, he be, and she be," but he found it was that way in Gaelic, which had been spoken by many of the original

settlers of the American South: *tha mi, tha thu, tha e, tha i.*
He also found that, just as in southern dialect, verbs tended
to have an "a'" attached. *A' dol* and *a' tighinn* were the
same as a southerner saying, "a-going and a-coming." Learning this was an odd sensation, as if he'd known it all along
and now merely realized it.

The sun was nearly set when Dylan found himself getting
colder by the second. He needed to return to the castle. He
pulled his plaid around his bare shoulders and let Sinann lead
him back. His brain buzzed with Gaelic words, and emotions
tugged him in several directions. He wasn't eager to admit
this place and time weren't as strange as he'd at first thought.

He made it back to the barracks by the light of the rising
moon, and found his shirts waiting on his bunk. Shivering
now, he put them both on. He was climbing into his bunk
when Malcolm entered the long, dark room.

"A Dhilein!" By now Dylan recognized the address form
of his name in Gaelic.

He replied in kind for the hell of it, *"A Chaluim!"*

Malcolm chuckled, then said in English, "Get your gear
together. You're leaving with us now."

"Huh? Leaving for where?"

"You'll find out on the way. Get ready, and meet us—"

"I'm ready now." *Gear? What gear?*

"You'll need your *sgian dubh.*"

Dylan felt for his knife under his arm. It and the sporran
on his belt and the clothes on his back were all he owned.
"Let's go." They went.

CHAPTER 7

Malcolm spoke in a low mutter as they clattered down the wooden stairs to the castle's inner bailey. "A messenger from Killilan has arrived with news of the Laird's sister-in-law, who is Deirdre MacKenzie. She's in her confinement, and it looks . . . nae good." Confinement? Dylan searched his vocabulary of archaic English and found nothing that made sense. Malcolm went on, "She's in need of her sister and niece. We're to escort them immediately." Dylan guessed Mrs. MacKenzie was ill.

Dylan then saw the horses saddled in the bailey, with Caitrionagh and her mother, Una, already mounted. The sight of Caitrionagh took his breath away. She sat tall, her cloak secured around her shoulders and her chin set against the fear for her aunt. The look in her eyes was far away and filled with worry.

Out of nowhere, Sarah hurried up to him and took his hands. "Be careful," she said.

Taken by surprise, Dylan stammered that he would try. Sarah smiled and squeezed his hands, then stepped away to let him by. He peered at her for a moment. Her gaze overflowed with emotion, and he was afraid of what it might be.

Had Sinann been right about her? He shook off the thought. It was too strange. Too . . . creepy.

Malcolm swung aboard his horse, leaving Dylan to ride an animal he was sure would kill him at the first opportunity. Almost as tall as himself at the shoulders, it tensed and sidled as he approached. He'd never ridden before, unless one counted the pony photo his mother had made when he was small. The horse snorted, and Dylan decided his only choice was to go with a complete bluff. Caitrionagh was watching. With as much assurance as he could muster, he reached for the reins, grappled for purchase on the English-style saddle and managed to get a foot in the stirrup. He hauled himself aboard.

The horse skittered sideways, but he held on with his knees and it settled after a moment. Slung over the horse's back in front of the saddle was a pair of leather saddlebags. Provisions, he guessed. It appeared they would be gone awhile. Malcolm urged his horse forward to take the lead, then Una, Caitrionagh, and finally Dylan brought up the rear as they moved between the gatehouses and over the drawbridge. He figured that with any luck, his horse would simply follow the others.

At the drawbridge, where the horses' hooves thudded and echoed on the wood, he made the mistake of looking back at the castle. Sarah stood beneath the stone arch and waved. He now had to wave back, and obliged before facing front again. This wasn't right.

The ride was long, cold, slow, and often too dark to see as they passed through the occasional wood. The full moon rose behind jagged peaks, but was sometimes blocked by pines.

In the clear, though, Dylan noticed Caitrionagh looking around more than might be usual for someone who knew the terrain. She looked back at him often. No words, just looks. He didn't know what to make of that, and the trail was too narrow and rocky for him to ride in tandem with her to talk. So he only smiled at her, not sure what it was she saw when she looked.

The horse beneath him had a habit of tossing its head and heaving great, snorting sighs that felt like a giant balloon inflating between Dylan's knees. He thought he might be holding on too tight, but whenever he relaxed his thighs the horse sidled and tossed its head again. More than once, when Dylan lost his concentration, the horse slowed or tried to veer from the path. He figured keeping control of the animal's head was all that kept him from being scraped off on a low branch or high rock. As the night wore on, though, the animal tired of its games. Dylan hoped it had figured out who was boss, for he was tiring of them, too. He wanted to wrap his plaid around himself because of the cold, but needed to keep his arms free.

The track rose and fell, and wound in so many directions Dylan could no longer tell which way was which, nor did he know what time it was. The moon moved, but it seemed to go several directions. He passed the time by mumbling his numbers to himself in Gaelic. Sinann had taught him as far as thirty-nine. "*A seachd deug air fhichead . . . a h-ochd deug air fhichead . . . a naoi deug air fhichead.*" Then back to one. "*A h-aon . . . a dhà . . . a tri . . .*"

Malcolm seemed to know exactly where they were and brought them all to a stop after what must have been several hours. They'd reached a clearing among gnarled pine trees, where it appeared other travelers had pitched camp in the past. A mound of ashes inside a circle of rocks indicated just how recently. Even Dylan could tell it had been only since the last rain, which in these parts meant within a day or so. Malcolm dismounted and felt of the ashes.

"Cold. It was last night they were here."

"Think they'll be back?"

Though Malcolm looked around for signs of current occupation, he said, "No reason to think they will. It's a common enough spot for people to stop, but not a place to make a home."

Malcolm went to help Caitrionagh and her mother, and they dismounted without speaking. Dylan hauled the leather bags from his saddle, then Malcolm took his own bags to dig through them. When Dylan set his on the ground, Malcolm said, "Take the horses over there, out of sight, and hobble them. You'll find the hobbles in that bag, there. Then remove the saddles and bridles, and set them on a rock or tree where the horses won't step on them." Dylan realized his lack of experience with horses was obvious. Malcolm continued, "Then get us some deadfall. Dry as possible."

Dylan went to do as he was told. He felt Caitrionagh's eyes on him until he was out of the clearing, and ached to return her gaze. The horses made no fuss about being hobbled, a huge relief to him as he bent among hooves and swishing tails. Even easier was the job of getting the animals to spit out their bits and stand still for the saddles to be removed. Still Dylan was certain putting them back on in the morning would be a much trickier process.

Finding dry wood was less easy, this being a common spot for people to stop, and it took him awhile to locate some that was suitably dry, large enough to be of use, yet small enough to be portable. He returned to the clearing with an armful.

They ate their food cold, for it was bannocks and cheese, then lay down, lined up with their feet toward the fire, the women in cloaks and the men in their plaids. Malcolm and Una lay in the center and Dylan and Caitrionagh were on the outside.

This close to the fire was the warmest Dylan had been since his arrival in this century. He couldn't tell whether it was just the fire, if he was acclimating, or if it was Caitrionagh's presence that banished the cold. His imagination ran away with the fantasy of sharing his plaid with her, and he warmed even more. The fire dimmed, and they faded into sleep.

Dylan popped awake at a feeling. He couldn't tell what it was, but something inside him wanted him awake. The fire had fallen into coals that were still warm but shed no light. The predawn sun was turning the sky a lighter shade of black. He lay still to hear. Nothing.

Huh. He closed his eyes again, but couldn't keep them closed. The feeling was a bad one. One of the horses snorted and stamped, and that decided him. There was something out there. He reached out to touch Malcolm's elbow, and the old man awakened without a sound. They both listened. Still nothing. But Dylan could tell Malcolm sensed it, too. The elder man felt for his belt buckle to free himself from his kilt. Dylan did the same.

Then they heard it: ever so slight rustling in the woods around them. There were at least two of them, one on either side of the clearing. Malcolm looked to one side, then to the other, and his hand moved toward his sword as he focused his attention on the trees nearest his side. Dylan looked in the other direction, and reached for his *sgian dubh*, which suddenly seemed pitifully small. He readied, not tense but prepared. The sky was purpling, and the trees around them were coming into visibility. But nothing moved.

A savage yell went up. A cold shock galvanized Dylan. Three men burst from the trees and sent the horses into paroxysms of screaming and rearing. Malcolm, before he was off the ground, skewered one and engaged another. Dylan threw off his kilt and ran for the third one, engaging him by waving his arms and shouting. Then, like a boy teasing a large dog, he dodged the attack he'd provoked. His opponent's broadsword clanged against a rock at Dylan's feet.

The game now was avoidance and deflection, keeping the guy busy until Malcolm could help. In the predawn light, the attackers were little more than purple shadows. It was difficult to anticipate assaults, but the disadvantage worked both ways. The attackers couldn't see either.

Dylan's little knife was no match for a broadsword. But the intruder wielded that sword as if it were a club, or a much larger claymore, which was Dylan's only advantage. His moves were telegraphed well enough that Dylan was able to simply not be there when the strike came. Swordless, his fencing skills were worthless to him now, and he worked as if he were unarmed. Kung fu moves enabled him to escape the long blade and confound his opponent by misdirection. He deflected with his knife only when necessary, and with quick, glancing blows.

It angered his opponent that Dylan wouldn't stand still and die. He swung faster and harder. Parrying strokes jarred Dylan's arm, and his knuckles were sliced open again and again. He circled, hoping to confuse, but the intruder kept coming. From the corner of his eye he glimpsed Caitrionagh picking up something that might have been a large rock. His heart froze. Was she trying to help? If she came too close to the flying blades, she might be hurt. He backed off from his opponent, just quickly enough to encourage him to follow, until the intruder was out of Caitrionagh's reach and temptation was removed. He checked the corners of his field of vision. Where the hell was Malcolm? Dylan didn't dare look. He couldn't take his eyes off his shadowy attacker.

Finally, in frustration, Dylan decided it was time to end this. He feinted and fell back to avoid the parry and counter. Another feint in rhythm, then he fell back again. The third attack wasn't a feint, and he pressed forward instead of retreating. He thrust his knife deep into his opponent's throat, twisted, and ripped sideways.

Blood burst and flew everywhere. Dylan staggered back. The other man gave a choked scream as he fell. The air was filled with a fine mist that stank of iron. It covered Dylan, and he blinked it from his eyes and wiped it from his face with blood-covered hands. When he could see, he stood back and tried to turn away, but couldn't. He watched the man die. Writhing and gurgling on the stony ground in the pink light of the rising sun, the man stared about with bulging eyes, as his hands tried to stop the red flow so he looked like he was choking himself. His panicked gaze found Dylan. Great horror yawned in Dylan as the man's struggles weakened and the awful sounds went silent.

The stillness of the body was appalling. His gut heaved as he realized he'd destroyed a human being. He forced it down, but the knowledge soaked into him slowly, and stained every corner of him. He looked to Malcolm, whose opponent had fled at the screams of his fallen comrade. The first wounded man had run early on. Only the dead man was left. Malcolm looked at him, then at Dylan, who expected reproach. But instead there was only admiration in the older man's voice.

"You went against a broadsword with a *sgian dubh*? You're a daft one, lad, and God knows why you're not dead. I've never seen the like of that!"

Dylan had to cough to find his voice. "I killed him." He wiped his face on his sleeve, which came away red.

"Oh, aye. He's dead all right. And to hell with him. He

asked to be killed, did he not?" Malcolm waited for an answer, and when none came an edge crept into his voice. "Is
it not true?" He indicated with his chin the women they'd
been charged to protect, who also stared. Then understanding
lit his eyes. He grabbed the dead man by a forelock of hair,
to hold his face up to the dim light. "Seumas MacDonell.
He's an outlaw, under sentence of death for the murder of
his pregnant sister."

Dylan's face must have shown his disgust at that, for Malcolm shrugged and continued as if sister-killing were a common thing among some clans. "Well, she was in no way
married nor betrothed, nor, by all accounts, is it likely the
child was anyone's but his. In any event he was tried and
convicted of the crime of murder, and on his way to Glasgow
for an appointment with the Maiden, when he made his escape and has had the run of these mountains since. 'Tis a
good thing you've done."

When Dylan didn't reply, Malcolm lowered his chin and
peered directly into his face. "He was an outlaw. A murderer,
and he would have killed you for your horse and provisions
if you hadnae stopped him. He was a man, but one who had
lived entirely too long. Is it nae true?"

Dylan straightened and raised his chin. "True enough."
He couldn't bring himself to stop staring at the dead man.
The smell of the blood made his stomach curl into a knot,
and he swallowed to keep the bile down. He forced himself
to look away, and wiped his knife blade on his already bloodied shirt.

Malcolm reached down for the fallen sword, then for the
man's plaid to wipe off the spattered blood. He presented the
weapon to Dylan. "Here. You've won yourself a sword, lad.
Handle it the way you handle that dirk, and you'll have
naught to fear from any man."

Slowly, feeling as if in a dream, Dylan took the sword
and held its grip. It was a fairly old and worn double-edged
broadsword with a heart-shaped basket hilt of pierced steel,
lined in leather. The grip was covered in leather bound with
twisted wire. He made a mulinette to the side and found the
weapon well-balanced. He could get used to a sword like
this. A wry smile curved his mouth when he thought of how

he'd once thought he would do anything for an authentic seventeenth-century broadsword. He looked again at the dead man and his mouth tightened. Not this. He would never have done this just for a sword.

Malcolm became busy. He buckled on his kilt without bothering to pleat it, hung his sword baldric across his chest, and restored his blade to its scabbard at his side. Then as he kicked dirt over the nearly dead coals, he pointed with his chin to the scabbard and baldric worn by the dead man. "Get them, and anything else of use he might have, then gather the horses. The sun is almost up, and it's best we be gone before someone else comes to try your little dirk."

Dylan obeyed, then slipped his sword into its scabbard at his side. The worn sporran on MacDonell's belt contained nothing but a wooden cup and a leather drawstring purse containing two pence. He slipped the cash into his own sporran, and left the cup and purse. He turned to Malcolm. "We'll be taking the body, then?"

Malcolm considered for a moment, then said, "Them as might care enough to bother with burial are currently cowering in the woods. They can have it when we've gone. When we get to Killilan we can send a gillie with a message to the MacDonell Laird with the news of the disposition of Seumas's case."

Dylan nodded, glad he wouldn't have to touch the carcass to lift it onto a horse. He turned to the horses and eyed his mount, but when he approached it the animal seemed to sense he was in no mood for any guff. There was no skittering this morning, for which Dylan was glad.

The riders pressed on. As the terrain opened up some, the trail widened enough for Caitrionagh to fall back beside Dylan. "Hold out your hand," she ordered.

"Huh?" He was tired, muddled, and not interested in doing much thinking at the moment.

"Hold out your hand. The cut one."

He looked at the knuckles of his right hand and only then realized they hurt. Though the tiny guard on his dirk had taken the brunt of the sword's blows and kept his fingers attached to his hand, three deep gashes had been opened. He'd forgotten about them and the pain had receded to the back of his mind. They'd stopped bleeding, and were now beginning to stiffen.

"Give me your hand," she repeated as she poured water from a skin into a small handkerchief. He held it out, and she wrapped the knuckles with the wet cloth. "It will start bleeding again, but then I can bind it and the wounds will close properly." She looked at him with those eyes. They cut clean to his soul, and seemed to like what they saw. Something in his gut untied, and conviction filled him. If necessary, he would kill a hundred men to keep her safe, and he would do it gladly.

All he could think to say was to thank her. "*Tapadh leibh*," he said. She gave a sudden smile to hear him speak Gaelic.

They arrived in Killilan when the sun was at mid-sky. People swarmed from the small peat house where they stopped, greeting Malcolm, Una, and Caitrionagh with great joy, and peering at Dylan with curiosity. The chatter was in Gaelic, but Dylan was able to pick out the words *paisd* and *glé mhath* in addition to the name Deirdre. The English word Malcolm had used, "confinement," suddenly made sense, and he remembered it from the movie *Gone With the Wind*. Deirdre had just had a baby. Furthermore, she was doing well, a translation supported by the happy faces all around.

A gaggle of chattering women hurried Una and Caitrionagh into the house, while Malcolm and Dylan dismounted to remain outside with three other men. Their horses were taken away by a boy of about ten, who pulled on the reins and hauled his charges along as if he weren't outweighed by a couple of tons. Malcolm and Dylan were invited to wash up in a bucket after their long, dirty, and bloody ride. Malcolm made introductions as they each rinsed their faces and necks.

It was little more than a recital of everyone's names, but Dylan scoped out the men quickly. The wall-eyed Alexander MacKenzie, who appeared to have had no sleep for a week, was obviously the baby's father. William MacKenzie looked enough like Alexander and was close enough in age to be his brother, and probably was. The older man, also named Alexander but with the last name of Sutherland, echoed the sunny look of Una and Caitrionagh and Dylan took him for

Una and Deirdre's father, Caitrionagh's maternal grandfather. The men all sat outside on three stools, an upturned bucket, and a stack of dried peat, and Alexander the younger, whom everyone called *Ailig Og*, passed around an earthenware jug.

Malcolm, usually the most reticent man in any group, was doing most of the talking today. Dylan concentrated hard to understand the Gaelic, picking out words he knew, and realized it was the story of the morning's ambush. During the telling, the three men stole glances at him which gradually turned from narrow skepticism to surprise, then to grinning admiration. When the jug passed to him, he was encouraged to take a solid drink.

Dylan sniffed it, and smiled. He'd tasted white lightning before, while visiting cousins who lived up on the ridge near Kentucky where stills were not uncommon even in his own century. This wasn't "corn likker," there being no American corn here yet. It was probably made from oats or barley, but it was sure enough homemade whiskey, and as powerful as the moonshine his more immediate family produced. He took a small mouthful, and though he swallowed carefully it made a path of fire to his stomach that almost made him cough. But the cough he turned into a mere throat-clearing. Strong whiskey on an empty stomach seeped into his stained corners and cleared away much of the horror of the morning. Some food and some sleep would be very good, but for the meantime whiskey was enough.

Una came from the house with a full, round bannock. The loaf was about the size of a vinyl record album, and with a hole in the middle. She placed the oat bread over the door, and shoved a thin iron rod through the hole into the peat wall of the house. Then she went back inside. Dylan stared at it long enough that Malcolm explained in a low voice, "It keeps the faeries out, so they won't take the baby away and leave a changeling."

Dylan nodded. Now that he believed in faeries, he was certain this was also true.

Caitrionagh came with some strips of linen to bind the cuts on his hand. The swelling had gone down enough for them to close properly. When she was done, he watched her walk back into the house, and let go a sigh without thinking. Silence fell among the men, who now stared at him. The Mackenzies and Sutherlands looked hard into him, but he thought there might be some understanding in Malcolm's eyes. Dylan put his gaze back on the ground, sorry he'd given himself away.

Food came: fried haggis in slabs on wooden plates. Dylan was hungry enough to eat anything, and decided haggis was pretty good if one didn't care that it was made from sheep parts one would hesitate to feed to a dog. It was definitely the spiciest food he'd had in a while, and it was good and hot. It went down with the whiskey just fine.

The men ate and talked, then drank some more whiskey and talked some more. The sun sank into the mountains; more food came and was eaten. Still the men talked. Dylan, sleepy and drunk, had to give up his attempts to decipher the Gaelic, and nodded off with his back to the peat wall of the house. Several times he caught himself, but more whiskey was had by all and it went down easier with each trip around. He had to close his eyes, just for a moment.

There was no telling when he awoke. He only knew it was dark, very cold, and he was alone, facedown on the sod by the house. He'd fallen from his stool and slid down the outside of the house. There were bits of peat all in his hair and down his neck. First he tried to pull his plaid around himself and go back to sleep, but it was far too cold for that. He struggled to his feet, barely able to keep erect, and staggered into the house where he found the other men crashed out on the floor. The hearth fire was low, but he could see well enough to find an unoccupied space. There he curled up, pulled his plaid around him, and fell unconscious again where it was relatively warm.

In the morning he was the last one awake, and only came to when a foot shoved his backside and Malcolm's voice demanded in English that if he was going to sleep the day away he should do it where he wasn't underfoot.

Dylan sat up and ran his fingers through his hair. His head throbbed, and his stomach was sour enough that when one of the women handed him a bowl of parritch he almost set it aside. But his time among these people had taught him

above all that one ate when one was offered food. The first
week he'd spent in this century, where raiding the refrigerator wasn't an option, he'd been a little hungry all the time.
And he'd had great cravings for sugar and caffeine. Those
had passed, and he'd learned to eat more at meals whenever
possible. Skipping a meal was out of the question. He made
himself swallow the oatmeal, and made himself keep it down.
When he began to feel more human, he decided he needed
to find a garderobe or its peat-construction equivalent.

He looked around, wondering what the facilities might
look like. The house was only a single room with dividers
that didn't reach the ceiling. Planks sectioned off the corner
where the animals lived, and a wicker sort of wall obscured
the bedroom, which the women had commandeered and
where they now all giggled and chattered in whispers. The
five men had all slept on the dirt floor, around the hearth
which was little more than a shallow hole dug in the floor
beneath a gap in the thatching above. Everything lurked in
shadows, for the sun didn't make much headway through the
small windows in this close, earthen hole.

Dylan, peering through his hangover, focused on a dark
corner and witnessed Ailig Og moving his bowels into a
wooden pot atop a short stool, his sark bunched up and dangling between his knees. Dylan looked away. Uh uh. Not
ready for that. He climbed to his feet, adjusted his kilt, and
went outside to find a place to relieve himself in private.

As he ducked out the low door, there was a voice from
above. "There you are!"

He turned, and was not surprised to see Sinann perched
on the roof thatching, munching on a piece of bannock she'd
torn from the loaf over the door. "Here I am," he agreed. He
looked around, wishing there were outhouses in Scotland,
then found himself astonished he was wishing for outhouses
instead of toilets. A porcelain bathroom with running water
and toilet paper seemed like an impossible dream. He took
a stroll down the slope where some trees and thick underbrush near a small creek were likely shelter.

"I looked everywhere for you yesterday morning!" She
fluttered behind him.

"You found me. What do you want?"

She ignored his question and continued to rant. "I'd like to know what you mean, running off like that. I looked everywhere for you. I had to ask Ranald where you'd gone, that's how desperate I was."

He stopped walking and peered at her. "Where did you think I was going to go? Home?" He looked back between the white birch trunks at the peat house and decided there were enough trees between himself and it.

She only frowned. "Ranald. You had me talking to *Ranald*!"

"Relax, Tink. I'm not going anywhere you don't send me. I—"

Sinann grabbed his right hand and gasped, "Who did this?" A bit of pink had seeped through the bandages, but Dylan didn't think they looked bad at all.

He withdrew his hand. "I was in a fight. Some men attacked us and I killed one of them."

"*You?* You killed someone? Defending your family, I have nae doubt."

Dylan nodded.

She beamed and fluttered off the ground, and looked like she might burst with pride. "That's my lad. I knew ye had it in ye." Dylan frowned. He sure hadn't known any such thing. Sinann continued to enthuse, "Was he English? Please tell me he was English."

With a sigh he turned to lift his kilt and ignored the question. "You always show up when I'm not fully dressed. Why is that?"

"*Och*, laddie, be assured that if I wanted to glimpse your bare *thóin* I would see it at my leisure."

Dylan laughed. "Right."

Sinann's eyes narrowed and she muttered under her breath in a language Dylan didn't recognize as Gaelic. She waved her hand, and his belt buckle slipped open.

As he reached for it to keep his kilt from falling off, his plaid fell from his shoulder. He grabbed for it, but all the buttons on both his shirts flew from their holes, one after another. He managed to get his belt buckle secured around his kilt again, but when he tried to button his shirts the belt popped open and fell to the ground.

By now Sinann was screaming with laughter. The entire *feileadh mór* followed the belt, leaving Dylan grasping his shirtfronts to keep them together as they tried to slip from his shoulders. They jumped and jerked as if someone behind were yanking them.

"All right! You win! You've made your point! Stop it, it's cold!"

His shirts relaxed, and he shrugged them back onto his shoulders.

He narrowed his eyes at her, and began the tedious job of putting his kilt back on. "How come you can't do that to the English army and win some battles for these people you're so hot to save?"

Her eyes snapped with anger. "Be assured that if I had the power over that many men at once, every *Sassunach* north of the Border country would find himself without his stitches in an instant. But, alas, things just dinnae work that way and more's the pity, for it would be entertaining in the extreme."

"I thought women in this century were supposed to be demure. Modest."

She laughed. "Women are women in any century, and I've lived through enough of them to know."

He buckled his kilt around his waist and stood. "Is that why Sarah was making goo-goo eyes at me when I left Ciorram?"

There was a long, stiff pause, and he waited for an answer. Then she said, "Was she?"

"Yeah. Very weird." He draped his plaid and secured it in his belt. "A month ago she was crying her eyes out over her dead husband, and now she's looking at me like a lovesick puppy. You wouldn't know anything about that, would you?"

Sinann hesitated again, then said, "Why would I?"

Dylan thought about pressing her, but changed his mind and shrugged. "Dunno. I just thought it was strange." He settled his belt around his waist, and headed back to the MacKenzie house, leaving Sinann to follow or not follow as she chose.

They stayed in Killilan for a week while Una and Cai-

trionagh visited with Deirdre. The men of the household
spent their days working around the house, restacking dried
peat, repairing tools and utensils, and other post-harvest activity, and in the evenings hung out by the hearth and talked.
The women stayed by Deirdre's bedside, and the baby made
one brief appearance among the men to be admired. Una
brought the child, who was wrapped in wool over a linen
baby shirt, and relinquished him to Ailig Og.

The men gathered around the new father, who held his
newborn as if the child might slip through his arms and fall
to the floor. William made a joke that Dylan didn't understand. Sinann, hovering to see, explained he'd said what a
tragedy it was the child looked like his father. Dylan chuckled, and everyone peered at him for being so slow.

The baby was a marvel of miniaturization. Dylan had
never in his life seen a person this young, and it seemed
almost impossible a human so tiny could live. But there he
was, breathing and making faces and everything. It was fas-
cinating, like gazing at a work of art that was always changing. He'd always liked kids, which in his business was a good
thing. The way they soaked up what he would teach was
what made teaching more worthwhile than just about anything else he could do. But four years old was as young as
he would allow a kid in his classes. This baby was something
wholly new to him.

Before long the child was retrieved from his father and
returned to the company of his mother, and the men returned
to their talk.

Dylan had never seen a group of people who could be so
quiet during the day, then open up with a flood of chatter
once the work was done. He'd already learned that *céilidh*
was what they called the informal evening gathering where
there was gossip, music, and storytelling, and each evening
during the visit the men had a small *céilidh* where there was
plenty of talk and as much ale. They sat on stools before the
fire, which threw dancing orange light and deep shadows
against the walls.

Sinann stayed by Dylan's side to interpret. Only Malcolm
spoke enough English to converse with Dylan, so the conversation was entirely in Gaelic. But soon Dylan was shush-

ing Sinann with a raised hand, and attempting to speak in Gaelic himself. It was halting, but Malcolm, William, and the Alexanders were patient and even seemed pleased he was trying. They spoke a little slower than usual, and if Dylan repeated a Gaelic word Malcolm provided the English for it. Dylan still didn't understand everything, but now he could get the gist of a conversation without giving himself a headache.

They were talking politics tonight, their faces serious in the close, smoky air and shifting light. William, as he packed a tiny amount of tobacco into a small pipe, defended the Queen to his Jacobite brother, pointing out that she was the daughter of James II. This was sneered at by both Ailig Og and his father-in-law, who declared that Anne's half brother, being male and the *son* of James II, had the true right to the throne. William gave little shakes of his head as he lit a piece of pinewood in the fire and held it to his pipe, then crushed it out once the tobacco was smoking.

The real trouble, Dylan gathered as he listened, was that religion had its big, fat foot in the controversy. The throne had been handed to Anne after her sister and brother-in-law, Mary II and William III, had died without children. Dylan gathered the reason for the disruption of the rules of succession after the forced abdication of James II was that Anne was Protestant while her brother James was as Catholic as his deposed father, and unwilling or unable to pretend he wasn't. Their uncle, Charles II, had been secretly Catholic while publicly Protestant, but James wasn't likely to pull that off. Catholic France was making a lot of noise in support of James, but because of various treaties with England wouldn't step in with arms for an uprising to gain him the throne. Young James was screwed coming and going.

Then the talk turned to speculation as to who would succeed Anne, since none of her seventeen children had survived.

"Fourteen children," said Ailig Og.

"No, seventeen," insisted William.

Dylan said, "Very many. Too many."

The other men agreed, and let the minor issue drop. Ailig

Og suggested the next monarch could be James, by simple succession, if he outlived Anne.

Dylan said, "George of Hanover."

The other four men fell silent and stared at him, and he would have felt stupid if he hadn't known he was right. Malcolm said, "George of Hanover?"

Dylan had to revert to English, and Malcolm translated, "The Elector of Hanover. Great-grandson of James I of England, through James's daughter, Elizabeth."

That brought gales of laughter, and even Malcolm smiled. William declared the idea ridiculous and Ailig Og reached over with a broad-fingered hand and patted Malcolm's silly colonial cousin on the head. Dylan shrugged and said in Gaelic, "You will see." All too soon.

At the end of a week Malcolm and Dylan escorted Caitrionagh back home, leaving Lady Ciorram to return accompanied by her brother-in-law at a later date. They left at dawn to make the trip in one day.

They arrived at *Tigh a' Mhadaidh Bhàin* in the early evening, just as supper was over and the clan was gathering. The three travelers were greeted and fed, and gossip from Killilan was shared with the Ciorram Mathesons. More and more people from the glen came, and more torches and candles were lit as the room filled. Dylan ate in silence at a trestle table, listening to the Gaelic chatter, and happened to see Malcolm in a dim corner with Iain Mór, in conference. When they returned to the *céilidh*, Dylan was mildly surprised when the conversation quickly shifted to the fight in which he'd obtained the sword that now hung with the other men's swords near the entrance of the Great Hall.

The onlookers turned to him, almost as one, and demanded he tell the story. Gathered before the hearth on stools and benches, some of the men and children perched on tables, in a *céilidh* that included many folk from the village, the local members of Clan Matheson looked to Dylan for their evening's entertainment.

He shook his head. "I'm not . . . I don't think . . ." Over Dylan's protests, Iain Mór hauled his bulky frame from his chair by the hearth and decreed that Dylan would tell the story of how he'd saved the lives of his wife and daughter.

Then he sat back in the large, wooden chair to listen, the smile on his face confident Dylan would comply. Caitrionagh smiled, and Dylan thought he saw sympathy there.

Malcolm handed him a *quaiche* filled with ale. "Tell it, it's a fine story."

Dylan remembered Sinann's words: *There's no such thing as just a story.* He knew his next words would become his reputation. He was stuck. He shoved his plate aside to sit atop the table and face the room. A big slug of ale from the wooden cup bolstered him and gave him some thinking time, then he cleared his throat and began in English. Malcolm interpreted in a low voice. As he spoke, Dylan relived that horrible morning and the fear and disgust crept back. His chest tightened. It took effort to keep his voice even. He found himself making light of the fight as if it had been no big deal to defeat a man wielding a broadsword while armed with a blade only three inches long. Children were wide-eyed. Sarah leaned so far from her seat to listen, he thought she might slip off her bench and fall to her knees. He down-played the spattered blood, and ended the story by saying merely that he'd stabbed the man, who had then died. That simple.

There was a murmur of approval, and Iain praised the brave act. Dylan's ears warmed. He didn't much care for all this attention he was getting for having killed someone, even if the guy had been under a death sentence for a horrible crime. Then Iain announced, "By protecting my family you have proven yourself a brave man, *a Dhilein*, and a Matheson for true." He paused for a moment, thoughtful, then continued in the formal voice of a man who has decided something weighty, "Tonight you'll leave the barracks to live in the West Tower, and you'll be charged with the safety of my daughter."

There was a gasp from someone among the onlookers. Dylan looked, and thought it might have been Sarah, but her face betrayed nothing.

Iain continued, "You've shown you would defend her with your life, and with a skill unimaginable. There's no man other I would trust so well with what I hold so precious." Artair said a single word, which Dylan didn't understand, then muttered something to Coll. Coll said nothing in reply, but glowered under thick, white eyebrows.

Dylan was too stunned to respond to Iain's speech, and in any case didn't dare show his joy at the prospect of spending his days—and nights—with Caitrionagh. He struggled for a reply.

But Caitrionagh leapt to her feet and said in a low voice, in Gaelic that Dylan understood fully, "Father! No!" Her cheeks flamed and her eyes snapped with anger.

The gathered Mathesons murmured again, this time in surprise. It seemed everyone had assumed she would be pleased to have such a brave and skilled fighter as Dylan for a bodyguard. Dylan's heart sank, but he arranged his face to betray nothing.

Iain's voice was hard and he spoke English for Dylan's benefit. "I'll have nae argument from you, daughter!"

Caitrionagh's reply was in Gaelic, and Dylan gathered she didn't want him for a bodyguard, but would rather have Artair or Coll. Anyone but Dylan, it would seem. The two uncles in question both smirked. Artair opened his mouth to say something, but was interrupted.

"I'll hear naught from you, little brother," said Iain as he stood. "Nor you, cousin," he said to Malcolm, who hadn't shown the least interest in speaking. Iain's face darkened, and his already ruddy cheeks fairly burned. He turned to his daughter in great anger. "Cait . . ."

She ran from the room, through the tower door, leaving Dylan to lean elbows on knees, stare into his ale, and wonder what he'd done to deserve this. There was a deep silence among the clan while Iain fumed and muttered. Dylan shifted his seat on the table and feigned indifference, irritated by the treatment. But even more, he was mortified someone might think he was bothered by the girl's rejection of him.

He took a long draw from his ale, sorted some words out in his head, then slowly strung together enough Gaelic to ask the old storyteller for a tale of long ago. That broke the mood and brought smiles to a few faces, for there was always a new story to tell or an old story to tell in a new way. The old man began to talk of a battle against Vikings, while Dylan avoided looking in the direction Caitrionagh had taken.

That night Dylan took his newly acquired sword from the rack along the wall near the main entrance doors, and followed directions to his new quarters in the West Tower. It was about halfway up the tower, he guessed after following the stone steps up and around, where he found an alcove like the others, shaped like a lopsided wedge. But unlike the others it was furnished. A bunk stood against the wall to the right. A small hearth had been built into the other side, with stone that looked newer than the surrounding walls. An iron box filled with chunks of dried peat sat next to it, an iron poker leaned against the box, and within the hearth was a grate in which a couple of small chunks burned.

The bunk boasted linens and a blanket on its straw mattress, and beneath was a wooden trunk bound in iron, long enough for his sword and deep enough for just about anything else he could imagine obtaining in this century. Next to the bed was a short pedestal table on which a candle stood in a shallow copper holder. Dylan lit it from the fire in the hearth, then set it back on the table. At the tip of the alcove wedge was the heavy, carved door to Caitrìonagh's room, at an odd angle to the two walls. He stared at it.

Then he sat on the bunk and looked around. "Not big on privacy, are they?" he muttered. Anyone going up or down the spiral stairs would have a full view of the alcove, which had only two walls and no curtain. Still, it was a step up from the communal barracks where the stove was at the other end of the large room and bedclothes consisted of his own kilt. Here, at least, he had a trunk for his things, a fire to himself, and bed sheets.

He stared at the door. Caitrìonagh was just the other side of it, pissed off at him, and he had no clue why.

He shrugged. It wasn't his problem. He now had a job that wasn't seasonal, and he would do it to the best of his ability. He knelt to pull the trunk from under his bed and opened it. Inside he found a broken rosary of black beads with a black crucifix trimmed with silver filigree and corpus, some candles he thought looked like beeswax, and a book of English poetry bound in leather that was cracked and flaking at the edges. He removed the crucifix from the remnants of beads and put it in his sporran, flipped through the pages of the book and set it on the table next to the candleholder, then sniffed one of the candles to confirm that they were, indeed, beeswax. Then he laid his sword and sporran inside the trunk, closed it, and shoved it back under his bunk.

He stared at the carved door again. She was in there. He wanted to ignore her, but couldn't. He got to his feet to knock on that door, and said, "Caitrionagh." There was no answer. He waited a spell, then knocked again and said, "*A Chaitrionagh.*"

There was no answer. He gave up and sat back down on the bunk. He loosened his leggings and set them on the floor, then his shoes. His kilt and outer shirt he draped over the headboard of his bed. Then he stretched out in the one shirt and pulled the dark wool blanket over himself. This mattress was thicker than the one in the barracks, and was almost comfortable. The warm fire, soft bed, and long day, not to mention all that ale after supper, conspired to make him sleepy. He drifted off.

But when the door hinge creaked behind him, he was wide awake in an instant. He didn't move, but listened for every sound. There was none, until the door creaked again and the latch clicked. Then utter silence.

He rolled over on his bunk and watched his candle flicker and make dancing patterns of light and shadow on the walls. A wave of homesickness took him, and for a moment he thought he would die if he couldn't return to the place where he'd grown up, where he knew everyone and knew the rules, and could be sure of where he stood at all times. A place where he might have lived his entire life without squeezing someone else's lifeblood from his eyes.

He sighed, then blew out the candle.

CHAPTER 8

Dawn found Dylan in the Great Hall, performing his workout while the servant women of the castle prepared breakfast. The work at the hearth went slowly, for all were curious about the stylized movements and elaborate sword work of the formal kung fu exercise. The women stared from across the room and a gaggle of children crept in on him, also staring, until finally, for their safety, he had to stop and wave them back. The kids moved away, but they all still chattered to each other in Gaelic.

They thought he didn't understand, but his comprehension had grown. As he returned to his exercise, he gathered they wondered whether he had a mental instability that caused him to engage in dance that was neither dance nor ceremony. At a pause in his form, in a low stance, sword to the rear as he stared down an imaginary opponent, he called to them in his stunted Gaelic, "I am learn at the fight." That shut them up, and he continued in peace.

He concentrated on learning the weight and balance of his new sword, making it a part of him. Its previous owner had died for not knowing these things. Dylan would not make that mistake.

Sinann appeared. "So you've been moved to the tower, have you?" Dylan ignored her. *Step, lunge, step, retreat, re-*

treat, lunge. His shoes smacked the stone floor precisely, and rustled the straw and reeds scattered around.

"You'll have to slip away at night, then, if there are no more Sundays when you can come take instruction in the Craft."

Block, thrust, block, step, block. "No way, Tink."

"You must."

"I have a job. I'm not going to sneak away at night, and especially not to learn your *Craft.*" He slipped into a sarcastic, countrified voice. "You just find yourself another old boy to whup them Limeys. If you won't send me home, I'll just have to make the best of things, and I do got me some ideas." He glanced at the door that led to the towers.

"You cannae have her, *a Dhilein.* She's for a man with position. Money. Influence. She's to solidify Iain Matheson's power among the clans. She wouldnae marry another Matheson, let alone a poor one." She leapt into the air to hover close and whisper in his ear as if others might hear, "Not to mention, laddie, what she did to ye last night in front of the entire glen."

Dylan waved her away like a fly and gave her a hard look. "Quit spying on me, Tinkerbell." He shook off a rising anger and his movements grew in force. Sinann sounded far too much like his mother. He stopped his exercise, panting with exertion and emotion, scabbarded his sword, and bowed to his imaginary opponent. Then he made for the tower door. Sinann followed.

"Be angry if ye like, lad, but it's true. There's no denying it." The corridor made a T where, to the right, a door led to the North Tower where Malcolm lived and Iain kept an office. Dylan turned to the left and hurried past the doors of non-family living quarters. The kitchen help and other household menials lived in these rooms, crammed together in the wooden structure built against the north curtain wall. Stone was to his right, weeping with the damp, and to the left was musty wood. At the end of the corridor he hauled open the heavy door to the West Tower, and headed up the steps. Sinann followed, babbling on about how he wasn't right for Caitrionagh, but he didn't listen. It was about the same as tuning out his mother.

In his alcove, he put his sword in the trunk then pulled out his sporran. "Hey, Tink, I got a question." He shoved the trunk back into place and sat on his bunk.

She fluttered overhead and settled, perched on his headboard, and balanced by pressing her heels into the wood. "And I might very well have an answer, did I know what you would ask."

"How much is this stuff worth?" He took out his napkin with the silver coins and spread it open on his blanket.

"Oh, he thinks he's got a fortune for working in the fields, does he?"

He raised an eyebrow at her and curled his lip. "I'm crazy, not stupid. It's winter. I need a coat, and want to know if I've got enough to buy one."

"A waistcoat would be a good thing, as well."

Dylan made a face. "I hate those things. We don't wear them where I come from, but I tried one once and couldn't breathe in it. Couldn't hardly move, either, and that I can't stand."

"I daresay it must have been a poor fit."

He shook his head. "I just don't like them. An overcoat is all I need, thanks. So, do I have enough?"

She leaned over to peer at the spread of coins. "I'd say that depends on what sort of coat you mean. Those pieces with the queen, they're three-pence. The ones graced with William are one penny." Dylan's stomach flopped with alarm. Pence? Pennies? Four pence had been his daily wage, apparently. His accumulated wealth amounted to fifty-two pence. But Sinann continued, "You've got four shillings, four pence. Enough to buy a fine coat, or enough to buy a serviceable coat and another kilt."

"Really?" Put in those terms, a penny didn't seem so little. Dylan did some quick math. "So there are twelve pence to a shilling?"

Sinann nodded.

"How many shillings to a pound?"

She made an exasperated noise. "Have you nae money where you come from?"

He sighed. "We have different money. Like English money is different from Italian and French. Besides, where

I come from even the English have finally wised up and gone to the decimal system. So, how many shillings to a pound?"

"Scots, or English?"

"These are English coins, right?"

She sighed. "Twenty, then."

"How many in Scots?"

"Twenty."

Dylan threw her an exasperated look.

She spread her hands. "But in Scots a shilling is only as much as an English pence. There are two hundred and forty Scots shillings to an English pound. A Scottish pound is worth one shilling and eight pence sterling. And . . . have you any merks? Nae, I see you don't. In any case, a merk is worth thirteen and one-third pence sterling."

Whoa. Overload, even for a former business major. He held up his palms and nodded. "Okay, whatever. Let's stick with the English coins, because that's what I've got right now. So a serviceable coat would cost . . . ?"

"Three English shillings if you're wanting a good, heavy one but without decoration. You can get them less dear, but a thin one would be pointless to have in the winter."

"And a new kilt?"

"Eleven pence. Maybe more, maybe less. Far less if you let Sarah make it for you."

He chuckled. "I don't think so."

"And why not?"

"I probably wouldn't come through it with my virtue intact."

She laughed. "A selling point, to my mind."

He waved away the concept. "Forget it. I'll find someone in the village to make me a kilt. And a coat."

"Suit yourself." Her tone made it clear she was not pleased with his decision.

The carved door to Caitrionagh's room opened, slowly creaking, and she looked out. Her eyes were still bleary and her mouth soft from sleep. Dylan marveled she could be so pretty so soon after waking. He fell silent, and stood. She said, her voice groggy, "Oh. I thought I heard voices out here."

Dylan glanced at Sinann, but said, "I was just wondering

out loud where to buy a coat, and maybe a new kilt."

"For a kilt you just weave a length of cloth and sew the ends. Almost any woman could weave one for you. But for the coat, there's a woman in the village as does excellent work. I'll take you there today."

Dylan smiled and thanked her, and ignored Sinann's scowl. The faerie said, "Yer wasting yer time, ye fool."

Caitrionagh withdrew to her room and her door clanked shut, leaving Dylan free to whisper to Sinann in rising irritation, "Ask me if I care. It's my time to waste, and if you're so unhappy with it why don't you send me home? But, oh, that's right . . . you can't undo what you've done."

Sinann had no reply, but snapped her fingers and disappeared.

Dylan's job was to accompany Caitrionagh everywhere she went, and his charge had business in the village that day to take a basket of food to a distraught family whose mother was dying. Dylan accompanied her from the castle grounds, and had to take care not to look too pleased to do so.

Snow had come the night before, and it lay in a thin white blanket through which rocks and weeds poked in dark contrast. Dylan hugged his plaid around his shoulders against the cold air. He would be glad to have a coat soon.

Caitrionagh wore her heavy woolen traveling cloak and scarf, and seemed quite comfortable as she gossiped to Dylan, "Marsaili was nurse to Artair and Coll and myself, until her marriage to a man in the village."

"You mean that guy who knocked up . . ." Dylan blanched. "I mean, the one who disappeared shortly after that girl was banished? Seóras Roy?"

Cait's eye darkened and she scowled. "Aye, the one who went to Inverness after his whore, leaving Marsaili and their children alone to face her dying. Her sister works in the kitchen still, and comes to help, but the woman needs her husband and the children their father. Such a coward, he is. It's a wasting thing she has, and some even say she's possessed. My father would fly into a rage, were he to know where I'm going."

Dylan stopped dead in the track, and she paused to look back at him. "Then we're not going," he said.

She smiled and started again on her way. "Indeed, we are. And you willnae stop me."

He hurried to take her arm. "No. If your father doesn't want—"

"He's not the one who has a starving family, is he?"

"Then let me take the basket to her. But you can't—"

"Dylan . . ." She gave him a look that said he was being silly. He knew what she meant, that the gift wouldn't mean the same if he took it.

He said, "Is this why you were so upset last night? You thought I wouldn't let you go see Marsaili?"

A puzzled look came over her, then it cleared up and she said, "No. That was nothing." The early winter wind blew her scarf tail over her face and she moved it aside with her finger. "You should ignore it." She went on her way again, slogging through the snow in the lane, and he followed.

"Nothing? It didn't feel like nothing. Why are you being this way?"

"What way?"

He fell behind for a moment, sighed, then caught up to her again. "You can go, but don't you dare touch anything while you're there. And keep away from her. Don't let her get in your face—"

"*In* my face?"

"In front of you. Close." He shook his hair from his eyes and demonstrated by placing a palm in front of his nose. "If you promise that, you can go."

"And if I dinnae promise, I suppose you'll throw me over your shoulder and carry me back to the *Tigh* like a great, hairy Viking?"

He looked at her white-blonde hair and wondered how many of her ancestors had been actual Vikings and done that very thing. "I might." A smile played at the corners of his mouth, though he tried to keep it down.

A big smile lit up her face, but she said nothing and went on her way. He shook his head and chuckled to himself, and kept by her side.

The peat house where Marsaili lived was well down the glen and backed up against the steep southern slope, a dark and depressing place at this time of year even with the sun fully risen. There were two daughters in their early teens and a little boy, and the oldest girl had the worn look of a child who had grown up entirely too fast. Dylan had seen a lot of kids like this over the years, ones that wanted kung fu lessons to defend themselves from adults as well as bigger kids.

He stood by the door to do his bodyguard thing, and entertained himself with idle thoughts of Mafia gunmen alert to danger from rival families, while Caitrionagh visited with the sick woman.

Marsaili sat before the fire in a high-backed chair, her legs covered by a wool blanket. Even in the dimly lit room Dylan could see her face was gray and dry, and her lips were the same shade as her face. There was no coughing, which made him think it wasn't tuberculosis, and that was a relief. But he was no doctor, so the illness could have been anything. All he knew of fatal disease was what he'd seen on television, and he could only guess at what was killing Marsaili. He thought it might be cancer, and hoped it was at least as noncontagious as that.

As he watched her with Caitrionagh, he was appalled at the pain he saw in Marsaili's face. Where he came from, dying people were given the mercy of anesthetic, but here there was nothing more than whiskey or willow bark tea. He glanced around and saw a stone jug sitting on a trestle table, and was glad to see someone was keeping her in whiskey, at least.

Caitrionagh spoke in a low voice, which seemed to soothe Marsaili. Dylan let them have their privacy, but he watched Caitrionagh's eyes. There was sincere caring in them. This was far more than a gesture of noblesse oblige; she was tending to a friend. Though her voice stayed light, over the course of the visit he saw small lines appear in her face, showing the stress of watching her friend die. They stayed through most of the afternoon.

Done visiting, Caitrionagh stepped outside the house and stood for a moment to stare at the mountains surrounding the glen. She took deep breaths, and for a moment looked like she might cry. But she shook it off and turned to Dylan. "Now to order you a coat before your thin colonial blood freezes and we have to prop you in front of the fire to thaw you out." She giggled at her own joke, but he wasn't entirely certain it wasn't true.

She guided Dylan to a house among the cluster near the castle, where she asked the seamstress for a price on a coat and kilt. The front living area of the house was set up as a shop, the walls festooned with rolls of plaid wool and linen fabric, some natural colored and some dyed yellow, and patterns of coarse brown paper. Boxes of raw wool and balls of yet undyed yarn stood near a large, wooden chair. A pillow on the chair constituted the first thing he'd seen resembling upholstery since his arrival last month.

The woman, who Caitrionagh introduced as Nana Petti- grew, was short, dumpy, and the most sunny personality he'd met in Scotland. She chattered away in a kind of speed- Gaelic he couldn't begin to sort out, but his lack of reply didn't seem to bother her. She looked him up and down, then indicated he should turn around for her to take measure- ments. A few quick touches with a string marked with knots, and she announced in English as if she'd known all along he couldn't understand her Gaelic, "Four shillings, three pence for the coat, a shilling and two for the kilt." She spoke so fast and with such a thick brogue he almost couldn't un- derstand her English either.

Dylan blanched. Five shillings, five pence, total. He didn't have it.

Caitrionagh saw his reaction, and said to the woman, "He's not the Prince of Wales, you know, and needs naught of style. Besides, he's only got three shillings to spend." Dylan opened his mouth to correct, but she threw him a warning glance and he shut up. She said, "Both items for three shillings, or we let someone else do the work."

The sunny smile never faltered. "Then let them." Caitrion- agh took Dylan by the arm and made to leave, but the woman stopped them. "All right, three shillings eight. I can have it done in four days." Four days? It took that long to sew a coat? The woman was still smiling.

"Three shillings four," said Caitrionagh.

There was a long, thoughtful pause, then, "Only as your father is who he is, then done. Half in advance." Dylan pulled out his napkin filled with money, and counted out twenty pence. It was hard to get his mind around the value of these coins. As pennies, forty of them was the least he'd ever spent on clothing. But calculated in terms of days worked, he was handing over five days of his life, with five more in the balance. That was one bloody expensive coat and kilt.

The already cold day waned as they crossed the draw-bridge to the island where *Tigh a' Mhadaidh Bhàin* stood. But instead of going straight through the gatehouse, she veered off toward the shore where the willow tree hung over the water.

"Where are you going?" He said it in Gaelic because he could, and he followed her.

"Just to the tree."

"What for? It's freezing out here."

"It's barely nippy. Come." She ran down the slope, and he followed. The leaves had all gone from the tree, and bare branches dangled to the ground. Caitrionagh parted them as she moved, playing as if she were a child under department store clothing racks, with Dylan right behind. The ground underfoot crunched with ice. Then she hopped up onto the remnant of the castle's outer curtain wall, no more than a low strip of rubble a few feet wide that circled the island at the water's edge.

"What happened to this wall?" he asked from mild curiosity and for the sake of conversation.

She walked along it, and he followed. "You'll notice some of the village houses are stone. When this castle was last used for purposes of war the outer curtain was breached. See, over there by the drawbridge, where sappers dug a mine under it then set fire to the supports so it collapsed. The assault still failed and my . . . *our* Matheson ancestors retained the keep. The MacDonells were eventually beaten back. Rather than repair the castle, though, since the strategic value of such a stronghold had become not worth the rebuilding, they turned the fortress into little more than a very large house and began taking the stones from the outer curtain for other uses. Over the past century, they've used almost every stone, and the outer bailey is now grazing for sheep."

Dylan looked around as if he cared. "I see." He kept an eye on her, and within reach of her, lest she stumble on those stones and fall into the icy water of the loch. But, not wanting to appear to be hovering, he picked up some flat stones from the rubble underfoot and began skipping them across the water.

"Oh!" she cried, and reached for a rock he had in his hand. "Look!" She showed it to him. It looked like a donut. "A Goddess Stone!"

"A what?"

"It's a stone with a hole worn through it. It's magic!"

Oh, brother. "Really?"

"Indeed. Look through this hole and you can see if there are any faeries nearby."

Suddenly he was interested. *"Really?"* He put the rock to his eye like a monocle and looked around. Sure enough, there was Sinann, perched in the crotch of the willow right behind them. He waved. She stuck her tongue out at him.

Caitrionagh giggled. "You're funny." Then she put her hand to his chest and he froze, the Goddess Stone forgotten. Her eyes looked straight into his, and he could suddenly hear his heart pound in his ears. She murmured, "I need something," and opened his shirtfront. He held his breath. Her hand went inside his shirt. His mind flew to figure her out, what she was up to, but could grasp nothing. Still her fingers sought inside his shirt.

Then she grasped his dirk and pulled it from its sheath under his arm. "Hey!" he said, disappointed. He watched as she cut a piece of branch from the tree. Then she cut from the thin branch two pieces the length of her finger, and handed the knife back to him. She stuck one of the pieces between her teeth and handed the other to him.

Sinann's voice in the swaying branches overhead made his eyes narrow, but he didn't look up. "She's playing with ye, lad!"

"Ah." He slipped the Goddess Stone into his sporran, took the piece of willow branch, and put it between his teeth the way she did. "A toothpick." He chewed one end so it flayed like a brush. "Beats the snot out of picking your teeth with a knife, eh?"

She laughed and let him escort her into the castle. "Beating snot out? Such a way you have with words, *mo caraid!*"

He laughed and glanced back at the tree, but if Sinann was still there he would need the stone to see her. He said to Caitrìonagh, "Tell me what that was about last night."

She paused in her chewing on the toothpick, thinking. Then she said, "You shouldnae put much store in it."

"So you didn't mean what you said?"

"Nae." A smile played at the corners of her mouth. "But if the castle were to know that, we would be watched far too closely to suit me. I'd much rather let them all think I barred my door against you every night and never spoke to you if I could avoid it."

Dylan kept his expression neutral, but his heart lightened. "Am I to take it, then, that you would *not* bar your door against me?"

She turned and tapped him across the arm with the remainder of willow branch in her hand, as if it were a whip. "I said not to put much store in it. I simply prefer the prying eyes look elsewhere. That is all."

Dylan nodded as if he believed her, but saw the flush in her cheeks that told him things she wouldn't say with words.

Winter struck in earnest soon after Dylan took delivery of his black wool coat and kilt of rust-and-black tartan, and he was glad for the warmth of the heavier kilt in addition to the coat. The people of Ciorram took to their homes, and there was no longer any unnecessary traffic to and from the castle. Aside from the occasional trip to deliver food to Marsaili and her family, Caitrìonagh never set foot beyond the gatehouse by the drawbridge.

In her mother's absence she spent her days supervising the household staff. Each day she also set aside some time for her needlework. Dylan spent his own days within earshot, sometimes in a chair just outside the room where the women did the sewing, sometimes on the stone steps inside the kitchen that led to the animal pens in the bailey.

Sigurd the collie kept him company, and he taught the dog to fetch a deer bone he'd rescued from a soup pot one morning. Siggy was tireless in his retrieval, but when his arm wore out the dog would flop down by Dylan's side to rest and chew on the bone.

At Christmas time Dylan found himself in the right place at the right time to sample every holiday dish in preparation. Caitrionagh seemed to enjoy feeding him, and he gained back some of the weight he'd lost in the fall. Since his arrival he'd been dismayed by the lack of anything sweet, and Dylan guessed the commerce in cane sugar from the southern American colonies had not yet made it this far north. The cravings had gone away weeks ago, and he figured his sweet tooth had died of starvation.

One frosty December day, Dylan was sitting in the kitchen, on the steps with Siggy stretched out on the step below his feet, watching Cait supervise the help. Her arms were up to her elbows with oatmeal dust, for she helped with the grunt work as well as the decision making. As he studied her, she reminded him of her father: born to take charge and tolerating no guff. But she leavened her orders with a charm she certainly hadn't inherited from Iain Mór. Dylan followed her every move with fascination.

Then Caitrionagh brought him a bannock with something like pink cottage cheese smeared on it.

"What's this?"

She smiled. "Ye've never eaten *crannachan*?"

He shook his head. "Where I come from it doesn't get much better than peanut butter and strawberry jam." He wasn't sure peanut butter had been invented yet, but doubted he would cause a serious time anomaly by mentioning it and didn't much care if he did.

Caitrionagh frowned. "Butter of peas and nuts? How strange." She shrugged. "Try this."

He took a bite and his eyebrows went up. His sweet tooth awoke, the happiest it had been since October. "Man, this stuff is great!" It was heavy, whipped cream with oatmeal and raspberry preserves, and there was a bit of that toasted oatmeal flavor to it. Cait had spread it on the bannock over a slathering of butter. It was the best thing he'd tasted since coming here. Cait dusted oatmeal from her hands and went back to work, satisfied by his reaction, and he watched her go. The sway of her hips under her wool overdress took his mind quite away from the *crannachan*. She turned, and smiled at the look on his face. He came back to himself, then remembered to swallow and took another bite of the bannock.

Siggy whined and slobbered, eyeing Dylan's food. Dylan grinned at him. "Uh uh. Mine." He took another bite, almost finishing it. "Mine, all mine." But in the end he didn't have the heart to take the last bite, so he handed it over to the dog. Siggy wolfed it, looked for more, and when he saw there was none, flopped back down on the step at Dylan's feet. Dylan would have liked some more, too, but contented himself with watching Caitrionagh work.

These particular Mathesons being Catholic, Dylan had little choice but to attend Mass with them whenever the parish priest made it out to Ciorram, which was every month or so, not necessarily on Sunday. Though Catholicism was a mite alien to his experience, and though his former-hippie, former-Jesus-freak, finally-Methodist mother would not approve, he viewed mass as a chance to learn about Caitrionagh, her life, and her beliefs. Besides, Methodism wouldn't even exist for another half-century, so he would be hard put to find a congregation if he were inclined to look. The intense conflicts between the Presbyterians, Episcopalians, and Catholics in Scotland being what they were at the time, Dylan was not eager to rock that particular boat.

So, to the end of fitting in, he acquired a sturdy linen cord on which he hung the ebony and silver crucifix he'd found in his trunk, which he wore under his shirt and never removed. In time he became somewhat attached to it, regardless of what his mother or the local Presbyterians might have said about the graven silver image.

With his new job, his pay more than doubled to nine pence a day, and he was now able to insist on cash. At Christmas he spent some on presents, and received a few as well. From Iain he received a fine, foot-long dirk with a triangular blade and an etched silver hilt, which he now carried in a steel scabbard inside the straps of his right legging. From Caitrionagh there was a new sark of bleached linen she'd embroidered in intricate white-on-white at the collar and cuffs, which he now wore on Sundays. And from Sarah, some writing paper and ink. Those he kept stashed in his trunk, not sure how to address the issue of letters home, because there was nobody to receive them. Also, he was not entirely comfortable with the idea of exchanging gifts with Sarah.

At a little over a pound sterling per month, less the weekly penny he paid Seonag to launder his kilts, sarks, and bed-clothes, and the other weekly penny he paid Gracie to bring him a bucket of hot water for washing every evening, by mid-January he'd accumulated two English pounds and a few shillings in cold cash.

The weather worsened after New Year's, and the darkness seemed never ending. Now even the scant light that had come through the few windows was blocked by deep overcast. Fresh air was rare, respiratory infections ran rampant, and Dylan noticed the food was changing. Everything fresh was gone. Meat was now all salted or smoked, the oatmeal had that dull *been around* flavor to it, and even fresh baked bread seemed a mite hard and tasteless. Dylan started looking for bugs, and hoped the fact he never found any was a true indication there *weren't* any.

It was the late evenings Dylan treasured. After the *céilidh* when there was one, with the castle quiet and no traffic on the West Tower stairs, he waited on his bunk in his sark, stretched out face-down with the book of poetry opened before him on the floor as if he were reading it, his chin resting on the mattress box. He rarely read anything, but only stared at the words until the carved door to the chamber would open just enough, and Cait would sit on the floor with her back against the stone opening to talk to him. He never moved from his bunk, and she never opened the door so far that she couldn't slip it discreetly closed if someone approached from the hallway. Since the door was situated in the deepest corner of the alcove, Dylan could see anyone coming from down-stairs and greet them before they might see the door, and if anyone came from upstairs Cait would see their feet before they were down far enough to see the door. Anyone who happened by would find the door closed and Dylan reading by candlelight, alone.

Sometimes he read to her from the poetry book. Sometimes she read to him. Her voice so close and quiet, and her hair glimmering in the unsteady candlelight, she read, or talked of things she loved and hoped for, and asked him questions about America.

"What are the red savages like? I've heard they're ghastly murderers," she said one night early in February. She hugged her knees and rested her chin on them, her eyes wide as if she weren't sure she wanted to hear the gory details in answer to her question.

That was a hard one for Dylan. Indians in his own time tended to be as peaceful as anyone else, but he knew that while he and Cait sat in this castle there were attacks and skirmishes all over the colonies, and settlers lived in morbid fear of Indians.

On the other hand, this wasn't far from the time when his white ancestry merged with his Indian ancestry. He had no clue of the circumstances of that union, but had always assumed it had been consensual. Rape in this century, in that place, would probably have never made it into written record to be found by his mother so many years later.

What he told Cait was, "It can be dangerous if one lives outside the large towns. The Indians don't like us very well." True enough.

"But you never killed one."

"I never had to." Also true.

"Do you miss America?"

He did, but what he missed were things she couldn't comprehend if he told her. How could he explain television, or cravings for cinnamon-flavored jawbreakers? He missed french fries, but the Scottish people of this time didn't even yet know what a potato was. He said, "Have you ever wondered what it might be like to fly?"

She chuckled, low and quiet. "Fly? Like a bird?"

"Just like a bird. So high and so fast that you could go halfway around the world in a day. Would you like that?"

Her eyes glittered with excitement. "Halfway around the world? I've never even been to England."

"If you could fly, you could go to England in . . ." He made a guess, "oh, about an hour, I think."

"How wonderful!" Her eyes glittered in the candlelight

and her voice rose with excitement. "You should tell stories, you're so—"

"Full of it, I know."

"Full of what?"

"Manure." That made her laugh, a little too loudly, and he shushed her. Then he said, "What if you could pick up a machine and talk into it, and there would be another person miles away who could hear you?"

She really was getting into this. "My mother?"

That struck him. He'd not noticed before that she missed her mother, who was still in Killilan. "Yeah, your mother. You could pick up the pho . . . machine any time you wanted, and talk to her. And she could talk back."

Cait pulled her blanket a little tighter around her shoulders. "And could you talk to your mother in America?"

His heart went heavy. Did his mother even know he was gone? That is, *would* she know in 286 years? Would Sinann ever send him back to his own time, or would he be dust centuries before Mom might realize his absence?

Cait said, "You must miss your family terribly."

"I do."

She gathered her feet under her to stand, then came to sit next to him on his bunk. He sat up, not entirely comfortable with her that close but certainly not wanting to send her away. The alcove was private enough to give a false sense of security, but not private enough to make this safe proximity for them, especially at night. She took his hand, which kept him from standing. Her voice low enough to not be heard even from the stairs, she said, "I hope you have found a place with us." She kissed his knuckles where the scars were still pink.

He felt suspended in time, in that moment when everything changes and there is no going back. Nor wanting to go back. When he finally moved, it was to lean over and touch his mouth to hers. Her lips were tender, caressing. He was breathless, expecting her to back away.

She didn't retreat. Instead, she reached up to run her fingers into his hair. He pressed the kiss, and as his mind turned to mush he wished the suspension of time would last forever. She opened her mouth to him, and he pressed further. He wanted to drink her in. Take her into himself so she would be his . . . a part of himself.

But his better sense crept back on him. He had to let go of her and stand, though his knees didn't want to hold him. He cleared his throat and stared at the floor so he would be able to say what he had to. "You need to go in now. Alone."

She said nothing for a moment, then cleared her own throat to say, "Aye. For in the event of a nighttime wandering by Artair or Coll upstairs, your absence from this bed would be as condemning as my presence."

He looked into her face as she stood, and her eyes showed the same intensity he felt in himself. He said, "Good night." She replied in kind. He kissed her again, then watched as she returned to her room and shoved the door shut behind her.

A great sigh escaped him, and he collapsed onto his back on the bunk. He stared at flickering shadows on the ceiling until the candle guttered out, then he stared into the darkness for a long time.

Winter wore on. Dylan borrowed a bow and some arrows from Robin Innis, and on days when he could excuse himself from Cait's presence he took them to the stand of oaks near the summit of the wooded north slope and practiced. Since in the Highlands the bow, dirks, and swords were still used for hunting more than were guns, it wouldn't do to be so completely ignorant of the bow as he was. He needed to teach himself to shoot and hope he wouldn't look too lame when he had to do it with people around. It was a long, tedious process that earned him a badly bowstring-slapped coat sleeve and some frustration looking for lost arrows in the snow.

Over those cold weeks, the life of the clan had its high and low points. A daughter was born to one of the tenants, but she was weak and died after only a few days. A great controversy then arose in the village, for the baby had been baptized by only the midwife and died before the priest could do it officially. Everyone in Ciorram had a strong opinion as to whether the baby had gone to heaven, which gave rise to shouting matches and hard feelings among the snowbound Mathesons. Dylan considered the question academic and found the high emotion on the subject an irritant. Then he saw the bereaved parents in the Great Hall one evening and decided, for their sake, that he hoped their little girl was in heaven.

A fever swept through the *Tigh* and village, taking with it Marsaili's younger daughter, Sarah's littlest son, and Nana Pettigrew's old mother. The weather hardened, and the people of the glen grew silent and close. Sarah's loss moved Sinann to redouble efforts to talk Dylan into an interest in the widow.

"She needs ye, lad."

Dylan was alone in the Great Hall with his workout. The winter sun had not yet risen, the hearth was not yet lit, and the torches in sconces along the stone wall made no dent in the cold. His breath puffed out before him in dense clouds. These days a warm-up never meant working up a sweat, and he always did well if not shivering. He said, "She needs someone who loves her, that's what she needs."

"And I suppose you cannae stand the sight of her."

"I care about her. She's a good woman. Her kids are . . ." His voice failed and he stopped to stand for a moment with his eyes shut at the thought of the two-year-old who had died. "Her sons are great kids. But . . ." He fell silent as the tower door creaked open and a woman entered. It was too dark to see all the way to the end of the hall, but as she approached, Dylan could tell by her carriage it was Sarah. Speak of the devil.

"Don't let me interrupt you," she said, and hovered just beyond the reach of the torch light.

"I was just about finished."

"You were not, you liar," said Sinann.

He cut her a sharp glance.

Sarah said, "I enjoy watching your exercises. It's a pretty dance you do."

He didn't know whether to thank her, or what. He chose to get off the subject instead. "How are you feeling today, Sarah?"

She sighed and shrugged. "The loss is a terrible one. It's true there is no worse pain than having arms empty of a child."

"I can't even imagine it."

"Dinnae try. There are enough of us already who know how it feels. Far too many."

Silence fell, and Dylan thought it best he move along before anyone came to find him alone with Sarah. He scabbarded his sword and bowed politely to her, making a gallant leg and flourishing an imaginary hat. "Alas, I must take my leave, Madame. Have a nice day."

She giggled as he made for the door, and Sinann shouted after him, "Coward!"

He sure didn't know what that damned faerie expected of him.

The deaths of that winter, the utterly inhospitable landscape, the cold that never quite went away no matter how close one sat to a fire, had their effect on Dylan's spirit. Eventually even he began to wonder if the sun would ever return. He now understood how people had once believed in vampires and werewolves, in ice queens and giants and dragons, for the winter was long and invasive and there was little protection from disease, cold, and hunger. Inside the castle, Dylan could know there was nothing outside but snow and rock, but on a visceral level he found himself able to believe monsters lurked in the icy darkness.

He was not surprised when one day in March a real monster did approach him as he left the wooded hill after bow practice, in the form of the red-coated English Captain on horseback. Dylan had reached the burn, which he would follow down iced-over rocks and tree roots to the glen floor, and his way was blocked by Captain Bedford. "Good afternoon," the *Sassunach* said, brimming with the sort of cheer Dylan hadn't heard since Christmas. He seemed well-fed and healthy, which only made his presence that much more annoying.

Dylan declined to reply. He only stared up at the mounted officer and wondered if he could get past without being shot, or if he should run the other way. Instead, he did neither and waited to see what was wanted.

Bedford said, "You're the new Matheson, I hear. The one from the colonies."

Dylan still kept quiet. Bedford had information from somewhere, and Dylan was curious where.

After a period of waiting for an answer, the officer said, "I can imagine the sort of welcome you received from your . . . *kinsmen*. Another mouth to feed, another opinion in the mix, another in competition for their women. It can't have been pretty."

"I hold my own."

Bedford leaned back and sucked air between his front teeth in an irritated hiss. His mount shifted its weight. "Yes, but wouldn't you like to do *better* than . . . mere survival? You appear a bit smarter than your cousins. They wish to overthrow the lawful Queen, but you've lived elsewhere, haven't you, and you've not been brought up on lies. I expect you must know an uprising can't succeed."

Dylan knew exactly that, and more surely than this guy did, but this condescending prick was getting on his nerves. "What do you want?"

"Information."

"I haven't any. And if I did I wouldn't blurt it to you." Dylan understood Bedford had pegged him as the weak link in the Matheson clan, due to his American birth, and that pissed him off. He raised his chin. Fat lot this clown knew.

"There is money to be had."

"Big deal. How about you move your nag out of my way and let me by?"

A white line of suppressed anger appeared around Bedford's already tight mouth. "It wouldn't be wise to dismiss my proposal out of hand. If I should let it be known you gave me information—"

"They wouldn't believe you." Dylan tilted his head in impudence, having no patience for this unsubtle ploy. "See, unlike yourself, I *earned* the trust of those people. They don't give it easily, and they don't take it back easily, either. That's what it means to be a kinsman. But you'll never know what that's like, being English and all."

Bedford was silent for a long moment. Then he said, "Very well. Run along to your cousins. But mark me, you'll wake up one morning with a knife between your ribs, and you'll be sorry you let yourself believe they gave a damn about you." He sidled his horse to make room on the path for Dylan to pass, and as he did so Bedford said, "The clans can't last."

Dylan knew that was so, but also knew it was irrelevant. He didn't have it in him to betray the people he was learning to call his family.

CHAPTER 9

Stolen kisses with Cait helped the dark months pass for Dylan, but they were too few and too far between. The talk at *céilidh* was of royal pardon and pension for certain Jacobites, for peace with the clans was sought by Queen Anne and the Crown wished to put behind the horrors of the battle of Killiecrankie and the massacre at Glencoe a quarter century before.

Dylan's little stash of coins grew, and he enhanced it by fishing through a hole he knocked in the frozen loch and selling his catch to the castle kitchen. Occasionally he caught an eel, but nobody would buy those. So the eels he cleaned and cooked himself, the meat spitted kebob-like over the fire in his alcove. He was able to talk Cait into trying the eel, and she liked it, but everyone else in the castle called him "daft."

The small silver pieces in his sporran grew in number and weight until Dylan asked Malcolm to exchange them for larger denomination coins. Pence became shillings, then shillings became gold guinea pieces bearing Anne on the front and four shields on the back. A guinea, he learned, was worth twenty-one shillings. Never having seen a real gold coin before, Dylan began to feel well off. In typical American mindset, even typical of Americans of that century, he now thought in terms of acquiring some property. Perhaps then he could ask Cait to marry him.

He'd never entertained *that* thought before, about anyone. Not even Cody, though she'd brought up the possibility once in a "hey, why not?" sort of moment shortly before she'd married Raymond. Marriage as a concept had never interested him. But now it was all he thought about. His days revolved around Cait, and his nights were spent yearning to go through that carved door which stood between them.

The nights were long and cold, and the late evenings were more and more of a strain on self-control. Talking was less satisfactory by the day, and more often Dylan read to Cait from the book of English poetry. She sat, bundled in her blanket, inside her door frame, and he lay on his belly on his bunk with the book laid open on the floor and the candlestick beside it, his chin on the edge of the mattress box. His voice was low, lest anyone overhear, and he read a poem of devotion, the speaker declaring he would live and die for his lover. Here Dylan's voice faltered. He'd read this one to her before, but each reading cut closer to the bone. He found himself reading it tonight with more conviction than anything he'd ever said before.

He looked over at Cait, surprised to see her eyes swimming in tears. Her head leaned against the door frame, and she repeated the last line, but her voice failed, thinning as she choked.

"What's wrong?"

She shook her head. "Naught. I'm a silly goose. My heart is too filled, and so it hurts."

He rested his chin on the edge of his bed again, and gazed at her. He'd never seen a woman look at him like that before. He'd seen lust and sometimes friendship, he'd dealt with more than one student with a crush, and of course there was Sarah's needy stare, but he'd never been the recipient of the sort of devotion he now saw in Cait. He was at a loss for a reply, though he wished he could find the words to tell her he felt the same way.

When Cait had gone to bed, Dylan asked Sinann whether he should give her an engagement ring.

"A what?" She perched at the foot of his bed, and he'd

mumbled his question as he'd begun to drowse. "A *which* ring?"

"Engagement. Like when you promise to marry someone."

"Oh. Betrothal. I'd say yes and no." Dylan frowned at her, and she explained, "Yes, it's done and nae, you shouldnae give her one. She's not for you, lad."

"Let's just assume you're wrong."

"But I'm not."

"Let's just assume." He leaned up on his elbow, and his voice went hard. "So, assuming she'll say yes, I'll need a ring. Two rings; one for engagement and one for the wedding."

"*Och*, nae, one ring will do. In many ways a betrothal is as binding as marriage. And lavishing jewelry will make you seem wasteful. Indeed, it would *be* wasteful."

"Where I come from, we use two rings, and one is set with a diamond. At least one diamond."

"Oh, for the riches of where you come from! How can you stand to be amongst the destitute?"

His eyes narrowed at her, but he ignored her needling and said, "Where do I find a ring?"

"You don't, in these parts. Even Lady Matheson wouldnae have a spare one just lying around handy and a' that. Though you might ask the smith. If there is silver to be had—"

"Gold. It's got to be gold."

"Yer daft."

"Where I come from—"

"Oh, aye, where you come from the streets must be paved with the stuff."

"What about my coins? I have several gold coins. One of them could be made into a ring."

Her eyes went wide. "An entire English guinea you want to spend? Not to mention what it'll cost for the work!"

"It doesn't have to be a heavy ring. The smith can take what's left of the gold."

"He'll give you a wire circle, he will."

Dylan made the guttural noise of disgust he'd picked up

lately from the other men. "No, he won't. Not if he values his life."

"All right, ye fool, spend your gold on her. I promise, though, it'll end badly. She's nae for you, that one. Just you see."

"We'll see." He lay back on his mattress and smiled.

Dylan talked to the village smith the next day. Tormod Matheson was one of Iain's tenants, who, as part of his rent payment, also did metal work on the occasions it was needed. Those occasions were seldom, since almost everything was made of wood, straw, stone, or animal parts. Tormod's work was mostly weaponry, and even then his were the more crude dirks rather than fine swords.

Nevertheless, Dylan handed over one of his guineas and requested a wedding ring be made of it, with the excess gold going for payment of labor. He then assured the smith if he was not happy with the ring, Tormod would become an equally unhappy man. Three days later the ring was delivered to Dylan by Tormod's young son, wrapped in a wad of dirty linen.

He went to a garderobe to open it, and the dim winter light through the arrow loop glinted from the plain gold ring. Nothing fancy, no engraving, and the surface was hammered, but it was, by God, shiny and in its simplicity seemed to radiate power. Promise. His heart lifted as he folded the cloth around the ring and slipped it into his sporran.

Later that day in the kitchen Cait handed him a bucket and informed him she needed to go to the well, on the other side of the bailey. On the way her face betrayed nothing, and neither did his as he followed her. It was cold out by the well, but it was protected from the wind and with the two of them there was always body heat. The well was tucked into a corner of the bailey between the West Tower and the non-family living quarters. No windows looked down on it, and the only approach was through a narrow passage. In the entire castle, this was the only place they could be alone and relatively undisturbed. If they couldn't stay long, it was because people would notice their absence.

Behind the well, Cait turned to him and opened his coat, and he kissed her as she came inside. His blood raced and warmed against the winter cold. She pulled back, and he kissed her cheek then touched his lips to her mouth. She said against his mouth, in Gaelic, "Do you love me?"

Lips still touching, he said, "Oh, yes." He wondered why she had to ask.

She leaned back to look into his eyes. "Will you tell my father, then?"

He was about to say he would scream it from the rafters, when he realized what she was really asking, and his heart soared. To her, or to any woman of this time, the issue of "love" was far more than warm fuzzies and a safe, steady date. If she loved him enough, the question of whether he loved her in return could make or break her future and that future would depend entirely on him. To tell her father he loved her would mean asking to marry her. That conversation with her father was not something to be done lightly, nor asked for capriciously. He said, "Yes. I want to marry you."

Her face flushed with joy. "You don't wish to return to America, then?"

He flashed on how she would cope in his century, and nearly laughed, but shook his head instead. "I wouldn't ask you to leave your family so far behind."

She kissed him, then snuggled into his arms. He held her, and his mind flew with what lay ahead. Months ago he'd given up hope of returning to his own time, but now he would have to give up wishing for it as well. His future was with Cait now, and it seemed brighter than ever before in his life.

She freed herself from his coat and picked up the bucket to fill it. He reached for his sporran and said, "I've got—"

"We must go. We've been here too long already."

She was right. They had to return to the kitchen right away, or there would be whispers. They could talk later, in the alcove when the castle was quiet.

That night they talked at length, she in her usual spot on the floor just inside her door, and he sitting on his bed, listening. She thought her father might award Dylan a tenancy on some of his land, and if he didn't offer it she assumed she could talk him into it. They would build a house, plant oats and barley, raise sheep and cattle and many, many children. Cait's eyes brightened by the candlelight of Dylan's alcove as she spoke. He had the ring in his palm and rubbed the tip of his middle finger on it hard, over and over, waiting for an opening. Finally she paused for breath, and he stood. "Cait, come here." He held out his hand.

She blinked at him a moment, then climbed to her feet and hugged her blanket around her shoulders. "Aye?"

"Just come over here for a moment and sit." She obeyed, and gave him her hand as she sat on the edge of his bed, a puzzled smile on her face. Then he went to one knee in front of her and said, "I don't know how you do it here, but where I come from there's a certain way one goes about these things. Back home we'd be doing this over a candlelight dinner, with soft music in the background, roses. . . ." He paused and glanced at his table. "Well, okay, we've got the candlelight." She was peering at him, puzzled, but the curl to her mouth now suggested she had a suspicion of what he was getting at. He shrugged and opened the hand with the ring. "Say you'll marry me."

She lit up with a smile. "I'll . . ." Her jaw dropped open when she saw the ring. It took a long time for her to close her mouth, and Dylan barely restrained the laughter that rose. "Where did you get that?"

"I had it made. For you. Will you wear it?"

She slipped it on. The band was a mite loose, but he figured she would then be able to wear it into old age even if her hands thickened. She should wear it forever, was his opinion. He leaned down to kiss her palm, then pressed his cheek against it. She stroked his head, and pressed his cheek to her knees, then began smoothing his hair around his ear and his beard against his face. Her hands on him was sublime pleasure, and he wished to stay here forever, just like this, being touched by her. She then leaned down to his ear and whispered, "Stay with me tonight, Dylan. Come to my bed."

He sat up, and back on his heels. More than anything he wanted to go with her, but he also knew it was a bad idea. Every part of his body yearned for him to say yes, but he forced his mouth to say, "No. It's not a good time. It's too risky." In fact, they'd spent entirely too much time already where they could be caught. She protested, but he stood and drew her to her feet. With several more kisses, which did not help his case, he urged her back to her room. She went with reluctance, then he closed the door, undressed, and slipped into his bed alone.

He had almost drifted off when he felt a presence. The tiniest sound of bare feet on wood brought him around, and he grasped the silver dirk under his pillow while peering into the darkness. There was a shadow approaching Cait's door. In an instant Dylan was out of his bunk and smacked the man against that door, then grabbed him by the scruff of his shirt, hauled back, and spun him around. The dirk at the intruder's throat, Dylan nearly cut before he recognized the voice of Artair begging for mercy.

A sound came behind him, and Dylan throttled Artair with his left as he turned to hold off the second man with his dirk. It was Coll he stopped at the point of the knife.

"What are you two doing here?" Dylan demanded.

Neither answered right away. Dylan's grip tightened on Artair's throat, who croaked, "Let me go, ye daft bastard!" He wriggled under Dylan's hand.

"What are you doing here? Make it good, or I'll cut you."

Coll said, "We're making sure."

Dylan turned to peer at Coll, but could see no expression in the darkness. "Sure of what?"

"Just making sure our apple-squire cousin is doing his job and not taking advantage of his position."

"What's that supposed to mean?" He loosened his grip on Artair's throat in order to not kill him.

"What it sounds like," Artair gasped, now able to breathe. He felt of his sore throat and tried to pry Dylan's hand off but failed. His teeth clenched. "Be glad I didn't find ye niggling her."

Dylan blinked at the strange use of that word, but got the meaning well enough and slammed Artair's head against the wall. Cait's youngest uncle groaned. "Take that back. She's not like that. You know she's not, and Iain Mór would kill you for saying she is."

Artair growled, "Will ye go whining to him, then?"

"No, I'll kill you myself if I hear it again. Now, get out of here." He hauled Artair off the wall by his shirt and shoved him into Coll, who staggered back. "Both of you, clear out. Leave Cait alone, or I'll have to wonder why you're taking such an interest in your niece's bed."

The two skulked back to their rooms, but Dylan knew they weren't gone for good.

Dylan sat back down on his bunk, and alarm surged. Artair and Coll could tell something was up, and it was only a matter of time before the truth would get out. Tormod had been warned not to tell of the ring, and wouldn't necessarily have known who the ring was for, but someone had done the math. Artair and Coll had fully expected to find Dylan in Cait's bed tonight. Now Dylan wondered how well he'd put them off the scent by not being there. If Iain learned of the engagement now, and especially if he heard it first from the wrong people, Dylan could well be refused permission to marry Cait. He had to move quickly, to establish himself, to learn what he needed to have a farm, a home for Cait.

He began picking brains on the subject of farming, and engaged Malcolm at every opportunity. The old man seemed amused that the young man from the colonies knew so little about farming and cattle, but obliged with answers and advice. Many an evening they spent in the stable, leaning back on broken chairs, discussing the ins and outs of the family business, while the rest of the clan gathered in the Great Hall.

Malcolm sometimes asked questions in return. "Tell me, Dylan, do they practice reiving in the colonies?"

Dylan frowned, trying to remember what "reiving" was, then it came to him. Cattle reiving was what would soon be known in America as "rustling." He said, "No. People get hung for that over there."

Malcolm laughed. "Aye, they get hung here, too, but only if they're caught at it by those with influence in Edinburgh. Everyone else looks on it as sport. We take from the MacDonells, the MacDonells take from us, the MacLeods take from the MacDonells, we take from the MacLeods. It all evens out in the end. It's less burdensome than taxes and more efficient than charity for feeding those in need."

"Social welfare." Dylan said this in English to put the point across.

Malcolm had to think about that for a moment, then nodded and said, "Aye. Well said."

"But you can get killed doing it."

"Ye can get killed digging a well, too, but that doesnae stop people from digging them. Reiving is an old custom, with strict rules that everyone knows and abides by. It's only done to cattle. Take anything else, and it's thieving. If you're caught with the goods, restitution is made, and nae argument. If the *spréidhe* are tracked onto your land and ye cannae show a track leaving, then you are responsible and must give restitution. Ye never take more than the other man can afford to lose."

"Or it defeats the purpose of the custom."

A grin crossed Malcolm's face. "You're smart, for a colonial lad."

Dylan laughed and took a deep breath of the musty scents of old straw and horse manure. Here he was, with a business degree from Vanderbilt University, chatting about cattle rustling like it was a gentleman's sport. Anymore, he wasn't sure he shouldn't have majored in history. Or, perhaps, animal husbandry. He'd never even been a member of 4-H. Never even had a dog.

He looked down at Siggy who dozed at his feet. Well, he never had a dog until now.

He said, "How come you aren't married, Malcolm?" A shadow crossed the older man's face, and Dylan added, "You were once, then."

Malcolm sighed. "Aye, I was. To a Fraser girl with a fire in her eye and a figure so soft and generous a man could lose himself."

Dylan stifled a grin. "And did you?"

A smile curled Malcolm's mouth. "Oh, aye, indeed I did. There were times I thought I'd never find my way out." That brought a guffaw from Dylan, and Malcolm continued softly, "She bore many bairns, but only three lived past their first year."

Dylan's heart sank as he realized none of those three were still around. He figured Malcolm would let it go at that, but his eyes had gone dreamy and he continued to talk. The words came slowly, as if he were picking his way through a minefield.

"My daughter was a bright and lively girl, filled with excitement, always the chatterer, always up to something. She lived to the age of four, when she was kicked in the head by a horse. It was quite accidental, just bad luck the animal became cross at that moment.

"The grief of our only daughter dying nearly killed my wife, and she was never the same again. During the typhus epidemic the following year she finally succumbed. I'd sent the boys to the *Tigh* for safety from the typhus, and after burying their mother I gave my working land over to tenants and came here.

"Then, the first year that my younger son went to the *shielings* he was murdered in his sleep by MacDonell men raiding the cattle." Malcolm's voice began to falter, but he told the rest of the story. "Just a few years ago my one remaining son died in a raid at the hands of the dragoons down the glen."

On a hunch, Dylan said, "The same raid where Iain's father died?"

Malcolm nodded, his gaze on the floor, and there was a long silence. Then he looked over at Dylan. "Donnchadh was my uncle and my Laird, and losing him was bad enough, but there is nae more terrible thing than to hold in your arms the bloodied body of your child. I've done it three times, and my only solace is that it cannae happen to me anymore."

It took several moments for Dylan to find his voice, then he said, "You never remarried?"

Malcolm shook his head. "I've never loved but one woman. Some men are made that way, and give over their soul so completely there is none left for anyone else." His head tilted as he peered at Dylan. "I think you ken it, do ye not?"

Dylan hesitated in answering, not sure what Malcolm knew or was just guessing, but he finally nodded. "Aye. I do."

*　　*　　*

Now that Cait had accepted the ring, Sinann gave up talking him out of marrying her and provided pointers on establishing himself as a farmer. They spoke Gaelic now, because Dylan liked the practice.

"So you've given up this nonsense of wanting to go home, then?" She perched on his headboard, and he kicked back on his bunk with his bare feet on his pillow and his hands laced behind his head. Dawn had not yet broken, Cait was still asleep, and Dylan decided to invest his workout time today in questioning Sinann. He chewed a willow stick.

He shot her an evil glance. "I hate you for bringing me here. I don't belong in this time and I will never fit in. But, by God, I love Cait and since I'm stuck here I'll be happy to make her happy."

"And safe."

"Of course."

"Then you'll also be happy to get rid of the *Sassunaich*."

He let out an exasperated noise and with his tongue moved the willow stick to the other side of his mouth. "You know I can't do that. Queen Anne is going to die in a few months, and after that it will be open season on Jacobites."

"Open season?"

He took the stick from his teeth and looked at it. "Uh . . . they'll be hunted." Then he returned the chewed stick to his teeth.

"Oh. Aye."

Dylan continued, "The best thing I can do for Cait is to get her out of her father's house, where she stands in the line of fire for persecution."

Sinann was horrified and stood on the headboard as if ready to fly at him. "You have knowledge of what will happen to Iain Mór?"

He shook his head. "Not specifically him. But he's a Jacobite, the Crown and the Privy Council *suspect* he's a Jacobite, and lasting peace between the Scottish and English won't even begin for another thirty years. My aim is not to just be his tenant, but to buy a piece of land outright. Kicking free of the Jacobite cause is the only way to stay alive. It's the only way to keep Cait safe."

"Coward!"

"Realist."

She sat again. "You've got to go to war against the English. Like the great Cuchulain, who was a hero to his people, who defeated monsters and men alike."

"Cuchulain was a myth."

"As I am?"

Dylan sighed and tongued the stick to the corner of his mouth again. "You got a point there, Tink."

"You think you know everything of the world, do ye, lad? You think your Bible has all the answers? Is that why you willnae learn the Craft?"

Dylan was silent for a moment as irritation rose and he held it down. Then he said, "Why are you so hot to teach me this stuff?"

"Because you can use it against the English. Against Bedford. You can use it to defeat them."

"What makes you think I can even *do* it? I don't have any magical powers."

"Ye do, lad. There's a power in all things. There is power in every rock, every plant, and every creature. Every *man*." Her tone was beginning to get through to him. She was neither sarcastic nor angry, and that made him listen because she was so rarely anything but. She thought for a moment, then said, "Tell me, lad, can you believe in miracles?"

This was a hard question. Dylan took the stick from his mouth as he thought, then said, "Yes. But I don't believe I can make them happen."

"And I say you can. I know you can, because I've seen other mortals do it and with no more power than what you're given. Christian mortals they were, as well."

"Saints."

She shook her head. "Nae saints. Ordinary men as pure in heart as yourself." He looked at her to see if she was needling him, but she was serious. He returned his toothpick to his mouth as she continued, "The only question is whether you *want* to try. And ye cannae be afraid. Your Yahweh wouldnae let you come to harm. Do you think he would give you a power and not expect you to use it?"

"Yes. I have the power to murder, but I believe it's evil."

"Nae. You have the power to *kill*. How you use that power

decides the good or bad of it. You have killed, but you're nae evil. You used that power to stop a terrible thing from befalling yourself." Her voice went low. "And to keep an even worse one from your beloved Cait. It's the same with every power granted to every creature of this earth, including myself. The evil is not in the using of it, but in using it for evil. And there are some as would say the knowing the difference is what makes you *human*."

Dylan stared at Sinann, and didn't reply. This he wanted to believe. She was making sense, but he was still unsure of what to do.

Finally, she said, "Hear me, lad. We're of one world, all of us. You once told me you dinnae want to hear about the *Sidhe*, but I can tell you where to read of them. Go find Malcolm's Bible, and take a look at the book of Genesis, chapter six, verse four."

Dylan opened his mouth to tell her to bug off, but before he could say it she snapped her fingers and did exactly that.

The following morning he asked Malcolm to see his Bible, and was told to find it on the shelves in the North Tower. Dylan climbed the steps to Malcolm's chamber and searched the books till he found the frail, old, yet cumbersome copy of the pet project of England's first Stuart king. He turned the delicate pages to Genesis 6:4 and read, *There were giants in the earth in those days; and also after that, when the sons of God came in unto the daughters of men, and they bare children to them, the same became mighty men which were of old, men of renown.*

Dylan stared for a long moment at the text, then whispered to himself, "I'll be doggoned. Cuchulain and the *Sidhe*."

Finally spring crept into Ciorram, first showing signs when the snows turned to cold rain in March, then to less cold rain in April. Peering through the garderobe hole one morning, Dylan saw someone in the garden below, digging and distributing matter from the pile below across the turned soil. Even over the dank odor of the stone and fertilizer he could smell fresh-turned earth and new growth all around. The grass was greening and the white roses on the rail fence were in bloom again.

All through the castle, shutters were thrown open and fresh air circulated. Cattle were driven from their biers, bone thin and hardly able to stand. Dylan helped some of the farmers shove, cajole, and almost half-carry their beasts outside to the pale new grass. Preparations were made for the young folk to take the livestock to higher pastures later in the season. Early in the month the sun popped out for a day and stirred Dylan's memories of what it was like not to ache from the cold. That day the castle work routine went to hell while people made excuses for walks to houses in the village or around to other parts of the loch.

Even Dylan slipped away. Cait was weaving cloth with the other women, which he knew was an all-day activity, and his presence was barely tolerated, let alone needed. He took a freshly laundered shirt and kilt, and a chunk of soap, and strolled to the stream behind the ruined tower in the next glen. There, he stripped to his skin and immersed himself for the first time in over six months, then soaped and scrubbed every inch of his body. It was the coldest bath he'd ever taken, and his balls climbed so far up he thought he'd never find them again. But he sat on a smooth granite boulder with the mountain stream pressing at his back, flowing and splashing all around him.

A tune he'd been hearing lately was stuck in his head and he mumbled it to himself as he scrubbed, *"Glaschu bheag . . ."* He tried to remember the words. *"Dol 'na lasair . . ."* Something about Glasgow in flames and Aberdeen . . . somethingorother. Oh, well, it was heaven to be clean all over, to reach all the spots that one simply can't get when washing from a bucket. He leaned back to wet his hair, and soaped it thoroughly.

He also scrubbed his beard, which had grown to a respectable if not particularly impressive thickness. Another way, besides his coloring, in which he differed from the old world Mathesons was that his was not the thick, bushy facial hair sported by the rest of the clan. His straight-haired beard lay against his face, more smooth than bushy. He soaped, then took his *sgian dubh* and trimmed his mustache so it would stop falling into his mouth while he ate. Then he rinsed and spat.

Once clean, he went inside the ruined tower and stretched out, naked, in the sun, in the center of the grassy floor. The ground beneath him smelled fresh and green, and the earth warmed him. He drowsed, and wondered if life in any century got better than this.

Sinann's voice woke him, "*Och*, it's skyclad he is, and ready for Beltane, sure."

Dylan didn't budge, but said in a lazy voice, "Ogle all you like, Tink. I can't be moved to care."

She made a guttural noise of disgust. "You take all the fun out of the teasing."

Dylan chuckled. "Oh, well." He stretched like a cat, then rolled over to sleep like one.

But Sinann wouldn't leave him alone. "Have you thought about the learning of the Craft?"

Face-down on the grass, he muttered, "I have."

"And what is it you've been thinking?"

He rolled back over and sat up. It took a minute to focus his thoughts in the drowsy sunshine, but he had to admit to himself that, whatever else he'd been taught to believe, he was faced with the reality of Sinann. Even if he was certain he had some of the answers, he obviously didn't have all of them, so maybe he shouldn't dismiss her teachings out of hand before finding out what they were. He said, "You really think it will help?"

"Oh, aye. Most assuredly."

"I won't worship the *Sidhe*."

She snorted. "*Och!* Nobody's asking you to, lad! Do what you like, for a' that. It makes no difference. Learn from me, but never worship me. I leave that to who needs it."

He sighed and said, "All right. Let's do it."

She leaped to her feet, giggling, and did a little dance Dylan would swear was a jig. He reached for his clothes, but she said, "Those willnae be necessary, if it's all the same to you. You were enjoying the sun, so continue."

He looked at his kilt and sark, and shrugged. "Okay, Tink, acquaint me with the ways of the *Sidhe*."

"First there must be a fire." Dylan groaned. She said,

"Take that dead branch over there and break it up. It needn't be a large fire." Dylan obeyed, laid the broken pieces in the stone hearth. Sinann lit them with a snap of her fingers. Dylan hoped the smoke wouldn't attract the attention of the soldiers in their barracks, but his concern was allayed when he saw there was very little and it was diffused by the breeze above the stone walls. The barracks was upwind, so they wouldn't smell the burning, either.

"All right, novice, kneel before the flame."

Dylan knelt, sat back on his heels, and took a deep breath. It was comfortable here. Said Sinann, "This tower is a magical place, you know. A great hero died on this very spot, and his name was Fearghas MacMhathain. One dark day while the other men of the clan were away with the cattle, he alone with his sword fought a hundred invaders from Killilan in the glen below. Single-handed, he held off the enemy."

"Single-handed?"

Sinann's eyes narrowed at him. "It's true, what I'm telling you. Vikings, they were, big and bold, and ready to plunder Glen Ciorram from east to west, and rape the women and carry the children off for slaves. But Fearghas, he came at them with his enormous, great sword, and the ugly northern brutes fell as young oats before a high wind.

"However, during the battle he took a wound, which he ignored, though it gave him great pain, until the fight was over. Then, standing among the bodies of his vanquished enemy, he dinnae wish to fall among them. So he carried himself, all bleeding and broken, to this tower where he crumpled to the earth and died, and his life-blood soaked the very ground upon which you kneel. When the *Sidhe* saw this—"

"That would be you."

She frowned at him, but said, "Aye. That would be me. And some others. The *Sidhe* saw this and lamented, 'Oh, what a terrible thing this is, for so great a warrior to be cut down.' And so when the body was taken away by his mourning clan, all wailing and keening, the blood remained. And does so to this very day."

Dylan stood in a hurry. "Huh?" He peered into the grass

where his knees had been. "Blood?" He poked his toe at the impression of his knees in the grass.

"Have a look."

He knelt again and parted the grass. Though the tips of the blades were the bright green of spring growth, at the middle began dark streaks of maroon that thickened and brightened to solid red at the roots. He pulled apart the dense growth, and found the earth beneath was also red. He poked his finger into it and pulled up a small clod that crumbled in his fingers, but was as red as blood spilled a moment ago. He'd seen red clay many times in his life, all over Tennessee and Georgia, and this wasn't it. This was blood-colored dirt.

Sinann continued with her story. "Since that day, no invader has entered the tower."

"The English have never been here?"

"I said no invader, did I not?" Dylan conceded she had. "For centuries this was a sacred place, until the priests came and carried the people away to their churches. But it is still a place of power, where a man who knows how can draw from that power and take it with him. This beneath your feet is the blood of your ancestor, *a Dhilein*, and the earth of your origin. It's your heritage, no matter where you were born."

He let the earth crumble in his fingers and fall to the ground. His voice was soft with awe. "Okay, where do we start?"

"Get your silver dirk, lad. We start with the consecration of it. Hold it before you, resting the blade and the hilt on your hands outstretched." Dylan obeyed. "Now hold it in the smoke of the fire. Imagine, as you do so, all the impurities going upward with the smoke. All the bad energy of those who used it before you, gone." Dylan closed his eyes and focused. From his eastern studies he knew enough about bad energy to imagine the evil leaving his knife. There seemed an awful lot of it, too.

Sinann then said, "Now hold it high in your right hand. You're right-handed, are you not?" Dylan nodded and held up the dirk. Sinann went on, "Let the sun shine on it. Feel the rays fill your body. Feel the strength the sun gives. This, you see, is why it's just as well you're skyclad." Dylan took a deep breath, and could feel the glorious sun inside him as well as on him. The dirk glinted in the daylight.

"Now," she said, "hold it in your hands in front of you, between yourself and the sun. Without staring, see the shape of the dirk against the sunlight, and feel the strength flow from the sun, through it, into you; then back out to the sun again." Dylan was breathing hard now. His skin tingled and he quivered with the energy. He felt like laughing, but only gasped for air.

"Now point the dirk to the ground and with a deep breath blow into the hilt. Three breaths of life you give it, then hold it high again and say, *"A null e; a nall e; Slàinte!"* Dylan repeated each phrase after her. "This is my dirk; my soul and my strength. May it serve me well. Let it be powerful as the sun. I name this dirk . . ."

"I name this dirk . . ." He looked up at her. "Huh? I have to name it?"

"Aye."

He thought fast and hard. He'd never named an inanimate object before. And for some weird reason the only name he could think of at that moment was of a Christian saint who had been borrowed from Celtic paganism. "Brigid. I name this dirk Brigid."

Sinann smiled. "Good choice, laddie." She gestured to the dirk. "Now you must sleep for seven nights with it under your pillow."

"I sleep with it every night under my pillow."

"Good lad. Carry it with you always. Never let it be taken from you."

Dylan held the knife, Brigid, and let the sun glint from . . . her.

CHAPTER 10

The weather had its ups and downs during April, and a cold snap dumping a little late snow was in progress when Dylan, as he took some air at the kitchen door that led to the animal pens, saw a number of strange men enter the bailey through the castle gate. They were escorted by Robin Innis. It was apparent they weren't Mathesons, at least not ones closely related to the local clan. They were haggard and dirty, as if they'd come a long way, and moved across the snowy bailey with a lanky, casual air.

Dylan leaned against a pole supporting the thatching over the pens and crossed his arms. To him, these men wouldn't have been out of place wearing straw cowboy hats, faded Levis, wrinkled leather boots, and belt buckles the size of Montana. One of them had a willow stick clenched between his front teeth that dangled like a long piece of hay, still with a couple of leaves on the end that danced as he walked. Robin led them through the large doors to the Great Hall. Dylan was about to return to the kitchen, where Cait directed preparations for supper, when he heard a whistle from across the bailey. He looked, and Malcolm gestured to him to come.

Dylan hesitated, and glanced toward the kitchen. Though her mother had returned from Killilan and was once again in charge of the household, Cait was well occupied with super-

vising supper preparations, elbow-deep in bowls filled with
flour. The sharp smells of hot grease and boiling greens filled
the air. He looked out at Malcolm, who waved again for him
to come. Dylan went. He shoved the kitchen door closed,
vaulted the low rails of the pens, trotted across the bailey,
and followed Malcolm into the Great Hall, where the visitors
had been seated and given some ale. He shook snow out of
his hair.

Iain entered the hall from the towers, and greeted the men
heartily with handshakes and nods. They all seemed to know
each other, and Malcolm named Dylan to the visitors. At
Iain's frown, Malcolm said, "He'll be accompanying us."

"And what of my daughter?"

"She'll be safe enough. Our prodigal will grow lazy if we
let him remain on his backside much longer." There was a
general chuckle, and even Dylan had to smile. His job paid
well, and being with Cait was a joy, but sitting and standing
around all day when she was busy was boring as hell.

Iain grunted, then returned his attention to the visitors,
who turned out to be MacLeods from south of Glen Ciorram.
There were ten of them, led by a quiet man named Donnchadh an Sealgair. *Duncan the Hunter.* They were all pale
men, but with a tendency toward green and brown eyes, and
brown hair. Their plaids were varied in color, but predomi-
nantly green. Having been in the century for several months
now, Dylan knew the colors of a man's tartan had less to do
with his clan identity than his wife's preference in weaving,
so a similarity in setts meant little more than similar taste in
women.

Malcolm and Dylan settled into the group, on benches, or
leaning against a table. For a while it seemed to Dylan he'd
been hauled in there just to hear gossip, but he knew there
had to be a reason for his presence. So he listened patiently
to news of MacLeods who had married Matheson girls, and
MacLeod women who now lived in Ciorram. Food was
brought for the visitors, and there was political discussion of
the Queen and her policies. Also there was news of arrests
by the English soldiers, of cattle reivers who were successful
or unsuccessful, and talk of how the *Sassunaich* were not
amused by the goings-on of anyone Scottish, it seemed.

Long after the MacLeods had arrived and supper was eaten by all, the talk finally turned to the business at hand. Dylan learned the MacLeods and the Mathesons were planning a *creach*. He perked, honored now he'd been let in on this. In the fine, old tradition of the Highlands, they were going to steal some cattle. Dylan knew the trip was necessary because of the many head the Mathesons had lost that winter. Said Iain, "Artair and Coll report the MacDonells' pastures being somewhat crowded, and could most likely do without so many animals eating their grass."

"But," Dylan said, "what are we going to do with a bunch of winter-skinny cows?"

Malcolm grinned, apparently amused at the Mathesons' colonial cousin. "Pasture them in a small glen back beyond the peat bog until they're fat enough to sell. Then we take them south a ways, to Glenfinnan," he nodded at Donnchadh MacLeod, "and trade them out for MacGregor *spréidhe* brought up from the Trossachs. That way we dinnae have the MacDonells coming around identifying their wee pets."

Dylan grinned. "Sort of like cow laundering, eh?"

Malcolm and the others let out a loud guffaw. "You have an Irish way with words, lad!" He slapped Dylan on the back, and for the rest of the evening and well into the night, Dylan listened carefully to the plans for the raid.

The next day they spent sleeping, then the following night the selected reivers set out on foot in a northeasterly direction, armed with swords and dirks. Dylan, Malcolm, Artair, Coll, Robin Innis, Marc Hewitt, and four other Mathesons walked in silence with the ten MacLeods, accompanied by Dylan's Sigurd and Iain's white collie, Dìleas. They crossed rocky slopes and skirted peat bogs on a route Malcolm seemed to make up as he went along. By the moonlight, Dylan kept a close eye on the landscape as they traversed it, for he was the only man present who had not spent his life traveling these mountains and his survival might one day hinge on being able to find his way around.

Cooking fires would give them away, so they ate cold oatmeal from their hands. The closer they came to Mac-Donell territory, the more careful they were of not announcing their arrival. It rained off and on, and Dylan fought the chill of wet wool in the night. By day they rolled themselves in their plaids and slept on heather that barely mitigated the damp of the ground. After the second day, Dylan discovered if one was tired enough and determined enough to rest, one could sleep anywhere and under any conditions.

On the third evening they lay low among some trees and waited for sunset before moving in on the hundred head of MacDonell cattle, which a MacLeod scout had reported ahead in a secluded pasture. There had been little talk on the trip, and now Dylan dozed in the silence, his back to a sun-warmed rock and Siggy's head in his lap.

Robin, sitting nearby, commented in a low voice, "That Sigurd seems to have attached himself to ye."

Dylan opened his eyes and looked down at the drowsy dog. Though Siggy had slept in the Great Hall with Iain's dogs since Alasdair Matheson's death last fall, during the day he could almost always be found somewhere near Dylan.

Artair said, "Alasdair's dog and his wife, both. I wouldn't be surprised if you turned up with his land before the year was out."

The MacLeods stirred, interested in the exchange and the ominous tone in Artair's voice.

Dylan let his hand slip to Brigid's hilt and informed Artair, "You'll be taking that back, now—"

Malcolm said, "Set it aside, the two o' ye! Quiet down or ye'll have the entire MacDonell clan down our necks."

Dylan and Artair both sat back, but Dylan would have been just as happy for an excuse to cut the snotty kid.

They all slept, and the full moon was high when they set out to rustle the MacDonell herd. This was the tricky part, separating the cattle from those charged with their care, especially while the cattle were not yet driven to the remote *shielings*. According to intelligence brought back from the scouting foray, three teenage boys occupied a tiny hut tucked between two rocky knolls near the pasture. Donnchadh, two of his MacLeods, and Marc were dispatched to overpower and bind the cowherds.

Silence was essential now, which meant keeping the cattle from panicking. If yet another blood feud was to be avoided, the boys would have to stay unhurt, though the MacDonells would certainly try to kill the reivers if the *creach* were discovered or tracked. If the village were alerted, there would certainly be blood and no matter what happened then, some of that blood would eventually be Matheson. Slowly, easily, the Mathesons and MacLeods, and their well-trained dogs, urged the cattle to a walk and guided them northward from the pasture.

The false trail was taken for several hours, their route chosen carefully to avoid MacDonell households and to suggest a retreat toward Fraser lands. Then Malcolm guided them to higher, rockier ground. An hour later they began a wide circle that led them southward again. It wasn't enough to simply make it home with the cattle, they had to shake the MacDonell trackers *before* crossing into Iain Mór's lands. If the cattle could be tracked into Matheson territory but not out of it, Iain would be responsible for restitution regardless of whether the *spréidhe* were found and identified. Furthermore, during the following days they had to pass through enough grazing to keep the cattle on their feet. Speed was essential, to make it out of MacDonell territory.

The group pressed on, more slowly than on the approach, but covering more distance before stopping to rest. The route was different, over rocks that wouldn't show tracks and through treacherous bogs that would close over behind them if crossed properly.

At a narrow pass, Donnchadh slapped some of his men on the shoulder and five of the MacLeods dropped out of the group. They climbed to a rocky outcrop above, and settled in as shadows under the moon. Dylan asked, "What are they doing?"

Malcolm replied, "Just assuring we're not followed."

Dylan nodded, and continued with the herd. But before long, the hair rose on the back of his neck. He didn't like the feeling, and muttered to Sinann who rode the back of the animal next to him, "Hey, Tink. What's going on back there?"

Her voice was close and quiet. "I'm sure I have nae idea."

"Should I fall back and see?"

"Dear lad, always attend to what your gut tells ye. Go."

Dylan tapped Robin's shoulder and pointed with his chin

back along the trail, and with Sinann flying behind they retraced their route to the MacLeod ambush detail. The Mathesons heard the clang of swords before they were close
enough to see anything, and rushed toward the fray with
theirs drawn. When they arrived, the MacDonells had been
subdued and all but one run off. That one lay across a boulder, at the mercy of a MacLeod who had his dirk hauled
back to kill the struggling boy.

"No!" Dylan ran to stay his hand, and hauled hard against
the man's swing. The young MacDonell scrambled from under the loosened grip, and scurried into the darkness toward
home.

The MacLeod spun on Dylan and shoved him off, his eyes
wide and dark and his face screwed up with rage. His eyes
shifted down, and Dylan on reflex parried the dirk thrust at
his gut.

"Hey!" In the same motion he stepped in and with his
elbow knocked the man back a few steps, then held him at
the point of his sword. The other four MacLeods drew
swords, but Robin stood back to back with Dylan. Dylan
said, "What in bloody hell is going on here? That was just
a boy!"

"A boy to grow up a MacDonell. And it's nae concern of
yours," the senior MacLeod said.

"You *want* them to come after us?"

"Again, ye mean?"

Sinann threw in her two cents. "Last year the MacDonells
made a raid on the MacLeods and killed three men. I daresay
it's already a blood feud."

Dylan said, "You're right, it's no concern of mine. But
Iain Mór said no killing. If you want to carry on a feud, do
it on your own time. Leave us out of it. I'll not have the
MacDonells coming after *Tigh a' Mhadhaigh Bhàin* for your
killing."

The MacLeod gave him a withering look. "I wouldnae
expect an outlander such as yourself to ken."

"You're right, you can't. What you can expect me to understand is that I was told by my Laird there would be no
blood. Hear this, MacLeod, I will not let you kill anyone on

this trip. Come back later if you have to chase down skinny boys for vengeance."

The man glared at him for a moment, then sheathed his dirk. Dylan scabbarded his sword, then the rest of the weapons were put away. Slowly, keeping eyes on each other, they began the walk back to the herd.

Near dawn the reivers came to a river that had risen in the rains since their passing days before. Malcolm, Dylan, and Donnchadh went to the front of the herd to assess the situation, and debated the pros and cons of resting before crossing.

"The men and beasts are near exhaustion," said Malcolm.

Donnchadh replied, "But to stay invites attack by the MacDonells, a likely thing since this fellow from the colonies let the young one go earlier." He narrowed his eyes at Dylan, who ignored the remarks.

Malcolm peered at the brown, rushing water. An increased depth of only a foot made the difference between wading across safely and having to fight for footing. The men were tired, and so were the cattle. Dylan looked across the herd and saw them sluggish, with heads down. They all needed sleep. But he knew putting this river between themselves and the MacDonells would possibly shake the pursuit. They needed to push onward. He was not surprised when Malcolm gave the nod to cross.

The cattle were reluctant, and went into the water panicky. The dogs were carried across, draped around the necks of two Mathesons. The icy water pressed heavily, and the rocky bottom made poor purchase. One of the kine broke loose and floated away, bellowing in terror. Another followed, and Robin foolishly reached out for it. Outweighed, he was pulled from his footing.

Faster than thought, Dylan grabbed Innis's collar with one hand and dug into the riverbed with all his strength. He pulled and held on with both hands against the heavy drag of rushing water. His fingers, numb from the cold, clenched in Robin's sark but began to slip. Robin's struggle to find footing yanked against Dylan's hold. He leaned back against the current until the water rushed over his head, held his breath, and dug into the bottom with his toes and hauled hard.

Robin came within reach of one of the cattle, and grabbed a fistful of shaggy coat. Dylan surfaced and saw Robin would be all right, but kept hold of the exhausted man's sark as they continued across.

Slowly they made it onto the opposite shore and stood, shaking and dripping. "Thank you," said Robin.

Dylan nodded and watched the last of the cattle climb the bank. "It's good we only lost the two head." Robin nodded, and nothing more was said.

They stopped to sleep only once, and on the last day of travel made a hard, fast push into Glen Ciorram. As they passed just within sight of the barracks of the English dragoons, there being no other way into the glen with so many cattle, Dylan wondered out loud whether they would have any trouble from the Captain.

"I expect so," said Malcolm, apparently not much disturbed by the idea.

"You figure the MacDonells will go to him?"

At that Malcolm laughed. "Nae. Some Lowland clans might, but by no means all of them, and it's certainly not like the MacDonells to go·running to Her Majesty for defense. More likely they'll come after their cattle or steal ours. That's why we must hurry, and put the *spréidhe* where they cannae be found. The day after Beltane, the young folk will be off to the high pastures with them. Come June or July, we make the trade with the MacGregors."

As they made their way down the glen past the church, and the castle came into sight, Dylan's thoughts turned to Cait and he felt less cold, tired, and hungry. It was like coming home, a feeling he hadn't known in what seemed forever.

They drove the small herd across oat fields to a tiny track that cut behind the steep hills along the south side of the loch shore. The trail was seldom used, steep, thick with birches, oaks, and ferns that grew between the hills. The plan was to shelter the herd in a narrow glen deep in these hills. The cattle would spend the night, then half would be parceled·out the next day to Matheson pastures and the other half taken south with the MacLeods.

The herd went in single file along the track; the men were spread even more thinly. One of the kine veered from the herd to bolt up a ravine, and Siggy cut out after it like a black and white streak. Malcolm turned back and gestured to Dylan, but it was unnecessary. He was already off, following the two animals up the steep ravine that narrowed quickly as it rose. A tiny stream of snow, melted from white peaks, trickled over rocks at his feet as he picked his way along.

The dog had cornered his charge against a boulder and was worrying and herding it back the way they'd come. Dylan had to climb to his right to let them pass. He caught a whiff of something that smelled horrible.

He'd encountered some rank odors since coming to this century. Poorly cooked food, piles of composted human excrement, pustulous sores, farts, and unwashed bodies were inescapable parts of daily life now. But this was a stench that set off alarms in his head. Something had died nearby, something big. Dylan climbed over the boulder and coughed as the sickly-sweet odor of rotting meat invaded, thick enough to taste.

Though his instinct was to get as far away as possible, instead of following Siggy back to the herd he went farther up the ravine to see what had died. Perhaps if it were a deer there might be antlers to salvage and sell for knife handles and spoons. A couple of the men in the barracks did pretty good work, carving antlers, horns, and hardwood. He pulled Brigid in hopes of finding something he could use, and climbed over another boulder.

What he found made him take several steps backward. He coughed and gasped to get the oily stink out of his chest and mouth. For a moment he thought he would vomit, but closed his eyes to calm his hitching stomach. Then he opened them. Wedged between two pieces of granite jutting from the ground, bloated and ghastly pale, was the body of Marsaili's husband, Seóras Roy.

CHAPTER 11

He barely recognized the face. It was mostly by knowing the man was missing that he was able to connect the puffy, red-bearded carcass with the frightened man he'd seen the morning of All Saints' Eve.

Something else caught his attention. Three fingers were missing from the corpse's right hand, and one from the left. Taking shallow breaths, he reached down to pull back the ragged shreds of linen from over the chest and found an exposed rib cage crawling with squirming, scurrying bugs. Seóras had been missing since November but wasn't very far decayed. No doubt he'd been frozen in snow all winter. His skin was gone and the flesh below fetid, but Dylan could still see how the man had died. The sternum and several ribs were busted all to hell. That, and the defensive wounds on the hands, told him death had come from stabbing. Furthermore, Seóras had probably been disarmed before his death.

Dylan returned to the herd and reported his find. Malcolm climbed the ravine to investigate, and came to the same conclusions Dylan had. He sent Dylan and the other Mathesons on with the herd, and returned quickly to the castle with the MacLeods, the body wrapped in his own kilt, carried gently by three men to keep it intact.

Once the herd was safely tucked away, the Matheson reivers returned to the *Tigh*, where the men of the clan were in an uproar over the murder. Torches dotted the bailey. The Great Hall swarmed with clansmen arguing about what to do and what must have happened. The women hovered at the fringes, mostly out of sight. Dylan looked for Cait, but failed to find her.

The stinking corpse had been put in a winding sheet and laid on a trestle table in the Great Hall, near the large doors that opened onto the bailey, which were now thrown open because of the stench. Nobody paid much attention to the body in any case. Iain Mór was in the bailey with Malcolm, Artair, and Coll, in tense discussion with several other men including Myles Wilkie. He was the father of the banished girl, Iseabail, whose baby by Seóras Roy had reportedly been born in Inverness in early January. The man stared at the ground and sucked on his lower lip.

Iain was saying, "Can ye deny there was a desire in you to do it?"

Wilkie said nothing but stared at the ground as tears filled his eyes.

"Can ye swear to me an oath ye dinnae do it?"

There was more silence, and the men waited. Wilkie finally looked up at Iain and said, "He shamed us all."

Iain crossed his arms over his broad chest. "As did yer daughter. The entire business was an ugly and shameful one all around. I expect keeping a closer watch on your own responsibilities might have prevented it."

Dylan's gaze went to the ground as he wondered what the Laird would say if he knew his own daughter was secretly betrothed to her bodyguard.

There was another long wait for a reply from Wilkie, but none came. Iain then said, his tone pointed, "Do ye wish for a trial, then, Myles? To keep the English Captain happy?" Dylan gathered a trial wouldn't have been offered if not for the presence of English authority, and Iain appeared angry enough to execute the wretch himself right there.

Wilkie shook his head. "Nae, Iain. Dinnae let the Crown have my kine. Please, I've little enough. Leave me to the judgment of God and let my wife keep her home."

Iain nodded. "Ye'll hang, then." It was a request for

agreement as much as a pronouncement. Wilkie nodded, as if a deal had been cut, and Dylan realized it had. A sort of plea bargain in which *nolo contendere* still meant death, but no conviction also meant no confiscation of property because no guilt had been found. The man would die, but his wife would live. Iain said to the men standing by, "Take him to the guardhouse and put an extra man to watch him." To Malcolm he said, "Send a messenger to Inverness for the hangman."

Myles Wilkie was led away to the barred cells in the gatehouse. The crowd of men dissolved, leaving Dylan alone, stunned at what he'd just witnessed. The body had been discovered only a few hours earlier, and the killer was already found and sentenced without trial. There was no doubt even in his mind the girl's father had done it, and no doubt in anyone's the man would hang without a fight.

As he made his way to his bunk in Cait's alcove, he whispered to Sinann, who had also witnessed the scene, "Why didn't he deny the murder?"

She fluttered backward as he walked and peered at him as if he'd said something unutterably stupid. "Should he rather burn in hell?"

"If he did it, wouldn't he go there anyway?"

"Swearing to a lie would only cause him to die unrepentant, whether he died now of hanging or later of something else. Now he can pay for his evil deed, repent, and perhaps be forgiven by your Yahweh."

Dylan collapsed onto his bunk for some sleep, but instead lay awake, trying to get his twentieth-century mind around what had happened. When he finally slept, it was a fitful doze filled with nightmares of hanging.

The following day Dylan, in the midst of his workout, stopped cold with his sword raised when Captain Bedford strode into the Great Hall like he owned the place and made for the North Tower corridor. Two dragoons entered behind him and stationed themselves by the door. Dylan swallowed his shock in a hurry, then intercepted the *Sassunach* with the point of his weapon. "Where might you be going?"

Bedford halted and peered at him. His expression was

neutral, but the contempt in his voice wasn't disguised at all. "Get out of my way."

"I can't let you go in there. Furthermore, the guard is going to be in deep trouble for even letting you past the gatehouse."

"Don't be ridiculous. Let me by before I have you arrested." A smile curled his lip and he sounded like he relished the idea.

"I don't think so." Though he knew the American concept of privacy didn't wash in this time and place, there was still no way he was going to have this limey wandering around loose in the castle.

Malcolm came from the North Tower corridor, his lips pressed together at sight of Bedford. He turned to Dylan and said, "Let the Captain make himself comfortable by the fire, Dylan. The Laird will be with him shortly."

Dylan scabbarded his sword, then pointed with his chin to the rickety armchair by the hearth at the other end of the room. Bedford hesitated a moment, then gave a curt nod and strode across to the chair.

It was a short wait, then Iain Mór burst from the corridor door and bellowed as he crossed the hall, "What on God's earth do you want now?"

Bedford stood, and waited for Iain to approach. He stopped before the Englishman with his arms crossed and his chin out. "Well?" The contrast between the two men, one bulky but fit and one slender but fit, was striking.

"You've sentenced a man to hang."

"I have." The underlying tone also said, *So, what?*

"He's not been tried."

"He asked for the judgment of God."

Surprise flickered over Bedford's face. When he replied, it was with a new tack. "The punishment, then, is *peine fort et dur*, not hanging."

Dylan had no clue what that meant, but Iain's next words set him straight. "Piling stones on a man until he's crushed to death is not an English custom I care to allow into my glen. A quick hanging will do. You can arrest me if ye like and carry me off to Ft. William, and ye can confiscate my prisoner, but the man will be executed regardless. Unless ye're willing to have a number of your men die trying to take me from here, just for the sake of making sure one Scot dies like an Englishman, you'd be well advised to let this one go. *Captain*." The hatred in the Laird's eyes gleamed, and his cheeks were ruddy with rage. Iain was talking to the man who had killed his father. Most likely he would have murdered the Captain on the spot if he might have gotten away with it. Dylan noted that Iain was unarmed, and thought the Laird must have left his dirk behind as a precaution against his own unleashed temper.

Bedford said nothing for a long moment, then seemed to come to a conclusion. He sighed and said, "All right, Ciorram, have your hanging. But mark me, there will come a day when your inherited jurisdiction will no longer be held valid by the Crown."

"When that day comes, Captain, then you may stop me from hanging murderers. But until then, I'm the Laird of this glen and I shall rule my people as I see fit." The Captain opened his mouth to speak, but Iain Mór overrode him. "*And even then*, Captain Bedford, the English had best have a care for the kinsmen themselves. For I dinnae rule by simple authority. I rule by their will."

"Thank you, I've read Machiavelli."

"I expect ye have."

There was a long silence as the men stared at each other with palpable hatred. It was the *Sassunach* who spoke next. "Very well. Hang your kinsman. While you can." With that, he turned and marched from the hall.

Iain stood where he was for several minutes, staring into the fire. Malcolm and Dylan said nothing. Finally, Iain said, "Dylan, 'tis a good thing you found poor Seóras Roy. Now the Captain has something to occupy his mind other than the MacDonell cattle you drove past his barracks yesterday."

Malcolm laughed, and even Dylan had to chuckle.

Over the next couple of days the sheep were shorn of their winter wool. The ground was still too cold and soggy for plowing, but slowly the village of Ciorram shook off its winter sleep.

In the midst of the awakening of life, a wooden gallows was built in the castle bailey.

A week after the discovery of Seóras's body, a man rode in with a large pack slung across his saddle. The hangman from Inverness had arrived. Dylan watched people fall silent as the man passed, keeping to his path without a glance at anyone until he dismounted, stopped Marc Hewitt, and asked to see the Laird. The gallows had loomed over the lives of the Mathesons for days, and even Dylan felt a sense of relief it would soon be gone.

The following morning, before dawn, the clan gathered in the bailey for the execution. Dylan didn't want to go, but also didn't want to explain why he didn't want to go. Cait was determined to witness the hanging, so he went with her and told himself he wouldn't watch, though he knew it was an impossible vow to keep.

The gallows was nothing more than a high wooden piling set in the ground, with a cross beam bolted to it and a ladder leaned against it directly under the beam. The rope had been slung the night before, measured against the gallows and the man to be hung. From the noose it ran up through a hole in the cross beam, then down to the upright where it was tied to a cleat. Mathesons gathered around the contraption, huddled in plaids and cloaks against the morning chill, all of them nervous and some of them near tears for the man who was their neighbor and cousin. Dylan was appalled to see children had been brought to the spectacle. The only Matheson that seemed to be missing was Ranald, and that was a relief.

As the sky lightened to blue, the crowd parted to let through the hooded hangman and his charge. The condemned was ashen-faced, but otherwise calm and under control. He climbed the flimsy ladder until his head was higher than the noose. The hangman climbed up behind to tie Wilkie's hands, then up a couple more steps to place the noose around the man's neck. The ladder sagged beneath the weight of two men. The noose was pulled snug, then the hangman backed down the ladder. Wilkie looked over to where the ladder rested against the upright, and bounced on it a little. It jumped and banged against the upright.

Iain Mór stood nearby and said in a voice to carry across the gathering, "Have ye anything to say, man?"

The condemned looked down at the hangman who was ready to pull the ladder from under him. He said, "Nae," and jumped on the ladder so that it bounced off the upright, as he kicked it. It fell, and so did he. He reached the end of his rope just before his feet would have touched the ground, and the snap of his neck was audible. He dangled, twisting slowly, and all the air seemed to leave the witnesses. The man's neck stretched, and one shoe tip touched the ground, which stilled the twisting.

Dylan finally looked away when he saw urine drip down Wilkie's legs. It made a dark puddle in the dirt.

Cait whispered to Dylan, "Have ye never seen a hanging before?"

He shook his head.

"They let murderers live where you come from?"

"Sometimes."

Her shocked look at that made him realize there were some things about this century he would never understand.

CHAPTER 12

Once the executed body had been buried, the hangman paid, and the gallows removed, life in Glen Ciorram lurched back to normal for a few days, then moved on to the festive. In the castle kitchen preparations began for a festival which Dylan gathered would be on May 1, two days away. Some called it May Day, others Beltane. The entire glen was abuzz. He could sense an infectious excitement in Cait, and she gave him long looks as if she didn't care who saw. He returned them. She often found excuses to touch him, a hand on the arm or a shoulder against his chest. The excitement rose in him, and he wanted to shout to the world that she would be his wife.

The celebration of spring took place among the thin stand of pine trees at the crest of the wooded hill just north of the village, where a gigantic bonfire was lit at sundown. Everyone in the glen went, even the crippled and ill who were carried miles to the festivities by relatives and sat, bundled, on stools and chairs brought for them. Pipers raised lively song to the heavens, loud even in the open under the spreading crowns of the tall, gnarled trees. Drums recalled the pagan, almost savage origins of the festival, and stirred something deep in Dylan's belly.

Ranald was his raucous, annoying self, but nobody

seemed particularly annoyed by him tonight for his chatter fit right in with the spirit of the party. Ever-present and underfoot children ran and squealed with laughter at the outskirts of the crowd, and it was still hard to tell which kids belonged to which villagers, even though he could now put a first name to every face in the glen.

Dylan's heart soared, and he realized this was what he'd always sought but could never find in the Games in Tennessee. He and his friends had never accomplished more than a dabble in semi-familiar culture, and had never fully understood why many of those traditions had ever existed. But now he was among people for whom this celebration was part of the collective soul. He watched the dancing and singing and felt something of his own soul settle into its proper place, as if the missing piece of his heritage had finally been found and put back. He felt whole.

A line of men formed under a tall oak tree, with Malcolm at one end, who gestured to Dylan to join them. When Dylan tried to decline and held up a palm, Malcolm insisted, gesturing again. When Dylan still wouldn't go, Malcolm went over to collect the reluctant cousin, pulling him by the arm into the line. The other men began to dance, and Malcolm and Dylan joined in. Everyone was well on the way to intoxication from whiskey as well as ale, so they were not a graceful lot. Dylan kept his eye on Malcolm's feet and hoped nobody noticed he was a hair behind everyone else. The wail of the pipes made his heart pound, and his soul soared. Quickly, for the dance was a lot like the Appalachian clogging he'd learned as a boy from an aunt up on the ridge, he picked up the steps and began to enjoy himself. When he caught a look from Cait, he laughed out loud and his feet were just a little lighter.

Once the fire died down, some people began to jump over it. Couples ran hand-in-hand, and some women made the leap by themselves. Dylan had heard of this, and knew it was a custom that had roots as some sort of pagan fertility thing. When Cait moved into position to try it herself, he could feel his shock all the way to his toes. He glanced around at the crowd, and found a few faces as surprised as his. Nobody looked in his direction, though, and that was a relief since it was obvious Iain Mór was not pleased to see his unmarried daughter jump the fire.

She took a running start and leapt, and made it with only a slight stumble at the far side. Quickly she shook cinders from her skirt and stomped them out on the ground, then smiled at the onlookers. Color was high on her cheeks, and she laughed with joy. Dylan could hear the mutterings and jests, but he ignored them. Cait was simply in high spirits and would be forgiven the indiscretion, he was sure. He wished he could sweep her into his arms and kiss her, right there in front of everyone, so the entire glen would know she'd be married soon.

But again he was hauled into a circle of men who began an a cappella singing Dylan knew as "mouth music." He'd heard this particular song before at a *céilidh*, but had never sung it, and found himself giddy trying to keep up with the clip of syllables that went so fast they were almost nonsense. The men's voices sounded almost like the low register of the pipes. The repeats were a maze of similar lines changed just slightly each time sung. They moved with an almost mathematical progression until the entire thing was repeated once. Then, like most of these songs, it would probably come to a sudden ending. Dylan focused to find the pattern as he sang, and when the whole was repeated he began to smile because he finally knew where he was. Then the ending came and he quit right with everyone else. There was a moment of dead silence, then the men all looked at him and laughed. Dylan grinned. They'd expected him to keep going and give himself away, but he'd tripped them all up. Malcolm slapped him on the back and he laughed.

The dancing continued, and Cait took a turn. God, she was beautiful! Her chin held high and her body straight and proud, her face lit up with a happiness he wished would last forever, she danced with such grace he couldn't take his eyes from her. Afterward she rested, standing near her father, her cheeks aflame, and her eyes shone the color of star sapphire.

Her ring was nowhere in sight, which did not surprise him. He wondered where she hid it. Though he knew why she couldn't wear it in public, he still found it annoying. For all his adult life he'd had girlfriends, or not had them as he or they wished, and it was strictly between himself and the woman in question. Though his mother had always butted in with opinions, he'd never thought it was any of her business who he slept with and had always done as he'd pleased.

But here, everyone in the village had an opinion of every coupling, and the immediate family, especially, had a vested interest that was very real and weighted with economic and political considerations. It was the most irritating thing about this century, even worse than the incessant cold and that lunatic faerie.

The party was still lively when Dylan noticed Iain, Artair, and Coll taking their leave. Malcolm had already retired. Iain had hold of Cait's arm to take her home, but she shook her head and gestured to Dylan. It appeared she was asking to stay late. Iain considered it, then nodded and left with Artair and Coll, chatting with various villagers on his way out, like a politician.

Not much later, Cait disappeared and Dylan suspected where he might find her. He backed to the rear of the crowd, which was clapping rhythm for another dancer. It took several minutes to make it look like he was only milling among the villagers, but once he was behind everyone he moved more quickly toward the rocks jutting at the edge of the hilltop. Darkness hid him, and he stood for a moment to watch the dying bonfire.

A woman's voice came from the darkness behind him down the slope, and he turned toward her. Then a man's grunt made him stop, and the woman's giggle made him wonder who in hell was down there. He crept to investigate the thicket, and he recognized the voice of Seonag Matheson chattering in praise of whoever was making her giggle. Dylan smiled, tickled to hear quiet Seonag so cheerful. She was usually unsmiling, and had a lost, sad sort of look.

The man spoke her name in a husky voice, and Dylan realized he was eavesdropping on Marc and Seonag getting laid. He backed off and eased down the slope toward the rushing burn. He stifled a drunken giggle himself, amused to learn those two were involved, for he never would have guessed by their public behavior.

Soon there was another rustling in the denser woods ahead

and Cait's whispered "*A Dhilein!*" He descended toward the sound, and found her down by the burn, in a clear spot where moonlight glinted on the bits of golden hair that peeked from the front of her snood. She picked up her skirts and rushed to him, threw her arms around his neck and kissed him with the full passion of the evening. Joyous laughter rose as he kissed her in return. She pressed her body to his, and the laughter became a moan. Then she pulled away and drew him along. "This way. Come with me." She stepped onto a stone to cross the burn.

He pulled the other direction. "No. This way. The woods are too crowded." He knew where he wanted to go, and she followed without hesitation, picking up her skirts with one hand and gripping his hand with the other. Up he led her, along the burn, over rocks, lifting her over tree roots, to the tiny glen where the ruined tower stood, gleaming gray and silver in the moonlight.

Cait hung back at sight of it. "Nae. This place is enchanted. Faeries live here." Her voice quavered, and her eyes were wide, staring at the moon-washed stones.

"I know. Don't be afraid." He kissed her and touched her bright hair. "The faeries are the good guys." He chuckled. "Mostly."

That made her laugh, and she followed him, close behind, hip to hip, as if to put him between herself and any faeries that might jump out. Which, he knew, was a possibility if Sinann wanted to cause trouble. He led her through the gap in the stones, and watched her look around in wide-eyed wonder. "You've never been here before?" Dylan glanced around and hoped Sinann might have the grace to take herself elsewhere for tonight.

Her voice was soft with awe. "I've never been inside. When I was a child I once came to glimpse it from under the trees. Over there, up on the little hill. I never was brave enough to come so close." She turned and looked, then turned again and ventured away from Dylan to investigate under the branches of the oak that grew through the window. He followed her as she said, "I was always too afraid of the wee folk, for they will take you away to their home and enchant you so that a night is like a lifetime, and when you go home everyone you knew is dead and gone. I could never bear that, to lose my family and the time on earth given to me."

A chill skittered up Dylan's back. He coughed to clear his throat, then had nothing to say. He slipped his arms around her waist from behind, then nuzzled her neck and murmured, "I'll keep you safe. As long as I live, I'll never let you come to harm. I swear it." He pressed his palms to her belly and held her against him. If he could only hold her like this for eternity, she would be safe from the world.

She turned to him and placed her palms against his chest. "I know." His hands rested against the swell of her hips, then he pressed one to her yielding breast. A smile curled his mouth. No bra in this century, only a woolen overdress and a linen shift. She pressed his hand to her with her own, and her softness was luxury. He kissed her, freely for the first time ever. No angry uncles would venture here to catch them *in flagrante*. Cait tugged on his hand, down, until he sat with her on the grass. Then she reached for his belt.

Suddenly he was the one who faltered. The thunder in his heart was almost unbearable, but he made himself stop for a moment and shake the whiskey from his brain. He put his hand over hers against his belly. He'd lived with these Mathesons long enough to understand the enormity of this. She was offering the most valuable thing she had, which, once gone, would be gone forever. "Are you certain?" *Please say yes.* Wanting her was a fire in his gut that had smoldered for months, but he would rather wait than give her regrets. After all, they surely would be married before long and the waiting would then be over. He ran one finger up under the edge of her blouse sleeve and hoped she wanted this as much as he did.

She kissed him. "You're to be my husband, and you will be my only. Waiting will merely put off what must be." Her smile widened. "And tonight is Beltane. Waiting will bring us to nae better time." Her hand went to his belt again, and this time he let her. He couldn't think of an argument against her, and didn't care to try. He shoved his plaid from his shoulder and let the kilt and belt fall behind him as she unbuttoned and wriggled from her own clothing.

Her body was soft and warm in his hands, and she quivered at his touch. He wanted to do this slowly, to learn and explore her, but his own urgency matched hers and it was all he could do to wait until the clothing would be set aside. He removed his shoes and leggings, then pulled his shirt over his head. "Skyclad" was how Sinann had put it, and the night air on his skin felt just like that—as if the sky were his cloak.

Cait lay back and drew him with her. He was her first, and he swore she would be his last. She bore the pain with only a single squeak, then relaxed under him as he moved slowly and with care. Her warmth covered him and filled him, suffusing him with joy throughout, as if his soul had already gone to her and his body was now rejoining it. He moved faster as she responded with short, breathless words of love. Being so close, and knowing how she cared for him, his heart was touched in places he'd never guessed he had. The century ceased to matter. Time became forever. Existence was *now*.

For a long time afterward he held her, heady with the scents of disturbed grass and her own sweet skin. She was a rag doll in his arms, and he could barely move. It was a pleasure just to feel her breathe against his chest. He reached for his plaid, to draw it over them, and they slept.

It was dawn when Dylan awoke, half surprised to learn the night before hadn't been a dream. He rubbed the cold from the end of his nose and leaned up on one elbow to gaze at Cait, asleep in his arms, under his plaid where it was warm and their bodies soft with sleep. He pressed his lips to her hair and she stirred. Then she snuggled to him with a sleepy moan, and reached for him under the plaid. Her hand was gentle and he needed little encouragement. They made love again as the east sky outside the gap in the wall began to glow pink and the world awoke to a new spring day.

There was the slightest touch of blue in the sky, though the sun wouldn't be visible for a while yet, when they dressed to return to the castle. Hand-in-hand they made their way down the burn, then slipped silently along the stone dikes that defined tenancies in the glen, and crossed the drawbridge quickly in hopes of going unseen. Dylan, not having his sporran with him, whispered to the night's watch, "A shilling for you later, Robin."

Innis, who sat on a stool with his whittling, dropping shavings between his feet, didn't look up as he replied, "Nae. I'll not need bribery from you. Take her in, and be swift about it before Himself awakens." He gestured with his knife and took quick, careful glances at Cait.

Dylan grinned. "Thanks, friend." He urged Cait onward. To avoid the Great Hall where breakfast was in preparation, they climbed the empty prison tower of the gatehouse where there was a door onto the battlement. Across the top of the curtain wall they hurried, above the stables and barracks. The bailey below was empty of movement this early, and still deep in purple shadow. They crossed to the West Tower and descended in silence past the chambers of Cait's parents and her young uncles, to her own room and Dylan's alcove.

There they found Iain Mór sitting on Dylan's bunk, cleaning his fingernails with a long, sharp dirk. His elbows leaned on his knees and he gave no acknowledgment of their arrival. Cait and Dylan pulled up short. "Father," she whispered.

CHAPTER 13

Iain didn't look up, but continued to dig dirt from his nails. His elbows rested on his knees, and his heavy eyebrows met over his nose. *Iain Mór Crosda*, thought Dylan, and, perversely, he nearly laughed. *Big, Bad John.* He knew what was coming, and knew Cait's father wanted her out of the way. So did he.

"Cait," he whispered, "go on inside." She shook her head and stood her ground, but he squeezed her elbow. "Trust me," he said. She looked into his face, and he repeated, "Just trust me." She went, and he closed the door behind her.

He turned back just in time to avoid Iain's dirk. Dylan dodged, and it slammed into the door next to his head. As Iain yanked his knife free, Dylan drew Brigid from his legging and circled fast to avoid being cornered in the alcove, then backed away. "I love her, Iain."

"Which matters not in the least, lad. That doesnae make you any different from a dozen other men who would do what you've done."

"She loves me in return." Dylan backed down the stairs. "That makes me different."

Iain still came. "That nevertheless gives you nae right to decide for her, or for the clan, who she would marry. I'm her father, and I will do the deciding."

Dylan took a deep breath and made himself relax in readiness and confidence. He had to know he would succeed, or the fight was already lost. "Me. I want to marry her, and I won't let her go."

Iain let out a roar and came at him. Dylan parried and nearly fell down the tower steps in his hurry to get away backward. He retreated, feeling his way down each dark step as he guarded his back. Iain took random swipes, which did little more than keep Dylan on the defensive. They were easily parried.

At the bottom of the tower, Dylan bypassed the door that led to the corridor behind the non-family living quarters. He needed open ground and room to maneuver. He continued to back around inside the tower toward the door that led to the stables. Iain saw his plan, and launched a series of attacks meant to back him past the door and corner him in the bottom floor room of the tower.

Dylan parried furiously, not willing to attack and risk hurting Iain, but not eager to be cornered, and perhaps be killed. He suddenly fell back a step and let aggressive Iain overbalance, then stepped in and shoved the older man away from the door. He ducked through it, ran under the stairs of the tack room with Iain right behind him, into the stable, and through the wide double doors to the castle bailey. There he turned to make his stand, in a spot where he stood a chance of defending himself without damaging Iain.

Iain's frustration at losing his chance to kill Dylan away from prying eyes showed in his reddening face. "You want to marry my daughter? *You?* Would I let her marry a man who makes a pledge then throws it away like so much refuse?" He took a swipe at Dylan's face, but sliced only air. "And a penniless one for a' that."

"I promised to protect her, and I have. I want to keep protecting her for the rest of my life. I swear on my soul I'll never let her come to harm. She needs me. Can't you see she'll never be happy with someone else?"

Iain's eyes went wide and he seemed to swell with rage. "Well, now, aren't ye just so full of yerself as to burst? So ye're arrogant enough to think ye're the only man on all the earth who can make my Cait happy?" He took another swipe at Dylan's face. Dylan fell back to avoid the blade. He circled to get the rising sun out of his eyes, but Iain wouldn't let him, and they sidled toward the stable. Iain feinted, trying in vain to get Dylan to retreat. Dylan dodged the knife. On the third feint they clashed dirks again and Dylan stood his ground.

He didn't know how long he could keep this up without hurting Cait's father. The look in Iain's eye was murderous. The older man wouldn't be satisfied until he'd drawn blood, and Dylan had to resign himself to that. At the next attack, he blocked with his left forearm instead of the dirk. Iain's dirk put a deep lengthwise slit in it.

Dylan let out a shout of pain to satisfy Iain with his victory. He was surprised at how much the wound hurt. Brigid thudded on the ground and he grabbed the wound. It felt like it had gone to the bone, and he hoped he was wrong. He held his bleeding arm and shouted, pissed off now, "Yes! I am the only one who can make her happy!" The pain was a fire that crept past his elbow, and he wondered if he'd made an error that might cost him his life. If he bled to death, the question of him marrying Cait would be easily settled, and not in his favor.

He pressed hard with the heel of his other hand. Blood smeared his arm and his hand and dribbled onto his kilt. He looked Iain in the eye and said again through gritted teeth, "I *am* the only man who can make Cait happy. If I wasn't dead sure of that, I would want her to marry someone else. Anyone else, as long as she was happy. We both want that for her, Iain. For God's sake, and for her sake, let her have it. You're her father; let her be happy."

Rage drained from Iain's body, and he stared at Dylan's arm. He wiped his blooded dirk on his kilt, then slipped it into the scabbard at his side. Without a word he headed for the entrance to the Great Hall, leaving Dylan standing alone in the middle of the bailey.

Artair and Coll were outside the Great Hall, watching with hooded eyes. They stood among the castle residents who had gathered at the entrances to the bailey, silent in their shock. Dylan watched Iain go, and saw the Laird's half brothers follow him into the Great Hall. Then he picked Brigid off the ground, wiped the dirt onto his kilt, returned her to the scabbard in his legging, and turned his attention to stopping his bleeding.

He went back the way he'd come, to the West Tower, and found Cait on her way down the steps, hurrying with her skirts in her fists. "I told you to stay in your room," he said, suddenly very tired.

She paused on the steps, and her voice took on an offended edge. "No, you dinnae. You said naught about staying. I saw it all from the battlement. Here, you're hurt!" She'd brought a kerchief with her, and pressed it to his arm. Together they went to her chamber. He hesitated at the door. She peeled back the kerchief just enough to see that the bleeding hadn't quite stopped, then pressed it again. "It'll need sewing," she announced.

"I know." He shuddered. *Drugs!* Oh, how he wished for drugs! Morphine, Lidocain, Demerol, Novocain, anything! Aspirin, acetaminophen, ibuprofen . . .

"In here. I have things for it." She guided him into the bedroom, where he'd never before ventured. The bed was large and of heavy oak, and an armoire stood beside a stack of trunks. The room was shaped like Malcolm's, except it had shuttered arrow loops instead of windows. She wasn't high enough in the tower to rate glass windows, which, in the days of siege warfare, would have been a weakness of the castle on the lower floors. Her hearth was near her door, and he could see his own hearth had been built to share her chimney on the other side of the alcove wall. She gestured that he should take a seat in a wooden chair by the fire, and she rummaged through a trunk at the foot of her bed. From it she produced a box, and from that box a needle and long linen thread that she wet in her mouth, twisted, and poked through the eye.

He coughed and said, "Um, do me a favor? Would you boil that before sticking it in me?"

She almost laughed as she tied a knot at the end of the thread. "Whatever for?"

He shrugged. "Yeah, I know it sounds silly, but would you do that for me?" He resurrected his "cute teacher" smile and hoped she wouldn't ask too many questions he couldn't answer.

There was a moment of hesitation, as if she weren't sure he wasn't joking, then she took a small three-legged copper pot from the hearth and filled it from the ewer on the table across the room. She then dropped the needle and thread into it and set it back in the hearth, over the fire. "Is this some strange, American religious custom? Have you all gone over to heathen ways, then?" Her voice was teasing but pointed enough that he needed to explain.

He checked on the bleeding, then pressed the kerchief again. "No. It's just to make it more clean. I don't want to be poked with a dirty needle any more than . . ." he thought a moment for a comparison, "than, say, you would want to eat dust." She made a face, and he said, "Exactly. Not healthy."

"Not *tasty*."

He chuckled. "It's not tasty because it's not good for you. Neither is a needle with dirt on it, and sometimes dirt is too small to see."

"Evil. We call it evil hereabouts."

"And so it is." Dylan thought the word was not inappropriate in reference to germs and disease. "Boiling things makes them less likely to make us sick. Less . . . evil." His voice brightened to get off this morbid subject, particularly as it concerned his own arm, "So we'll just wait for that there water to boil, and hope this bleeding stops in the meantime." He checked the wound again, found the bleeding had slowed but not quite stopped, and put pressure back on.

She sat on the floor next to his chair with her legs curled under her and put her chin on his knee. "You've won, you know," she said. "He neither killed you, nor did he tell you to leave. He'll let us marry, as soon as he gets over his anger."

Dylan hoped she was right.

Once the needle and thread had boiled enough to make him happy, she poured out the water into her washbowl and picked up the suture by the thread. Truly sterilizing it was out of the question, but Dylan hoped the boiling would at least reduce the potential for infection. It took a minute of blowing on it before she could touch the needle, then she reached for his arm.

She wasn't timid. The stitches went deep, meant to hold. Dylan closed his eyes and focused, concentrating on breathing steadily and not letting his mind drift to anything else, and the pain lessened until he could no longer feel it. It was a long cut, and took thirty stitches or so, all run together like a neat embroidery line along the inside of his left forearm near his elbow. When she was done and leaned in to bite off the thread, he relaxed. The pain came roaring back, and he groaned.

"Let me help you clean up." She dipped a towel into her washbowl and began wiping blood from his arm and hands. Her touch was now light and painless, and the warm water felt good. He leaned close as she worked, and touched her hair where a shining lock framed her face. She looked up at him, and he kissed her sweet mouth. She would be his wife, and he thought his heart could burst for it.

Artair's voice at the door was filled with disgust. "At it again, the two of you?" Dylan and Cait separated. Dylan sucked on his lower lip, furious at feeling guilty for a simple kiss. Artair lounged against the door frame like a hoodlum, arms crossed over his chest and head cocked. "Were you to bring yourselves under control and at least feign decorum, the Laird would have an interview with his daughter's suitor. Alone." He shoved himself erect and made his exit as quickly as he'd come.

Dylan squeezed his eyes shut and sighed. Here was the moment he'd dreaded for months. The knife fight had been easy compared to this.

Iain Mór kept an office on the first floor of the North Tower, where he conducted business and handled paperwork relating to the management of his lands and tenants. By a single, curt word from the Laird, Dylan was bade to enter, which he did with as calm a bearing as his physical training afforded him. He'd changed out of his torn and bloody sark, and into his good one with the embroidered cuffs. The one Cait had given him. He was unarmed to indicate goodwill.

Iain, smoldering with anger that made Dylan shudder, sat in a large, red-upholstered chair, hunched over a heavy table

stacked with papers and books. He appeared busy with a
letter of some sort, and declined to acknowledge Dylan's
presence. Beside the pot of ink into which he dipped his quill
was a wooden box filled with quills, some used and stained
with ink, some still feathered and clean. Against the stone
walls were tall bookcases, filled with leather-bound volumes
for reading, and large, bound record books.

A movement in shadow caught Dylan's eye and he
glanced to find Malcolm tucked away inside an arrow loop
behind the desk, sitting on the deep stone ledge with his back
leaned against the side and one foot propped opposite. Dylan
pretended not to notice, choosing to wait and see what would
develop. He turned to examine the room while Iain fussed
with his papers.

It was the most luxurious room Dylan had yet seen in the
castle, appointed to impress those who came on business.
Upholstered chairs stood before a cabinet filled with wine.
Dylan guessed the wine would be from the continent, French
perhaps. His gaze fell on a sword displayed on the wall behind Iain's desk, and his breath was taken quite away.

It was huge, and glittered of silver hilt and polished steel.
At cursory glance he put it at early seventeenth century or
late sixteenth, a broadsword with a hilt that preceded the
basket-hilt design in that it was more reminiscent of the
swept-hilt lines found in rapiers. *Very* unusual. And very
beautiful. The knuckle guard and swirling quillons bore an
intricate etched and pierced design, the grip was bound in
wire, and the pommel was pierced in an exquisite pattern of
whorls that echoed the curves of the quillons. It was the very
sort of masterwork he'd always wished to have in his collection, and here it was all shiny and real. He had to force
his gaze from it to look at the rest of the room.

One wall was hung with a tapestry of a forest scene that
caught his eye for its size. A white unicorn galloped among
dark, twisted trees, and a man rode that unicorn. He was
large, almost dwarfing his mount, and sported a bright, red
beard and flowing red hair, just as Sinann had described
Donnchadh Matheson. In one hand he wielded a sword and
in the other a white rose. The plaid of his Great Kilt flew
behind him like a Highland flag as he galloped.

But what drew Dylan's attention, and held it, was the figure hovering over the mounted man, on whom his gaze was turned. It was a faerie, glowing white and shimmering in the darkness. On closer inspection, a shock of recognition hit him. It was Sinann. There was no doubt—the face was hers.

He turned to Iain and indicated the man on the unicorn. "This is your father, Donnchadh Matheson, is it not?"

Iain was unable to hide his surprise, and his eyes went wide before he regained control. "What makes you think that?"

Dylan shrugged, not wanting to give away his connection to Sinann. "I'm guessing. The bard has mentioned him and the white faerie." It was a lie, but Iain might not know that. "Who made this?"

Iain shrugged. "The tapestry was a gift from faeries. The day my father was buried, this appeared where you see it now. I've not dared take it down."

Dylan gazed at the image of Sinann, and before his eyes the figure turned and winked at him. He shuddered, then struggled to keep his voice steady as he stared at her. "Do you believe in faeries?"

Iain replied, "Of course, I do. They brought the tapestry, did they not?"

Dylan chuckled as the faerie in the tapestry resumed her pose. "Aye, they did, sure enough."

Iain grunted and set his quill aside. He crossed his arms over his chest, leaned back, and finally got down to business. "So you want to marry my daughter." To the point. Dylan had come to expect that from the old world Mathesons, a trait lost to his own branch of the family. All the Mathesons back home, as well as Mom's folks, liked to hem and haw around every issue and never quite say what they meant. They therefore rarely got anything accomplished.

He turned to reply. "Yes." Equally blunt. When in Rome . . .

"How will you support her?"

"I have money. Enough for a small piece of land." A very small piece in a high, rocky glen to the south. He was still in negotiation, finagling a deal through Malcolm that, if he didn't do some fancy footwork, would most likely include five years of labor as payment to a MacLeod Laird. But Iain didn't need to know all that yet.

Iain's eyebrows raised. "I see I've been paying you entirely too much."

"I'm careful with my money and have no vices beyond a bucket of hot water of an evening. I know how to use my money so it will increase. Your daughter will never go hungry."

"She's accustomed to more than just safety from hunger."

"She's also an adult who knows that fortune comes and goes. As part of the clan we will all ride things out together."

There was a dark pause, then the anger in Iain's voice took on an uglier edge. He leaned forward on his table. "You fancy yourself a landowner, then, do you? You hold with the English laws that are destroying the clans, where land is owned by few and those who control it have no responsibility to those as work it."

"You own your land."

"By English law only. By the law of the clans and my lairdship, I only rule the land for the sake of my people. Even the poorest of my tenants eat of a winter if there is any bread to be had by the clan. That is something as cannae be said by the Lowland scum who would wrest from me ownership and then evict tenants whose families have worked the land since the time of our first king, Kenneth MacAlpine. It is for the sake of profit they do this, to line their embroidered pockets with gold and silver while people starve all around them."

Dylan nodded that he understood. In a few years hundreds and thousands of those starving people would flee to America and make homes in the mountains of Appalachia. That he knew that was nothing he could tell Iain. So he simply said, "I don't wish to separate myself from the clan." Indeed, it would be foolish to live in these mountains without the protection of Cait's father, for the small farm he had in mind would be vulnerable to raids and one man alone could never hold off neighboring clans.

"Then, as a landowner, you would keep your allegiance to me?"

Dylan opened his mouth to answer in the affirmative, then shut it again. Iain was asking whether he would go to war if called. Knowing Iain was a Jacobite, he couldn't in honesty promise to fight for the cause that would destroy many families over the next three decades. He said, "My allegiance is to Cait. Her safety is what I will swear to."

"If you would be under my protection, you would also be beholden."

There was a pause and Dylan thought hard, but there was no getting around it. In order to marry Cait, he had to pledge himself to military service. He nodded. "Aye. It's true. As a landowner I will promise myself."

Iain sat back in his chair, relaxed now, as if securing Dylan's pledge had been the entire purpose of the meeting. But then he glanced at Malcolm and said, "You're aware that, as I have nae sons, Coll is heir to the lairdship of my holdings."

Dylan nodded.

"And, were he to die without male issue, Artair would become heir by order of birthright."

Again, Dylan nodded and wondered what Iain was getting at.

"Also, you must be aware that, being young and reckless the both of them, and Artair with his unruly tongue, they stand a good chance of neither of them living to make a marriage to give them legitimate heirs."

This was news to Dylan. Expecting young men to die before marriage just wasn't part of his cultural background. He shrugged and said, puzzled, "Which means . . . ?"

"Which means, laddie, that, as Roderick's son, you become the next candidate for the lairdship. It's been suggested that's the real reason you made the journey from the colonies."

Dylan let out a short bark of a laugh as he remembered what Malcolm had said the day after his arrival, about whether he'd expected to find so many male cousins. At the time he'd thought his relationship to Iain had been meaningless in terms of the lairdship because of having been born in America. Only now did it occur to him that his citizenship was considered British. The United States didn't exist. Vir-

ginia was a British colony, and under the Treaty of Union
with Scotland signed seven years before there was no legal
difference between Scottish and English citizenship. Tech-
nically, a British subject was a British subject. Therefore,
under English law as well as clan law, he was in line for the
lairdship just the same as if he'd been born in Scotland.

Astonished, his jaw dropped open. "I told you. I was
brought here against my will. It's only because of Cait that
I want to stay at all."

"Easy enough said, lad."

Dylan chewed on the inside corner of his mouth for a
moment. This wasn't anything he'd expected. He wasn't sure
how to respond. Then he rolled up first his left sleeve, revealing the purpling wound with its thirty stitches now pink
with blood, then his right, baring his good arm. "Care to have
at the other one?" he said.

Anger rose in Iain. "Perhaps I should have killed you."

Dylan slipped his plaid from his shoulder so it hung in
the crook of his arm, and opened the front of his shirt to
expose his chest adorned with the black-and-silver crucifix.
"Go ahead. Put your dirk right there. If what you want is to
get rid of me to make sure your title doesn't go to an American, get your sword and stick it in me now, because I won't
live without Cait. Screw the land, fuck the title, but I won't
live without Cait." He paused a moment as he realized something. He let go of his shirt and continued, "You won't,
though, because she'd hate you for it."

Iain's brow knotted and he sucked on his lower lip. "She
would get over it."

Dylan went with his faith in Cait. "If you believe that,
then go ahead and kill me. But you know her better than that.
You know she's as stubborn as you are and will hate you
forever if you put me away." He stood hipshot, as if he didn't
care what Cait's father might do. "You know she loves me."

Iain Mór turned to grab the silver-hilt sword from its wall
bracket, and in one motion slipped the scabbard off and laid
the edge of the sword aside Dylan's throat. The younger man
held his ground and only blinked as the sharp edge stung his
skin. Iain's eyes flamed and he spat his words. "You come
to me with my daughter's blood on your prick, I *should* kill

you." He stopped and stood, panting for a moment, his face reddening. Dylan said nothing, and moved only to breathe. If Iain was bent on killing, then Dylan would die and that would be the end of it. Death would be preferable to living without Cait. It was a long, tense moment as Iain considered his next move.

Finally, the older man withdrew the sword and laid it on the desk before him. He sat back down in his chair, elbows on the desk, and pressed his lips to teepeed fingers. After another long moment he leaned back and looked into Dylan's face. He said, "If you had the title, and the land, would you care for it as I do?"

Now Dylan was puzzled again. "If I had it?"

"I cannae leave my holdings to Cait. All I can do is provide her with a dowry befitting her. The title and the bulk of the clan holdings must go to a male heir. But Coll and Artair are nae my sons. So I can more easily say before my death *which* male heir should receive the lairdship, and the clan would most likely follow my wishes. Provided my choice is a reasonable one."

"You can disinherit Coll and Artair?" This was a complete surprise.

Iain shrugged. "If they are both unsuitable, the clan willnae follow either of them, and that is all there will be to that. If Coll inherits but is weak, Artair will try to take the lairdship from him. It could split the Mathesons, and even lead to war within the clan. As Laird, I must consider the future of all my people, not just my daughter. Something you would do well to learn yourself."

"What about Malcolm? He's your first cousin as much as I am." More, were the truth known.

"Malcolm is a Taggart, and a Matheson only through the female line. The clan would never accept him."

Malcolm finally spoke, his voice sounding hollow inside the arrow loop, "Also, I'm an old man. You, Dylan, are not."

There was a long silence while Dylan chewed on this, then he said slowly, "If I took over, Artair and Coll would both come after me."

"Oh, aye, they will," said Iain.

"But you are not weak." Malcolm said it as if it were

something Dylan should have thought of. "When you marry Cait, and become Iain's right hand, you will almost surely be seen as his preferred heir. You are strong enough to hold the clan together. Then, on your passing, the lairdship will go to your son, who will also be Cait's son. Iain's grandson."

"You think the clan will accept a stranger?"

A look crossed Iain's face that told Dylan this was indeed the weak spot in the plan. But the Laird said, "I'm not dead yet, young Dylan, nor am I going anywhere soon. There is time, and in time the clan will accept you if I encourage it."

Dylan couldn't help but glance at the silver-hilt sword on the desk before him, and Iain said, "That sword comes down from my great-grandfather. *Our* great-grandfather. It's English, made by Clemens Horn for King James VI of Scotland after he'd become James I of England. It was presented by the King to our ancestor for service to the Crown, and has been handed down from father to son for a hundred years. I wish for it to go to a man who is worthy of it."

The world as Dylan understood it did a complete turn-around. "This morning you wanted to kill me."

Iain's anger rose again. "I still want to kill you, and will do it gladly if you give me any more trouble." Then he continued in a tone of frustration, "You took something very precious to me, and thwarted a well-laid plan in the bargain. Nae for a moment should you think this willnae cost me." He looked over at Malcolm again, then continued more calmly, "But now, having had time to think on the possibilities, I can see that your caring for Cait might be a gift from God. A recompense for the young sons I lost as children, and an opportunity to pass the clan leadership to someone who won't lose it to those who would harm the clan."

Dylan took a deep breath and his mind raced. In the space of just a few minutes he'd gone from resigning himself to death, to entertaining the possibility of inheriting Iain Mór's lands and title. But now as he thought it through, he realized both Artair and Coll would have him dead before they would accept what Iain proposed. Furthermore, aligning himself politically with Iain Mór would put him within the notice of the Crown and the Privy Council as a Jacobite, only a year and a half before the next doomed uprising.

He came full circle and once again knew his days were numbered.

CHAPTER 14

The meeting ended, Dylan was told to move his belongings to a room in the North Tower, as he was no longer charged with guarding Cait. When he went to pick up his things from the trunk in his alcove, he took her hands and murmured into her ear what had transpired between him and her father. "Not only are we to be married with his blessing," he said, and he squeezed her hands in his, "but he's talking about making me his heir."

For a moment her face went slack with astonishment, then she squealed with joy and hugged him, which almost swept away his confusion. His life was changing, morphing into something unrecognizable, but the one thing that mattered, Cait, was unchanged. She loved him as much as he loved her, which was considerable. She said as much, over and over, chattering on about how wonderful it was all going to be.

When she calmed enough for him to get another word in he said, "But I've got to move into the North Tower." He let her go and kissed her hand, then saw she wore his ring. He kissed it, a joyful chuckle rising as he did so, then turned and knelt to collect his things from the trunk.

She set a fist on her hip. "Of course you've got to leave. It wouldnae do to have you sleeping outside my door. Some-

thing *unseemly* might happen." The sarcasm in her voice
tickled him, and he grinned up at her. All that waiting was
probably now wasted. The entire glen certainly thought
they'd been sleeping together for months.

He shrugged and laid his spare kilt on his bunk, folded
in quarters, then his spare sarks and the poetry book on top
of it to roll them together. Then, with his *sgian dubh* strapped
under his arm, Brigid in his legging, his baldric and sword
slung across his chest, his sporran on his belt, and his coat
over it all, he tucked the rolled kilt under his arm and leaned
down to give her a kiss.

"Dinnae be silly, it's not goodbye," she said. "I can walk
with you to your room."

He smiled and shook his head. "Bad idea. We've given
them enough to gossip about; they don't need more. I'll see
you at supper."

She frowned. "But Dylan—"

"Don't be arguing with me, my love. Not on this. I'll see
you at supper." He kissed her, and he left the West Tower
for good.

When he arrived at his new quarters in the North Tower,
he found Malcolm in the alcove outside his door, squatted
on his heels against the wall. He stood as Dylan approached.
"Congratulations, young Dylan."

Dylan stood for a moment, assessing Malcolm and deciding how much to give away of what he'd inferred from the
afternoon. Finally, he said, "Thank you, Malcolm. But why
did you do it?"

The older man shrugged and glanced around at nothing,
wanting to be honest, but still careful. "It's a sad thing my
cousin has no sons living. He would have raised a chief to
hold the clan together in these times of disaffection and over-
whelming attack from Lowland scum and *Sassunach* laws.
Neither Artair nor Coll was raised to the responsibility, and
all they see is the wealth that comes with the property. They
neither of them truly understand what it means to manage
and protect people when there are too many of them for the
land to support." He shifted his weight and glanced down
the stairwell as if concerned with eavesdroppers. "You, on
the other hand, are smart enough and caring enough to do

right by the clan, and strong enough to not let those other two tear it apart. Iain dinnae see that at first, and now he does. That's the long and the short of it."

Dylan had one more question. "Why have you never doubted I'm Roderick's son?"

Malcolm smiled, as if this were an easy question. "Two reasons. Firstly, I've seen how you treat people lower than yourself. You respect them, and you respect yourself as well as your superiors. I *want* you to be Roderick's son so that the Ciorram Mathesons will have a strong leader once Iain and myself are gone, and will continue to have them in your sons and grandsons. And secondly," he chuckled, "like Sigurd, I know a Matheson when I see one." He slapped Dylan on the shoulder and went on up the stairs toward his own chamber. "I'll see you at supper."

Dylan had a queer feeling that he was being railroaded, but when all was said and done, he figured he was on a track he wanted to follow.

His new room was huge by the standards to which he'd lately become accustomed. And it had the luxury of privacy—a door he could actually close. Though it was directly below Malcolm's chamber, it had arrow loops for windows instead of glass, but if he leaned into one and put his face right up to the narrow opening, he could see almost the entire loch and granite mountains beyond. Someone had lit a fire in the hearth, which took the chill off the large room. He dumped his clothing on the bed, which was similar to Malcolm's but had a frame for bed curtains. No curtains, just the frame. And instead of an armoire there was a trunk the size of a large coffee table at the foot of his bed.

He looked at it and wondered if he would ever have enough things to need a trunk that big. His sword and clothing went into it, then his coat, sporran, leggings, dirks, and shoes. Then he looked at that mighty inviting bed, unbuckled his kilt, and put it in as well before dropping the lid. Then he collapsed on top of the wool blanket and drifted off to sleep. It had been a long, eventful night and an equally eventful morning.

He was awakened by Sinann's urgent and frightened voice. "Dylan! Wake up, lad! Hurry! Get up! Get up!" He leapt from the bed without fully waking and reached for Brigid but she wasn't there. He couldn't remember where *he* was. He spun a circle in the middle of the room, irritated, and growled, "Tinkerbell! What do you want?"

She laughed. "To see you fall over your feet. Aye, there's an obliging laddie." Her giggling was musical and irritated him to the bone.

He focused on her and made a disgusted noise. But he reached into the trunk for Brigid before crawling face-down onto his bed again with the knife under his pillow where she belonged. "I suppose you're here to gloat."

"Gloat? I'm here to give you something. For what do I need gloating?"

He turned on his side. "You've won. I'm going to fight the English. In a year and a half I'll probably be dead. If Artair and Coll don't get me first. Thanks, Tink." He threw her a sarcastic salute.

Sinann was tugging on the lid of his trunk. "I'm nae gloating, lad. I know your predicament." Her wings beat frantically as she tried to lift the lid.

Dylan sat up on his bed and reached over to help. "What are you looking for?"

She ducked her head into the trunk, and came up with his sporran. A short flight, and she settled at the top of the curtain frame.

"Hey!"

"I'm not after your money, ye sumph. Where's that brooch you had the day you came?"

"It's in there. What do you want with it?"

She found it, held it aloft, then tossed the sporran to the mattress below where it gave a loud clink of his money. Dylan leaned back on his elbows to watch as she held the brooch in both hands and bowed her head.

"What—"

"Shhh!" She held the brooch above her head and began murmuring to herself. There was a long moment, then the steel in her hands began to glow. The light increased until Dylan had to shield his eyes from the unaccustomed brightness. When it died down, Sinann dropped to the mattress beside Dylan and held her hands out to him.

"What did you just do, Tink?" Dylan didn't trust anything she did, especially if it involved magic.

"It's now a talisman. The thing means something to you. It represents the clan, does it not?"

Dylan nodded.

"The clan is your protection. None can live without support of family."

Again, Dylan agreed. "So, what have you done to my pin?"

"It will protect you in the way the clan does. When you wear it, you cannae be seen by those who would harm you."

Dylan took the brooch. "Not seen? Like, invisible?"

"Completely invisible. As long as you keep still."

He knew there would be a catch. "I guess that lets out sneaking up on people, then."

"It does, indeed. Like the clan, its protection works only if you stay in one place."

Dylan chuckled. "Oh. A hint. I guess I'll be sticking around for a while."

Sinann laughed with joy and spread her arms as her wings lifted her into the air. "Oh, yes!" she cried to nobody in particular. "He's come to lead the Mathesons to victory over the English!"

Dylan groaned and rolled over to bury his face in his arms.

At supper he sat with Cait, and though the entire castle stared he couldn't wipe the grin of happiness from his face. No matter how he tried to control it, he couldn't keep his mouth from curling at the corners. Cait's sunny smile lit up the room for him, and it was all he could see. Or cared to see.

The *céilidh* that evening, with Mathesons gathered from all over the glen, turned formal when Iain Mór stood to make the announcement everyone seemed to know was coming. Dylan sat, straddling a bench, with Cait settled on it between his knees. She leaned back in his arms with her head on his shoulder and their hands twined against her belly. As she relaxed into him, it became almost as if he couldn't tell where he ended and she began.

By the hearth, holding his silver flagon bearing an etched

image of a bear, Iain cleared his throat and composed himself. Cait squeezed Dylan's hand, and he squeezed back but didn't look at her. This could go smoothly or turn ugly. He caught a glimpse of white overhead, and looked up to see Sinann's smiling face. She hovered over them all like a guardian angel.

"It has come to my attention," intoned Iain, "that my daughter and a certain young man have taken a liking to each other." Everyone in the room turned to gawk at the pair, and Dylan kept his eyes on Iain, who continued, "Tonight I consider myself a fortunate man in that I can heartily approve of my daughter's choice." A wry smile crossed his face and his voice took on a conspiratorial tone. "For we all know that Cait does what she likes and would marry him regardless, even were he a beggar." There was a ripple of laughter in the room. "Therefore it is with joy I am announcing the betrothal of my daughter to our kinsman who was born in Virginia across the sea but is a Scot just the same, Dylan Robert Matheson." A luxuriant roll was given to both R's in "Robert." Then he turned to Dylan and Cait, and raised his flagon. "*Tha mo beannachd-sa agaibh.*" With that blessing, he drank.

The room erupted in talk, some surprised, some pleased, and some not so pleased. Dylan glanced over at Artair and Coll, who, not surprisingly, were red-faced and muttering to each other.

Sarah leapt from her seat and ran the length of the Great Hall to disappear into the corridor to the towers. Dylan watched her go, then looked up at Sinann for an explanation. But Sinann didn't seem to have noticed the retreat.

Iain called for silence, and when the hubbub had died down he said, "The wedding will take place after three Sundays when we will be graced by the company of Father Buchanan. If there be nae impediment," and here his eyes narrowed briefly at Dylan, "the priest will join the two, and the lad will take his place as my new son."

A curse was heard from the direction of Artair and Coll.

Iain ignored it, and continued, "Young Dylan, needless to say, will nae longer be safeguarding my daughter's virtue." Again there was laughter. "Rather, he will have charge of the castle guard, and responsibility for the security of the premises." Translated into modern terms, Dylan understood he was to be the "sergeant" of Iain's small clutch of men retained to guard the castle, Dylan's nine former bunkmates. Iain raised his left hand in an awkward knife-edge and said, "And perhaps he would be so kind as to teach our men of that strange sort of fighting he does."

Dylan chuckled. Once again he was blessed with kung fu students.

There was much singing that night, many sweet songs of love won and lost. Sarah's oldest son, Eóin, displaced Cait in Dylan's lap to spend the evening chattering to him and Cait of his surviving brother, who was four years old. Dylan happily carried his third of the conversation in Gaelic, and it gave him intense pleasure to think that he and Cait would surely have children of their own one day. A dozen or so, he hoped.

The next morning Iain sent word around to Dylan, Malcolm, Artair, and Coll that their presence was requested for a hunt.

Dylan, who had gone to his room for his sword, said to Sinann, "Short notice for a trip like this, isn't it? I'm told we're supposed to be gone for a few days." Provisions were being prepared and he had just come from borrowing Robin's bow and quiver of arrows again.

She sat cross-legged on the bed and shrugged. "You've upset every relationship in the castle. There's not a man in the glen who willnae be affected by your marriage to Cait because you're now closer to the Laird than you were. Iain Mór will want to see how you get along with his closest relatives while on this new footing. It's a test, lad."

Dylan sighed. Coming up through the rankings in martial art was nothing compared to this.

The snows were retreating, but the landscape was still cold and soggy. The hunting party descended to a lower glen where woods were a bit thicker and deer would be found. The walk was long, and at midday they stopped to eat. After a hard rain in the early morning, through which they slogged without stopping, the sun came out and the air bordered on muggy as the landscape and their clothing dried. The men sat on a stretch of exposed rock that had dried and was now warming. Iain struck up conversation with Malcolm while they ate.

"Next month we're to move the MacDonell *spréidhe* south to Glenfinnan. Ramsay has agreed to take them on to Edinburgh. The English will buy them, and then he can obtain other kine to be brought north."

Dylan glanced over at Sinann, who was listening in, but she only shrugged. She didn't know who Ramsay was, either.

Malcolm said, "Will he be coming here?"

Iain shook his head. "Nae. And a good thing, if you ask me."

"You havenae told him, then?"

"When the time comes. When I must."

"When it's done, ye mean."

Dylan interrupted, since they were making no effort at keeping the conversation to themselves. He figured if they were going to talk in front of him he should know what was going on. "Who's Ramsay?"

Iain opened his mouth to reply, but Artair said, "Iain. Do you think it wise?"

The Laird glared at his younger half brother. "I'll ask you, do you think it wise for a gillie such as you to question me? Get some hair on yer balls, and then tell me what's wise and what isnae."

Artair shut up.

Iain turned to Dylan and said, "Connor Ramsay does business with us, and sometimes does special errands. Though he's close to some on the Privy Council and publicly a Whig, he's secretly a supporter of James."

Dylan frowned. "Publicly a Whig? Can you trust him?"

Malcolm sniggered into his bannock and threw Iain a look.

Iain shrugged. "He's not betrayed us yet, and were the Crown to learn of his trafficking in intelligence and arms, he would be hung for a traitor."

Artair said, "And were he to betray us, he would be shot for a traitor. Worse, perhaps, if the wrong man found him out." Artair's tone made it clear he would be the man to do worse than shooting to a traitor.

That brought an appreciative chuckle from the other men, each of whom Dylan figured would volunteer to do the deed if needed.

Iain continued, "He's wealthy, and privy to information we can use. We'll trust him until we have reason not to." With that, he climbed to his feet and announced they would press on.

At nightfall they came to a small clutch of houses in a wooded glen. This was still land controlled by Iain, but the tenants here were not familiar to Dylan. Being an entire day's walk from the castle, these Mathesons came to Glen Ciorram only on the rarest of occasions.

The hunting party found shelter that night in a peat house occupied by a family with seven children. There were larger families in Ciorram, so Dylan wasn't surprised to see the seven kids slept in two beds stacked like bunks. The hunting party was fed salted beef and slept on the dirt floor of the public room, wrapped in their plaids. Early the next day they struck out into thick woods where faint trails ran through thickets of ferns, toadstools, moss, birches, prickly gorse, and majestic pines. Everything here seemed covered with moss. As a Boy Scout Dylan had been taught to tell north by checking what side of the trees moss grew on, but here it grew on all sides. The darkness of the thick parts of the woods would make it unutterably easy to get lost.

Each hunter was armed with a sword, dirk, and bow, but Iain, Coll, and Artair also carried muskets that reminded Dylan of Daniel Boone's Kentucky Long Rifle. Each gun had a barrel almost as long as a man was tall, and the stocks were inlaid with brass in ornate designs. Coll's musket was entirely steel, and the stock sported deep, swirling grooves. Raised on TV shoot-em-ups, where guns were supposed to be convenient and rarely needed reloading, Dylan considered the powder horn, wadding, and balls of the flintlock a monumental nuisance, and the single-shot nature of these guns made them a waste of effort and expense. He was just as happy with the arrows and his blades, and would rather eat beef than venison anyway.

The woods were thick, but the hunters moved with care and in silence. Once Iain found fresh spoor of a quarry, Dylan and Malcolm were placed in a spot overlooking and downwind of the deer track while the other three men circled wide to beat bushes. They were half an hour or so getting into position, and Dylan waited with Malcolm in disciplined silence. Not a word was said, and the men were alert but relaxed.

Then the noise began, far off in the trees. Swords slapped branches and undergrowth, and loud voices filled the air. Dylan and Malcolm each nocked an arrow in anticipation. A rabbit hurtled past, but they ignored it. Birds rose into and above the trees, out of reach. Another rabbit passed, and Dylan began to wonder if those were all they would find.

But a larger creature came crashing through the brush as the voices approached behind it, and Malcolm raised his bow to aim. Dylan did likewise, though he still couldn't see what the animal was. The beaters were hot on the trail of the game. Then a small deer broke from the foliage, reddish-brown and shaggy, fleeing for her life, and Dylan let fly his arrow.

The next thing he knew he was floating in nothingness, Sinann's voice was pleading for him to wake up, and his head felt as if it had been cracked open like a coconut. He tried to speak, but could only groan. He found himself lying on the ground, and Malcolm pressed something lightly to the side of his head just above his right ear. Dylan finally formed the words, "Wha . . . happen?"

"You've been shot. The ball put a crease in your scalp and took off the tip of your ear. It's bleeding like a heart wound, but you'll live. You were insensible for but a few moments."

Dylan grunted and struggled to sit up, then took the cloth from Malcolm's hand to hold it himself. He looked around at the Mathesons standing over him, all of them white-faced and silent. His eyes narrowed at Artair. "Who . . . ?"

Iain said quickly, "It was me. My ball is the one that went astray. I'm sorry for it."

Dylan knew a lie when he heard one, and it was not in Iain's nature to lie well. Sinann confirmed it. "Dinnae believe him. It was Artair trying to murder ye. Ask to smell his gun. Go ahead, smell it. Iain never fired."

Dylan glanced at her and declined to follow her advice.

He knew it had been Artair, but wondered why Iain was
protecting him. He also wondered if Malcolm knew what had
happened or if he was merely taking Iain's word on it. But
to press these issues would be pointless at least, and possibly
even dangerous. His head wasn't in any condition for thinking in any case. He merely nodded slowly in acceptance of
the apology. He then said, "The doe?"

"Malcolm's arrow found her, and Coll's sword finished
her. We'll stay here for a few days while you—"

"I'm fine. I can make the trip back now."

"Would you not rather—"

Dylan was as firm as he could make his voice, which he
heard as if from a distance. "I wish to return to the castle.
I'm fine."

Iain said, "Very well, we'll return in the morning."

Dylan looked at the unhappy Artair and vowed to keep
an eye on him.

CHAPTER 15

The walk back to the castle was a hard one. Dylan fought dizziness most of the way. But he concentrated on staying conscious, and putting one foot in front of the other, and gradually the sick feeling cleared as they neared Ciorram. By the time they reached the castle he was fighting only weariness. Artair and Coll carried the doe hung from a pole, and at every opportunity Artair made cracks about himself and his brother being the only fit men in the group. By sunset, Dylan would have been happy to take both their heads, and Iain informed Artair that if he didn't shut his mouth he might shortly have it full of fist.

Their arrival in the castle bailey caused great excitement as people came to see the kill, and to query after Dylan's injury. The doe was hauled away to the kitchen to be butchered by a couple of Dylan's guardsmen. Artair and Coll disappeared, and Malcolm hung around Iain in the Great Hall as the Laird told the story of the hunt. Dylan shrugged at the exclamations of concern and distress over the bloody bandage around his head while he searched faces for Cait.

Then a shriek drilled his brain, and he turned to find Sarah wide-eyed and pushing her way through the onlookers. "Dylan! Oh, no! Dylan!" When she reached him, she threw her arms around his neck and began to sob.

"Sarah . . ." He pried her arms from his neck and held her hands together where they couldn't grab him again. "Sarah, don't be so upset."

Her sobbing was loud. "You've been hurt."

"I'm fine." He wanted to tell her she had no business being this upset, but that would seem cold. He was touched by her concern, but her wailing was inappropriate and an embarrassment. He looked around for Cait, desperate to break free of Sarah. "Where's Caitrionagh?" he asked.

"I'm here." Cait was right behind him. He let go of Sarah and turned to take Cait into his arms. She said into his good ear, "Are you sure you werenae too busy for me?"

For a moment he wasn't sure she was joking, but when she smiled he did also. He kissed her, then murmured into her ear, "I was nearly too *dead* for you, and it's a good thing your uncle is a lousy shot."

"I was told my father—"

"No, it was Artair."

That gave her pause, and her voice went low and frightened. "If that one wants to kill you, he won't stop until one of you is dead."

Dylan kissed her and squeezed her hands. "Don't worry. Nothing will happen." He kissed her hand, but her eyes were still worried.

Later that night, after blowing out the candles in his chamber, he lay in the dark, thinking about Sarah. Something was wrong there, something off-kilter, and he figured Sinann was behind it. He said into the darkness, "Tink."

No answer.

He repeated, "Tinkerbell."

Still no answer.

"I know you're there." She'd followed him in before disappearing, as she had always before followed him to bed. He never knew if she stayed the night, but she was always there when he fell into his bed.

Her voice came from the curtain frame above, "What is it?"

"What did you do to Sarah?"

There was a long silence. Just when Dylan was about to

repeat his question, she said, "She would have fallen in love with you regardless."

He sighed. "What did you do?"

"It was only a slight charm."

"You put a love spell on her?"

"A small one."

Now he groaned. "Why?"

"You needed a reason to want to stay. I couldnae let you spend your life here without a family, and there were Sarah and her boys, all right there and perfect for you. How was I to know Her Highness would tumble for ye?"

"And by the time you saw that Cait and I were in love, it was too late. You'd already done it."

"True, and you know what happens when I try to undo what I've done. I wouldnae wish to see you murdered."

Dylan was suddenly very tired and sick. "Is she going to be like that forever?" He felt like he'd just run over a puppy.

"I cannae say. She can shake it off if she's a mind to, but I daresay she isnae inclined to fall out of your spell."

"*Your* spell."

"It's you she loves."

"It was cruel. You shouldn't have done it. Now I've got to do something to make up for this."

"You could marry her instead of Her Highness. That way, perhaps Artair will stop shooting at you."

"Shut up, Tink." Dylan rolled over to sleep. But he did not sleep well.

During the next few days he settled into his new job as sergeant of the guard. Brought up in a world where the concept of military meant strict discipline, close-order drill, and uniformity, he had to make a conscious shift to thinking in terms of an eighteenth century Scottish guard. These were not the crack Highland troops that would later become the pride of the English army. The nine men under his charge were independent, belligerent, and naturally violent, more like pro wrestlers and street punks than soldiers. On the plus side, these qualities became assets when coupled with strong loyalty, bravery, and work ethic. They would do their job, but it was up to Dylan to figure out how to tell them what that job was at any given time.

Kung fu training was made optional for the *Tigh* guard. Since the Chinese mind-set of calmness and economy of motion and energy was diametrically opposed to the full-on berserker approach common to Scots of the period, there was no sense in forcing the lessons on anyone. Only two of the men, Robin Innis and Marc Hewitt, came on the first morning Dylan offered instruction during his workout. Both were in their twenties and of open-minded, better than average intelligence. Also, they were both men Dylan already liked.

For the sake of leaving room in the Great Hall for the women preparing breakfast, the men conducted their sessions of a morning in the bailey outside. Spring rains would be a hazard, but even Dylan knew by now that in Scotland one got rained on or one got nothing done at all.

On the second morning some boys came to line up in the bailey beside Robin and Marc. Sarah's son, little Eóin Matheson, came; an older boy named Coinneach Matheson, who was the son of a tenant; and a teenager named Dùghlas Matheson, who was either Coinneach's brother or first cousin, Dylan couldn't remember.

So as not to pick on the littlest, he addressed all five students as he had the men the day before. "You understand, now, that this isn't a sometimes thing. You can't learn it all in a day and you can't learn it by coming only on some mornings." The boys and the men all nodded. Dylan continued, "Also, in order to learn this you've got to forget everything you've already learned about fighting. That doesn't mean you can never do those things again, but for now, while you're learning, you have to start from the beginning." Again, they all nodded. A slight breeze kicked up and he was glad for the bandage around his head, which kept his hair out of his eyes. A crowd was gathering in the bailey as they had before, and now Dylan noticed Sarah with an injured look about her. He needed to do something about the situation, though he had no idea what.

He started his students from the beginning, with the horse stance, feet at shoulder width, knees slightly bent, shoulders back, arms relaxed. "See," he demonstrated, "like this you become harder to knock over. Your balance is under control." He walked up to Robin and gave his shoulder a push.

Robin rocked back, but maintained his footing. Dylan continued, "See? He's relaxed. Now watch." He stepped to Marc and shoved, and Marc was forced to take a step back to keep his balance. Dylan's voice lowered so he was talking only to Marc. "You're too stiff. Too tense. Relax your joints. Feet pointing the same direction." Marc relaxed. "Yeah, like that. You're getting it." He shoved Marc again, and this time the young man held his ground.

Dylan stepped back to the front, but Eóin shouted, "You didn't shove me!"

"Oh." Everyone snickered and Dylan smiled, then went to give Eóin a tiny shove. The boy held his ground like a hero. For the sake of form, Dylan also shoved the other two boys.

On the third day the class was joined by Artair. Dylan touched the strip of linen bandage around his head and had a bad feeling of what the snotty teenager might be up to, but today Artair's unruly tongue was still. He learned the moves with an intensity and aptitude that gave Dylan even worse misgivings. He didn't like this one little bit. Nevertheless, he taught Artair as he did the other students.

Over the next two weeks Artair did his best to ingratiate himself with Dylan. Dylan saw what Artair's game was. All along the kid had aligned himself with his older brother in order to be close to the lairdship once Iain Mór was gone and Malcolm would be out of the picture. He would probably not inherit, but he could have the power and business advantages of being Coll's right-hand man. And that would also give him an edge for a successful clan uprising if Coll proved weak enough. But now that Dylan was an important factor, Artair aligned himself with the new heir presumptive. If there should be another attempt on Dylan's life, suspicion wouldn't fall on him. And, if Dylan lived to become Laird, he would be his right hand man. Dylan played along, waiting to see what more might happen.

Preparations for the wedding geared up a week before the event. Everywhere he saw Cait, she shone with a happiness that made him want to laugh aloud. When they held hands at supper he kissed her palm and thought he might die of impatience before they were married. His joy was almost unbearable, and the waiting was sweet torture.

He occupied himself with his new job and with the business of securing the property he and Cait would live on. In the interest of keeping Cait close to home and Dylan where he would be of use and visible, Iain agreed to sell Dylan a piece of a small glen adjoining Glen Ciorram, next to Alasdair's former property. Dylan wasn't sure he wanted the land that would surely be next on the Whig agenda of creeping expansion, but it was better land than the MacLeod property he'd been negotiating for. It was also nearer the *Tigh*, and wouldn't involve a labor debt. The land was set to change hands after the wedding.

Once he and Cait were married, the house would be raised by the clan. Like every other young man approaching marriage, Dylan now had to ask around for his stock: roof tree, household items, and livestock. Cait's dowry was a few head of cattle, a pair of sheep, and Sigurd the Collie. Nobody started with nothing, but even with the dowry it would take hard work to start the farm, and more hard work to maintain it. The day after his wedding he would be a landowner with a family to support, and as poor as everyone else. He couldn't wait.

Meanwhile, Sarah's broken heart was apparent to everyone, and there was talk that Dylan had made promises he'd not intended to keep. He approached her in the Great Hall one morning after breakfast to straighten things out with her. People were still coming and going, and most of the women were clearing breakfast.

"Sarah, might we talk?"

She carried several dirty bowls and spoons, but stopped when he spoke to her. He wished she would look up, but her gaze stayed on the floor.

"Sarah, I have a feeling there has been some misunderstanding between us."

She opened her mouth to speak, but no sound came out. He watched her struggle with her emotions, patient but wishing he were anywhere else.

A shout went up from the hearth and a toddler, screaming with laughter, went tearing past with a knife in his hands. "Whoa!" Dylan blurted and bent to scoop up the little boy and disarm him in one motion. The little one kicked and screamed at his capture, but Dylan held him around the middle with one arm and looked around for a responsible party. Seonag hurried up in bustling skirts to retrieve the squalling boy and the stolen kitchen knife, and returned to the kitchen, scolding.

Dylan returned his attention to Sarah, who finally was able to say, "Nae misunderstanding. It's nae your fault. I'm the silly one to think a one such as yourself could ever want a widow with three . . . *two* wee sons."

Dylan stifled a groan. He groped for a reply, unable to look her in the eye, mentally cursed Sinann, then finally said, "Not silly. Just unlucky that things worked out differently than what you'd hoped. For what it's worth, I care deeply for you as a cousin and have high regard for you as a woman and a mother. Your boys are fine lads and will grow up to make you proud." He made himself look into her face.

She finally looked at him and smiled, but there was still pain in her eyes. Her mouth opened to speak, then closed. It took a moment, but she opened it again and said, "I wish yourself and Cait all luck and happiness, and many healthy children."

"Thank you."

Sarah then hurried away with the dirty dishes, leaving him to feel like he'd just backed over the dead puppy.

That Sunday Dylan was free to take some instruction with Sinann at the *broch*. It was a rainy May day, but Sinann promised to keep him dry. True to her word, no rain came into the *broch*. It all collected and ran off somewhere at the height of the oak tree, and the ground inside was dry. Dylan poked with the toe of his shoe at the blood-red grass and wondered if it ran red when wet.

"Okay, what today?" In previous sessions she'd taught him things such as how to read portent in a hearth fire; that it was bad luck to circle "widdershins," or counter-clockwise, rather than "deiseil"; that a crow's presence meant death; and that graves were never dug nor allowed to be open on Sunday because it meant another one would be dug within the week. She'd taught him the power of thought, and how the *maucht* of his thinking could be directed to cause things to happen.

Though much of it echoed his eastern studies, still some of it struck him as no different from common superstitions involving black cats, ladders, and umbrellas. Yet he did what she asked to humor her.

"Today you ride the wind."

He laughed. "Okay. With what, a broomstick?"

"With your soul. Come, center yourself."

Dylan had kept his kilt on, for it was just a little nippier than he cared for when skyclad. He stood, facing southeast where he could sense the morning sun through the overcast, in a horse stance. Eyes closed, he took deep breaths and felt the power of the earth rise through his feet and into his body.

When he felt calm, Sinann said softly, "All right, lad, lie on your back." He obeyed, and gazed up at the raindrops disappearing overhead. It was almost hypnotic, the way none of them reached the ground.

"Now you need to relax your body, bit by bit, and ease your mind into almost sleeping. Not to sleep, but to be half-waking. Close your eyes."

He obeyed and felt very relaxed indeed. Her voice continued softly, "Now, I'm going to give you a bit of help here." He felt a tingling that was not uncomfortable, and he felt so good he never thought to ask what she'd done. She continued, "Riding the wind, you can go anywhere. You can take yourself out of your body and go anywhere you wish. You can . . ."

Her voice faded as he drifted away and the world became hazy.

From somewhere came Cait's voice. "Dylan? Dylan, wake up." She shook him, and he opened his eyes. "What arc you doing here?"

He'd fallen asleep. *Oh, no.* He looked around. Sinann was gone. Cait looked worried, soaking wet, having come through the rain outside the broch. Somewhere she'd lost her snood and her hair had come loose to hang around her face. He reached up to kiss her and said, "I came here to think, but fell asleep instead." He pulled the Goddess Stone from his sporran for a quick look around, and found Sinann perched on the stone block above his head. "Ye fell asleep, you goof," the faerie said. "I told you not to do that." She pointed with her chin to Cait. "Tell her to leave."

"I hope you're not thinking you've made a mistake. About the wedding, I mean." Cait said it with a smile, but her voice had an edge he'd come to know meant she wasn't entirely kidding.

He laughed and ignored Sinann as he returned the stone to his sporran. "My only mistake was in not spending the day with you."

"Well, then," came Sinann's voice, "if ye willnae send her away I'll have to get rid of her myself." With that, the rain above was set free.

"Uh oh," muttered Dylan. He drew Cait down onto the grass with him and rolled on top of her as water came crashing over them. He grunted as the weight of it hit his back. Cait squealed and shivered at the cold. The rain continued to come in sheets, and he helped her to her feet. "Come on," he said. "Let's go back to the castle where it's warm." He threw Sinann a cross look, and she snapped her fingers and disappeared from his unaided sight.

Dylan looked down at where he'd lain, and found a puddle forming, swirling red. He shuddered.

He and Cait hurried back along the burn in the rain, then into the glen where the downpour almost obscured the castle. The *Tigh* stood as a gray shadow surrounded by misty, slashing rain so heavy it almost seemed as if the loch itself was encroaching on the air. Cait's hand in his was cold and slippery, and he gripped it hard to keep her with him.

But she stopped, and dug in her heels when he tried to urge her along. When he looked back at her, her eyes were wide and her mouth dropped open. He turned to see what she was staring at.

They were still half a mile from the castle, but through the rain Dylan saw a white form trotting across the drawbridge. A dog.

Cait's hand tightened on his, and she began to shake with a violence that shocked him. She said, "*Am madadh bàn.*"

He peered through the rain. The white dog trotted to the gatehouse, turned three circles widdershins, then settled by the stone wall as if it were his accustomed place. It was a huge animal, shaggy and long-limbed like some sort of wolf-hound, though he'd never seen a white one, and it appeared to be on guard. Then, as they watched, it melted into the rain and mist until there was no more sign of it than if it had never been there. A shudder took Dylan, and he was rooted to the spot. Cait clutched him, trembling.

"It's a bad sign." She began to cry. "Dylan, it's a bad thing. A terrible thing is going to happen." He held her close and she sobbed into his wet sark.

Though he was as shaken as she, he tried to calm her. "Shhh. It will be all right. Nothing terrible is going to happen." He made her look into his face and wiped strings of wet hair from her forehead as the rain tried to flush it all back. "And even if something bad happens, we'll be together. We can handle anything if we're together, right?"

She hiccuped and nodded.

He tugged on her hand. "Come on. Let's get inside and dry before we catch our death. That *would* be a terrible thing."

She followed him, but at the gatehouse both gave wide berth to the spot where the dog had been.

The next day, the Monday before the wedding, Artair came to Dylan after the morning workout in the bailey and asked if he knew the way to Killilan. Dylan nodded. When he'd gone in November the return trip had been entirely by daylight, and he'd been again with Malcolm and Robin to retrieve Cait's mother. Over the past two months, since the snows left, Dylan had walked the local terrain and his knowledge of the topography had grown. "Why do you ask?"

"Marc was to go to Killilan for the purpose of escorting Deirdre Mackenzie to the wedding, in the absence of Ailig Og, who cannae attend. He is now indisposed with a fever and cannae make the trip. Iain Mór asks if you would go fetch her instead." He stood before Dylan with his fists on his hips.

The last thing Dylan wanted just then was to be away from Cait. "Me? He wants the groom to get her?"

The habitual sneering tone came to Artair's voice and he shifted his weight. "Too proud to escort your kinswoman to your own wedding? Or is it only . . ." He stopped short, blinked rapidly then said, "Sure, it would be a gesture of good will to your future mother-in-law."

Dylan chewed on the inside corner of his mouth and glanced around the bailey as he thought about it. Artair's snide attitude aside, escorting his future mother-in-law's sister to the wedding *would* be a gesture of goodwill toward Una and Iain. He nodded and said, "All right. I'll go." One day there and two back would put his return at Friday.

In his room the next day, readying to go, he called for Sinann as he strapped his *sgian dubh* under his arm and hung his sword across his chest.

She blinked into vision, sitting cross-legged on his bed.

"Tink, I need you to watch Cait for me."

"Am I your servant, to be ordered about?"

"I'm not kidding. This is important. I'm going to Killilan to bring back Deirdre MacKenzie for the wedding. I don't trust Artair, nor Coll for that, and I need you to make sure she's safe until I get back."

"And if she were in danger, what would I do for it then? Put a love spell on her, I suppose?"

"Let the others see you, and tell them Cait needs help."

"Nae, that willnae help. Those cursed witch-hunts have made it near impossible to catch the attention of a mortal these days. I could scream myself blue in the face and not a body would let on they could hear."

"Then get Ranald to raise some noise. He's good at that. Iain will listen if even Ranald screams that Cait is in trouble."

Sinann's voice turned to disgust. "Ranald . . ."

Dylan thrust a finger in her face. "Do it, Tink. No guff. Make sure she stays safe."

Sinann sighed and nodded. Dylan hurried downstairs to the bailey where Cait waited by his horse with a stuffed bannock wrapped in a napkin for him. He thanked her and slipped it into his sporran.

"Can't another one of the men go?" She ran her palms up the front of his sark, and he thought again of how much he didn't want to get on that horse and leave.

But he'd promised he would go. "It's your mother's sister. And, besides, I'll be back in a couple of days. We'll be together when it matters." He held her hands together and kissed them, mostly to make her stop driving him nuts. Much more of the touchy-feely stuff, and he wouldn't be able to get on the horse, let alone ride. He kissed her mouth and whispered in her ear a promise to be fulfilled on their wedding night, then mounted the horse and left for Killilan.

Dylan's horsemanship skills had improved greatly since his first ride to Killilan, and he was now used to the idea of a thousand-pound beast between his legs. He'd learned so quickly as to wonder whether there might be something to the idea of ancestral memory. His paternal grandmother's people had, back in the early nineteenth century, owned a Thoroughbred farm near the Cumberland River, and had often raced their horses against Andrew Jackson's. But over the next hundred and fifty years the tradition of horsemanship had passed from the family. During the Civil War the Yankees commandeered the horses, which nearly crippled the farm. A recovery was attempted, but then racing was outlawed in Tennessee at the beginning of the twentieth century and the farm eventually folded. But now, for Dylan, riding was another one of those things, like swordsmanship, that seemed to click into place like it was supposed to have been there all along.

He rode at a trot through a wooded area along the narrow trail that would take him partway to Killilan before he would have to cut over the shoulder of a mountain where there was no track, then down a winding series of glens and hollows. Walking would be more direct and take no more time, but he would be returning with Una's sister and so needed a horse. Only the rich rode in these mountains, and carriages were nonexistent because the lack of roads made them useless. Dylan guided his mount carefully, and by mid-morning had made some fair distance from the castle. His mind was on accomplishing his errand in good time that he might be back in Cait's company soon.

He was not the least prepared for the sight of the redcoated English soldier who stepped from cover of the close forest and pointed a flintlock musket at his face. More Redcoats followed. A total of four armed men ranged across his path. They were Bedford's dragoons.

CHAPTER 16

Dylan pulled up and his hand went to his sword. His horse danced at sight of the strange men.

An English voice from behind warned, "Stand down, Matheson!" Dylan wheeled to find Captain Bedford on horseback, with three more soldiers with guns, also mounted. He stayed his hand and raised his palm to indicate it was empty. "Dylan Matheson," said the Englishman in an accusatory tone.

Dylan nodded. "Aye." He felt a surge of alarm, but he stayed calm. He'd done nothing. They would let him go, he was sure. But the guns made him wary.

The blond officer nodded to one of his men, who approached Dylan's horse. The animal shied, and the officer barked, "Control your mount, or I'll have it shot!" Dylan tightened the reins and urged the horse still with his knees as the man on foot reached under his saddle blanket.

"Got it, sah!" the soldier crowed, and yanked something from underneath.

Got what? Dylan wheeled his horse to see the soldier with a fistful of letters. He recognized the paper as the stationery Sarah had given him for Christmas which he'd never used. The letters were handed to the officer, who broke open one of the seals and scanned the page. Then he read aloud, beginning in the middle of a sentence, ". . . the return of the rightful King James . . . imprison Her Majesty . . ." He looked at Dylan, his eyes wide at the appalling words. "Bloody murder! Here's an arrogant bastard! Take him, men!"

Dylan didn't wait to argue. He dug his heels into his horse's ribs and wheeled to flee, barreling through the line of men on foot. Shots went off like firecrackers all around, and as balls whizzed past his head the horse grunted and went limp between his knees. Thrown headlong, Dylan rolled as he hit the ground, regained his feet, and plunged into the woods at the side of the trail.

He ran, crashing between trees and through undergrowth down a short slope, splashing through a shallow burn, digging into his sporran as he went. Fingers flying, he took long strides up the other side. Finally he found what he was after and pinned it to his plaid. Then he stepped behind an oak tree and leaned against it, perfectly still, concentrating on nothing but controlling his breathing and making no sound.

The English soldiers went crashing past up the slope, and never saw him. At the top when they broke from tree cover, they realized they'd lost him and spread out to search the area. Some of them came back down toward the burn. He stood still, listening to their shouts and curses, and prayed none of them would brush against him. They trampled ferns and peered up into branches. Their boots slipped on mossy ground. They poked their bayonets into thick stands of bushes.

The Captain dismounted and came into the woods with his men. He stood, gazing about, as they searched. He was so close Dylan could smell the laundry soap on his uniform. He turned, peering into the trees, as still among his noisy men as Dylan. Facing him, Bedford's pale blue eyes seemed to look into his, and it was all Dylan could do to not bolt like a rabbit. But he kept still, like Sinann said.

Finally, Bedford called his men in. The Redcoats gave up and moved away down the trail back toward Ciorram. Dylan was alone in the woods. He sank to the ground by the tree and rested his forehead against his knees. What now? Who had done this to him? Artair? Or Iain? He'd made it clear he'd had plans for Cait he'd considered preferable to marrying Dylan. Had it been a mistake to think Malcolm had succeeded in changing the Laird's mind? Just how much had Iain had at stake with the other match he'd made for Cait? Malcolm had warned him to beware of those who would want him dead for being too close a relative, but Dylan had been so wrapped up in becoming one of the clan he hadn't seen the real danger.

He raised his head. He had to get back to Cait. He stood and began to walk back to the castle. Avoiding the trail, he kept a parallel course nearby. A Vietnam war movie he'd once seen had shown how soldiers never walked along trails for fear of ambush. Using this trail was what had given the soldiers the drop on him to begin with, so he kept to the woods and made his way slowly to the castle.

He arrived at Glen Ciorram near dusk. From the wooded slope above the village, under cover of the bare trunk of a pine tree, he could see the detachment of English soldiers clustered outside the castle gatehouse. They'd set up a small camp on the meadow, with a fire for cooking and a tent for the Captain. They weren't going anywhere for a while, not even back to their barracks. He didn't dare approach. Not today, in any case. He was at a loss now. Where to go? Where would he be safe? Was Cait all right? He wondered what was going on inside those stone walls.

The sun was setting, and he couldn't just stare at the English soldiers until they spotted him. He turned and made his way to the *broch*. There he could rest and think of what to do.

But when he rounded the hill by the stream, he saw a thin line of smoke rising from the *broch* into the air. Someone was there. He drew Brigid and circled away from the entrance to the oak tree. He climbed its trunk to the branch that had grown through an upper window, and carefully stepped along it and through to see what lay below.

In the center of the tower floor, Cait sat, huddled and shivering, by a small fire, staring into it. "*A Chait.*" Dylan hurried to her down the interior steps.

She looked up and her breath caught. Her skirts in her fists, she leapt to her feet and ran to meet him at the bottom of the steps. She threw her arms around his neck, weeping and talking so fast he couldn't understand her. Her clothing was soaked and ice cold. He kissed her and smoothed the tears from her face.

"Shhh. Take it easy. Shhh." He lifted off his baldric and let the sword drop to the ground, unbuckled his belt to unwind his *feileadh mór*, and put it around her shoulders. "Here, you're freezing. Get out of that wet dress." Her teeth chattered as she unfastened her overdress and let it and the shift drop from her shoulders to the ground, then pulled his kilt around herself. He held her until she was calm enough to talk. When her sobbing eased, he led her to the fire and sat with her next to it. "Are you all right? What happened to you?" The danger from the English slipped his mind in his worry for Cait.

More sobs escaped her, and she shook her head. "They want to hang you. If you go to the castle they'll kill you. They have letters—"

"I didn't write them."

She nodded. "I know. Father knows, as well. He's . . . he's . . ." Her face crumpled again as she tried to speak through sobbing. "They've killed Coll."

Even with Dylan's concern for himself and Cait, that hit him with a shock. "Coll? How? Who?"

"When the *Sassunaich* came looking for you and searched the castle and the village, they dinnae find you. They told us what they'd found under your saddle, and Father was furious. He guessed what Artair and Coll had done, because he knew you could not be guilty of the treason they accused." She looked up at him, "You, of all of us, are the one who argues with Father against the cause. So he knew any seditious letters in your possession had to have been put there by someone else, and I knew Coll had saddled your horse. When the soldiers left to set up their guard outside the gatehouse, Father ordered Coll to be put into the prison tower. Coll drew and fought. And lost." Fresh tears came, and she trembled in Dylan's arms.

"Who killed him?"

"Robin Innis."

"Good." Though Dylan wasn't quite ready to assume the

innocence of Iain, he was glad Coll's brother hadn't been the one to kill him. He held Cait while she cried again. When she recovered he asked, "How did you get out of the castle without being followed?"

"A rope ladder is kept for escape purposes down the North Tower garderobe. Gracie pulled it up after me, and will let it down again when darkness is complete. I swam from the island." She held his sark in her fists and looked into his eyes. "They're waiting for you to return. You cannae go back." There was a moment of silence, then she sobbed and added, "Ever."

His heart sank as his future crumbled.

Her voice was low and gentle, and she laid her hand on his chest. "Dylan, we cannae be married now. You're an outlaw. They will kill you if they ever find you."

He didn't want to believe his life was over. "I didn't do anything."

"It matters not. They'll kill you because they can, and because they dinnae care whether you did anything or not. The Captain's only interest now is that you never *appear* to have gotten away with sedition. Since you appear guilty, you must bear punishment. If he gets his hands on you, you'll die or be imprisoned one way or another. And it would be in his best interest if you never lived to stand trial. You cannae stay here. You must return to Virginia."

As the world turned to dust around him, his mind cast about for what to do. Going home wasn't an option. His home in Tennessee wouldn't exist for a long time yet. He held her tight, afraid to let go.

She loosened his hold, then opened the kilt to bring him inside. It was warm there, and soft. He kissed her. "Love me," she said. She helped him pull his sark off over his head and they lay back. He untied his legging straps and stripped the sheepskin and leather from his legs, kicked off his shoes, and eased into her arms and kissed her. His mind gladly slipped into a place where the English couldn't come.

Cait rolled over on top of him. She took his hands, and pressed them to the ground at his sides, indicating he should keep them there. He shivered as he lay there, waiting to see what she would do.

The kilt still draped across her shoulders, she leaned over him to feel of his chest. She tried to fluff his appallingly straight chest hairs, without success, and brushed a nipple ever so lightly. He shuddered and reached for her, but she pushed his hand away and felt of his nipple again, apparently fascinated it could go erect. Breathing became difficult for him.

Her voice was low and husky. "I've never touched a man like this before." Dylan in fact had never *been* touched quite like that before, having known mostly women who expected him to do the touching. He'd always been pleased enough to oblige. She said, "I wish to know you, all of you, to remember you always."

She explored him like a new toy, tugged on hair here and there, made him giggle by poking his armpits, pinched muscles, stroked skin, and all she would allow him to do was lie there. She reached down to squeeze parts of him that made him quiver and gasp, and when she kissed him there, took him into her mouth, he moaned and dug his heels into the ground. In a daze, he lifted his head and reached out to feel of her golden hair that shone in the firelight.

She returned to his mouth for tongue-sparring kisses, and straddled him so he eased into her warm body. He put his arms around her waist and held her to him, and wished he could put his entire self into her and stay forever.

Their lovemaking was bittersweet this time, with none of the joy of before. It was a mutual comforting, to put in temporary abeyance the grief they both knew lay ahead. Afterward, he arranged his plaid over them and they slept for a short time.

He awoke during the dead of night when even the creatures of darkness had gone to rest and the world paused for a silent moment before dawn. Cait had dislodged herself from his arms and was on the other side of the fire. When he stirred, she looked up and gave him a thin smile. He watched her walk back, a golden goddess in the moonlight, wide shoulders back and hips swaying with an unselfconscious stride. She slipped in under the plaid to lie with her back to him. He wrapped himself around her and their legs entwined. He murmured, "I'm going to beat this, Cait. They can't get away with this."

She did not reply, but rolled onto her back and looked into his face. With one finger she traced the line of his eyebrow. Her gaze was dreamy, and she said, "I love how your brow curves up when you are angry or puzzled." That took him aback, and she said, "Aye, like that."

He chuckled and rubbed the eyebrow.

She continued to trace a finger over his face. "And your lip." Her finger touched his lower lip. "Your mouth is a delight." He couldn't help a grin at that, and she said, "I love to see you smile."

Then he stopped smiling. "Quit memorizing my face. I'm not going anywhere. Ever. I'll be right there with you on the day you die. I swear it." He kissed her hair, settled beside her with his arms tight around her, and dropped back to sleep.

The next time he woke, it was sunrise. Cait had dressed and left, and the ground where Dylan lay was very cold and hard. He dressed, then reached into his sporran for the bannock he'd intended to eat on the road to Killilan the day before. But instead his fingers found something damp, which he pulled out to examine. It was a letter, bearing his name in Cait's hand. A warm feeling stole over him to have word from her, but it turned to a cold sweat as her ring fell from the folded paper.

> *A Dhilein, my love, when I told you why we could not marry, I gave only part of the reason. You know my father had made plans for me to marry someone else before he learned of our own plans. Now that it is no longer possible for me to marry you, he is taking me to Edinburgh in the morning to marry Connor Ramsay. Connor is a wealthy merchant in the city. As luck would have it, Father had never informed Mr. Ramsay of our engagement, and so the marriage will be none the worse for that, at least. Please forgive me for telling you in this way, for I could not bear to see your heart broken. Know that, whatever my name and whatever my circumstance, my heart and my soul will be yours unto my death.*

Dylan's body clenched, and rage turned his vision red. He started to crumple the letter but stopped. He turned, wishing for something to hit, someone to hurt, but there was only himself. With a deep, shuddering breath, he carefully folded the letter and replaced it in his sporran. Then he ate his stale provisions, and as his head began to clear he thought of the future. It was so deeply unsure, he couldn't know if he would survive what he now knew lay ahead. So he looked around at the *broch* and its stray fallen stones.

One large one lay under the spreading branches of the oak tree, and Dylan went to it. Squatting, he dug his fingers under an edge and lifted. His back strained, and for a moment he thought he would fail, but by stubborn will he turned it onto its side. Creepy-crawly bugs slithered and scurried at the intrusion, but Dylan ignored them. He took his money pouch from his sporran, and removed the five gold guineas, leaving only one silver threepence. One-by-one he laid the guineas in a row on the ground under the stone. He thought a moment, then pulled Cait's letter from his sporran and dropped it on top of the coins. Moving around to the other side of the rock, he shoved it back down exactly where it had been and smoothed the growth on the side that had been pressed. When he finished, the stone looked as if it had never been moved.

He looked around with the Goddess Stone for Sinann and wondered where she was. He would need to tell her of the money so, in case of his death, she could make sure Cait received it.

Then he untied the cord on which hung his crucifix, slipped Cait's ring onto it, then tied it again and slipped it all back under his sark. His baldric slung across his chest, he went after Cait.

The detachment of English soldiers was still bivouacked outside the castle. Coming around the foot of the wooded hill, hidden by trees, Dylan saw Bedford standing outside his tent, his interest focused on the castle gate. Other Redcoats stood by, their muskets ready. Dylan slipped into the glen, by one of the near houses, and made his way toward the loch, zigzagging down dikes and strolling like one of the villagers. Those working in the fields who saw him recognized him, of course. But nobody uttered a word to him, nor about him, except Marsaili's daughter who was coming from Nana Pettigrew's house. She hurried over to tug on his sleeve, and whispered that a soldier was visiting the seamstress. He thanked her and climbed over a dike to put it between himself and that house.

Cait was in the castle, and there was no way for him to get in except through the gatehouse. He stopped at a vantage point by the last house before the drawbridge, hidden by a copse of holly. Storming the gate would be suicide. His gut churned, and he bit his lips until he tasted blood. Needing to see Cait and talk to her was a fire in his blood. He could hardly see for wanting to get past those soldiers.

Then his heart leapt. The castle gate slowly opened, and through it rode Malcolm, Iain, and Cait, with Robin bringing up the rear. It was a somber group, and they stoically bore search and interrogation from the Redcoats before continuing on their way across the drawbridge. Dylan slipped along the dike toward a peat house and waited.

When the horses passed him, he stepped out of hiding and reached for Cait's hand. "Cait!"

She was shocked to see him. Iain reined his horse and said in a low voice, "Get off her, lad!"

"Cait, I've got to talk to you."

"Get off, I said!"

"Dylan . . ." Cait squeezed his hand, but then tried to pull free. "Dylan, I love you. Get away, or they'll kill you. Dinnae let them kill you! I couldnae bear it!" Her eyes were dark with deep sorrow, and the pain in them cut to his core.

Iain drew his sword. Malcolm tried to warn the Laird off, but Iain spurred his horse toward Dylan.

"Cait, don't do this." He didn't know what he expected her to do, but he couldn't just let her go.

Malcolm went after Iain, who wouldn't be swayed. The Laird growled, "I'll kill him!"

Cait's voice went panicky. "Dylan, please! Get away!" Her horse surged forward and broke their grip, leaving Dylan in the middle of the lane.

At that moment a dragoon stepped out of Nana's house across the way. Surprised at the scene before him, it took a moment for him to react. But then he unslung his musket, aimed, and fired at Dylan.

The ball caught the back of his left legging. He swallowed the cry of pain and surprise as his leg went out from under him, and he knelt as a fire of agony roared up his leg. Cait screamed. The shot brought the attention of the Redcoats across the drawbridge, and more shots whizzed past him. Cait's horse danced, and Dylan realized she was in the line of fire. While the English reloaded, he ducked behind the nearby house. Iain, Malcolm, and Robin closed ranks around Cait and kicked their mounts to a gallop as they herded her away from the scene. She shouted his name after him, and it tore at him to run away.

Dylan's leg gave out again after only a few more steps and he fell headlong. His legging was dark with blood at both ends of the wool, and his shoe squished with wetness. He scrambled to his feet again and made a few more yards dragging the bad leg. The soldiers chased him to the middle of a field, almost to Tormod Matheson's house, which sat at the foot of a wooded hill. Tormod was in the doorway and waved to him that he should take refuge inside.

But Dylan stopped running and shook his head. He would never make it unseen, and even if he did, Bedford would surely have the village searched again and they would find him. Whoever gave him refuge would be arrested as well. His leg no longer held him. His fingers fumbled at his sporran. He staggered as the world tilted. The talisman of invisibility was just there . . . somewhere. He dug deeper. There it was. But when he turned, the soldiers were already upon him, fire in their eyes. They had him trapped, for he couldn't get away and remain invisible.

He faced his pursuers on one leg, and held up his hands, gasping for air. The world was already going dark when one of them ran up and tried to clock him on the jaw with the butt of his musket. Dylan dodged it easily by reflex. *Come on, either knock me out or give it up*, was his last thought before the angry dragoon finally connected and his consciousness ended.

CHAPTER 17

It was a slow, five-day trip south to Ft. William. Dylan was in irons: heavy, hinged cuffs of iron locked to his wrists and connected to each other by three long, thick, iron links. Captain Bedford made the journey with his prisoner, along with three other dragoons. The trip might have been shorter if not for the English horses, which were ill-suited to the rocky terrain. Dylan ate and slept with one hand free but the other cuff attached to one of the men. Escape might have been possible, were he healthy and could overpower his chainmate to run, but his leg was agony to his hip. *Walking* wasn't an option, let alone running.

The first night, with his one free hand, he managed to remove the sheepskin from his leg and found the ball had made a bloody tunnel just beneath the skin and come out the other side. The bleeding had stopped on its own, but the muscle was too stiff to use.

The thought of infection terrified him, but because he wasn't allowed to clean the wound he didn't know whether to keep the legging on or off. In the end he figured he'd either have an infection or not and there wasn't much he could do about it. He put the legging back on so as to not lose it, though he did turn the bloody side to the front, away from the wound.

They fed him hardtack, the same as the soldiers ate, but quite a bit less of it than they took. By the fifth day he was dizzy from hunger, and the gait of the horse caused a jolt of pain at every step. Every nerve was alert to damage. It was a mixed relief when they arrived at their destination, the stone fort that was *Sassunach* Central for Scotland during this century.

The garrison was small but bustling, at the shore of a narrow loch, with a small town of wood and turf houses outside the gate. It stood at the foot of a granite mountain that rose straight up from the edge of town. Dylan was taken through a peaked stone arch to the outer bailey, then through the smaller gate to the inner parade ground. Wooden barracks buildings stood on two sides of the three-sided area. One much sturdier structure occupied the third, leaving the rest of the southern battlement clear.

The place was crawling with Redcoats. They brought to mind bright, blood-red roaches, scurrying this way and that about their official business. Dylan's vision swam, and his head throbbed. He wondered again about infection, and that made him even more ill.

The blond, periwigged Captain hopped lightly from his horse, apparently in good humor. He ordered Dylan sent to a holding cell while he presented himself to the commanding officer of the fort. A very young soldier in a red coat far too large for him came to take their horses. Bedford hurried off to the lone building on the south face.

Dylan was hauled from the horse, but his left leg folded under him. His right leg trembled as it tried to take all his weight. One of his escorts held him up, and half-dragged him across the yard toward the building where Bedford had gone, which Dylan took to be an administration building. But instead of approaching the front door, they took him around to the side, through a narrow gap between it and the next building, where stone steps descended into the foundation. From his escort he was treated to mutterings in Cockney English about "bloody, stinking, lazy, bum-bulling, murderous, heathen Scots."

In the wedge-shaped area between the buildings was a small two-wheeled cart leaning on its tongue, and inside lay

what Dylan thought was a pile of rags. But on second
glimpse he realized it was dead bodies, a couple of them in
linen shirts stained in various shades of reddish-brown and
blackened blood. Flies swarmed and crawled over faces too
pale to be human anymore, and Dylan couldn't be certain all
the arms and legs were still attached to the bodies. He wanted
to look away as he passed, but found he couldn't.

Down the steps, beneath the army offices, was a small,
dank, stone basement. The smell of the loch outside was
strong and fetid there, and added to it was the stench of
human waste and decaying body fluids. Heavy, wood doors
studded with iron lined the short corridor into which two
wooden support pillars intruded. The soldier on guard opened
one with a set of large, clanking keys.

The cell was dark, lit only by one high, barred window.
The stone floor was damp, and there was a long, iron bar
that ran the length of the small room secured to the floor.
Several sets of leg irons were attached to this bar, and the
dragoons secured Dylan there by both feet. He wobbled on
his right leg, barely touching his left to the floor for balance.
Then the Cockney straightened and leered. "Don't go no-
place, now."

"What, and miss your smiling face?" Dylan reached out
to pinch the soldier's cheek, and had it slapped away.

"Daft 'ighlander." The soldier took his leave and the room
darkened with the door closed.

Dylan slid down the stone wall and sat in the thin film of
muck on the cold, stone floor, finally alone. At least, he
thought he was alone. As his eyes adjusted to the darkness,
he saw a shape across from him that looked like it might be
a man slumped against the wall. But it sure didn't move
much. Nor did it sound like it was breathing. Smell was no
indication, for the place stank of urine, feces, vomit, and old
blood in addition to the dank stone and mud. It could have
been a rotting corpse leaping with worms and he wouldn't
have smelled it. But the longer he stared at the shape, the
less alive it appeared. He screwed his eyes shut and wished
Sinann were here.

Once, before the dim sunlight through the high window
died, a soldier came in to give him water ladled from a dirty

wooden bucket. He sucked down as much as he was allowed, and was still thirsty when the Redcoat plopped the ladle back in the bucket and left. Dylan sat back against the wall and waited some more. Once the light was gone, the fort was quiet and there were no more visitors to the dungeon. It had been morning when they'd last fed him.

He began to think now, as the initial shock of his arrest wore off and it became clear there was no escape, no cavalry to the rescue, no realization on the part of the English this was all a mistake. Once again his life as he had known it was over. It was also possible his life would soon be over, period.

They'd taken his sporran and his weapons, but left the crucifix around his neck and Cait's ring because they hadn't found them under his sark. Eventually they would, though, and the crucifix would be history for its silver and the ring for its gold. Dylan groped under his sark to find the cord and pulled it over his head. His fingers fumbled at the knot, numb and trembling, but he finally untied it and lifted the ring from the cord. Then he retied it and returned the crucifix to his neck.

The ring lay in his hand, a dim gleam in the failing light. They weren't going to take this from him if he could help it. They could take his life, but not this. He could think of only one place to hide it. He slipped it into his mouth for a moment to wet it as much as he could in his dehydrated state, then leaned over on his elbow and lifted his kilt. Lips bit together, he slipped the ring into his rectum. Sitting upright again, he felt just a little less defeated. Now he at least had a shot at being buried with Cait's ring. He wrapped his plaid around his shoulders and huddled against the wall to wait for what might come.

He slept some and woke in the cold several times. The shape across the room never moved, and he determined that whatever it was had died if it had ever lived at all. One time when he awoke, a bluish light wandered in through the window and he knew it was almost dawn. He slept again, but wasn't much interested in waking afterward. The cold stone made inroads on his aching bones, and every cell of his body hurt.

He was awakened by a soldier with a bucket, from which was dispensed a bowl of thin gruel. Dylan drank it, and didn't care that it tasted like dirty water. He was too hungry to care what they fed him. The soldier left him to his meal, and when Dylan was finished he set the cup in his lap and dozed again. Sleep was good. It was a place where the English couldn't come.

The day passed. He received more water, then struggled to his feet to pee as far away from his spot as the shackles would let him. Moving his bowels wasn't even an issue, he'd eaten so little since leaving Ciorram. Then he spent another cold night. Breakfast came in the form of another cup of gruel. Dylan was appalled at how grateful he was for the food, but refusing it never crossed his mind. It was keeping him alive. For what, he wasn't sure, but for now dying was not what he wanted.

Sometime that day, the door opened and a silent soldier came to unlock Dylan's leg irons. He didn't bother waiting for Dylan to struggle to his feet, but hauled him up and pinned him to the wall for a moment for him to find his legs again. The left one wouldn't hold him, and he limped to the door with the soldier half-carrying him by one arm.

He was taken down the corridor, past other cells, then through the door at the end of the hall, which led to a long, narrow, and windowless room lit by a number of candles in sconces. Still silent, the soldier hauled him to the center of that room where a thick wooden pillar, like the ones in the corridor, stood. An iron ring was bolted to it at a height of about seven feet. Dylan was taken past the pillar, turned, and shoved against the wood, facing it and the door. He leaned on it as the soldier unlocked one of his irons, brought his arms around to the other side of the pillar, and threaded the shackle through the ring. Then he restored that shackle to Dylan's wrist, turned the key on it, and left him standing there with his arms just over his head. The Redcoat exited the room, leaving him alone.

Dylan's heart raced. He struggled to swallow his fear, but his mind was ragged with pain and hunger. The best he could do was hold panic at bay, but it waited like a tiger, for an unguarded moment, to attack.

He had no idea how long he stood there. His arms ached and his legs trembled with the effort to keep him from dangling by his wrists. He hooked his fingers through the ends of the middle link on his shackles and let the ring and his arms take some of his weight. Eventually the door opened, and in came two Redcoats: Bedford and the guard. It seemed not many of the garrison soldiers frequented the dungeon, for Dylan had only seen the two guards. Today the Captain was accompanied by the charming cockney fellow, who carried a long bundle wrapped in linen. He set it on the table by the door, then stood by at attention.

Bedford stood, straight but relaxed. He sighed and blew out his cheeks as he stared at his prisoner. There was a long moment when Dylan hoped that was all he would do, but disappointment was inevitable.

Bedford took another deep breath and said, "First, let me make it plain I know you're innocent."

Dylan screwed his eyes shut. Somehow, that was more frightening than anything else the *Sassunach* could have said. He wouldn't be here, then, if his guilt or innocence were an issue.

The officer continued, "You've been brought here because you know things I want to know. And you will die here unless you tell me those things." His voice carried the certainty bred into aristocracy.

Dylan tried to speak but had to cough to reclaim his voice. "I know nothing. Zip. Zilch. Nada. And even if I did I'd not tell you, you bastard."

Bedford clucked his tongue. "How very rude. We'll have to teach you manners, I suppose." He glanced at the guard, who stepped around the pillar behind Dylan.

The dragoon's hands came around to unbuckle Dylan's belt. He yanked the *feileadh mór* from his body, and threw it and the belt into the corner behind him. Bedford tossed the soldier a knife and Dylan's sark was slit up the back and arms. It, also, was yanked from his body and dumped on the floor at his feet. Dylan stood before the two men, naked from the knees up.

He pressed his face to the well-worn oak and concentrated on not caring. If he didn't care what they did to the outside of him, they couldn't touch him on the inside. But he trembled as much from fear as from the cold. He held his chains tight to keep them from rattling, and took deep breaths.

Bedford spoke as he circled Dylan in a slow stroll. "Now, we all know Iain Matheson of Ciorram has Jacobite sympathies. You know it, I know it, the Hottentots of bloody *Africa* know it. The only reason he hasn't been arrested and his lands confiscated is that so far he's managed to keep a low enough profile to stay out of serious trouble."

"That, and whoever it is you have inside the castle isn't feeding you enough information," Dylan said.

Bedford coughed and proceeded as if Dylan hadn't spoken, but his voice carried a new tension. "However, we have reason to believe your *Laird* is part of an information and supply network operating in the Highlands. I want to know the names of Iain Matheson's cohorts. I want to know what they call themselves, the names they go by as they plot their sedition, and I want to know who is passing privileged information to the Jacobite clans."

Dylan nearly gasped, but caught himself. Ramsay. He was talking about Ramsay. Dylan's brain flew with scenarios in which he would tell Bedford all about Connor Ramsay. Ramsay would then be arrested and perhaps executed. Cait would be free, and so would he. He opened his mouth to speak, but then closed it.

To implicate Ramsay for the passing of information would be to murder Iain Mór, who was equally guilty of receiving it. Both would be hung for treason and their properties all forfeit. Cait would lose her father and her home, as well as her husband and his property. Also, the entire Matheson tenancy in Glen Ciorram would be evicted and destitute. Dylan couldn't do that to the clan. He groaned and said, "I know nothing."

Bedford sighed, paused for a moment as if thinking, then said, "I'm not sure you understand your position, Matheson. You see, you are not going to trial. You will not be hung. In fact, you are not even here. As far as anyone in that God-forsaken place you now call home is concerned, you died of an infected wound on the way here and were buried in a nameless field with not so much as a rock to mark the place.

"So you see, we can keep you here indefinitely, with no relatives petitioning for your release. No public outcry at your ill-treatment. No legal ramifications whatsoever. In short, I own your life." He chuckled. "For whatever that's worth."

Dylan said nothing. Bedford's contempt was palpable and his gaze drilled into him with a hatred beyond comprehension.

The Captain continued. "Most men in your position would be quite eager to tell me all they know, since talking does happen to be your only chance at release. Besides, it's what one expects from Scots, really, to turn on each other. You're a batch of raving barbarians, the lot of you. Surely you know your *kinsman* was ever so eager to have you arrested. Came to me personally with the information you were transporting communiqués to Killilan. Unfortunately, the letters were nothing more than diatribe. Enough to get you hung, but not enough to implicate anyone who is actually guilty of anything. However, resourceful as I am, I seized the opportunity to take into custody someone who might know something."

Dylan bit his lower lip and continued to say nothing.

After a long silence during which Bedford picked invisible lint from his uniform and appeared to have forgotten Dylan's presence, the officer said, "Have you noticed my promotion?"

A sigh escaped Dylan, and he peered at the Redcoat. He didn't know enough about English army insignia of the period to be able to tell, but he guessed. "Major?"

A wide smile cut across Bedford's face. "Yes. Though I was close to it to begin with, having been posted so far into the countryside had not brought me sufficiently within notice of my superiors. I haven't advanced nearly as quickly as I should have. Your capture may have given me the edge I needed, and now I am over more than just that little company in the wilderness. I would like to show my appreciation by allowing you an opportunity to tell me what you know so I can release you. Then you can go running back to your dirty friends. I'll wager it's the best offer you've had in at least a few days."

Dylan stared for a moment, then said with as much insouciance as he could muster, "You know what, Jeeves, your good-cop–bad-cop act needs a whole lot of work."

Bedford couldn't have understood the comment, but he did seem to get the sense of ridicule. Frustration built in his tense demeanor. Anger showing in jerky, sudden movements, he turned to the table and opened the bundle on it. Inside were Dylan's belongings: his sword, baldric, dirks, and sporran.

His voice took on an edge. "Here's the offer, Matheson. Give me the information I ask for, and I'll let you go. Simple as that. Talk to me, and you can have your things back, even your weaponry. In fact," his voice had the lilt of a game show host awarding prizes, and he reached under the sporran for a piece of folded fabric, "I'll even let you have a fresh, new shirt." He shook out the fabric, which turned out to be a white silk shirt with ruffled sleeves and neck. "I'd call that an excellent bargain, in exchange for someone you can hardly call cousin anymore."

When Bedford offered the weapons, Dylan realized it was all a lie. The man had no intention of ever letting him go, no matter what he did or said. Releasing him with his sword and dirks was unthinkable, and therefore a lie. He still said nothing, and knew for a certainty his life was about to end.

The edge in his voice sharpening, Bedford said, "You've never been flogged, have you? No, I can see you have not." He gestured with a graceful hand to Dylan's bare back. "You might want to think about this a bit before refusing my offer. Men have been known to die from flogging, particularly when the one ordering the punishment is not constrained by silly little rules regarding the number of strokes and waits between floggings and such. Surely there is nobody in that broken-down castle who means that much to you."

Dylan screwed his eyes shut and tried not to think about Ramsay and Cait. Nor Coll, who was dead. He thought about Iain, and the people he'd come to know this past winter. He thought of Sarah and little Eóin, of Gracie, of Seonag, of Robin and Marc, and of Malcolm, who had trusted him almost from the very beginning. They were his clan, and his death would be to protect all of them. He opened his eyes and glared at Bedford. With a deep, shuddering breath he said, *"Faodaigh thu a' póg mo thóin!"*

Bedford laughed, though anger flashed in his eyes. "Why, how generous of you! And what a lovely arse you have for me to kiss!" He strolled to lean against the pillar into Dylan's face, almost nose-to-nose. His breath stank. "But I'm afraid I must decline, for bestiality is not among my many vices. I'd as soon thrum a pig as dirty myself with a Scot of any gender. Not to mention I don't happen to be bent quite in that direction. But it's good of you to offer." He glanced at the soldier, then strolled back to lean on the table and continued, "So, since you refuse to cooperate, my only alternative is to proceed. Remember, you have only yourself to blame for this." He nodded to the soldier.

Searing pain slashed across Dylan's back. A surprised yell escaped him and his knees went out from under him. He hung for a moment, paralyzed by agony, then hauled himself to his feet. Bedford nodded again, and the whip came down a second time. Dylan lost his weakened legs once more and gasped as he hung. His arms trembled as he pulled himself up, only to be struck a third time.

Dylan wished to pass out. Each stroke of the whip, in expert hands, landed in a fresh spot. As he bled the tip picked up that blood and cut deeper on the next stroke for being wet. His blood ran freely down his back and thighs, and over his leggings. Soon there was a puddle of it, making mud of the straw on the floor and soaking into his ruined sark. His shoes slipped in it. He hugged the pillar for support. The strokes came slowly, spaced unevenly so each was a fresh surprise. The agony was heightened by anticipation. Time stretched until it seemed he'd spent his entire life in pain, which would never stop until time ended.

His eyes screwed shut, he struggled to remove his mind from the pain. Cait. He focused on Cait. Her soft skin, her musical voice, the way she'd made him feel when they were together at last. He took himself away from Ft. William, away from the Redcoats, and away from the whip that was cutting deep swaths in his back. The pain dimmed.

When Bedford was satisfied, or bored, he called a halt and left the room. The soldier remained at guard, the whip rolled up in his hand. Dylan's mind returned and the agony descended on him in an avalanche. He continued to hug the pillar, to keep his weight off his arm sockets. He gasped at the ongoing pain, and pressed his mouth to the pillar to keep his silence. He feared if he said anything it would be to give the *Sassunaich* what they wanted. Tears stung his eyes and ran down his cheeks into his mouth, and he didn't care. He just didn't care. Loyalty to his people had been bred into him for millennia, and it was one thing his American ancestors had not lost. He would die before telling the outlanders anything that would hurt Cait or her family.

Time passed. Water was brought. The guard changed. Dylan's mind grayed out. He fell into a state that was almost a doze but not really sleep. He regained his legs, but still hugged the pillar for the sake of protecting his most vital organs. The wood was smooth on his belly, polished by the bodies of other victims. He wondered how many other men had lost their lives while chained here.

The cold was deep inside him now, and his teeth chattered with endless shivering. The blood drying on his buttocks and legs itched and stung, and his outraged muscles stiffened.

And he waited.

It felt like he'd been here all his life, that his entire existence had never been anything but pain. Eternity was now. But when was now? How long had he actually been in the room? He sifted through the shards of his splintered mind to remember. It became horribly important to know the date. If he could remember the date, he could know the rest of the world existed and he was a part of it. If only he could remember the date, he would know he was still sane.

May 1. Beltane. His arrest had been the Tuesday before the wedding three weeks later, which made that May 15. Five days to Ft. William, he remembered by the five times they'd fed him. They arrived on May 20, the day he and Cait had expected to marry. He squeezed his eyes shut and struggled to set that aside, and continued his calculations. He'd spent one night in the cell, a day and another night, then was brought to this room and flogged on May 22.

The air went out of him when he realized the date, and

what a mistake he'd made in trying to remember. May 22 was his birthday. He'd just turned thirty-one.

Dylan's mind retreated from the world, and he waited through the cold night.

He was shivering hard by the time Bedford returned, accompanied by the Cockney dragoon. The night watch departed. The sconce candles, most of which had guttered out long ago, were now replaced and light returned to the room. Bedford said in a chipper voice, "Have we changed our mind yet?"

Dylan declined to answer.

A sardonic edge crept into the cheer. "Have we a mind left to change?"

Still Dylan was silent.

Bedford sighed. "Very well." He mumbled an order to the soldier, which sent him out of the room. He returned, with something that looked like a smoking hibachi. There were metal rods sticking out of the fire. "Over there," the Major said, and the soldier set the contraption on the floor. "Adjust him."

The soldier's keys jangled in his hand and he unlocked one of the shackles. Dylan's back and shoulders screamed with pain as he lowered his arms. Then he was turned around and shoved back against the pillar, his arms over his head, and his irons put through the ring again and secured. Now he stood with his back to the pillar and his hands secured behind his head. There was no longer any play in the chain and his stiff shoulder sockets felt as if they'd been bent in a direction they weren't meant to go. The wounds on his back reopened and blood flowed again, and his back made wet, squelching noises against the wood when he moved to adjust his weight.

Bedford chuckled. "If you know anything about the history of your people, Matheson, you'll appreciate this. When your King James I, not ours, but King of Scotland only, was murdered in 1437, one of the conspirators in the assassination was executed by this method. Pincers were heated until glowing, then used to tear the flesh from his body bit by bit. Finally an iron crown was heated 'til red and placed on his head, a fitting end to a man who had betrayed his king. A traitor. And that's what you are, as well. A traitor to your Queen, and you deserve to die like one."

By this time Dylan had no thought of the Queen, James, or anyone else in power or pretending to it. His only thought was, one way or another, he had to make the pain stop.

The fire was brought around to where he could see it and the tool in it. It was a pair of tongs, the business end only an inch across, but heated in coals that glowed red. His pulse thudded in his ears, and he began to moan. "No. No more." The pain bent his mind back on itself until he thought he would scream and never stop. His chest heaved for air. He could smell the coals and hot iron. He knew it would shortly be his flesh smoking and stinking. "No," he moaned. "No . . ."

"You're ready to tell us, then?" Almost absently, Bedford strolled over, reached out for the crucifix, and yanked the cord from his neck. He gave it an appraising once-over, muttered, "Damned papist," then tucked it into a pocket.

Dylan bit his lips together and screwed his eyes shut. He hoped they'd weakened him enough for him to pass out quickly. He felt like he was floating, and there was a buzzing in his head. If only he could leave his body and never come back. If only . . .

"No? All right then. Don't say you weren't warned."

Tears squeezed from Dylan's eyes, and he voiced gasps, on the verge of screaming. When he opened them, the soldier stood before him with the soot-covered pair of tongs in his gloved hand. In that instant Dylan decided it was time to die, and more quickly than these two would have it.

He pulled his weight onto the chains, and struck out with a snap kick to the soldier's gut. The Redcoat doubled over and dropped the tongs. Bedford laughed. "Oh, he'll regret that, won't he?" As the soldier bent to retrieve his tool, Dylan chambered again, cocking his leg in readiness for another kick, hip to front as if protecting his genitals, his weight still on the chains. The muscles of his torso stretched, pulling against his arms secured behind his head. He trembled with the pain, but held his position. As the dragoon straightened, Bedford's voice was still amused as he said to his soldier, "Watch out. . . ." But when the soldier looked up, Dylan

struck with a side thrust that drove the English nose into the
English brain and sent him into the far wall where he slid
down it, dead, his mouth and chin covered with shiny, red
blood.

"Good God!" Bedford sounded very surprised and deeply
offended. Dylan heard the rattle of a sword being drawn.
Here it came. He would be dead in about a minute.

A scream like a tin whistle made him look up. "Tink!"
There she was, hovering over him. Faster than Dylan could
think, she waved her hand and his shackles flew open. He
fell to the floor, and Bedford's attack missed. Dylan rolled,
kicked out at the overbalanced Major, and tangled his feet
so he tripped.

Hope of escape threw a rush of strength into him. He
scrambled to his feet for his own sword, which lay on the
table, and removed the scabbard from it. Armed now, he
turned to face his adversary just as the *Sassunach* regained
his feet. In these close quarters there was little room to maneuver, hopping and limping on one leg. Bedford kept the
pillar between them, probably expecting Dylan to make a
dive for the door, at which point Bedford could then chase
him outside and raise the alarm. Dylan was smarter than that,
and knew he would have to silence the Major before touching
the door.

He made quick forays to the other side of the pillar, but,
aside from a little sword clanging, accomplished nothing. He
didn't want Bedford circling to the door side any more than
Bedford wanted to be on the same side of the pillar as Dylan.

Sinann hovered. "Kill him! Kill the bastard!"

Dylan never took his eyes off Bedford, but said, "I hope
you're talking to me, Tink."

Bedford gave a small, puzzled frown.

"Kill that English bastard!"

Dylan's teeth clenched. "I'm trying!"

When it became apparent Dylan wasn't going to bolt,
Bedford came from behind the pillar to attack. Dylan parried
and staggered, much weaker than his opponent. But he had
one advantage: he wasn't afraid of being hurt. He was already in excruciating pain and knew if he didn't nail this guy
he would die. Bedford, on the other hand, was still hoping

Dylan would make for the door. Dylan attacked instead.

Caught by surprise, Bedford tried to retreat but wasn't fast enough. Swords clanged, and on riposte Dylan captured the English sword and threw it aside to attack again. Dylan's sword caught Bedford in the chest. The Redcoat let out a cry, then went down, coughing. He lay there, struggling to breathe.

Dylan didn't hesitate, but turned to the table and pulled on the shirt that lay there. He collected his kilt from the floor and rolled Brigid and his sporran into it, threw the baldric over his shoulder and scabbarded his sword. Then he lifted the key ring from the jailer's belt. "Let's go," he said to the faerie, then immediately turned back. "Wait a minute."

"*Och*, let's go!"

"Wait." Dylan went to the table. "Where did he put it?"

"Put what?" Sinann's voice was panicky. Bedford still writhed on the floor, gurgling and coughing blood.

"The cross." Dylan went to the dying Englishman and patted his coat, then reached inside for his crucifix. "Damned thief."

Bedford passed out. Though he was still breathing, it wouldn't be long now.

"Let us *go!*" Sinann nearly shrieked.

He stuffed the crucifix into his bundle, then he opened the door, and found the corridor empty. It was lit with candles in sconces, and Dylan slipped down toward the outer door, where he stopped. He leaned on the wall, gasping, and indicated the door. "See if the coast is clear."

"If the which is what?"

"Look to see if anyone's out there."

"Oh, aye." She raised her hand to snap her fingers, then stopped and said, "Were you a smuggler in America?"

"Just go!" His strength was fading fast as the adrenaline from the fight left his system.

She blinked out, then blinked right back. "The coast is clear." He unlocked the door then hauled it open, pulled it shut behind him, and crept up the stone steps. This end of the building formed a "V" with the building next to it, with a narrow opening to the parade ground and a wide exposure to the fort wall. It was morning and the fort was alive with

soldiers about their business. "Okay, Tink, how am I supposed to get out of here?"

She flapped her hands. "Fly, ye sumph!" She waved a
hand, and his feet lifted off the ground. This time he was too
weak to keep his balance, and he curled into a ball, hugging
his knees as he rolled and wobbled into the air and over the
wall. His heart leapt as he spotted a sentry at the point of
the battlement to the south, not ten yards away. But the soldier's attention was on the loch. Sinann let him down at the
base of the wall, and he rolled under a gorse bush. There he
rested for a moment, hidden by the thick, yellow blossoms
and thorny branches that snagged his shirt and put thin
scratches in his skin. But being stuck by the gorse was better
than the alternative, and was nothing compared to the
screaming pain in his back.

When he opened his eyes and saw Sinann peering under
the bush at him, he said through gritted teeth but in the softest
whisper he could manage, "Where the hell were you?"

"You told me to watch Cait. You went to Killilan."

"I was with her. She came to me that night. Where were
you?" Guilt crossed over Sinann's eyes. Dylan said, "Tinkerbell . . ."

"Well, you couldnae expect me to not go looking for you.
When that *Sassunach* bastard came to the castle, and I kent
you were in trouble, I went after you."

"And left Cait."

There was a long silence and her eyes flickered, then she
said, "Aye."

Dylan said, "But you didn't find me."

"You had disappeared thoroughly. I looked everywhere."

"Except the *broch*. Which was where Cait headed first
thing. You would have found me if you'd stuck with her."

There was a very long silence, then he whispered, "How
did you finally find me?"

"You know, that tapestry in Iain Mór's place of business
comes in handy on occasion when I need to spy while phys-
ically elsewhere. Late in my search for you, there was a
conversation in that room."

"You listened in and they were talking about me?"

"Aye."

Her lack of elaboration on the subject made him suspicious. "What was said?" For a moment he thought she wouldn't answer, so he pressed, "Was Iain part of the frame-up?"

She frowned. "*Frame-up?*"

"Um . . . did he help get me arrested?"

She shook her head. "But I cannae say he's overly unhappy about it. Coll is dead because he drew on Robin Innis, but Artair willnae be wasted in that way. Iain Mór is satisfied his plans for his daughter have worked out, Artair is the heir presumptive, and you have been forgotten by Himself, though not by the rest of the clan."

That was puzzling. "What does that mean?"

She sighed. "It means that, aside from the Laird and his brother, you are well mourned by your kin. Malcolm Taggart was right in thinking you could fill the lairdship. Every soul in Glen Ciorram was in tears and wailing of a broken heart at your arrest."

"Really?"

"Aye. But never mind that. You've rested entirely too long. Get moving! The guard has moved to the other end of his post." She gestured for him to get up.

He wanted to pursue the subject of broken hearts in Ciorram, but realized she was right and there would be opportunity later to question her. He tried to get up, but found it too painful. "Let me just lie here for a while."

"Nae! They'll find Bedford and his cohort, and, as the English tend to frown on people murdering their soldiers, they'll be after you any minute now! Get up! Get up, I say!" She grabbed his shirt and pulled on it. He groaned and swatted at her, but she dodged and pulled again until he was out from under the gorse. He wished he would faint from the shrieking pain of his back, but had no luck.

"At least make the pain go away. Wave your hand and make it stop hurting."

She sighed. "Would you have it so you never felt anything at all for as long as you lived?"

"Yes. Please. Just make it stop."

"Nae. I willnae do it. The hurting will go away soon enough."

Dylan groaned.

"You see that water down there?" Dylan nodded. "You must go into it, for the fort is surrounded on three sides by water. As it's a sea loch, it'll hurt a bit. . . ." Dylan threw her a look which she ignored. "But have nae worry about keeping afloat." Sinann resumed pulling, and finally he was on his feet, staggering and limping toward the water.

She was right, the water hurt a bit. He gasped at the fresh pain. Sinann said, "Leave only your mouth above water. I'll take you to the other side." Dylan rolled onto his back and felt a pressure at the back of his head. He was able to go limp, clutching his belongings to his belly, and slowly he moved toward the shore on a promontory to the north. As he crossed the inlet to the north of the fort, he saw a boat unloading supplies at the quay outside the sally port. English soldiers hurried back and forth, directing workmen in breeches and coats with their crates, barrels, and animal cages. Dylan squeezed his eyes shut and tried hard to not look like a face floating on the water.

When his head bumped shore, he rolled onto his knees again and Sinann urged, "Now, hurry! Into the shrubs!"

He climbed to his feet and obeyed, no longer willing to argue. In the safety of some reeds and deep heather, he crept slowly on his belly until he found a game trail, which he crawled along, following wherever it might lead. It led to the other side of the promontory where an estuary dumped a river into the loch. He then stood and followed that river inland for fresh water. The salt on his back and the thirst of his body drove him on, though he was dizzy with shock. The sun sank behind him, and in the distance he heard a hue of whistles and shouts. His absence had been discovered.

"Keep going," said Sinann. "It'll be a while before they entertain the idea you could be outside the walls."

The alarm spurred him on, up the glen that wound between towering brown hills that bore a veneer of green spring growth. When the water of the river stopped surging to shore and began to run downhill, Dylan waded into it.

"Careful!" Sinann shouted, and he was buoyed again. But the fresh water was a relief on his back and he drank all he

could hold. By the time his thirst was satisfied, he was ready
to sink below the surface and stay there.

"Get up!"

"Nuh uh."

"I said, get up! You've come all this way, and now the
Sassunaich are going to pick you out of the river like a piece
of flotsam. You've come too far, lad, to give up now!"

He sighed, gathered his strength, and hauled himself onto
the bank where he resumed his trek away from the fort.

Eventually he was well into the glen, but Sinann still
egged him forward. He groaned and sank to his knees on the
sod near the river. "Fly me."

"If I could lift you more than a few feet, I'd have you
back in Ciorram before sundown. But I cannae, any more
than I could carry you on foot. So get moving."

But Dylan was exhausted. There was not a square inch
on his body that didn't scream agony, and he'd not slept in
two days, nor eaten in three. He moaned and shook his head.

"Make it as far as those woods over there. Get into cover,
at least."

He looked. There was a cluster of trees ahead. He summoned his strength, and with trembling muscles hauled himself mostly to his feet. With a staggering gait, clutching his
wad of clothing and weapons, he made his way toward the
protection of the woods. Each step was agony. When he
made the tree line, he collapsed among the bracken and toadstools, and passed out.

There were voices. Dylan hoped they were angels. He
wanted to be dead. He didn't want to return to the world
of pain he knew awaited him. But the voices were Scottish
and spoke Gaelic. He took heart that at least they weren't
English, but also knew there were a few Scots who wanted
him dead. One of the voices said, "Is he from the garrison,
do you think?"

"I pray to God they didn't do this to him at the Banavie
tavern. Wake him up and see who he is."

Before anyone might touch him, Dylan opened his eyes
and groaned. Two men stood over him—he could tell by the

number of feet in front of his face. The first voice said, "Aye, you're alive, then."

He groaned again, hoping they would take that as a yes.

"Who might you be, lad?"

It took a moment to find his voice, then he rolled just enough to peer up at them. He could focus with only one eye. "If I answer wrong, will you just leave me, or run me through?"

"Depends, I expect, on how wrong the answer is." Both men were red-haired, but it was the younger one who asked the questions. Two pistols were thrust into the man's belt. The older one was shorter than the younger, but was built solid and had the air of someone born to take charge.

Dylan took a deep breath and said, "My name is Dylan Robert Matheson, cousin to *Iain Mór nan Tigh a' Mhadaidh Bhàin* in Glen Ciorram."

"And, Dylan Robert Matheson, is that some strange, northern accent you're speaking with? Or would it be a bit more *southern*?" The question was pointed. The interrogator was expressing a suspicion Dylan might be English pretending to be Scottish.

"I was born in America." He left it at that. They could run him through if they wanted; he didn't care. He collapsed back onto his face again.

But they didn't run him through. Instead they reached down to help him up. He still clutched his wad of belongings, and one of the men relieved him of it before they lifted his arms around their necks and carried him through the woods to a nearby clearing.

A fire burned cheerily, fed on small, dry sticks, and threw a thin line of smoke into the tree branches overhead. A game bird was spitted over it, and the smell of cooking food cut through the pain so his mouth watered to the point he couldn't help drooling. The men let him down onto the sod near the fire, then stood to either side. He ran the back of his hand over his mouth, and his lower lip cracked. Face-down on the ground, he couldn't see the men's faces as they went about their business. The older one finally spoke again. "Dylan Matheson, cousin to Iain Mór of Ciorram, I'm eager to hear how a man in your condition escaped from the garrison and made it so far up Glen Nevis."

Dylan sighed. "I flew." He looked around for Sinann, but didn't see her. "I was rescued by the wee folk, who have no liking for the English."

The men both laughed, and the older one sent the younger to fetch a skin of water. Then he knelt behind Dylan and tried to peel the bloody shirt away from his back. It felt like he was ripping skin off, and Dylan bit his lip hard to not make a sound. "*Och*," said the older Scot. "It's a thorough job they did." He tugged gently at the cloth, but it wouldn't come.

Dylan muttered into the sod, "I'm at a disadvantage here, Mister . . ."

"Oh, aye," said the older man. "I apologize. My friend here is Alasdair Roy, and my name is Rob Roy."

CHAPTER 18

Dylan lifted his face from the ground and turned, startled, to stare at the man. His elbows were trembling under his weight. He whispered, almost to himself, "MacGregor . . ."

The man grunted and said, revealing no emotion, "You've heard of me, then."

"I've heard of you." Dylan still stared. Anybody the least familiar with Scottish history would know the name of Rob Roy MacGregor. "What are you doing so close to Ft. William?"

MacGregor grunted. "Minding my own business, lad."

"Oh. Aye. I apologize." Dylan's gaze went back to the ground, but he stole another glance at MacGregor. The man didn't look the least bit like the guy who had played him in the movie. But Dylan shook that off as an idiotic thought. He was in the presence of one of Scotland's greatest heroes—perhaps the most revered Gael since Cuchulain himself—a Jacobite leader whose resistance activities had given him the reputation of a real-life Robin Hood.

His reverence dulled in an instant when MacGregor took the collar and tail of Dylan's shirt and yanked the fabric away from his back. He routed the shout of pain that rose in his throat through his nose where it became no more than a snort.

He collapsed to the ground again, and his brain went fuzzy as spots swam before his eyes. But then the shirt was pulled over his head and water was taken into the sleeve of it so MacGregor could clean his back.

Dylan clenched his teeth against the pain as MacGregor wiped blood from him.

"May I ask how it was you attracted the ire of Her Majesty's minions?"

Dylan pressed his face to the ground. "They thought I knew something I might be willing to tell. They were wrong."

MacGregor and his friend chuckled. "Who was it ordered the dirty work?"

"An officer stationed up north, near Ciorram. Captain . . . I mean, Major Bedford. I don't know what his own orders were. I think he may have been working on his own."

MacGregor grunted. "I've nae heard of him." He muttered to his friend about "Mary's jar," and Alasdair went to fetch something from a cloth bag that sat away from the fire. When MacGregor opened it, there was an earthy, animal smell. Then he began dabbing whatever it was on Dylan's back.

Dylan's eyelids drooped as the pain eased.

"If he was working on his own, that would be illegal. Without a conviction or sanction of any kind, I mean."

It was Dylan's turn to grunt. "I'll just have to sue the sonofabitch, then, won't I? That'll teach him."

Again the red-haired men chuckled. MacGregor finished spreading the goop and said, "There's still a bit of blood, but that'll stop quick enough. The salve will keep your shirt from sticking to you while you heal."

He handed the bloody shirt back to Dylan, who sat up and pulled it on. Wet and dirty as it was, it was better than sitting around naked. And it would dry soon enough. His kilt and sporran were still wet from the river, but they'd both been wet before. He wrapped the plaid around himself like a blanket, and the cloth immediately began to warm and dry, sending a thick smell of sheep into the air. He took the crucifix, tied the break in its linen cord and restored it to his neck, then checked his sporran and found everything there except the threepence. No surprise. He figured he was lucky to have anything back at all. Including his life. And especially his weapons. Besides, the bulk of his money was still in Ciorram, and he'd not yet had to retrieve the ring.

"I expect your sympathies lie elsewhere than with the Crown, then?" MacGregor's companion said.

MacGregor said, "Alasdair, let the man eat."

Alasdair fell silent while he served up pieces of the game bird, and Dylan ate with a relish he'd never known possible. His long-empty stomach balked at the solid food, but, taking deep breaths, he refused to let it come back up.

When the meat was gone, Dylan lay back on one elbow, sucking idly on the marrow of a leg bone, and thought about Alasdair's question. He knew the Jacobites would fail. Scotland would be part of the United Kingdom for at least another three hundred years, and there was nothing he, nor Rob Roy, nor anyone, could do about it.

However, the English musket and the English whip that had each brought him nearly to death had put a mark on his soul that would never be erased, nor forgiven. He'd seen the hatred in the eyes of the Redcoats, and knew they thought the occupants of this land to be no better than animals. All through this century, as through centuries already past, their aim would be the genocide of the Gaels. The killing would be systematic and ruthless, and whatever innocent lives might be saved in resisting the English occupation would be worth the Jacobite struggle.

He cleared his throat and said, "You ask me how I feel about Her Majesty's red-coated pigs?" He twirled the bone in his mouth, then pulled it out to look at it thoughtfully.

"Aye?"

"I say, long live King James VIII, and death and damnation to every *Sassunach* north of the Borderlands."

The other two nodded, and repeated, "Long live the King." Dylan had a sense that Alasdair wanted to talk, but MacGregor wasn't ready yet and hushed him.

Very quickly, sleep overwhelmed Dylan. He curled up in his plaid by the fire, still clutching the bone, and went to that place where the English couldn't come.

The next time he knew consciousness, he had no idea where he was nor how long he'd slept. He lay on what felt like a rack, made of pine branches covered with ferns. He was no longer in any clearing. All he could see were mountains covered in heather and dotted with granite chunks large enough to hide a small house. He was lying alongside the south side of such a boulder, in a hollow given minimal cover by some gorse. He couldn't move, and his entire body felt boneless. Thirst was his first thought, and he asked for water. A *quaiche* was put to his lips, but he was only allowed to sip once, then once again when he asked for more. He tried to look around, but his eyes were gummed shut. He went to rub them clear, and found his hands were trembling.

"Where are we?" He could barely croak out the words.

"Rannoch Moor. You've been ill. We had to carry you."

"How long?"

Alasdair shrugged. "Couple of days. We couldnae leave you behind, and we couldnae stay or else be taken by the Redcoats ourselves. If you've heard of Rob, you'll know why."

Dylan nodded. Sometime the year before, MacGregor had been outlawed for a debt he didn't owe, ruined by the Marquis of Montrose who had wanted his land and had gotten it.

Alasdair continued, "You had a fever. For a while it looked as if we might not have to carry you any farther. But we're in a safe place now where you can gather your strength." His voice took on a mild, teasing tone. "Then do yer own walking."

Dylan sat up, pleased to find he could. He took the *quaiche* from Alasdair and sipped some more. When the water hit his stomach, hunger raged. "Something to eat?" His voice would go no more than a whisper.

Alasdair smiled. "A good sign." He took the *quaiche* with the water, and reached into his sporran for a small cloth bag. Then he dumped a handful of oatmeal from it into the cup. He stirred the mush with his finger, and handed it back to Dylan. It was lumpy, and held together as Dylan picked globs out with his fingers. Hungry as he was, it tasted heavenly.

While he ate, he looked around. There was no evidence of MacGregor. As if reading his mind, Alasdair said, "Rob went on ahead, for he'd pressing business at home. I was to stay here until either you could walk, or I could bury you."

Dylan was oddly grateful they would have bothered to bury him, but much more pleased it appeared he would be walking out of there. He lay back down on the bed of branches, which turned out to be a stretcher of some sort, the branches and ferns laid over a frame of saplings lashed together. He slept again.

For two more days he and Alasdair kept their camp. The red-haired man asked some questions about his time at Ft. William, and Dylan answered them, but on the whole there was little talking. Dylan slept and ate, and slept some more.

On the third day a call of nature made him decide he felt strong enough to stand. Alasdair went to help him, but Dylan waved him off and struggled to his feet like a newborn colt. Feet planted wide, he stood by the fire and swayed. His back itched and his leg ached dully, but he still felt better than he had since . . .

His heart sank as he thought of Cait and their last night together. But he took a deep breath and looked around. He said, to Alasdair, "Are we ready to go on?"

"Do you think you can do much walking?"

He looked around as if it would help him get his bearings. "How much farther do we have to go?"

Alasdair shrugged. "Oh, two or three days' walk. If you feel up to it, we could start in the morning."

Dylan nodded, and went around to the far side of the boulder.

"Where are we going?" asked Dylan as they walked the next day, up the long slope to a mountain pass, headed south. Cait's ring now hung with the crucifix on the cord around his neck again, having been retrieved the day before and cleaned with a splash of whiskey he'd bummed from Alasdair. The red-haired Scot hadn't commented on the sudden appearance of the ring, but had given a firm opinion on the waste of perfectly good whiskey.

Dylan could have stood another couple of days' recovery, but knew neither of them had the luxury of lounging around Rannoch Moor much longer. If he could walk, then he needed to do so. He limped heavily, using for support a staff cannibalized from his stretcher.

Alasdair said, "We're going to Glen Dochart, I might as well tell you. It's nae secret where we've taken refuge."

"You're all outlaws?"

He laughed. "Oh, aye. The lot of us. But not all started out that way. Some of Rob's men are nothing more than jobless lads with nowhere else to make a living. So they come to reive cattle from the Marquis of Montrose, under the protection of his political rival, Iain Glas of Breadalbane. He's a Campbell who is cousin to Rob's mother. As long as we're in Campbell territory, that Whig Montrose willnae dare bring men to take us."

Alasdair's voice took on a pointed tone. "It's a good place to be, for a man as can take care of himself. Rob does well for us, and pays, besides food and a roof, half an English shilling a day on days you're occupied, plus a share of the price when the *spréidhe* are sold."

Dylan was struggling to keep up Alasdair's pace, but refused to call for a rest. He said, "And you're telling me this because . . ."

There was a moment's pause, then, "Because Rob wishes to offer you employment if you're of a mind to take it. Before he left, he told me that if you live it would be because you're either blessed with uncommon good luck, or else you're the toughest young lad he's ever clapped eyes on. Either way, he would like you among his men."

After the first flush of pride at the invitation to work for the legendary Rob Roy, Dylan remembered the man had also commanded Jacobite troops at Sheriffmuir. That defeat would put an end to next year's uprising. A few months ago he would have declined because of that. But now, outlawed and stripped of everything he'd had to lose—not to mention a fair piece of his hide—his outlook was changed. He looked around for Sinann, knowing she must be there, wishing she could appreciate what he was about to do. "Aye," he said to Alasdair. "I'll work for Rob." It looked like he was going to be fighting for the Jacobites at Sheriffmuir after all.

Rob's home at Glen Dochart was a low, thatched house of mortared stone, which stood facing the meandering River

Dochart on a flat glen bottom surrounded by towering, heather-covered granite. The southern slope of the glen was more heavily forested than anywhere Dylan had seen in Scotland before, but the house was in the clear.

Dylan and Alasdair arrived at sunset when the family was inside, eating. Some chickens roosted on the stack of peats outside, and when the door opened Dylan could smell one of their brethren roasted on the household fire. Alasdair went in, and a few moments later returned with MacGregor.

Now that Dylan was standing, he was a bit surprised at how short Rob was. MacGregor's height was probably about five feet nine inches, a few inches below his own six feet. But he had a bearing that made him seem taller, and long, muscular arms that Dylan saw would make him a formidable opponent with a sword.

MacGregor seemed elated and just a little surprised to see him, shook his hand, and with a warm smile welcomed him to his employ. "How is the back healing, lad?" He seemed genuinely concerned with Dylan's welfare.

Dylan shrugged, glad now that he could. "It's much better. That salve you put on it did a lot of good."

"I'll pass your appreciation to Mary, for it was she who sent it with me." He then addressed Alasdair. "Take him to the barracks house, and see he's made comfortable. Then I'll see you back here straight away." With that, and a nod, he returned to his house and his supper.

The barracks house was behind and upstream from the MacGregor home, a peat construction set against a hill, which looked like a part of the hill itself. Thick moss grew in the thatching, along with some grass, which at the moment was grazed by a goat that lifted its head and stared at them with dull yellow eyes as they approached. Alasdair chased it off with shouts and arm-waving, then said to Dylan, "Goat dung seeping through thatching in heavy rain is never a pleasant thing."

They ducked through the low door into the dimly lit barracks to be greeted by four men at their supper. The hearth lay at one end of the room under the chimney hole, and there was a trestle table in the middle where the men sat on stools. Two candles were set directly on the table boards among the

drippings of previous candles. They provided the only light.
Five sets of bunks stood against the walls, making a total of
ten beds, seven of which had straw mattresses. Other than
the beds, table, and stools, there were no furnishings, nor
was there room for anything else. The single window was
open to the night, having no glass nor shutters.

"Gentlemen," there was a snickering which Alasdair ignored, "welcome our new friend, Dylan." The lack of a last
name identification was not lost on Dylan. "He's fresh from
the dungeon at Ft. William, so he willnae be sleeping on his
back for a while, now." The mood in the room changed from
wariness to understanding, and a couple of the men nodded.
They each obliged with "*Hallo, a Dhilein*," and Alasdair
asked which bunk was available. One large man with shaggy
black hair and no nose pointed to a set in the far corner, the
only pair with a top bunk empty of personal belongings. Dylan went to deposit his sword and sporran while Alasdair
directed him to help himself to the stew on the fire. There
were wooden cups and spoons stacked on the table. Then he
went to his own supper.

Dylan investigated the stew, and scooped some from the
iron pot. He straddled a stool and sat with the other men,
and smiled amiably before digging in. Mutton. Dylan had
developed a taste for mutton over the past several months,
and this was better than Gracie's. He looked around at the
other men and said, "I thought there would be more of us."

No-nose grunted, then said, "Rob can muster a thousand
men if need be. The retainers amount to about fifty or sixty,
but he keeps us scattered for the sake of safety."

"Ah." Dylan ate some more, then said, "You all got
names?"

They chuckled and grinned, and No-nose said, "Oh, aye.
We're called all sorts of names." Dylan smiled in appreciation of the joke, and No-nose obliged with introductions. He
indicated the dull-looking fellow with reddish-brown hair
across from him, "He's Cailean nan Chasgraidh" *Colin of the
Massacre*. From his age Dylan guessed he was a survivor of
Glencoe. The big one continued, "This fellow over here is
Alasdair Og." *Young Alasdair* was, indeed, very young and
had no beard yet. "That's Seumas Glas." *Pale James* was

pale, but had deep rosettes of pink in his cheeks and a robust build. "I'm known locally as Murchadh Dubh." *Black Murdo*. Dylan hoped he was named for his coloring and not for his personality. He also wondered at the lack of nose.

Murchadh continued, "You'll want to shave that off."

Dylan felt of his beard which, though long enough, had never achieved anything better than a modest cover. He had no idea what it looked like on him, but he could tell the hair was straight and lay flat against his face. "How come?"

"If you've been to the garrison, you've been seen by nearly every Redcoat in the Western Highlands. Shaving will give you a different appearance." Murchadh turned back to his stew. "Besides, that raggedy crop isn't worth the growing."

Dylan scratched his chin and would have said something equally smartass in reply, except that what Murchadh said was true. He did need to change his appearance, and his beard wasn't much to brag about. He asked to borrow a whetting stone, and when one was tossed to him he went to his bunk to sharpen his *sgian dubh*.

Seumas, the only clean-shaven man present, also threw him a copper pot and said, "Go fill this from the well and put it on the fire. Once you've trimmed, the shaving will go easier if you put a hot rag on it first." He spoke as if he were talking to someone who had never shaved before, which for Dylan was just as well. The last time he had shaved, it was with aerosol cream and a disposable safety razor. He did as he was told.

Out by the well, he glanced over at the front of the stone house where MacGregor and his family lived. Two horses had arrived since sunset, and there were many voices coming from the house. He wondered what was up.

Sinann popped into existence, sitting on the edge of the well. Dylan jumped, startled. "Where have you been?"

"Right here. You didn't need me, and it was plain you did need to not be seen talking to yourself, and were in no condition to apprehend that fact. So I removed temptation and disappeared until you were alone."

Dylan nodded toward the house. "What's going on in there?"

"I've no idea. Care for me to find out?"

He nodded. Knowledge was power, and if there might be a way to not lose next year it would be his knowledge of the situation that would change things. "Tell me what you can. I need to know more if I'm going to do any good in the uprising."

She smiled. "I'm proud of you, lad. I knew you'd come around."

He did not reply, but returned to the barracks with his pot of water and a creepy feeling in his gut.

While the water heated on the stove, Dylan trimmed his beard as close as he could without cutting himself. Then he sharpened the knife again until he was satisfied it might not shred his face. He pressed the towel dunked in hot water against what was left of his beard until the edge was off the heat, then began to shave. It wasn't as difficult as he'd thought it would be. He cut himself only once, just at first, but then got the hang of holding the knife correctly. The beard came off and left his face bare for the first time in ten months. Then, while he was at it, he whacked the ends of his hair to get them off his shoulders.

He pulled off his shirt and washed it with the remaining hot water in the pot, wrung it out, and hung it to dry from the edge of the overhead bunk. It was irretrievably blood-stained, and he detested the ruffles, but it would have to do until he could have a new one made.

The next morning Dylan awoke stiff and sore, as he had every day since his arrest. Three days of walking after his illness had done him little more good than to let him know he wasn't likely to die. His feet were sore and his left calf didn't want to flex. He sat at the edge of his bunk and tried to point his toe, but could get it only halfway there. If he was ever going to be worth anything to anyone again, he needed to loosen up those muscles. It was time to resume his workouts.

At least, he needed to work out some of the worst kinks. One thing about Glen Dochart was that it had more level ground than any glen Dylan had yet seen in Scotland. In the flat area between the barracks and the house, he began at dawn with his sword at his side, stretching, moving, concentrating. The scabbed-over skin of his back was tight, and each movement of his arms pulled at it. He moved slowly, lest any of the wounds reopen. Carefully, he retraced the patterns he'd known so well for so long. He began the painful process of reclaiming the body—and the soul as well—they'd tried to take from him at Ft. William.

He heard a muttering nearby, familiar to him now as the sound of eighteenth-century Scottish people witnessing for the first time an Asian form of fight training. He ignored it, but saw Murchadh circle behind him and knew the challenge was coming. Still concentrating on his form, he hoped his leg was up to what would come next.

Sure enough, the big Scot grabbed him from behind, in a bear hug. Dylan flipped him with very little effort, though his back protested the abuse. The Scot landed on his back, looking up at Dylan with a dazed expression. "How did you do that?"

"Magic." He took a relaxed stance, left foot forward, with his weight on his bent right leg, arms hanging loose at his sides. He was ready for Murchadh to get up and come at him again. "Didn't Rob tell you I was saved from the English by the wee folk?" He heard Sinann giggle, but couldn't see her and couldn't spare the time to look around.

Murchadh stood and pulled a knife. Dylan sighed. He'd had quite enough blood lately to last him awhile. He refrained from drawing Brigid, figuring he could take the guy without any trouble. He dropped to a horse stance and began a move called circling fists, leaning from one side to the other, then back. Like the mulinette with a sword, it was to confuse and misdirect.

Murchadh circled, and Dylan turned with him, until the big Scot made a lunge. Dylan sidestepped, grabbed the extended knife hand with both of his, pulled, and twisted, which brought Murchadh off-balance and to his knees. The knife dropped to the sod, and Dylan shoved his opponent onto his back with his foot to pin him and keep the arm extended. His left leg ached with his weight, but Murchadh was defeated without blood.

"Let me up."

Dylan turned the man's thumb back some more, to let

him know he was serious. The thumb was strong and he had
to pull hard. Murchadh should have been groaning, but he
made no sound and his mouth only trembled. Dylan said,
"Back away. I don't want to hurt you."

"Aye. You'll have nae trouble from me. I swear it."

Dylan let him up, and their employer's voice rose from
the gathered onlookers. "Might we see what the lad can do
with a sword?" He stepped out, a big smile on his face.

"If it pleases you." Dylan drew his sword.

"Try Seumas, then. He's our best."

Seumas stepped into the clear. A sword was tossed to him,
and he immediately went *en garde* and circled with a big
grin on his face. Dylan saw that Seumas's sword was an old
claybeg that had once been an even older claymore cut down
to become a shorter, one-handed weapon. Due to the outsized
tang—the part of the blade inside the hilt—it would be clum-
sier and less well balanced than Dylan's broadsword. But it
was still small enough to be fast and heavy enough to do a
great deal of damage if Seumas had a hit. Dylan wasn't sure
what the rules of engagement were here, and so had no intention of letting that blade anywhere near him for a touch.

He stood in a hanging guard, left foot leading, weight on
his right foot and his sword held over his head with the tip
dropped. His idea was to invite attack and see how his opponent moved, thought, and felt. Seumas attacked fast and
Dylan found himself parrying frantically, retreating, until he
sidestepped like a matador and, overbalanced, Seumas went
blundering past. Dylan couldn't resist smacking him on the
ass with the flat of his blade on his way. Then he faced on
again to take the next assault. Seumas laughed at his own
expense, then set his teeth to attack.

Dylan's arm began to tire; this was happening too soon
after his illness. Breathing came hard. He knew he had to
win quickly or risk injury. He began a series of forays that
were high, leaving his lower right quadrant vulnerable. Seumas took the bait right away, and attacked low. Dylan, ready
for it, parried and captured Seumas's blade against the
ground, then stomped on it to disarm. The claybeg whapped
against the grass, Dylan grabbed Seumas by the shirt front,
and held the broadsword blade to his throat.

"Yield! I yield!" Seumas still grinned, though he sounded like he thought Dylan would cut him. Dylan wondered how much danger he'd really been in and how much damage Seumas would have done if he could. He let go and picked up the claybeg to restore it to his opponent.

There was applause from the onlookers, and Rob shouted, "*Seo Dilean Mac a'Chlaidheimh!*" Here is Dylan, Son of the Sword!

Dylan laughed, and figured there were worse things he could be called. Some of the onlookers repeated the name, "Mac a'Chlaidheimh," and seemed to think it fitting. Seumas gave him a huge smile and a hearty slap on the back. Dylan's face went gray with pain, but he gritted his teeth in a smile just the same.

As the crowd dispersed, Rob and Alasdair stood in conference. Then Alasdair yelled for Dylan, Seumas, and Murchadh, who presented themselves. "Come, we've business to attend to. Get rations from Mary, collect your gear, and meet behind the house." It sounded like they were going on a trip.

CHAPTER 19

Dylan realized it would be a long trip when he acquired and hefted his ration bag of oatmeal.

The men went to the barracks for their gear, and Dylan mourned the loss of the coat he'd left at the *Tigh*. He hoped he could get a new one before winter. The ration sack of oatmeal went into his sporran, his baldric over his shoulder, and he was ready. Alasdair and Rob awaited them behind the house, then the five of them struck out over the hills to the south.

There was no word as to where they were headed, and no indication of what their business was. Dylan didn't ask. He walked along in silence with the others. At night they slept in a heat-conserving huddle, wrapped in their plaids. In the mornings they ate globs of cold oatmeal from their hands. Once Alasdair shot a grouse, which they shared. The terrain here was more wooded than up north, and gradually the trail became less steep. On the third day they crested a hill and through the trees Dylan saw an immense stretch of low hills. The mountains had given way to the Lowlands. It had been a long time since he'd seen a horizon this wide. They descended.

The men still avoided worn tracks and roads, and wended their way across farms and between the hills. On the fifth day out they approached a farm, with the stealth of a hunter stalking his prey. Ahead was a herd of shaggy, black cattle. Rob counted them and relayed the information to Alasdair. Then they faded back and circled to another herd, which was also counted.

Dylan began to wonder why Rob needed four extra men on this job. Surely one or two could have counted cattle as well as five. And two would have traveled less conspicuously. But on the sixth day his unasked question was answered. They approached a small cottage, this time not with stealth. The five of them walked to the door where they were greeted by a barking dog and a middle-aged woman.

When she saw Rob her hard, lined face lit up in tearful joy. She welcomed him with a hug, and invited them all to hurry inside. The men ducked through the door to stand just inside while Rob moved away into the room by the hearth to speak to the woman. The conversation was low and brief. The woman carried on, trying not to cry but failing to keep the tears from her face and her voice. Then Rob reached into his sporran and produced a leather drawstring pouch. From it he counted silver coins into the woman's hand. She fell silent, her other hand over her mouth. Tears pooled on it. Rob closed the money into her fist, kissed her cheek, and turned to leave.

Just as they were all about to duck out the door, Rob turned back to the woman and said, "Be certain you get a receipt for the full rent. Dinnae let them leave here without giving you a receipt." She nodded, and they left.

The five of them went about half a mile down the track from the cottage, and there Rob called a halt. He gestured to an oak tree with branches that spread over the trail, and Alasdair set to climbing it. Once settled in a solid crotch, the man reached for the flintlock pistols in his belt to begin priming them. The other four retreated to a position on the other side of the track, in a fern thicket shaded by oak and pine. There they sat on the side of a slope and waited.

It was a long wait. Nobody spoke. Dylan's left leg began to ache, but he closed his eyes and concentrated on more pleasant things. Cait. He wondered what she was doing at that very moment. In Edinburgh, by now, and married to that . . .

He shook his head to clear the anger that rose. This was not the time to be distracted. It wasn't clear to him yet what was afoot here, but it figured that Rob had brought his two best swordsmen and his most skilled marksman on this cattle-counting foray for a reason.

Two or three hours after they hid—Dylan estimated by the progress of the sun—there was the sound of horses approaching, headed toward the cottage. The men waited, and let them pass. Once the horses had gone on their way, the four came out of the thicket. In a low voice Rob consulted Alasdair in the tree.

"How many?"

"Two. Armed with swords only. Perhaps dirks, as well." *Probably* dirks, as well, was Dylan's opinion. But no guns was a good thing.

Rob said, "Seumas Glas, Murchadh, behind this tree. Mac a'Chlaidheimh, come with me." Dylan had a moment's pause at his new name, then followed orders. They hid themselves behind a tree about fifteen yards down the trail. There they waited again, but for a much shorter time.

The horses returned from the cottage at the same casual pace as on their approach. The men were deep in discussion, in English, about where the woman could have gotten the money for her rent on the very day that had been set for her eviction. It was plain they were scandalized and disappointed, and thus were not paying attention to their surroundings.

They were even more scandalized and disappointed when Rob stepped out from behind the far tree, pistol drawn, followed by Dylan who drew his sword. The mounted men pulled up short. Alasdair dropped from the tree behind, and shouted a warning to the riders. They turned, saw Alasdair's two pistols as well as Seumas and Murchadh with their swords, and cursed. Dylan took his cues from the other swordsmen, who approached the riders with their weapons extended. For either horseman to have dismounted in any direction would have put him on the point of a broadsword. "MacGregor—"

Rob said, "Hand it over."

The man Rob spoke to was heavy-set to the point of pudginess, and wore a fanciful outfit of plum damask and velvet, plus a hat adorned with feathers that swished with every move. Living in the Highlands since his arrival had kept Dylan insulated from English fashion of the day. Though he'd seen such costumes in movies, he was quite stunned to see men wearing them in public and in seriousness. He shook his head and realized there were still many things about this century that struck him as utterly ridiculous. "Hand what?" said the Lowlander.

"Never mind the pretending. I know you've got it, so hand it over. Move smartly, and I'll let ye live. Not that ye dinnae deserve to die in any case."

The pudgy man sighed, then reached into his coat pocket for his purse.

"The rent money, you dunderhead. *And* the purse, if you please."

The other man was small and quiet, but watchful. Dylan kept an eye on him and watched his hands. The horses, shining specimens of a wealthy stable, high-strung purebreds, champed on polished bits and fidgeted.

Again the pudgy man cursed, and reached into a saddlebag for the silver. He threw both bags to Rob, who then pointed his pistol at the smaller man.

"And yourself?"

Palms raised indicated a lack of purse, but Dylan stepped closer and poked his sword under the edge of the man's waistcoat. The little one glanced at him and uttered a single word in such a vile tone, Dylan figured he was as well off not knowing what it meant. The other purse was handed over to Rob.

Rob hefted it in his hand and grinned. "I thank ye. Dinnae try to follow us, or your heads'll be blown off by my marksman friend here," he gestured to Alasdair, "and sent back to Montrose in a sack. Good day, Gentlemen." With that, he motioned for his men to follow him. They all scabbarded their swords to bolt into the woods.

It was not a stroll they took, getting away from Montrose's rent collectors. Making their way through the thickest parts of the forest and up steep slopes in order to elude pursuit on horseback, they ran when they could and crashed through foliage when they couldn't. Rob pushed them on, and when Dylan thought his leg would fold he pushed them farther.

Finally they were allowed to rest in a clearing well north of the cottage. Dylan leaned on his knees to gulp breath, and listened to the others' laughter and elated chatter of the rent they'd snatched from Montrose. The pain in his leg crept to his thigh, and he ran his fingers into his legging to massage his calf. Alasdair saw and said, "Are ye hurt, lad?"

Lips pressed together, Dylan shook his head. He looked around at the group and said, "Are you sure we shouldn't put a few more miles between ourselves and those men?"

The others laughed, and there was no more talk about Dylan's leg, which was fine with him.

What they'd just done began to sink in, and a genuine smile crept to his face. This was better than playing Robin Hood as a kid. Better than sparring without protection. This was having the freedom to put one's very life on the edge and win. He'd almost died at the hands of the Redcoats, and now, with his twentieth-century American sense of safety obliterated, he was exhilarated by the contest. He nearly laughed at the thought that Major Bedford might have created the Crown's worst enemy.

The following morning they struck out for Glen Dochart.

The day after their return was spent in prosaic pursuits. Dylan and the others were occupied with repairs on equipment and weapons, repairs on their clothing, cooking meals, and other things their wives might have done if they'd had any present. Dylan, Seumas, and Murchadh told and retold the story of the robbery, to the delighted audience of Cailean and Alasdair Og, who envied them the exploit.

Rob and Alasdair Roy were occupied throughout the day with the meeting that was now in full swing in the stone house. Quite a number of men had gathered there, and the men outside once or twice heard angry shouting. Dylan went to the well again for a conference with Sinann, who took her sweet time appearing. He was about to give up and go back to the barracks when she finally blinked into view.

"What's going on in there, Tink?"

"It's a row, and if it gets any worse they're like to kill each other."

"I can hear that much from the bunkhouse. Why are all those men here?"

"It's a meeting of the leaders of Clan Gregor. Archibald of Kilmanan, their chieftain, has died, and left no clear heir. Succession would dictate the chiefship go to Iain Og of Glencairnig, but it's the Queen's pension they're after. Her Majesty being in the habit of paying Jacobite chieftains to keep them quiet, they want the next chieftain to be . . . eligible. Iain Og cannot come out as a supporter of James; it would hurt his business concerns. But the pension is three hundred and sixty English pounds a year and the clan is not wealthy. They're electing a new chieftain who will bring the money to the MacGregors."

"Is Rob in the running?"

She gave him a withering look that condemned his stupidity. "Dinnae be daft. He's an outlaw. Not that he wouldnae be the best choice, from what I've seen in that house today. The clan would do well to have a man such as Himself leading them."

"So who do you think will get it?"

She shrugged. "I dinnae know that I care."

Dylan grunted, took his drink, and went back into the barracks.

The next day Sinann reported that Alasdair of Balhaldie had been elected chieftain, and that he would split the Queen's pension between the other claimants. For the next month it seemed the MacGregor clan would go on as it always had and that Rob's men putting their thorn in the side of Montrose would proceed, business as usual.

Dylan learned the ins and outs of Rob's protection racket, in which money was required of landowners who did not wish to have their cattle taken. It was called "blackmail," but without the evil connotation the word would have three hundred years hence. "Mail" meant rent, and, unlike the rackets run by gangsters, those who took money for the protection of cattle also guaranteed the safety of kine from other reivers. If a farmer under Rob's protection lost cattle to someone else,

Rob and his men went after them and either recovered the *spréidhe* or made good on the loss. Twice that summer Dylan went with his employer to hunt down cattle stolen from clients, and every head was recovered and returned to its owner.

There was another foray south. This time the men of Rob's immediate complement met with those from other parts of Campbell territory, and a raid was made on one of Montrose's properties near Stirling. Dylan estimated a hundred or so head of cattle were taken, and driven into the Highlands to be scattered and hidden.

The work wasn't quite as exciting as highway robbery, but was a mite less dangerous. It was the skilled planning of Rob and his lieutenants, such as Alasdair Roy, that kept the parties one step ahead of pursuit.

Summer was high when a gillie on horseback tore into Rob's dooryard, shouting. The young clansman leapt from his mount as the men emerged from the barracks and Rob and his family came out of the stone house to gape at what they were hearing. Dylan was as affected by the news as everyone else, though he had known all along it would come soon: Queen Anne had died the week before.

He went to the well for a conference with Sinann. When she appeared, it was with wide, frightened eyes. "I told you, Tink," he said.

"Aye, ye did."

"I can't change history. Now George will come from Hanover, totally clueless, and for the next thirty years the Jacobites will resist because he will leave the Jacobite Lairds no choice. His blundering will make them think they can succeed. A lot of people are going to die."

Anger clouded Sinann's eyes. "And how many will die if we dinnae resist?"

Dylan thought of Ft. William, of the men who had wanted to kill him out of hatred for all Scots, and wondered.

Men came and went from the stone house. For weeks the meetings were daily. Another raid was made, this time near Kippen, a little closer to home than Stirling. Rob didn't come on that trip, and the men were led by Alasdair Roy. The two oldest of Rob's four sons, James and Coll who were teenagers, came as well. It was Coll's first raid. The other sons,

Duncan and Ronald, were too young yet to participate in a *creach*, and stayed in Glen Dochart with their mother. Dylan did his job, earned his six pence a day, and watched the next uprising foment around him.

There was plenty of talk at night about the "Wee German Lairdie" that had come to occupy the throne of England, who spoke no English and had no idea why the Scots weren't getting along with their southern neighbors. His advisors let him remain ignorant, and his appointments systematically excluded anyone suspected of Jacobite sympathies. Disaffection among the Scottish aristocracy was rampant.

Late in the summer Dylan went with Alasdair Roy to collect mails from some particularly reluctant clients near Kingshouse. It was Alasdair's job to convince them to cooperate, and Dylan's role was to help Alasdair keep his hide intact by watching his back. Rob sent on this trip the minimum number of men required for this sort of job. Enough to give the appearance of confidence rather than brute strength. Yet the imagination of the clients aided them. In their meetings they tended to glance around, wondering where the rest of Rob's men were. Dylan would stand a bit back from Alasdair to keep an eye on the surroundings, subtle in his scrutiny, as if he weren't really paying attention. This gave the appearance of complacency that could only be interpreted by the client in one way. More of Roy's men must be hiding just beyond the trees or rocks nearby. It was only a guess as to how many had been brought to coerce the payment of mail. Thus each cattle owner paid without argument. Two days passed without incident.

But on the third day, while walking a track at the bottom of a glen near Kingshouse, Dylan and Alasdair were taken by surprise as they came around one of the many large boulders rising from the ground in that area. Two English cavalrymen lurking behind the stone rode down on them, demanding they halt and surrender their weapons. "Alasdair Roy!" one of them shouted.

Alasdair swore and reached for his pistols, but hesitated as both soldiers set their guns to their shoulders, already well-aimed. The range was almost point-blank. The soldiers grinned. Alasdair glared.

Dylan's heart galvanized. Letting himself be taken alive wasn't an option. Without a moment's thought, he ducked his head and spun in a high back roundhouse kick, striking the nearest horse on the muzzle. The surprised animal reared and neighed, backing away. The equally surprised soldiers had no idea what had just happened. They both fired. One musket ball flew wide and the other tugged at Dylan's shirt-sleeve then threw up a puff of dust in the trail.

Left with bayonets and swords, the soldiers slung their muskets and drew swords. But Dylan and Alasdair were already off and running. They scrambled up the steep hill to the north, which became ever more steep and craggy. The English horses weren't up to the climb, and the soldiers were forced to dismount to give chase. But Rob Roy's men knew the mountains well, and were Highlanders conditioned for travel on foot. One of the soldiers stopped to reload his musket, but by the time he got off a shot his quarry had ducked between two stones and zagged off into a patch of woods that gave cover as it took them behind another hill.

It was several miles, though, before Alasdair and Dylan stopped their flight. They were almost to Glen Dochart, well inside the territory of Iain Glas. So they stopped to rest for the night before going home.

They found a patch of heather between two boulders, wound themselves in their plaids, and lay down on it. Neither had said a word since the near disaster. But just as Dylan was about to drop off to sleep Alasdair muttered, "That was an ingenious move ye made, lad."

Dylan said only, "Aye." He was too angry at Sinann for letting the soldiers get the drop on him to talk to anyone but her. But he didn't dare have that particular argument in front of Alasdair. He wasn't even sure where she was. Probably hiding from the chewing out she knew must be coming.

Alasdair continued, "It's a strange sort of fighting. Like French, but only just. What is it?"

This was not Dylan's favorite subject. It came too close to areas of his existence he couldn't explain. But he said, "I learned it in the colonies. It comes from the East Indies. I've been studying most of my life."

Alasdair grunted in understanding. After a moment's

pause, he said, "You've a powerful hatred for the English, for a colonial with nae parents nor children kilt by them."

Dylan hesitated before answering, then adjusted the plaid around him and said, "I would have a family if not for them. I was to have married. But then I was arrested." Memories of last spring flooded him, and he sighed and pulled his plaid tighter. "Her name was Caitrionagh. I would have given my life for her."

Alasdair's voice went soft. "Is she dead, then?"

"No. After my arrest she was married off by her father to someone else."

"Does she ken where you are?"

"No."

"Does she care for you still, do ye think?"

There was a long pause before Dylan answered, then he said softly, "I hope so."

In October the cattle which had been lifted that summer from Montrose's lands were driven to Crieff, where herds from all over the Lowlands and southern Highlands were brought to market. When Dylan saw the little town, bursting at the seams with drovers and cattle—and the King's troops dotted everywhere like maraschino cherries in a fruit salad— he was reminded of Western films he'd seen of cattle drives with acres of land covered with caterwauling beasts. The main difference here was that the drovers were on foot rather than horseback, many wore kilts, and all spoke a dizzying mixture of Gaelic, Lowland Scots, French, and English.

The presence of the King's troops was overpowering. It gave Dylan the creeps to see so many of the red-coated bastards, putting their noses into everything they saw. He avoided them when he could, and prayed he wouldn't run into one that would recognize him from up north.

Watching the herd shortly after they arrived, Dylan and Seumas sat idly on a low stone dike that ran along a lane into the town proper. Dylan picked some pieces from the crumbling wall and tried to juggle them, but failed to keep them from banging each other. Over and over again he picked the rocks up off the ground, and tried again. Then he saw a clutch of Redcoats coming and put his gaze on the ground and the rocks back on the wall.

As the soldiers passed, Seumas greeted them with a big smile and a Gaelic vulgarism, which caused them to stop. Dylan's first urge was to throttle Seumas, his second to get the hell out of there. But he stayed put, wanting a chase even less than a hassle.

One of the soldiers said to Seumas, "What's your name?"

Still grinning, Seumas said, "I be of the Clan Murray, if it please ye. Or even if it dinnae." Dylan shot a glance at Seumas, relieved he at least had enough sense to not give his real name. Seumas was a MacGregor, but for two hundred years none of the clan had used the name south of the Highland line, the very name having been outlawed by the Crown over one misappropriated cow during the sixteenth century. Rob called himself Campbell, his mother's maiden name, and even the MacGregor chieftains used aliases to outsiders.

The soldier then turned to Dylan. "You?"

Dylan raised his gaze, and looked the Redcoat in the eye. He cleared his throat and said, "Dilean Mac a'Chlaidheimh."

That brought raised eyebrows from the Englishmen. The one speaking said, "I've never heard of that particular clan." He turned to his fellows. "They breed like rats up there, so now they've had to start new clans, eh?" That brought laughter from the other soldiers, then the speaker said to Dylan, "See that you tykes behave while you're here, right? And show a proper reverence."

Seumas was still grinning and gave a nod. "Aye, proper, indeed."

The soldiers went on their way, and Dylan socked Seumas in the arm. Seumas just laughed as he rubbed it.

Once the herd was sold and the drovers paid, Dylan took the opportunity, while in relative civilization, to buy himself a new coat. He'd replaced that damned ruffled shirt months ago. The cloth from the English shirt now functioned for him as a face bandanna and a money pouch, both items sewn for him by Mary MacGregor and dyed dark green for the sake of camouflage. His new coat was sheepskin, and in the end was cheaper than his old wool one because the fashion of the day was not for leather. A wool coat, smartly cut, would have cost him twice as much as the far warmer sheepskin.

While he was at it, he bought a new pair of leggings, for the old ones had never been quite the same after the bloody hole shot in the left leg. The new pair was warmer and fit him better, having been cut for him rather than poor Alasdair Matheson. His shoes, he decided, were all right for now, though the rubber on the soles was a mite thin and the insoles had been history for months. They'd last him another winter, then he would replace them with brogues of this century, which were entirely leather and made to fit more like moccasins than shoes. He didn't look forward to wearing shoes with no arch support, but would eventually have to.

On his way back to the empty field where his comrades were camped, he passed a high stone dike between two houses. Loud, raucous laughter rose from behind it, and Dylan thought there might be another cockfight going on. He'd happened past two others that week, and had stopped to watch, but found the sight of chickens killing each other less than entertaining.

However, this hilarity lacked the intensity of men betting on birds. It sounded more like anger than friendly competition. He was compelled to look. There he found a cluster of kilted men he knew to be of Clan Donald, with a jug of whiskey and a *quaiche* they passed between them, having fun at the expense of a man in breeches who spoke English with a Lowland accent. Dylan's skin crawled at hearing the language, as it had since his escape from Ft. William.

The Lowlander pulled himself to as full a height as he could, and in a voice of smug authority said, "And ye'll hand over that jug as well."

That brought a shout of fresh laughter from the drovers. One of them, his speech slurred by a great deal of whiskey already consumed, said, "Because the wee German Lairdie needs the money? Am I to be so concerned with the coffers of that bloody foreigner?" Dylan guessed that the Lowlander was a tax man attempting to collect on the jug of whiskey, what Dylan's more immediate ancestors would have called a "revenuer." The MacDonald drover continued, "I suppose it would bruise his wee feelings for us to not pay tax on our own whiskey."

The speaker was passed the cup, and he took a heavy

swallow. He addressed his comrades. "D'ye know what I'm thinking, lads? I think this here Whig is remiss in not drinking to the health of the true King, is what." He leaned into the Lowlander's face. "And such a social blunder for one so high up in the government as he is!" The laughter rolled, and Dylan found himself chuckling.

Only then did the excise man seem to realize his office held no water with these men, and his eyes began to shift with an inkling of fear. He took a step back, perhaps thinking of retreat, but one Highlander grabbed the back of his coat and another held a dirk to his neck. The one with the cup in his hand said, "Here, man, mind your manners and drink to the health of King James VIII."

The Lowlander tried to twist free, but the Highlanders held him and wrestled him to his knees in front of the man with the cup. On his knees, he protested weakly, but he was far outnumbered and surrounded by men armed to the teeth. "Say it," said the MacDonald.

The tax man mumbled, "To the health of James."

"His Majesty, James VIII, the true King," came the impatient prompt.

"To the health of His Majesty, James VIII, the true King." The cup was thrust in his face and he took a sip of whiskey. Then, almost too fast to see, the one with the dirk cut off the man's ear. The Whig screamed and crouched as blood ran between his fingers. Dylan flinched. But at the same time he thought of the government this pompous, stupid man represented, which had held Dylan prisoner without cause and covered his back with deep, knotted scars he would bear for the rest of his life. Something primal inside him cheered the blood.

The excise man was allowed to flee, followed by the hilarity of the Highlanders, and his ear was tossed after him. Dylan wasn't laughing, but neither was he sorry. He hoped the Whig would tell his story to other Lowlanders and Englishmen, who would then, perhaps, be a mite more respectful of the northerners.

Dylan returned to Rob's crew, camped down the high road a piece. He cut across a plowed field then scaled a dike to get to the field where the now-sold Montrose *spréidhe* had been. Their fire was shielded by the dikes and a few trees clustered at the edge of the field, where the smoke dissipated in the branches overhead. Most of the men were scattered about the large fire, eating slabs of mutton cut from a spitted carcass. Talk was loud and high-spirited, and a small cluster of drovers was gathered around a chess game. Dylan slipped Brigid from his legging to cut himself some meat, then found a spot on the ground next to a dike to eat it. He wiped the grease from his blade onto his kilt, then slipped her into the scabbard.

There was a lull in the talk and he said, "Some MacDonald drovers just cut the ear off a gadger up the road a ways." He tore off a bite of mutton. A *quaiche* of ale came his way, and he drank as well.

News of the ear-cutting was greeted with excitement and approval. Seumas asked, "Did he bleed well?"

Dylan swallowed. "Like a stuck pig. Screamed like a woman, too."

The MacGregors laughed, and a few crude comments about effeminate Lowlanders were muttered among the men. Rob asked, "Does he yet live?"

Dylan nodded. "They let him go and he ran." He took another bite of his supper.

Murchadh climbed into the field, over the dike on the tree side, then turned to help a young woman climb over after him. The men went silent. Murchadh called out to the twenty or so men present, "Who's next?" He gestured to Rob and continued, "I mean, them as have nae wives close at hand." Rob chuckled into his ale.

The woman looked around for a fresh volunteer and, finding none, made disappointed noises and stamped her foot. The pocket full of coins under her skirts jingled, and Dylan gathered Murchadh had been the last of the clients to be serviced that evening. It seemed each man had already had a turn. But then the whore caught sight of Dylan, and cried joyously in English, "Come, lad! Put yerself in my hands. I'll take good care o' ye!" She snatched up her skirts and showed him an ankle as if that were supposed to make him hot.

Danged if it didn't catch his interest, too. He smiled at

himself, he who had been raised in an era where nearly-naked women were everywhere, catching sight of a bare ankle and a dirty foot and his blood quickening at what else might be found under there.

He shook his head at himself and his hormones, swallowed the last of his mutton, and washed it down with the ale. Paid, fed, clothed, and on his way to a good night's sleep, he was in a cheerful mood. But he knew better than to curl up with a woman he knew was exposed to every communicable disease to be had among Rob's less than fastidious drovers.

Particularly Murchadh, whose lack of nose Dylan had learned was the result of what they called "the French pox," which he guessed was syphilis. Murchadh was in the stage when sores popped up in nasty places. Everyone knew he would eventually go insane and die. In this century, long before the advent of antibiotics, syphilis was as deadly, as ugly a death, and as incurable as AIDS would be in his own time.

And even if not for that, there was Cait always on his mind. No matter how well his body might respond to the whore, she wasn't clean, she wasn't Cait, and he wasn't about to take her up on the offer.

The woman, who was youngish and not bad-looking, picked up her skirts again and came to him. She flounced onto the ground at his feet and leaned toward him between his knees. Her bright red hair was somewhat the worse for wear from her earlier business exchanges, and much of it dangled around her face in limp curls and strings. In the past/future he'd seen photos of high-fashion models and movie starlets at awards ceremonies with that look, but here it wasn't a fashion statement and only meant sloppiness. She cooed, "Come on, big fellow. Come show us what yer made of."

Dylan pulled in one foot, leaving only his left knee up, and was glad his *feileadh mór* had enough folds to fall loose over his legs and hide his reaction to the girl. He looked around at the other men, who were waiting to hear his reply. Most of them knew about Cait, but he didn't figure they thought he would ever see her again. He knew they expected him to climb over the dike to dally under the trees with the whore.

He shook his head again. "Thank you, no." Not having seen a napkin since leaving the *Tigh*, he wiped mutton grease from his lower lip with the back of his hand, and wished this woman would go away. While his mind knew he would never go with her, his body had other ideas and he was more glad by the minute for the folds in his kilt.

One of the men said, "He's waiting for the next meeting of the Beggar's Benison." Laughter rolled among the men, and Dylan bit his lip. He knew little about the Beggar's Benison, beyond that it was an elite sex club in Edinburgh.

Another drover made a comment about "solitary vice," and Dylan felt his ears warm. Not that every man here didn't deal with frustration in private once in a while, but nobody wanted to admit it, not even twentieth-century, enlightened Dylan. That much about human nature would never change.

"Nae, it's one of these he's wanting." Seumas threw something floppy, which landed on Dylan's face with a cold splat. Dylan pulled it off and found it was a condom made of a sheep's intestine. "I used it but once," Seumas promised.

Dylan flung the thing back, and wiped his face with his sleeve. "No, thank you. I must decline. But I appreciate the thoughtful gesture." There was more chortling from the men, and Dylan found it harder to ignore.

The girl whimpered with disappointment, then smiled at him, revealing she had all her front teeth. Dylan had come to appreciate good teeth these days, since so few people here were able to keep theirs much past adolescence. His body responded, and he found himself smiling at her. She giggled and put a hand on his leg. He groaned and tried to forget it had been six months since he'd last been with a woman, and seven months before that waiting for Cait.

Then the whore reached under his kilt and squealed at what she found. He tried to scoot away, but was already against the stone wall behind him. Her eyes went wide and her mouth made a perfectly round O. "Aye, yer a handful, I'll say!" That tore it. Dylan was angry now, and no longer the least interested in this woman on any level.

Sinann squealed with laughter invisibly nearby.

He kept his voice even, but not without a struggle. "Let go." But she only squeezed harder and found with her thumb the spot that made all his joints go wobbly. He groaned.

It was time to end this. He yanked up his kilt and sark, disengaged her hand and, squeezing it hard enough to make her cringe, said, "What part of *no* did you not understand?" He tossed her hand away from him. Gales of laughter rolled from the men, and Dylan let his clothing back down. The girl climbed to her feet and fled, carrying on in a loud voice about lunatic Highlanders.

Seumas called after her, "Dinnae let it trouble ye, girl, the lad's in love, is all. He'll be over it before long." Then he winked at Dylan, who curled his lip then closed his eyes to wait for the ache to go away.

The following night, the last of the tryst, Rob gathered the men and a keg of whiskey, and led them to the center of town where a large stone cross stood. They made a ragged circle around it, the bung was removed from the keg, and wooden cups filled. The mood was one of celebration. A number of torches lit the square and threw tall shadows against the surrounding buildings. As a church bell tolled midnight, Rob started off with, "To the health of His Majesty, King James VIII." By that, he committed a treasonous act punishable by hanging. They all drank.

Another man raised his *quaiche* and shouted, "Confusion to Montrose!" The gathering cheered and drank to that as well. The toasts went on, and a piper started up. "To Iain Glas of Breadalbane!" shouted another MacGregor drover. The cheering and laughter rose, becoming louder with each toast. Dylan shouted, "Damnation to every Englishman north of the Borderland!" This was greeted with enthusiasm, and the men drank deeply. They could all be hung for this, and Dylan knew if they were caught the hangings would be carried out without delay. But he also knew there were worse things than execution. Besides, this wasn't the first hanging offense he'd committed that year. They'd have to catch him before they could kill him.

The party grew as drovers from other clans joined in and crowded the square. Shouts came from surrounding homes to shut the bloody hell up, but they went ignored as the whiskey flowed, toasts became more outrageous, and the men more cheerful.

"May Argyll be caught buggering George, and hung for treason!"

"To Argyll's nose hair, may it grow strong and healthy!"

"To the boil on Montrose's arse, may *it* grow strong and healthy!"

"May George fall down his garderobe and drown!" Laughter rolled until the men wiped tears from their eyes.

The sound of military drums quelled the hilarity some, for they heralded the approach of English troops. A thrill shot through Dylan, and he wondered if there would be a fight. He was ready for one, and fingered the pommel of his sword. But Rob seized the silence and raised his cup one more time. "To the health of those honest and brave felons what cut out the gadger's ear!" With a roar of approval, the men drank, then fled, scattering in all directions.

Dylan took off down a lane, but before disappearing into the darkened town he looked back to glimpse the red coats of the English army. Hatred, stitched into his bones by pain and bigotry, galvanized him as he made his escape.

CHAPTER 20

S nows came in November, and the raids stopped after one last *creach* on Menteith. Very little moved this time of year, so paid activity was at a minimum for Dylan and his four bunkmates. They stayed in the barracks and were fed well by their employer, but cash flow stopped. Dylan had a few shillings in his purse in addition to his share from the cattle sale. He hung on to his money.

Murchadh and Cailean, who had wives in the Trossachs, went to spend the winter at home, leaving Dylan, Alasdair Og, and Seumas Glas as the barracks' only occupants. The three drifted to the stone house of an evening, for the tradition of *céilidh* was as strong here as anywhere in the Highlands and everyone within walking distance came for talk.

With nothing much to do but talk, every bit of news concerning the Crown and the rise of Jacobite sentiment was hashed and rehashed often. New information was welcomed with excitement, and everyone who approached the house in Glen Dochart was questioned thoroughly for any tidbit. The tidbits were many. Foreclosure was the new Whig pastime. Public expression of support for James was now too common for the treason laws to be enforced. All of Scotland awaited the rise of new Jacobite leaders.

Winter passed, and unrest grew.

Toward the end of February, Dylan was sitting on his
bunk one night, cleaning and sharpening his sword. Not that
it particularly needed either, but there was nothing else to
do. Voices arrived outside the barracks door. He looked up
to see the door open to a blast of snow and wind, and Alasdair Roy let in a young man, whose face gave Dylan a
strange feeling of time displacement.

"Mac a'Chlaidheimh, see the lad gets a blanket and something to eat." Alasdair left before hearing a reply.

"Aye," said Dylan, who now stared. He'd seen that face
before. The newcomer nodded a greeting and found a bunk
empty of blankets to set his gear on. Then Dylan recognized
who it was, set his sword down, and stood. "Robin."

Robin Innis looked, peered across the dim room for a long
moment. When he finally recognized the beardless Dylan his
eyes went wide and he gave a shout of joy. He hurried to
shake his hand, then grabbed him in a huge bear hug. "*A
Dhilein!* You're alive! Thank the Lord! They said you had
died of sickness from the ball in your leg before reaching
the garrison!"

Dylan laughed. "No, I didn't die. The *Sassunaich* only
made me wish for it. What are you doing here?"

Robin glanced around the barracks, "Taking shelter in my
travels, carrying messages for Iain Mór."

Dylan sat on his bunk and gestured for Robin to pull up
a stool. "Tell me, what's the news at *Tigh a' Mhadaidh
Bhàin*?"

Robin took a stool from the table to straddle it, and filled
him in on the deaths in Glen Ciorram over the past year,
among them Marsaili. In a way Dylan was sorry to hear this,
but in another way he was relieved. She'd suffered a long
time. Her surviving children were now orphans. The teenage
daughter now worked in the castle kitchen, replacing a girl
who had married in August. The boy was apprenticed to
Tormod to learn smithing. Two new babies had been born
in Ciorram, one of which survived, and the harvest this year
had been a good one.

The political news was that, though Iain Mór's Sutherland
cousins were Loyalists, everyone expected him to side with
the Jacobites if war should come. Especially since some of

his own land had been taken for imaginary debts. "Also," Robin paused and his voice went low, "I come from Edinburgh with important news for Iain Mór." His tone gave Dylan to believe the news would interest him.

Cait. It was about Cait. Had her husband died? Was she in danger? "What is it?" Dylan's heart leapt in his chest.

Robin hesitated, then said slowly, "The Laird is a grandfather. A wee bairn was born to his daughter, about a month ago."

Dylan's heart seemed to stop, and for a moment he couldn't speak. Then he took a deep breath and managed, "A month ago?"

"The twentieth of January. A big, healthy boy. She's named him Ciaran."

There was a long silence while Dylan let this sink in. January 20 put the baby's conception at the beginning of May. Beltane. Cait hadn't married Ramsay until mid-June, nor even gone to Edinburgh until the end of May. A barely eight-month birth would not only not have produced a big, healthy baby, but in these days of medical ignorance the child most likely would not have lived at all. Ciaran was Dylan's son, beyond doubt. Furthermore, everyone must know it, including Ramsay.

He had to clear his throat to find his voice, then said, "Is she well?"

Robin nodded. "As well as can be expected. She survived her confinement with nae illness, and Ramsay hasnae denounced her publicly. But he doesnae treat her well. Nor does he treat the bairn like a son. He feeds them and shelters them, but his anger is great and his cruelty stops only at the taking of their lives. It's hardly a happy life she has."

A welter of emotions rose in Dylan, and he stood as if to do something. But there was nothing for him to accomplish, so he only fidgeted and paced. A son. He was a father. His beloved Cait was trapped in a home where she and her baby were not welcome. Murderous rage pushed everything else aside, and his one desire was to kill Ramsay.

Robin continued, "He ridicules her in public, and carries on in adultery in their home. And he beats her."

"She should divorce him."

Robin fell silent for a moment, then said, his voice thick with anger, "Shame on you, Dylan, for saying such a thing. Even were the Pope to allow it, which His Holiness most certainly would not, her father would decry it regardless and banish her as a whore. He could never accept his daughter as divorced."

"Ramsay is an adulterer."

Robin's voice went low again. "You know the way of the world, Dylan. Surely I don't have to tell you. . . ." Then he peered at Dylan as if seeing him clearly for the first time. With sudden insight, Robin said, "Stay away from them, Dylan. Ye cannae help."

Dylan turned his anger on Robin and leaned over the table. "He should die. He took them from me. That baby is mine. He's . . ." His voice failed and he straightened. The enormity of the child's existence swept over him like a tidal wave. And the loss came hard on it. Tears rose, but he fought them back. "I'm going to Edinburgh."

Robin stood and grabbed Dylan's sleeve. "No. You cannae. You willnae help anything. All you will do is make things worse for them both. So far Ramsay hasnae declared the baby a bastard, but if you go there he will. He'll have nae choice."

Dylan pulled free and drew on his coat, scabbarded his sword, and threw the baldric over his shoulder. "Good. Then I'll take her back to her father."

"You cannae do that to her. You're not that cruel."

Dylan paused and looked at Robin. "What do you mean?"

"She would be shamed her entire life, were you to do that. And impoverished as well. Surely you know she could-nae live in her father's household with a bastard baby. He'd turn her out. And the child as well."

"He wouldn't. Una wouldn't let him."

Robin nodded. "He would for a certainty, and his wife would have nae say. How could he lead his people if he let his daughter bear a bastard without shame? How could he hold himself up to them as a man of honor and morality?"

Dylan shook his head, thinking the world had tilted again and he'd slipped sideways into another dimension where it could be honorable to disown family. "Excuse me?"

"You heard me."

"This is crazy." Dylan made for the door.

"Dylan!" Robin followed him. "Dinnae be daft! It's night, it's winter, and you've nae provisions! Come back."

But Dylan didn't want to stay. He didn't want to hear any more about false honor, bastard babies, or Cait being hurt. He was going to Edinburgh. He walked into the night, where a buffeting wind tried to knock him sideways.

Sinann popped into sight, hovering just before his face flying backward as he trudged through the snow in a vague southerly direction. "Go back."

"Get lost, Tink."

Robin caught up to him. "Dylan, be reasonable."

"Listen to your friend, Dylan. He's right when he says you would ruin her by going there and claiming the child."

He glared at her. "You knew, didn't you?"

Robin said, "Knew what?"

Sinann said, "I kent naught. How could I have?"

Dylan made a disgusted noise and kept walking. The snow crunched under his feet.

Sinann landed in front of him in an attempt to make him stop, but he neither stopped nor strayed from his course. He forced her to take wing again or be trampled. "You'll die, Dylan! Even if you don't die on the way, they'll kill you when you get there! Then she'll be in greater danger than before, with the bastardy declared by Ramsay!"

"Dylan!" yelled Robin as he fell behind, unwilling to follow in the snowy night.

"Dylan!" yelled Sinann as she hovered before his face. He waved her off like a huge fly, and walked on.

There was a noise, like the breaking of a dead tree limb, and pain shot through his left leg. He let out an inarticulate shout, and collapsed in the snow. "Damn you!" He scooted along in the snow, trying to get away from the pain in his leg. "*Damn you!*" Red Fury and white agony filled him.

"I had to do it, lad," she said.

"Get away from me. Just get away from me!"

Robin hesitated as he was about to help Dylan to his feet. Seumas, Rob, James, Coll, and Alasdair Roy came from the stone house to see what was the matter. Robin knelt beside Dylan. "What happened?"

Dylan fell back in the snow and let out a bellow of pain and frustration that echoed from the surrounding snow-covered slopes.

The other men helped him back to the barracks, and onto his bunk. Lacking a blacksmith to set the bone, which Dylan considered a blessing, they splinted his shin tight. Sinann told him she'd given him a clean break, and Dylan didn't bother to thank her for the favor. Alasdair gave him enough whiskey to dull the pain, then the men left him to mutter in his sleep about the fucking *Sidhe* and what they could do with their damned faeries and *oh, please, God help them, God help them, God help them. . . .*

For the rest of the winter he recovered from his broken leg and from the shock of the news. Slowly he came to understand why it was so important he not claim the baby. As an outlaw wanted for treason, murder, and robbery, he could never give Cait and her child any amount of security. Their lives would be almost as endangered as his if he tried to keep them with him. He also knew that after the battle at Sheriffmuir they would be safest with someone politically close to the Crown and the Privy Council as Ramsay was. As bad a husband as Ramsay might be, he was still Cait's best bet for making it through the coming persecutions without starving. Misery was just slightly better than death, but it was still better.

In mid-April he began to walk without a crutch as the snows receded. While working out one morning, sparring with Seumas Glas, Seumas assured him that once James took his rightful place as king, they would all be pardoned and Dylan could claim his son.

Before he could stop himself, Dylan laughed and stood down as panic tried to take him. He turned in place and gazed for a moment at the surrounding mountains to compose himself. Seumas gave him a funny look, but Dylan couldn't tell him what he knew.

Seumas guessed what Dylan was thinking, though. "You believe we will fail?"

Dylan plundered his memory for what he knew that he

could tell. "Jacobite leadership is weak. There are no generals who can lead."

"There is the Duke of Berwick, King James's half brother."

Dylan shook his head. "He's a Marshal of France, and France has signed a treaty with the Crown, promising they won't give us aid. Berwick won't do it. Many Western Highland clans have sided with George. . . ."

Seumas's jaw dropped. "No! They can't have!"

Oops, had that happened yet? Dylan only knew it was sometime this year. He quickly backpedaled. "If they haven't yet, they will. I'm sure of it. Campbell of Argyll, especially, you know it. And that leaves nobody with the battle skills for leading the uprising."

"I hope you're wrong."

Dylan only wished he could be, for it would be that very weakness of experienced battle leadership that would lose them Sheriffmuir.

The leg healed well, leaving Dylan with only a slight dull ache during wet weather. Which, in this part of the world, was pretty much all the time. But he could use the leg, with only a slight limp. Sinann pointed out she might have broken the good one but chose the one that had been shot. He only looked sideways at her.

Cattle raids began as soon as the snows left, and Dylan joined them in late May. Robbing Montrose's rent collectors became more common, as well, and other political targets lost their purses along the way. Dylan became quite adept at the routine he called "Stand and Deliver."

On one such foray in late summer, not far from Glen Dochart, he, Alasdair Roy, Seumas, James, and Coll waylaid some soldiers transporting guns and swords near Callander. Word was, the English were on their way to Ft. William with dispatches as well as arms. Though the weaponry was the excuse for the robbery, the dispatches were as important to Rob.

There were six men on horseback, five uniformed and one civilian, and two *garrons* loaded with crates. The trail was narrow, with a steep, loamy slope to one side and a river to the other. Alasdair stepped onto the trail from behind a tree and stopped the procession by brandishing his guns, and the others surrounded the horses with their swords. The soldier leading the pack horses reached for his musket, and Seumas threw his dirk hard, striking him through the back. He struggled for a moment, eyes wide and hands grappling for the weapon, until his eyes glazed over. He slumped, and was silent. Moments later, blood began to drip from the hem of his red coat onto his saddle. While the Redcoat was dying, Seumas went to retrieve his knife, and wiped the blood off on the soldier's breeches. The horsemen shifted nervously, everyone knowing the raiders hadn't enough swords nor guns to keep all the English under control.

"Your guns. I want all the pistols handed to the young gentleman, over there." Alasdair barked the order, and Coll MacGregor went to collect the various pistols and muskets handed to him. He stuck the pistols in his belt and the muskets he laid on the ground, except for one he held on the men as he backed away.

Alasdair then ordered the remaining men to dismount and move away from the horses. He gestured to James, who mounted and took charge of the pack animals.

The civilian bolted, and Alasdair shot but missed. "Mac a'Chlaidheimh!" he shouted. Dylan, the closest, was already off after him. The fleeing man ducked into the woods at the side of the trail where it crossed a shallow stream. Dylan plunged after him, and scabbarded his sword to draw Brigid from his legging. The woods were thick and allowed no room for swords. He ran after the filthy Whig, eager to teach him whose territory this was. Over the past year he'd become familiar with most of the land between Glen Dochart and Stirling, and this area had been scoped out well in preparation for the robbery. He knew he was chasing his quarry into a trap. The stream they followed upward widened to a pool at the bottom of a tall waterfall. On three sides were granite cliffs, and the fourth side was blocked by Dylan and Brigid. The fleeing man skidded to a stop amid ferns and tall, gnarled pines realizing that the trail had ended. He turned, turned again, and finally confronted Dylan with a face slack with fear.

"Don't kill me! Please!" His tall, lanky body cringed in

abject terror of Dylan's dirk. His white, powdered wig sat askew, the queue visible over his left shoulder.

"Give me a reason why I shouldn't." Dylan held his dirk ready to do just that.

"I'm a Jacobite! I'm a supporter of King James VIII! Long live King James!"

Dylan's eyes narrowed. "Easy enough to say."

There was a pause in which the man seemed to consider his next words, then he said as if confessing, "I'm a friend of Iain Mór of Ciorram!" Dylan's interest perked. He lowered his dirk and the man went on, encouraged, "Iain Mór is a Jacobite! I provide intelligence for him and his fellows!" He pulled himself up as if posing for a portrait, and straightened his wig. In the haughty, almost condescending tone of the upwardly mobile, he said "In fact, I'm married to his daughter!"

Cold sweat broke out. In a voice that suggested murderous intentions, Dylan said, "Your name?" But he already knew the answer.

CHAPTER 21

"Connor Alexander Ramsay, of Edinburgh."

Dylan gripped Brigid in his fist. It was all he could do not to kill Ramsay on the spot. Through gritted teeth he said, "What in hell are you doing here?"

Ramsay blinked at the vehement reaction. But he seemed to gather his life was no longer in danger and relaxed into a loose-limbed stance of insouciance. He said, "I told you, I carry intelligence. I was accompanying the guard for safe passage to Ft. William, supposedly to meet with a Major Bedford. . . ."

Dylan's head buzzed and he shook it, puzzled. "Bedford's not dead?"

"Nae." Ramsay seemed surprised anyone would think he was. Once he was certain Dylan had decided not to kill him, he began picking at his clothes to straighten them. His breeches were doe skin and he wore a brocade waistcoat under a coat of green velvet. His wig was tied back in a queue, with a matching green ribbon, in the military manner. Ruffles erupted at neck and both wrists of his shirt.

Dylan shook off the bad news to concentrate on the immediate matter. "You're no friend of Iain Mór. I think you lie." He knew it wasn't a lie, but didn't want Ramsay to know how he knew it. "However, I think I'll let you live.

Put your hands against that tree, over there, and spread your feet." Ramsay did as he was told, gingerly as if reluctant to be handled by a ruffian. Dylan held the point of his dirk to the side of Ramsay's neck as he frisked him. There was a package hidden in the lining of his coat, and Dylan slit the lining open to get at it. They were the dispatches all right, folded into a leather wallet. Dylan opened the wallet and found the letters were in code, looking like random characters on the paper. Ramsay hurried to explain. "I have nae intention of leaving those with Bedford. After our meeting I am to slip away to Glenfinnan. A courier is to meet me there, to take these on to Ciorram."

Dylan knew Ramsay was suspect, or Rob would never have needed to send his men after the letters. He grunted and stuffed the letters inside his sark. He tied Ramsay's hands with a lace handkerchief he found in the pocket of the brocade waistcoat. Then he lifted Ramsay's purse, shook it for jingle and weight, and from experience valued the contents at about three or four pounds. He hauled Ramsay off the tree by his collar and gave him a shove in the direction from which they had come. He would see to it the letters made it to Ciorram, whether Ramsay had intended it or not.

They arrived at the trail, where the raiders had mounted the English horses and were holding the disarmed soldiers at gunpoint as they awaited Dylan's return. There was a murmur of approval when they saw he had captured the civilian. Dylan turned custody of Ramsay over to Seumas, then approached Alasdair for a conference. The leader leaned down from his mount to listen. Dylan was careful to stand with his back to the soldiers.

In quick, hushed Gaelic, Dylan said, "We have reason to keep him. Hold him for ransom."

Alasdair's bushy eyebrows went up. "Aye?"

Dylan nodded and reached inside his sark to show just the corner of the letters. "He carried the dispatches bound for the garrison. If the English know about them, and think the letters are undiscovered, they'll pay more for him. Their eagerness to buy back the courier might give an indication of how trustworthy he is."

The big, red-haired Scot grinned. "I like the way ye think,

lad." In English he shouted to the uniformed captives, one of whom carried their dead compatriot over his shoulder, "All right, *Sassunaich*, I've a message for you to take to your superiors. They can have their Whig merchant at the cost of a hundred pounds sterling, brought to this spot in a week's time. Start walking to the garrison. Any one of you tries to follow, he'll have his head blown off and his balls fed to my pigs, and not necessarily in that order." The soldiers stood, not sure they should leave their civilian charge. Alasdair shouted, "Quit yer gawping ye gowps, and get the hell out of here before I shoot the lot of you just to have your ugly faces out of my sight!"

That moved them. They began to shuffle along the trail, reluctantly, looking back at Ramsay. Dylan and Ramsay each mounted a horse, and with Alasdair's pistol trained at the soldiers the band of brigands took off in the opposite direction as fast as the pack *garrons* would let them, bringing the spare horses along.

Coll MacGregor was sent home to Glen Dochart with the booty. Once Coll was gone, Alasdair fell back on the trail to where Dylan followed Ramsay's horse and gestured for him to fall back even more. Out of earshot, he said, "There is a letter in the packet I want sent to Mar."

Dylan knew he was hanging himself, but said, "They all need to go to Ciorram."

There was a pause, then Alasdair said, "What did Ramsay tell you? I am the only one here who was told of Ramsay's special relationship with the Jacobites."

Dylan chewed on the inside corner of his mouth for a moment, sifting through the things Ramsay had said that Dylan wanted widely known. He replied, "He admitted he was a spy in hopes of release. But I figure he's not a well-trusted one, or Rob wouldn't have sent us after the dispatches. It was pretty easy to figure out."

Alasdair chuckled. "I hope the other men dinnae find it so easy. Though I dinnae expect they will."

The letters were ordered sent to Ciorram via one of Rob's men. The rest of the brigands went to an abandoned house near Lochearnhead, at the foot of the pass into Glen Dochart, arriving about nightfall. The horses were hobbled outside to graze. Dylan was given charge of the prisoner, and had him bring inside an armload of peat cannibalized from the crumbling wall on the byre side of the house. Seumas lit the fire under the smoke hole, then set to making a supper for the men, of bannocks baked on a flat rock.

A stray chicken from inside the byre flew up to roost on the boards separating it from the rest of the house, clucking and peering at the intruders. Seumas shushed the other men as he eased into position below the bird with his back to the wall, looking up. Like a snake he struck, and grabbed the chicken by the neck, then hauled it down and shook it hard, snapping its neck. It barely had time to get out one indignant cluck before it went silent and limp. He took it outside to pluck and clean it. Everyone was in a good mood now. Fresh chicken for supper.

They each picked out a spot on the floor, and Dylan sat Ramsay on the floor against the byre wall, his hands tied behind his knees. Though Ramsay insisted loudly he was a Jacobite, the men were not allowed to believe it was true and so Dylan kept him restrained and periodically told him to shut up. Seumas spitted the chicken carcass over the fire. There was little talk while they anticipated the meal, the scent of roasting meat filling the room. When it was ready they all shared it. Dylan stuffed a large chunk of meat into Ramsay's mouth and let him cope with chewing and swallowing his ration.

But when it came to feeding him a bannock, Dylan wasn't quite angry enough to watch him choke on a whole share. But neither did he feel like feeding pieces to him like a servant. He stood with it in his hand, debating.

Ramsay said, "Perhaps you could see your way to letting my hands loose so I can at least feed myself?"

Dylan looked over at Alasdair, who shrugged and nodded. So Dylan reached under Ramsay's knees and loosened the handkerchief. Then he handed the bannock over and went to sit against the peat wall.

In keeping with the habit of most of the men there, supper was followed by drinking and talking. The whiskey was passed to Ramsay as well, and the mood lightened for all of them. Tonight Seumas talked of wanting to marry a girl he'd

met in Glen Dochart. His praise of her beauty and sweetness
brought hoots from his comrades, but he laughed and declared them all jealous. Dylan's heart was heavy as he
thought of how he'd dreamed of marrying Cait, and realized
with a flush of jealousy that Ramsay was the only married
man in the room.

He turned to Ramsay and said, "You're married. Tell the
lad what it's like."

A sour look crossed Ramsay's heavy-lidded face, and Dylan wanted to punch him out. Ramsay said to Seumas, "Don't
do it."

Dylan's eyes narrowed. "You don't like being married,
then?"

Ramsay shrugged. "I suppose a wife has her uses. Especially if her father is wealthy and if she's pretty enough not
to embarrass one in public." Chuckling rippled through the
firelit room.

Dylan's cheeks burned, but he took a deep, silent breath
so as to not give away his keen interest in Ramsay's wife.
"Surely there's more to marriage than that. Even if you have
your differences, there must be a solace in good company."

"I've nae need of her company."

Alasdair said, "*Och*! Rubbish! Every woman has a certain
charm, if you know what I mean."

The others laughed, but Dylan stared at Ramsay for his
reaction. It was little more than a smirk. Ramsay looked as
if he'd smelled something bad. "Ever since the child, the
allure has . . . dwindled."

That brought a roar of laughter from the Highlanders, and
the redness of Ramsay's face revealed he'd not intended the
pun.

Dylan, not laughing in the least, said, "You have children,
then?"

There was a long pause, then Ramsay said, "Aye. One
boy. But having married a faithless woman somewhat takes
the joy from fatherhood." His voice was filled with pain, and
Dylan had a twinge of guilt that the man had been duped by
Iain into marrying Cait when she was already pregnant. That
much, at least, had not been Ramsay's fault.

But then the Whig said, "I won't disown the little bastard,

but I have disinherited him and will make him wish I had put him out. And his whore mother, as well. If ever she's too marked to appear in public, then that's nae matter. I never lack for feminine company and can do without hers if need be." The pain was gone from Ramsay's voice and replaced by the arrogance of vengeance. He was making Cait pay for her father's treachery.

Dylan screwed his eyes shut and his hand reached for his legging, to curl around Brigid's hilt. He was about to attack Ramsay when Sinann's voice came to him. He opened his eyes.

"Nae, laddie," she said. She crouched by his knee and put a hand over his hand that rested on the dirk.

The others went on talking to Ramsay as Dylan said, well under his breath, "Are you going to stop me by breaking my other leg?" He stared at the floor so nobody would see the murder in his eyes.

"Nae. I'm going to stop you by reminding you that your lovely lady needs this man, at least until you can take her away. You heard what he said. He's disinherited the boy and his mother. He's made an early will and most likely declared the bairn illegitimate. Kill him, and you will ruin the two people who matter most to you in the world. Wait until you are free to marry her." She shrugged. "Then kill him."

"I'll never be free to marry her. Even if I don't die at Sheriffmuir, I'm not likely to survive the persecutions after." He rubbed his thumb hard against Brigid's hilt.

Sinann squeezed his hand. "You cannae know that."

He finally looked at her. "I can't change history."

Her voice took on an amused tone, as if he'd just said something unutterably stupid. "I daresay you never read in a history book that Dylan Robert Matheson, also known as Dilean Mac a'Chlaidheimh, was killed at that battle or shortly thereafter." Dylan shrugged. She had a point.

She continued, "Let it be. For now." He let go of his dirk and relaxed against the peat wall behind him to sulk. But there was more: "Not only can you not kill him, but you have to make certain nobody else here does."

He shot her an evil glare, but said nothing.

The talk continued well into the night. When the Highlanders began to curl up on the dirt floor under their plaids, Dylan tied Ramsay's hands behind his knees again with the handkerchief. A bit more tightly than necessary, perhaps, but not tight enough to give him gangrene. Not before morning, anyway. He pulled his plaid around himself and lay down to sleep.

Sometime during the night he was awakened by the sound of wood against wood, and came fully conscious in an instant. Seumas raised a shout, and Alasdair went flying to the gap Ramsay had pulled in the byre wall. Dylan found Ramsay's handkerchief on the floor and picked it up. Rather than wait his turn to go through the hole, he drew his sword and ran out the front, then around to the back where the horses were.

Ramsay had slipped the hobble on one of them, and was mounting. Alasdair had his pistol primed, and was taking aim. Sinann's voice came from nowhere. "He must live! Dylan, you must protect him!"

Dylan ran at Alasdair and struck the gun to spoil his aim just as he shot. The ball went wide and the report spurred Ramsay's horse into flight. Seumas freed another horse and mounted to pursue. Alasdair turned on Dylan.

"What in bloody hell did you do?" He slipped the gun into his belt and pulled his sword. Dylan fell back to defend with his. Alasdair continued to shout, red-eyed with fury, "Tell me, young idiot, just what that was about! Are ye in league? Have ye turned Whig on us, lad? Or are ye simply daft? Gone soft in the head, have ye?" He circled, and Dylan wished he'd let Alasdair kill Ramsay. "Have ye an answer, lad, or are you going to die without speaking for yourself?"

"I don't know why I did it."

Alasdair's sword struck out, and Dylan parried. One clang, and they circled some more. "Not good enough, lad." The next attack almost landed, but Dylan parried and backed farther.

"I don't want to fight you." He didn't want to hurt Alasdair, who was a fine shot but a mediocre swordsman.

"Then you should have let me shoot." Another attack, and Dylan parried. "Why didn't you? Have we a spy in our midst?"

Aw, jeez. This he didn't need. He finally sighed and said, "I couldn't let you shoot him. We didn't bring him here to kill him."

"Neither did we bring him here to go running back without us getting our money. Why is it so desperately important to you that he live?"

There was a long pause while Dylan debated telling the truth. Alasdair made another series of attacks, backing Dylan against the house, until he could go no farther and they locked swords. Dylan decided he was keeping a secret that was not important enough to die for, and said, "That boy he was talking about last night . . . his wife's baby . . . that's my son!"

Alasdair's jaw dropped. He shoved off from Dylan's sword and stood down. "Ye jest, lad!" Dylan shook his head and leaned against the sagging wall, feeling like a spent balloon. Alasdair made a disgusted noise. "*Och!* He's the prick married your Cait?" Dylan nodded. The wheels turned behind Alasdair's eyes, and Dylan could see him come to the same conclusion Sinann had. "Aye, I see why you couldnae kill him. Ye have my sympathy. And Cait, as well, having to live with that spineless pig." He turned back to the direction Ramsay had taken and said, "Let's hope Seumas catches him. If not, we'd best hie out of here in a hurry."

Seumas returned without Ramsay, and the band packed up and returned to Glen Dochart.

It was just as well the ransom plan fell through, for they weren't back long when they were told to collect their gear again, all of them. All the retainers who wished to fight were invited to join Rob as recruits for the forces of King James VIII. They were headed for Glen Gyle, Rob's ancestral home, where his chieftain would send out the fiery cross to muster troops from Clan Gregor for the cause. About half of Rob's outlaws gathered. They struck out westward, carrying their weapons and their rations, and Dylan went with them.

Sinann appeared, hopping and running beside him as he walked. "You're going! You're truly going!"

Dylan's smile was lopsided, and he said with a bit of irony, "Look sharp, there, Tink. We're in the army now."

CHAPTER 22

D ylan found himself less than enchanted with his new status as a soldier. His pay was cut in half to threepence a day, and the daily ration was three loaves of bread. If he wanted meat he had to buy it or shoot it himself. He had appropriated one of the pistols taken from the *Sassunaich* the previous month, but thought of it as a waste of effort and expense to load and fire. And he wasn't much of a shot in any case. He only kept the pistol and a few powder loads and balls, for the sake of appearing well armed. Poaching was frowned upon but not punished, so whenever somebody else shot something large enough to share, Dylan bought in. Also, as always before, he ate vegetables and wild greens, though he took a terrible ribbing from the other men for it. Never mind that he wanted to keep his teeth. Having no cultural qualms over eating food fit only for poor folks, he figured that, since vegetables were food, if they were available he should eat them.

Like most of the other men, Dylan had a bonnet made, a floppy blue hat that fit snugly at the band and lay on his head like a deflated balloon. The color identified him as a member of the Jacobite army. His sark was ragged and his kilt had seen better days, but he had a bright, shiny new hat.

"It suits you," said Sinann.

He adjusted it on his head. "It's all right. Wouldn't want anyone to mistake me for an Englishman." He didn't care much for hats in general, but he did find that the wool kept his head warm at least.

Sinann laughed. "Have you seen your reflection lately, lad? You're a Highlander to the core of ye, and just from the look in your eye nae man would mistake you for a soft Hanoverian."

Dylan couldn't help smiling at that.

Life in Glen Gyle, among the men mustered by Rob Roy and his nephew, Gregor Ghlun Dhubh, consisted mostly of waiting. Then Rob was called to Perth and given the duty of transporting money for arms to Breadalbane. He took with him a small contingent of his best men, including Alasdair Roy, Seumas Glas, Alasdair Og, and Dilean Mac a'Chlaidheimh. They were well chosen for the job. Having been raiders themselves, they were well equipped to make sure the money made it safely to its destination.

Riding five of the best mounts in Gregor Ghlun Dhubh's stable, they crossed through Glen Dochart to Perth without incident.

Having successfully completed their first mission, Rob and his contingent became couriers for dispatches between the new Jacobite leader, the Earl of Mar, and his General, Alexander Gordon of Auchintoul. King James was expected to land near Dumbarton on the Clyde estuary near the western coast. Dylan was not impressed. While everyone around him waited in breathless anticipation of the grand entrance, he kept his irritated silence, for he knew the King would not arrive. Not in time to save his own cause, anyway.

During a stop in Stirling, the recipient of Rob's communiqué had gossip about chieftains who had entered the fray. Dylan was disappointed to hear that Iain Mór had mustered men for the fight. This was not good news, though it was also not unexpected, given Iain's hatred for the Sassunaich. But, as a northern chief outside the line of fire, he could well afford to let the western families take the brunt of the conflict. And Dylan wished he would. Many of the MacGregors, MacDonalds, Camerons, Macleans, MacDougals, and Stewarts had not sided with the Crown. The larger part of Clan

Matheson, particularly the Sutherland chiefs, were Loyalists and would survive, but Dylan feared horribly for the southern Mathesons of Glen Ciorram after the uprising.

By October Rob and his bodyguard were back in Perth, having crossed and recrossed the upper Lowlands and southern Highlands several times on their errands. Spending days and weeks on end in the saddle, Dylan grew accustomed to his mount. Riding became more than just a skill that came easy—it was second nature to him. He acquired a pair of woolen trews to protect his legs, but found them itchy and binding on his upper thighs. So he gave them up after a week. He wished for a pair of long johns, and sometimes wondered idly if cotton would find its way to Scotland during his lifetime.

The Jacobite army grew as Mar recruited more chieftains. Then Rob and his men joined up with Gordon's troops to assault Inverary in an effort to gain control over the seaward approach to the Clyde River, which was a maze of sea lochs and islands.

However, their orders came slowly, and by the time the Jacobites arrived at the castle, the Campbells had fortified the town. There wasn't much for the Jacobite army to do but take potshots at them from behind breastworks. In the return fire Rob sustained a minor crease on his forearm, and spent the next few days walking about with a bloody rag tied around it, in a bad humor, cursing Argyll at every opportunity. Then he and his contingent went with Gordon, who left some of his troops to keep the Campbells occupied at the castle while the rest plundered up and down the western shore of Loch Fyne for supplies.

Sinann's excitement grew as she saw the Jacobites gain momentum. She hopped and flew to keep up with Dylan as he helped carry supplies along the trail between the boats on the loch and the Jacobite camp about a mile inland. The men carrying boxes had spread out some along the trail, so Dylan felt comfortable talking to her in a low voice. He suggested she help him carry the large crate of hardtack he was hauling. Sinann waved her hand and suddenly the box was lighter on his shoulder.

"Thank you. I hope you didn't actually empty it."

"No worries. It'll be heavy enough, once you've set it down. It'll be needed when the King—"

"He's not coming, Tink."

"Ye lie."

"He's not coming. Not until the battle is lost and it's too late to save the uprising."

"But the dispatch from Mar—"

"Mar knows nothing. He's almost as clueless as that pompous German ass in London. He's the one who's going to lose us Sheriffmuir, him and his dithering. He's already lost us Inverary with his farting around."

"So slip a dirk between his ribs and that'll be the end of that. You've a talent for it."

Dylan stopped walking and stared at Sinann, appalled. "I don't think so! Whatever I might be—whatever I've become since you brought me here—I'm not a murderer! Take back what you said!" He loomed over her, threateningly.

"I don't—"

"Take it back, Tink, or I set this crate down, head for Glasgow, and hop the next ship to the colonies and to hell with your precious uprising!"

"I only meant—"

"Take it back. I don't want to hear any more about assassination. Ever. Take it back."

"All right, I'm sorry."

He walked on in silence, still angry, and she ran, hopped, and flew alongside. "You were certainly ready to murder Ramsay nae so long ago."

"I was wrong. You were right to stop me."

She made a noise of disgust. "Now he listens to me." There was a long silence as she struggled to keep up with his pace, then finally she said, "But what can you do?"

He sighed deeply. "I don't know. I really don't."

For several weeks Dylan and his comrades were occupied escorting Rob and the Jacobite communiqués back and forth to Perth, then back to Drummond Castle, then to Perth again, and to Auchterarder and back to Perth. Though Dylan asked as many nosy questions as he figured would be tolerated, and hung around Rob as much as possible, he was never privy to the information transported. So he continued in frustration of not knowing exactly where the mistakes were going to be made until they happened. Even the information Sinann was able to glean in her eavesdropping was always too little too late—and too often inaccurate by the time she reached Dylan with it. It seemed Mar couldn't make up his mind about even the smallest things. All Dylan could learn was the delays were hurting them, which every Jacobite in Scotland knew by now.

The Jacobite army was eager to fight, but frustrated by Mar's stalling and disheartened still further by Argyll's taking of Edinburgh. For Dylan, that news bordered on terrifying, as he wondered what was happening to Cait and the boy.

It was November now, the snows were close and creeping in from the Highlands, but still Mar waited for the arrival of the King. It wasn't until November 9 that the news came they would march soon. Dylan knew when, and he knew where. They were four days away from the battle of Sheriffmuir. His heart sank.

A messenger came running, breathless with orders from Mar for Rob to break off from the main contingent of MacGregors. He was to make a reconnaissance on the River Forth then rejoin Mar's army in a few days. A great weight was lifted from Dylan as he realized they would miss the battle. But that weight reasserted itself when he also realized he was the Jacobites' only hope. If he were to change the outcome of the uprising, he had to somehow change the outcome of this battle. He couldn't do that if he were off scoping out terrain with Rob. He went to MacGregor with a request.

"I want to fight with Balhaldie."

Rob was in conference with one of the MacPhersons, but excused himself, turned to Dylan, and frowned. "Why?" He clearly didn't like the idea of his men leaving him, even to go to the forces of another MacGregor. Though social structure and attitudes in Scotland were changing, it would still be another generation or two, or three, before Highland men would be used to the idea of fighting for, or beside, anyone but family. Dylan had been accepted by Rob Roy's MacGregors, but now he was leaving. This was not good.

Dylan cleared his throat. He couldn't tell Rob he knew if

he stayed with his friends he wouldn't reach the battle until it was too late to fight. He knew Mar was going to mess up badly but couldn't remember from his reading just what would happen. He only knew if he was going to affect the outcome of the battle and give the uprising a chance, he would have to stick with the main strength of the Jacobite force. So what he said was what he thought Rob would accept. "I want to be first on the field. I've got a score to settle, and I want to kill some Redcoats."

A dry smile curled Rob's lips, and he glanced at Mac-Pherson, who also had a smile playing at the corners of his mouth. Rob said, "You've never been in battle, have ye, lad?"

Dylan shook his head. Beyond the siege at Inverary he'd never been in a full-fledged battle. He knew they thought he was an overenthusiastic fool, but he let them think it. It would be easier for them to understand than the truth.

"You'll regret asking this." There was genuine sorrow in his voice, as if he had some premonition of Dylan's death.

Dylan nodded, certain Rob was right. He expected to die, but didn't want to avoid the battle then spend the rest of his life wondering if he might have done something to make a difference. If there was a chance to alter the course of history, to find a way to carry the tide long enough for the cause to last until James' arrival in December, he had to take it. For if the rising should succeed and James take his place as King of Scotland, it would prevent the next two uprisings in 1719 and 1745. Many Scottish lives would be saved and many clans would prosper where they hadn't done before.

And he had personal considerations. If James VIII were to succeed in his claim to the throne of Scotland, Dylan, as a Jacobite, would be pardoned of the charges against him. He would then be free to claim Cait and his son.

So he was strangely elated when Rob gave his consent for Dylan to march with the larger contingent of Mac-Gregors.

On foot now, Dylan continued to be anxious on the long march to the battle. He could tell where they were, and knew where they were headed. And though he knew what the end result would be, he had little idea of what would happen once they got to the battlefield. If only he'd had a history book in his hand when the sword had grabbed him from the future!

On the morning of November 13, he awoke from sleep at Kinbuck near the Allan Water, huddled on the ground with thousands of men he didn't know, shook frost from his hair, and rubbed circulation into his nose. Two years ago he would have been immobilized by this cold. But he'd since learned not to feel it so much and not to let his body clench with shivering, so he could be about his business. He ate breakfast quickly: a handful of oatmeal wetted in the river and mashed into a glob that he swallowed in chunks he picked out with his fingers. Having eaten, he rinsed off his hands and proceeded to load his pistol.

The firing charge went into the barrel, and he hoped it wasn't too much. He valued his right hand and didn't want the gun to blow up in it. Then in went the wadding and ball, which he tamped down with the ramrod. Tight, but not too tight. Damn, he hated explosives! Then he slid the ramrod back into place under the barrel, opened the priming pan, and half-cocked the pistol. He loaded the pan with fine priming powder, then closed it and jiggled the gun so the powder would go into the touchhole where it could ignite the firing charge inside the barrel. Then he slipped the pistol into his belt.

Fully armed now, he formed up to march with the rest of the men.

They moved away from the river, toward the rise. The terrain was rocky, with low, undulating hills rising to the muir. Ten thousand Jacobites swarmed over the hills, and as Dylan descended between each hill he lost sight of the muir above. He was on high ground, though, when a halt was called. The enemy was outlined against the sky to the west of the muir, tiny toy soldiers making a thin, red line on the horizon. The sight of them stirred something ugly in Dylan. Red coats equaled the enemy. Those English uniforms represented pain and danger. He'd suffered personally from the English occupation, and sight of those soldiers clenched his gut. His heart beat faster, and his soul hardened.

Readying for battle, the clansmen dropped their kilts and tied their sporrans into them to fight in their sarks. Dylan debated pinning his brooch to his sark, but decided against using the talisman. It required stillness to work, and if he were wounded and fell he might not be found. He had little money anymore, so the bag contained only a few pence, the brooch, Ramsay's handkerchief, the Goddess Stone, the flask of priming powder, and his ration bag of oatmeal. He buckled his belt in a loop to keep the sporran on it, then wrapped it in his rust-and-black kilt and left it on the ground at his feet as he walked away. His baldric hung across his chest, and Brigid was strapped to his legging. He carried his primed pistol in his right hand. Energy was intense among the Highlanders. The Jacobites were ready for blood.

When the order came to move again, it was to change direction and head up the slope and circle above the Hanoverian position. But Argyll was moving, too. The Jacobite Army didn't make the muir in time to gain the higher ground. Both forces formed up and readied to fight on the rolling ridge top. Dylan's heart slammed in his chest as they advanced to position.

Sinann appeared, marching beside him. "Look to your right, at the bottom of the muir," she said. On the right was a conical hill, very precise and pointed. The army made a wide berth of it. "A faerie knoll. Now look closer."

Dylan peered at the strange hill and frowned. A woman dressed in a flowing red gown stood at the peak of it. She watched the sea of men flow past. She seemed inordinately pleased at what was happening, dancing around the top of her little hill. "What is she doing?"

"That's Morrighan. Goddess of war."

Dylan grunted and returned his attention to what was ahead. "Well, she's going to be a happy camper today. A lot of people are going to die." Then he muttered, "You go away."

Grinning, she shook her head and marched at a two-step to keep up with his one.

"I said, get out of here."

Now she frowned. "What if you need me?"

"The best I could hope for from you would be to put me out of my misery quickly when the time comes. Go away, you might get hurt yourself."

"Silly mortal." She clucked her tongue and flew into the air. There she hovered over him as he walked. He could live with that. She would have him believe she was immortal, but he knew better. Long-lived and wily, but not immortal.

The battlefield was uneven moorland covered with heather and large rocks that were slippery with mud from other soldiers' shoes. The ground between the rocks was damp, almost boggy in places, and the trampled growth underfoot did not hold well in the mud.

The Jacobites, facing southwest now, lined up opposite the Hanoverians, and Dylan found himself and the other MacGregors on the left wing with the MacKinnons and MacPhersons. As Campbell of Argyll's troops formed up across the way, Dylan could hear the steady English drum cadence and saw, with a surge of blood lust, that his group was in opposition to units of red-coated dragoons. He was on foot, but he had experience dealing with men on horseback. The dragoon had a height advantage, but sometimes a man's horse could be manipulated against him.

At that moment the Jacobite cavalry on his left broke and galloped to the center, to Dylan's right. This was not good. It left only clan infantry against the opposing heavy English cavalry. Dylan took several deep breaths and tried to stop thinking about dying as the armies approached each other at a walk. Muskets, pistols, swords and dirks were brandished on both sides. Dylan, his pistol in his right hand, picked up his knee as he walked and drew Brigid with his left hand. Then the ranks halted. For one breathless moment they faced each other. Time stopped. Then there was a single volley of gunfire, and Dylan blinked. He had no idea which side had fired until smoke rose from the front ranks of the rebels.

Then the skirl of pipes lifted on the air and the Jacobite army surged forward. Dylan's voice joined the roar, and he ran to close the space between himself and the charging English cavalry.

There was no sense of tactics anymore, but only the focused desire to kill the enemy. Guns roared. Dylan fired his pistol at a charging dragoon, and the enemy soldier toppled. Then he dropped the gun and drew his sword, a roar of fury in his throat. The heather and stony ground made footing difficult and running dangerous, and gave an advantage to the four-footed horses. The clang of thousands of clashing swords was deafening. Dylan ran past others engaged, and a dragoon rode at him. He dodged to the rider's left so the right-handed cavalryman had a shortened reach, and parried easily. But the horseman wheeled, crowding him with his mount. There was no room among the flailing men to gain space, so Dylan stepped into the attack, his sword in a high guard, and with his dirk stabbed the dragoon's thigh. He pulled it out and stabbed again.

There was no immediate reaction, though blood surged and the Redcoat slipped in his saddle as he slashed with his saber at Dylan's head. Dylan parried with his dirk and attacked with his sword. It slipped into the Englishman's back. He stiffened with pain and the knowledge that he was ended. When Dylan retrieved his weapon, the dragoon fell from his saddle and Dylan turned to seek another opponent.

All was chaos. Dylan was no longer sure which way he'd come. His focus narrowed to staying alive, parrying enemy swords and cutting down anything in a red coat that moved. But as the afternoon wore on, the men in red seemed to overwhelm the men in kilts. In the dim distance the pipes called to rally at the battalion colors. Dylan fell back to make his way there, and found himself treading on and leaping over the bodies of Balhaldie's MacGregors, men he recognized as comrades. His unit was retreating in the face of a fresh charge of Lowland troops. They circled back down the slope the way they had come, now at a serious disadvantage with the enemy on higher ground. Dylan's hair stuck to his sweaty face, and he discovered his cap was gone.

Horses screamed, wounded, some dying. A dragoon charged at Dylan, sword raised, but a MacPherson swung and hacked the horse's tendon. The animal fell sideways, crippled. The unhorsed dragoon regained his feet and renewed his assault. Dylan, attempting to retreat, almost didn't parry in time. The Jacobite presence was thinning here, and he needed to get back to his lines. Tiring, he gave ground, but the soldier pressed him. The clang of their swords was lost in the din around them. Dylan parried frantically. The dragoon snarled at him, and came on with lightning speed.

Dylan backed against other men, and could go no farther. In a moment of indecision, Dylan made the wrong parry against a feint, and the Englishman ran him through.

For one seemingly endless moment, Dylan stared at the hilt pressed to his gut, and a distant, detached part of his mind took note of the chiseled face on the bowl guard, identifying it as a "mortuary" hilt. The bodiless head, sometimes thought to be that of the executed Charles I, was covered in his own blood. Then the weapon was yanked from his body. Once he saw that the clansman was done for, the dragoon turned for a fresh quarry, finding one in another MacGregor who had come to help.

Dylan's sword thudded to the ground on the hillside and he stood, the heel of his right hand pressed against his gut. His left hand clenched around Brigid's hilt and pressed against his right hand. "No," he said. "No, I can't die." But as blood ran down his back from the exit wound and down his leg, soaking his shirt so it stuck to him, he realized that even if he didn't die today from blood loss, he had at the most a few days before he would perish in a very ugly manner from peritonitis. And the blood pouring out of him, oozing between his fingers and dripping from the tail of his sark, made it likely he'd be gone in a matter of minutes.

He looked up to see Sinann, wide-eyed and speechless as she fluttered down to him. "I'm sorry," he said. "I couldn't change anything." He staggered, but tried not to fall. He didn't want to lie on the ground until he had to. The world began to spin. "No," he said again. "No . . . No . . ."

As if from a distance, Sinann's voice came and comprehension failed him. She was weeping as she said, "*A Dhilein,* you must go home."

The world blackened. Dylan knew he was passing from it and wondered if there would be a light to follow like everyone said. Shrieking pain wracked him, and he wondered how he could feel pain if he was dead. Then the light did come. All around him was brightness. Then that brightness differentiated into colors. The colors became faces. Familiar ones, though he couldn't place them. "*Chan eil,*" he kept saying, still denying his death as it was happening. "*Chan eil, chan eil. . . .*" No, no, no.

Heat. It was hot.

Someone screamed. Then he collapsed to the grass. More people screamed. Someone shouted to call 911. Someone else shouted that there was a fire truck in the parking lot. Hands lifted him. The world faded again, and he knew he was dying.

CHAPTER 23

Dylan awoke to a stench of antiseptic and plastic. And to pain. Intense pain. His gut felt like his insides would fall out if he moved. He wasn't dead, and had to think about it before deciding that was a good thing. He grunted and tried to get the plastic thing off his face. A nurse materialized by his side and removed it for him.

"Mr. Matheson, how are you feeling?" Mister? How long had it been since he'd been called "mister"? It felt strange. He looked at the nurse, who was pretty and dark-haired and wore deep purple scrubs. The color was so vivid he couldn't take his eyes off it. Everything was so bright. As if God, sometime during the twentieth century, had come through with a watercolor set and touched up everything. "Mr. Matheson?" The nurse still awaited a reply.

He said, "I'm not dead," and discovered his throat was sore and his voice almost too hoarse to be intelligible.

She smiled, as if he'd made a joke. "No, you're not. You've lost your spleen and a kidney, but you're going to be all right. Provided your other kidney stays healthy, you shouldn't even have any long-term effects from this. I'll get you something for the pain, then we'll move you into a room." She waggled a finger and drawled at him, "Don't you

go no place, now." She giggled and left him to grunt again
to himself.

He tried to sit up, but there were no pillows on the gurney
to lean against, so the effort was wasted. He lay back down
and waited to be moved. The pretty nurse returned with a
syringe, which he let her stick in his upper hip, though he
cared little about the painkiller. He'd taken far worse pain
than this in the past without it. His wounds and the surgery
incision were no more annoying than the catheter in his pe-
nis, which he found an almost intolerable invasion of his
body.

They took him to a private room, so he knew his mother
had found him and was pulling strings somewhere. When
he'd been a part of this century, his health insurance wouldn't
have covered a private room. He wondered how long he'd
been gone. Had he been missing for two years? Did he even
have a life to go back to? He looked around the room and
wondered. The TV was on with the sound off, and he stared
at it for a moment. Images flashed, one after another, and he
found it disconcerting. Confusing. He decided he didn't want
the entire world inside his room, so he reached for the remote
and pushed the green *power* button. The screen went dead,
and the room seemed peaceful.

The door moved, and his mother peeked in. "Dylan?"

"Mom." She came in, and he saw how panicked she'd
been and how relieved she was to see him alive. Her face
was white and her eyes red from crying. She looked terrible,
but it had been so long and he was so happy to see her it
didn't matter. He thought she was beautiful.

His voice cracked. "Mom, I'm okay. It doesn't even hurt."
Not anymore, at least. Whatever he'd been shot with was
kicking in nicely. She came to take his hand, and he noticed
how clean he was. Someone had scrubbed him down thoroughly at some point while he was out, but under his arms
he found orange-brown antiseptic left from his operation. He
felt his hair, and found it still full of dirt, sweat, and blood.
He ran his fingers through it in an effort to organize it for
his mother, but it did little good.

Mom sat on the edge of his bed to tell him how happy
she was he would be all right. He neither heard nor cared

what she said, he was so intent on watching her face. He had missed her so much! He only held her hand, not wanting to let go.

The door opened again, and Cody appeared. "Dylan?" She came into the room, and time warped again for him. She had on the same seventeenth-century outfit she'd worn at the Games on that day. . . .

"Mom, what year is it?"

His mother stopped in the middle of a complaint about how skinny he was and didn't he ever eat, and she laughed. "What *year*?"

He had to breathe hard to keep talking. "Just tell me. I've forgotten. Trauma does that, and they've got me on some wicked strong pain killers." Another deep breath. "What year is it?"

She uttered another nervous laugh. "2000."

"September 30?"

She looked at her watch. "For another few minutes. It's almost midnight."

He blinked at Cody. It was the same day. Sinann had returned him to the moment just after he'd touched the claymore. They didn't even know he'd been gone. He squeezed his eyes shut.

From the doorway his father's voice addressed his mother, "We need to get home, Barri." Big surprise Dad wouldn't come into the room. Dylan kept his eyes shut until his mother kissed his cheek and said, "I'll come back to see you tomorrow. You get some rest." He nodded, and watched her leave.

Cody stood there, twisting her collapsed kerchief hat in her hands. "We were scared to death, Dylan." She looked like she'd been crying, and might start up again if encouraged.

"How are you, Cody?" For her it had been hours, but for him it had been two years.

She gave him a puzzled smile, then sat on the edge of his bed. "Dylan, how in the world did you keep standing for so long?"

He frowned. "Huh?"

"After he stabbed you. You walked over to the sword and

picked it up, and nobody even saw you were bleeding. You said you felt funny, or something, then I blinked and suddenly you were on your way to the ground and covered with blood. It was like it all came spurting out at once." He grunted and made a face. "Oh, sorry. But, anyway, people were screaming and crowding around you, and I couldn't even see what they were doing. You were muttering something about canned eels, and some people thought you'd eaten something you shouldn't have. But they didn't see the blood. The firemen put you in the truck and ran the siren all the way to the hospital. I've been in the waiting room since they brought you here. Raymond is having fits. . . ."

Raymond . . . he of the polyester hair. Dylan remembered and nodded.

"Anyway, we're real glad you're alive. That guy should be put in jail."

"What guy?"

"Bedford."

Cold sweat broke out, but then Dylan remembered she meant the Yankee, the one who had inherited the claymore. "He didn't do it."

That silenced her for a moment. Then she said, "Yes, he did."

"No. It wasn't his fault."

"He stabbed you. It was only a sparring match, and he almost killed you."

"No. He did nothing. He never touched me."

"But—"

"*Cody*, let it be!" Her eyes went wide again, and he lowered his voice. "Whatever happened, it was between the two of us and doesnae concern anyone else. Do you understand?"

She considered it for a moment, then nodded. Then she smiled and said, "I think the Games went to your head. *Doesnae*?"

He sighed and smiled, and thought of how much there was about him now she couldn't know.

"Well, listen," she said, "like I said, Raymond is having conniptions so I'd better go. We'll see you tomorrow, all right?" She went to give him a hug, and he put an arm around her waist. But when her hand slipped around to the open back of his hospital gown, she gasped.

He lay back, flat against his pillows and muttered a Gaelic curse at his stupidity.

"Dylan? What happened to you? What happened to your back?" She reached for the shoulder of his gown and he tried to fend her off, but she murmured to him that it was all right. "Dylan, please let me see." He wanted her to just get out and leave him alone, but after a moment decided she was still his most loyal friend in this century. It wouldn't be so horrible to let her see. He rolled a little for her to look at his back, and let her reach for the gown again.

There was a dark silence as she stared, then she said, "These are scars. Old scars." Her voice was soft, in awe. "I've never seen ones like that before. Or that many. What *happened* to you?"

How could he explain he'd been whipped nearly to death two hundred and eighty-six years ago? He sat back up against his pillows and said, "Motorcycle accident?"

"When? Those scars weren't there last week during class. You wore a loose tank shirt that day, remember, and had to take it off because it tore. These weren't there. And since when do you ride a bike? Dylan, this is awful. This is way too much scarring to even be kinky fun gotten out of hand. This is torture. This is . . . impossible."

He sighed. "I can't explain it. I just can't."

"Dyl—"

"Please. Just let it go, Cody. I can't explain it. And don't tell anyone else. Please."

Tears had filled her eyes, and she whispered, "You know I won't. I just . . . I'm so sorry."

He squeezed her hand, and she kissed his forehead before leaving.

The following morning he awoke to more pain, the continued annoyance of that catheter, and the entrance of his surgeon making rounds. The thin, bald man in a white coat strolled into the room and addressed Dylan with a condescending tone. "Hello, Mr. Matheson, I'm Dr. French. You seem to have been a little careless around sharp objects

lately." He sounded just like the pompous sort Seumas used
to tease at every opportunity.

Seumas. Dylan's heart sank to remember his friend was
dead and had been for a long, long time. Dr. French probably
thought he was being funny, but he didn't look up from the
clipboard containing Dylan's chart for his reaction.

The guy had been here for thirty seconds and was already
getting on Dylan's nerves.

"Hey." Dylan looked around the room. "Where's my
stuff?" He knew when he'd been sent back to this century
he'd had Brigid in his hand. His cut and bloodied sark was
probably in the garbage and his sword had been dropped on
the battlefield, but the hospital better not have done anything
with his dirks.

"What stuff?"

"I had two dir . . . knives. Where are they? And a scabbard
on a baldric."

The surgeon didn't seem the least interested in helping
him. "You can talk to a nur—"

"Call the nurse now."

"You can—"

"Now."

Exasperated, the doctor turned from the bed and spotted
a cabinet in the corner. "I'll bet they're in there."

"Go look."

Dr. French sighed and went to look. Leaning against the
back of the cabinet was Dylan's scabbard, and on the shelves
were Brigid, his *sgian dubh*, his boots, wool stockings, and
his leggings. Those were all he'd worn into battle, except for
his sark. "Is that what you want?"

Dylan laid his head back on his pillows. "Yeah."

Dr. French sighed and returned to the bedside. "All right,
then."

"When can I get out of here?" Dylan asked, sharply.

The surgeon laughed. "Well, we'll see about releasing you
soon." It was clear the physician intended to discharge Dylan
in his own good time. "How about if I at least let you get
out of bed this morning?"

Dylan looked at him sideways. "How about if we get this
catheter out of my dick first?"

Dr. French was ruffled by that, which had been Dylan's purpose in saying it. He said, "Well, we'll do that as soon as we can. Meanwhile, let's—"

"Let's get the tube gone."

French considered that for a moment, then shrugged. "All right. I'll have a nurse come and take it out for you."

"Thank you."

Once the catheter was gone, Dylan felt less helpless and tied to the hospital, which improved his disposition a bit. He walked to the bathroom and back, and never even leaned on his IV tree. Back from the bathroom, he took a private moment to examine the surgery damage. The original cut had been small, made with a narrow cavalry sword, but in removing the spleen and kidney both entry and exit wounds had been enlarged. The front scar was extended only an extra couple of inches, but as he felt around to his back he found gauze bandages taped near his spine and around to his side. He shuddered and realized he did need the pain killer after all. Nobody from the eighteenth century had ever survived this sort of incision long enough to need anesthesia.

Sometime at mid-morning, there was a short knock on his door and a cop entered. "Dylan Matheson?" He was in plain clothes, but Dylan had come to easily recognize the look of a man who considered himself a watchdog of Law and Order. "I'm Detective Jones and I'd like to ask you a few questions."

Dylan said nothing.

Jones stopped in the middle of the room, clearly surprised at Dylan's lack of cooperation, and said, "You don't mind, do you?" He had the look of a bulldog, with a receding hairline he disguised by combing his hair forward in a cascading lock. Dylan stared at that lock. Maybe it was the drugs, or maybe it was a gut reaction to the cop's authoritative demeanor, but he couldn't get over how stupid it looked.

Finally, Dylan grunted and said, "Have a seat, Officer."

Jones dragged a plastic chair away from the wall under the TV to sit on, and opened a notebook he'd pulled from his coat pocket. "I want you to know, the man who did this to you is in custody."

"Let him go."

Jones sighed. "You won't press charges?"

"He didn't do it."

"We have witnesses who say he did."

"He didn't do it."

"Are you saying it was an accident?"

Dylan's voice rose. "He dinnae do it. Let him go. The man never touched me."

"Then how did you get stabbed by a broadsword?"

"It wasnae a broadsword. It was a cavalry saber with a mortuary hilt, called so because of the carved face on the guard, resembling the beheaded King Charles I. The blade was nae more than two inches wide, which, if I'd died, you could have told by an autopsy. But, since I dinnae die, you'll just have to take my word on it. That monstrous big Italian storta Bedford fought with would have made a much larger hole than what the surgeon found. You can ask him. Bedford did not come near me."

"Then how do you explain—"

"To the best of my knowledge, Officer, I'm not charged with a crime and need not explain anything at all to you. What you do need to know is that Bedford did not stab me, and I will swear to it if you try to convict him."

"I don't know who you're protecting, but I would advise you to—"

"I've not solicited your advice, nor am I likely to. I'll thank you to leave me in peace. Get the hell out of here and don't let the door hit your *Sassunach* backside on the way out."

"Mr. Math—"

"Good day, sir."

There was a very long silence, then Jones closed his notebook, rose, and left. Dylan lay back on his pillows, satisfied he'd put enough suspicion on himself to keep the police off Bedford's back. They could hassle him all they wanted, but they couldn't convict him of stabbing himself. As much as he despised the *Sassunach* Major, his descendant had done nothing. Dylan wouldn't let the Yankee be imprisoned for something he hadn't done.

Dylan wished he could get out of the hospital. The room was stifling hot.

It took five days for him to finally escape the antiseptic stench and hospital food, but even then he couldn't go back to the dojo. His mother deemed it too risky for him to be by himself, so she talked him into staying in her guest room, which had once been his own bedroom. When she brought him home, she suggested he go upstairs to lie down. He obeyed and, sitting on the guest bed, he looked around at the strange room that had once been the center of his world.

Mom had redecorated in the years since he'd moved out for good after college. He'd been twenty-two then, and it almost didn't seem like the same room now. Unless he looked out the window at the view he'd grown up with, it was like any other generic guest room with a single bed, brass lamps from the eighties, and an oaken chest of drawers that had never been used except as a suitcase stand. The closet was full of large boxes of Christmas decorations that made the room smell of musty cardboard and decaying pine cones. Dylan pressed his hand to his side to still the lingering feeling his guts would spill if he let go.

He was home, sort of. For five days he'd avoided thinking about Cait and the others he'd known in the distant past. It almost felt like a dream, except for the knotted scars on his back, the thin white line on his left forearm, the nick out of his right ear, the thick white mark at the back of his left calf. . . .

He slipped Brigid under his pillow, screwed his eyes shut and lay back on the bed to clear his mind and make the world go away for a while.

His eyes half-closed, he drifted. His body relaxed for the first time since his return. As he lay there he took inventory of himself: the broken parts, missing parts, the weakened ones, as well as the parts of him that were still strong and perhaps tougher than before. Gradually the various pains diminished, and the world faded into silence and darkness. But he wasn't asleep. His eyelids were not closed, but he couldn't see. Alarm surged and he leapt from the bed. All around him was grayness, like fog at night. He tried to see his hand before him, but there was nothing. He tried to *feel* his hand. Nothing.

He turned and peered into the mist. "Where am I?" he asked the air, but got no answer. "Sinann?" No answer.

Then there was whispering. Many voices spoke around him, but softly and in a strange language. All around him. "Who are you?" There was no response, just more unintelligible whispering.

Above the voices there rose a Gaelic one that cut to his heart. Cait. She was praying, asking God for the safety of her beloved. "Cait!" Dylan called, but she didn't hear and only continued until her voice faded into the others.

In the next instant Dylan again felt his body around him— the aches and injuries—and found he was still lying on the bed. He sat up, and had to press his hand to his side as his dozens of stitches tugged at him. He whispered Cait's name, but knew nobody was there to answer. He sagged back onto the bed and lay still.

After a while he was called to lunch.

When he was finished eating, his mother parked him in front of the television to while away the hours watching movies on cable. He slept some, mostly out of boredom, and picked a book from the shelves in the living room. Toward the end of the day, though, he found himself tensing the way he always had this time of day when he was a kid. It was almost time for his father to come home.

Then it was past time for him to come, which was familiar, too. He'd most likely stopped for a drink on the way, and in a sense that was something of a relief. It meant Dylan might escape dealing with the old man for the evening.

Kenneth Matheson finally walked through the door after Dylan had eaten his supper. His mother was most likely sick from not eating while waiting until her husband would be home. Dylan heard him downstairs, his voice angry and growing louder. He was probably still throwing back the whiskey, and Dylan hoped the ogre would pass out soon. Again, that was as it had been all his life. He closed the bedroom door and lay on the bed with his book open in front of him. He read the same page over and over until he fell asleep.

For the next week Dylan avoided his father. His wounds healed, muscle knitted, the ache lessened, and he began walking on the property. It felt good to move freely again, and walking long distances had become second nature to him over the past couple of years. He was almost ready to return to the dojo, which would be a relief.

After a long walk one day he returned for supper to find his father's car in the driveway. He sighed. Eating with Dad was never good for the digestion or the blood pressure. He went inside.

His father sat in his leather club chair, watching television. "Hi," said Dylan.

The elder Matheson looked up. "Hello." He spoke in a normal tone, which meant he wasn't too far into the bag yet. But there was a glass on the end table at his elbow, containing only ice, and not much of it melted. It wouldn't be long before more whiskey followed. A bottle, in fact, stood on the coffee table, waiting to refill that glass.

Dylan sat in the Lesser Chair, the one meant for guests. It was the one he preferred because it was on the opposite side of the room from Dad's chair. Mom always sat at one end of the couch, if she sat at all. Right now she was bustling around in the kitchen.

Dad returned his attention to the movie on TV. *Butch Cassidy and the Sundance Kid.* Butch and Sundance were fleeing the Pinkerton agents, taking their horses over rocky terrain to thwart the trackers. Dylan sighed. Been there, done that. He looked at his father and realized he knew as much about a couple of nineteenth-century American bandits as he did about his most immediate ancestor. As he stared, he wondered why he had to be that way.

He'd never noticed before, but he now saw his father had the blue Matheson eyes that had been so common among the family and tenants of Iain Mór, the same eyes Malcolm had said saved Dylan from imprisonment as an English spy. When he was a boy, nobody had ever told him he looked like his father, nor any other Matheson, mostly because his coloring came from his mother's side. Dad and his brothers all had medium-brown hair and light skin. It was a small shock to realize that having his father's eyes probably had saved his life.

Dad refilled his glass from the bottle on the table, and when he set it down Dylan's attention was caught by the name on the label. He leaned forward for a closer look, but he hadn't imagined it. The name on the bottle, in old English style type, was *Glenciorram*. He moved to the sofa to pick up the bottle and read the small print, but learned only that the single-malt whiskey had been distilled in Ciorram, Scotland. *Duh.* He set it back onto the table and shook his head to rid himself of the willies. He told himself not to think too much, and let it slide to the back of his mind.

They sat in silence while Mom put supper on the table, then went to eat at one end of the long dining room table. Mom sat at the kitchen end, and Dylan and his father took seats on either side. Then Dylan saw the swelling in her lip.

She'd covered it with dark lipstick, but there was no hiding that her upper lip was swollen to twice its size and had been split since he'd seen her that morning. Dylan glared at his father, who was oblivious. He wanted to reach across the table and haul the old man out of his chair, but his mother laid a hand on his. Her eyes entreated him to keep still. He sat back in his chair with his arms crossed, wondering if his father would catch on, or if he was too drunk to see the anger.

Mom did her best to crank-start the conversation, though Dylan and his father both did their best to kill it. Finally she gave up on the safe subjects of church and television and said, "Dylan, how did your Games go? Except, of course, for how they ended."

Dad chuckled, his mean laugh. Another glass of whiskey sat at his place, half gone. "Other than that, Mrs. Lincoln, how did you like the play?"

It would have been funny, if the joke hadn't been delivered with an ugly snarl. Dylan ignored it, though, and said, "It was terrific. There was this sword there—a real claymore. It had . . . quite a history." If only he could tell it.

Mom surely didn't have the first idea what a claymore was, except that if it interested him it must be Scottish. She gave a smooth social smile and said, "You certainly know an awful lot about Scottish history."

He coughed and nodded. "More than most, I guess."

"I think that's so wonderful." She probably did. There wasn't much he did she didn't think was wonderful. Even at his age he loved that about her. "I heard on the news this morning there's talk about Scotland becoming independent of the United Kingdom."

He smiled. "There's been *talk* of Scottish independence for about a thousand years. At this point it's probably too complicated to ever sort out. I don't think there will ever be complete independence, any more than the South will ever rise again."

Mom sighed. "Yes, all those wars they had. It's a shame, I think. Perhaps there was another way. Perhaps they could have changed the system from the inside."

Dylan shook his head. "They were too often not part of the system. England wasn't a democracy back then."

"But did they need to go to war?"

He shrugged. "Do you think Americans shouldn't have had the Revolution?"

"Well, that's different. The Americans weren't English."

"They were. They just didn't live in England. Neither do the Scottish. And Highland Scots were even more culturally disparate from the English than the Americans were at the time. They should not only have fought like the Americans, but they should have won like them."

"Oh, shut up," said Dad. "Who gives a damn about Scotland anyway? Pansy men in dresses, is what they are."

Dylan sat back and crossed his arms, his eyes narrowed and irritation rising. "Just so you'll know, Dad, Highlanders in kilts are considered among the most formidable soldiers on earth." He could feel his acquired Scottish accent slipping in, and let it come. "And they've been known to throw fear into an enemy before firing a shot just for their courage in attack. They've been called *Ladies from Hell*, and by people who have faced them. If ye'd ever fought with yer pants off, ye'd never call such a soldier *pansy*. But then, I've come to expect that sort of ignorance from you."

Dad sputtered, then half rose from his seat. "You little prick . . ."

"Knock it off, Dad."

"Stop it, both of you!" Mom's voice was panicky and she stared at her plate. Dylan glared at his father while the man sat back down and drained his glass again. There was a long silence, then Mom attempted a wobbly laugh and said, "Eat up, you men. I've made chess pie for dessert."

The glass was slammed to the table and ice went flying. "Dammit, is that all you could think of to make? Chess pie. It's always chess pie."

"Dylan likes it." She should have known better than to even try to talk to him when he was like this, but Dylan figured if she stopped talking to him when he was a drunken asshole, she would never utter a word to him.

"I don't give a rat's ass what Dylan likes. What about what I like?"

"I thought you liked chess pie."

He took a swing at her, backhand, and missed as she made an expert dodge. "I don't!"

"*Hey!*" Dylan half-rose from his seat.

"Dylan, I'm all right." Mom was frightened now, and her eyes began to swim with tears.

Dad sneered at Dylan. "Shut up and eat your supper, boy. We've got your *favorite* for dessert."

Dylan sat back down. He had to struggle to keep his temper in check. He stared at his plate and picked at the food there. His appetite had fled. Now all he wanted was out of there.

Dad got up to refresh his drink, and slowly weaved his way down to the sideboard at the far end of the table where there was a decanter. Dylan reached for his water glass and accidentally-on-purpose knocked it over.

"Oh!" Mom leapt to her feet. "Let me get a paper towel!"

"How about some more water, too, Mom." He needed her to be gone long enough. As she hurried into the kitchen, he slipped his hand over his steak knife and rose from his seat. As quickly and silently as he'd learned in the woods and moors fleeing English soldiers and Montrose's men, he moved to meet his father at the end of the table, where he grabbed the old man by his shirtfront, twisted the fabric in his hand, and shoved him backward over the end of the table.

Dad's eyes bugged out, and he sputtered. "What the hell?"

He tried to rise, but Dylan shoved him back onto the table. The centerpiece jumped, and the candle in it flickered. "Get your fucking hands . . ." But Dad went silent when the point of the knife was pressed just below his solar plexus, pointed up toward his heart.

Dylan leaned on his father's chest, securing him with a thigh between his legs. "Listen to me," he said quickly, in a low voice thick with murderous intent, "I'm only going to say this once. You are a disgrace as a man and as a Matheson. One who cannae lead without unnecessary violence is not a man at all, but a coward." Through his teeth he said it in Gaelic, "*Tha thu gealtach!*" He twisted harder the shirt fabric in his fist.

His voice was still low. He hurried to finish before his mother came back. "You will be civil to my mother. God knows why she loves you, but she does, and that is the only thing that keeps me from slipping this knife into your black heart and ending this right here. Now, I am telling you, if you are not as sweet as pie to her from now until you die, I will make sure you die very soon." He pressed the point of the knife again to emphasize his meaning. "Do not ever do violence to her again, under any circumstances. Are you understanding me?"

His father nodded, and Dylan hauled him off his back just in time to be caught at it by Mom. He began brushing his father's shirt to smooth the wrinkles, and said, "Dad tripped. You should watch where your feet are going, Dad."

His father was far too shaken to speak. He left his glass on the sideboard and returned to his chair. Mom mopped up the spilled water and provided Dylan with a fresh glass. Dad made an excuse to leave the table.

Mom stared after him, puzzled. "Usually, he drinks until he can't stand and I have to make him comfortable where he passes out."

Dylan said, "Perhaps it's time he changed his ways. Aye?" His stomach was in knots. He'd just threatened his own father's life, and knew he would carry through if he saw his mother hurt again. He watched Mom eat, and wondered what sort of man he'd become.

CHAPTER 24

The next day he returned to his apartment. His Jeep had been taken there from Moss Wright Park by Ronnie the day of the Games, so his mother dropped him off. But first she made him promise to come to supper the following night. He kissed her cheek, then let himself in through the front glass door. He stopped dead just inside and let the door close automatically behind him.

He'd forgotten what the place looked like. For two years he'd thought of going home, and the memory had changed until details went missing: the stack of folded floor mats against the mirrored wall, the bulletin board sporting fliers about events that were still weeks away, the broken office window. Damn, he'd forgotten about that. Ronnie had covered the hole with plywood while Dylan was in the hospital. The past few weeks his assistant had covered all of Dylan's classes, and it seemed he was doing a fine job of running things. Good old Ronnie.

Out of curiosity he stepped on the scale by the mirrored wall. Even with clothing and the weight he'd gained since his return, he was still ten pounds lighter than the day he'd left two years ago. The reflection before him was of an angular, tough-muscled man with edges he'd never seen before. He'd never realized how much extra weight he'd once carried. But now all of it was gone, leaving taut skin over a strong but economical build. Once again he was shocked at how much he'd changed.

He went up the stairs to his living quarters. The place smelled odd. Familiar, but not how he remembered it. A faint bit of mildew drifted from the public showers downstairs. Warm electronic scent emanated from the TV set. Burnt dust blew from the furnace vents. He went to turn the thermostat down until the heat kicked off. Ever since his return he'd been uncomfortable in the heat. People kept thermostats way too high around here, particularly for such a warm climate.

He looked around, remembering. He wanted to be glad he was home, but it was all too unsettling. Anymore, he wasn't even sure he was glad to have survived the surgery.

The kitchen was as he'd left it, of course. Nobody had been upstairs since the day he'd left. He perked up, remembering, and reached into a ceramic cookie jar on the counter for a cinnamon jawbreaker. He'd always loved these things, and had missed them horribly for the first year of his absence. He squeezed it from its cellophane wrapper into his mouth, and as the cinnamon stung his tongue and wafted into his head he smiled. *Oh, yeah!* He rolled the sugary lump around in his mouth as he wandered into the bathroom. The towel he'd worn two years ago was draped over the toilet seat still.

It was too quiet here. There should be voices. Children chattering under the conversation of adults telling stories. Telling about themselves. Telling about things that were, or about things that might not have been but were true just the same. *There is no such thing as "just" a story.* He longed for someone to talk to, and even more to listen to. Ginny was history. She hadn't even visited him in the hospital, not that he still missed her after two years. Cody had her own life that only included him to a point. Everyone's life included him only to a point. A dark, antsy feeling crept up his back. He tried to sit in his living room, but couldn't be moved to pick up the TV remote. He could go to bed, but he didn't feel sleepy. He went back downstairs, left the dojo, and walked to Main Street, to a lakeside restaurant that had a bar.

There were people here, and that made him more comfortable. He sat at the bar and ordered ale, though he knew asking for ale in Tennessee was like looking for grits in New York or a burrito in Glasgow. When it came he sipped it, and though it was weaker than he cared for it was still better than beer. He looked around the room at neon signs, dark corners, and the fellow Americans he'd chosen for company that night.

A young couple played pool on one of the tables in the room, and he watched them knock balls around. The fellow was teaching his date how to handle a stick, and for each shot he snuggled up close behind as if readying to bang her right there. Then the girl, while waiting for her turn, idly stroked her cue stick as if she didn't know her boyfriend was watching. The guy strutted like a rooster, absolute master of the table. Dylan found himself amused by the none-too-subtle body language, which shouted to the room that two people were getting laid later on. Times had certainly changed, for that sort of behavior around Cait would have gotten him killed.

But with a small shock, Dylan realized that the strutting and flirting was neither more nor less sexually overt than the courtship he and Cait had experienced. It was merely more public, and he and Cait might not have behaved any different from these two had they been free to let the clan know they were courting. The young man and woman playing pool here tonight were allowed to be obvious because nobody around them gave a damn what they did. Dylan thought about all the people in Ciorram who had cared deeply about himself and Cait, each of whom would have been, however distantly, affected by the marriage. He wasn't sure modern attitudes were an improvement.

Soon, though, the young man noticed that he and his date were being watched. He looked up at Dylan and a deep frown creased his face. Dylan realized he was being nosy. He held up a reassuring palm of apology, and faced back to the bar.

Another man sat at the bar, by the window overlooking the lake, alone and looking like he expected to stay that way. He appeared to be in his forties, but had a well-worn air that said he felt much older. Dylan could tell there was a story there, but also knew he'd get a fat lip if he asked to hear it.

Dylan stared into his glass and thought about the last two years. His time in the past hadn't been fun. He'd not wanted it, and hated it at first, but in the end he'd found people he loved. Cait, especially. She alone had been enough to make him want to stay. The yearning for her now was so painful as to make him wish Sinann had let him die at Sheriffmuir. The distance between them when she had been in Edinburgh and he in Glen Dochart had been bad enough. But now the insurmountable distance of centuries was setting him adrift in ways he couldn't even comprehend. She was dead, and furthermore had been dead for . . .

Ciaran came to mind, and Dylan's heart clenched. He was gone by now, as well. The realization slammed into him so hard the room spun. Whatever life that had been given to his son had been over for centuries. He shuddered and took a deep slug of his drink, then stared into it some more.

All of them. Their lives had gone on without him, and now they were over. And his was continuing. Every passing moment took him farther and farther from them.

Shaken, Dylan finished his ale and left the bar.

At home, he wandered restlessly around his living room and told himself he should go to bed. His side ached, and sent pain shooting all down his left leg. But lying down didn't appeal to him. He paced along the low balcony wall, and stopped in front of the tall bookcase at the far end. Most of his books were about Scotland, and it crossed his mind he might find some of them laughable now. He reached for one about Scottish battles, and opened to the index. Glencoe, Killiecrankie, Culloden, but no Sheriffmuir. He put it back and selected another. This time he found a tiny bit about the day he'd nearly died. *One* of the days he'd nearly died.

It told how the left flank of each army at Sheriffmuir had been routed by the right flank of the other, which made him blink since he'd been part of the Jacobite left flank. "Damn," he muttered to himself. But, besides the fact that Mar had ultimately withdrawn, which Dylan had known even before the charge, the book offered nothing. Certainly nothing to indicate what had caused Mar's retreat.

He returned the book to its shelf, then picked up the phone, sat on the sofa, and dialed Cody's number. After two years, he could still do it from memory. Raymond answered the phone.

"Hi. Is Cody there?"

"Hang on a minute, Dylan." There was muffled shouting for Cody, then the phone clunked down. Shortly it was picked up.

"Hi, Dyl. How are you feeling?"

"Like I could walk to Edinburgh."

There was a pause at the other end, then a short, unsure laugh. "Okay. That sounded like something I should ask about."

He hesitated before speaking, and she waited. Finally he scooted down to lie on the sofa and said, his voice low and quiet, "What would you do for someone you loved?" He pressed a throw pillow to his sore side.

"Anything. I'd do anything for Raymond."

"If you had kids, what would you give up for them?"

"Everything." She made a humming noise and said, "You know, these are pretty elementary questions. What are you getting at?"

What *was* he getting at? What could he say that she would believe? He decided to tell it and see what might happen. "Would you believe me if I told you I've been in love for two years and have a son who was born last January?"

She snorted. "Not you. You'd have told me. Nice try, Matheson."

"No, I'm serious. What if, during the blink of an eye, I went away for two years, fell in love, almost got married, and fathered a baby?"

Now she was giggling. "Whatever you've been drinking, Dylan, you'd better check to see if the can says *Sterno*."

Maybe this wasn't such a good idea. He tensed, but pressed further. "You know those scars on my back?" Breathing was hard now, and he felt giddy, finally talking about what had happened.

She stopped giggling. "Uh huh." Good. She knew he was serious.

"You saw them. You know they're there. And you know I didn't have them the week before you saw them, right?"

"Right."

"But that's impossible, right?"

She paused, then, "Right."

"You saw me walk away from a sword fight uninjured, but then suddenly I was run completely through and covered with blood."

"Right. That was very weird."

"I was also covered with dirt, and my kilt was gone. Right? Suddenly I was wearing a baldric I'd never had before, and leggings. I had a dir . . . knife in my hand you'd never seen."

There was a very long pause, then she said slowly, "I don't remember the other stuff, and I thought they'd taken your kilt off to see where you were bleeding. But now that you mention it, you were different. You looked different. In the hospital I was shocked you were suddenly so skinny, and you . . . well, you looked older. A whole lot older. I thought it was the surgery."

"Not the surgery. Cody, I went back in time to 1713, where I met and fell in love with a woman named Caitrionagh, and we had a son. The reason I have scars on my back is that in 1714 I was arrested and tortured by the English army. My kilt was left on the battlefield at Sheriffmuir, in Scotland, on November 13, 1715, the last big battle of the Jacobite uprising of that year. That is how I was run through with an English cavalry sword just before I was returned to this century."

"Dylan, you're scaring me."

"Cody, I'm sane. You saw the whole thing. You asked about the scars. You know they can't be explained any other way. That claymore you found? It was enchanted by an Irish faerie. I touched it, and it sent me back almost three centuries. I was there for two years."

Cody considered that for a long, silent moment. Dylan held his breath. Then she said, "They tortured you?"

He closed his eyes with relief that she believed him. His voice went soft and low, remembering the dungeon at Ft. William. "Yeah."

"And you have a son?"

"His name is Ciaran. I never got to see him, but I wanted to."

"A son." Her voice held awe, and it seemed to take some effort to grasp the idea. Then she said, "Jesus, Dylan, you might have descendants living in Scotland right now."

He pressed the pillow harder against his side as his gut clenched. "Cody, no. I can't think about that. I can't think . . ."

"The baby's mother; what was she like?" Cody laughed. "Is it true what they say about nobody bathing or shaving back then? I mean, did she have hairy legs and armpits?"

Dylan had to chuckle, and thought a moment. "You know, I never noticed. By the time I even saw her legs, things like that didn't seem to matter. And people did, too, bathe. Just not all at once and hardly ever with hot water. Everything else there smelled so bad that sweat just wasn't that big a deal after a while. I loved the way she smelled. It was like . . ." he searched for a description, "she smelled . . . like sex feels."

She gave a soft laugh. "You loved her a lot, didn't you? I always knew you would fall like a ton of bricks once it happened to you."

He had to chuckle though his throat was tight. "Cody, I would walk through fire for her. She was tall, and strong. She could probably kick *my* butt if she wanted, but she was the sweetest, gentlest . . . she had a heart so big and soft you could curl up in it to sleep."

He tried to continue, but helplessness choked him again. "Cody, there's nothing I can do. It's all screwed up now. It's like I'm living my life backward. It's like I've suddenly been able to see who I am, and now I've got to go back to being who I am not."

"What can you do?"

"I don't know."

"You need to do something, Dylan. You sound miserable. I can't imagine what you're going through, not being able to see your baby. Or Caitrionagh."

"Cody, I don't even have the words to tell you." But he tried. They talked into the night and he told her his stories of three centuries ago. He talked about Sinann and told the story of the white hound, and of Fearghas MacMhathain's battle with the Vikings. He told of the cattle raids and robberies. There was no talk of the men he'd killed, for that was something he could never hope to make her understand. But he did tell her of the knife fight with Iain, and the hunting trip when he'd lost the tip of his ear. He laughed when she berated herself for not having noticed the nick, and it felt good to laugh.

In that conversation he found no answers for his situation, but being able to confess to Cody helped clear his mind. The traffic on Main Street was silent by the time he pushed the "talk" button on his phone, set it on the floor, and curled up on the sofa to sleep.

But there was no sleeping. He lay awake, listening to his heart beat. The world was silent and still, but his heart was thudding loud enough to hear. He was alive, and would continue to live, but most things he held dear were long dead. He sat up, and a queer shiver ran up his back. His body vibrated with the energy of his existence and his yearning. He stood, unable to contemplate sleep.

Brigid was with the bundle of clothing he'd brought from the hospital, and he slipped her into his belt. Then he left the apartment by the back door and clattered down the wooden stairs to the raggedy grass at the back of the building. The willow tree by the water's edge rustled in the slight breeze, and Dylan felt of the almost bare branches and yellowing leaves as he ducked under to his rowboat. Willow bark tea. The memory was strong.

The oars leaned against his boat, and he set them on the ground. Then he lifted the side so the boat slid off the blocks, and carefully heaved it over and upright. It whumped onto the grass and tottered there before coming to a rest at a tilt. Then he set the oars inside and went to the prow to drag the boat across the grass and into the water. There, he stepped in and shoved off with an oar, then he set the oars into their oarlocks and pulled onto the dark lake.

The lights from the volleyball courts on Main Street hid the stars as he rowed. Reflections danced on black water, and became small and still as he pulled down the inlet, away from the causeway, toward the main channel of the lake. Houses on either side were dark. Quiet. Trees rustled, and the breeze tossed his ragged hair around his face. Goose bumps rose, and he shivered them down.

He knew the power of his surroundings now. The water below him, the air around him, and the stars above each had their place in his existence. He felt of them, and sensed he was out of time. He didn't belong here. They told him to go home, but had little to say about how to get there. The trip down the inlet was slow as the dark shore slipped by on either side, and the world was silent but for the tiny splash of oars and their creaking in the locks.

There was a small island, covered with underbrush and trees, where the inlet met the main channel of the lake. He landed on the rocky shore and pulled his boat up until it was hidden by growth. Then he climbed the small hill to the center of the island, where a clearing had been made by illicit picnickers, and a fire pit had been dug. During high school, he'd partied here with friends often. It had been a gathering place for telling ghost stories and making out. Tonight he had something far more important in mind.

He gathered deadwood that was good and dry, and made a small fire that threw a thin line of white smoke into the air. He added to it a green branch of a cedar tree that grew nearby. Brigid he laid on the ground next to it so he could pull his shirt off over his head. Then he kicked off his shoes, peeled off his socks, and unbuckled his belt. His jeans dropped to the ground and he stepped out of them, then his shorts joined the pile. He shivered. A fluttering grew in his belly, and he took a deep breath. He felt the air around him, the moonlight on his skin, and laid a hand over the crucifix that rested against his chest. Cait's ring was still with it, and felt warm against his palm.

His pulse picked up. He took Brigid and stood by the fire to clear his mind and center himself. The breeze was soft on his body. The cedar smoke sharpened the air and his senses. Then he pointed Brigid straight into the fire and walked three times deiseil around it, knelt, and sat back on his heels with the blade point in the dirt and his hands resting on her hilt. He took a deep breath and let it out slowly, then stared into the fire and emptied his mind of everything. All doubts that this would work left him. Doubt would make it impossible.

Finally he spoke in a soft monotone, "*A null e, a nall e. Slàinte.* Dirk of fire, dirk of power, your breath of life gives life." A shock like electricity ran from his hands, through his arms, then into his body. Pain shot through his gut, and he struggled for breath, then gathered himself and plundered his mind for the words that would focus the power. "The purity and sanctity of the fire is yours. By that power, take me to Caitrionagh. Rejoin that which was riven. Make my soul one with hers. By the power of the sun and moon, let this be done."

For several minutes he sat and only breathed. The night became so comfortable he might have slept sitting up. The warmth of the fire on his skin dimmed as his senses numbed. As he focused, the more he concentrated, the warmer Brigid became under his hands. Then she began to glow with a silvery, moonlike light that shot out in rays between his fingers. It bathed him, and he could feel the power of the *broch* enter him.

When all seemed still and his body was relaxed, he closed his eyes and allowed Cait into his mind. Lovely Cait, the other half of his soul. So far away, and so long ago. Patiently he took himself back through the centuries, across the ocean, distances that stretched his ability until he thought he might not make it. Or he might not make it back to his body.

Then he was flying. Wings outstretched to either side, the long feathers were shiny and black. The night air rushed past him, both exhilarating and terrifying. He glided on, toward Edinburgh. The sun rose on the day the battle was being fought and the moment he was . . . dying.

He lit on a windowsill of a large house and saw her, dressed as he'd never seen her before, like an Englishwoman. Her hair was in a kerchief, and she knelt on the floor. Her eyes were red with crying and swollen with purple bruises. His mind called out to her. "Cait . . ."

"*A Dhilein.*" She looked around, searching.

Shaking took him, and tears stung his eyes. "*A Chait.*" His feathers ruffled and the winter wind blew them all around. Her voice was inside him, all through his body. He vibrated with her presence. His chest heaved as he gulped air and clung to the sill with clawed feet.

"Dylan, where are you?" Fresh tears came.

"I'm right here, sweetheart." His throat was so tight he could hardly make a sound.

But she was confused. He could feel it. "Where? Where are you? I cannae see you. Dylan, we're needing you. It's fearful here. So very fearful. I cannae see you." She began to cry. "Dylan, I miss you so much since they took you. I miss you. . . . Oh, Dylan . . ."

"I'm not dead, Cait. They didn't kill me. I miss you, too. How can I come back? Tell me how to get back."

"Get back?" There was a pause, then the sobbing grew louder. He sensed she was confused and couldn't understand. She couldn't know what was happening, nor even where he was. "Come to us."

"I can't. I'm trapped here by magic. I have no way home."

"Make them let you come back. Ask the wee folk. They'll ken. Go to the *Sidhe*. The faerie folk will help you. Please. Hurry. He's like to kill us. The danger is great."

Then suddenly she wasn't there. The emptiness was appalling. With a wild rush, he snapped back over the years and miles. He couldn't breathe. Pain shot through him. The separation was unbearable. A cry split the night air in Tennessee. He slumped over, and Brigid fell to the dirt. Tears ran down his face, and sobs took him. "*Cait*."

He knelt on all fours with his forehead pressed to the dirt, and his body shook with sobs until he thought he would break into small pieces.

He didn't belong here. Probably, he never had. He belonged with Cait, in whatever circumstance he would find himself when he got to her. It was what he was for, and always had been. He needed to find Sinann. Whatever it took, he needed to find her and make her send him . . . home.

CHAPTER 25

Dylan had his will drawn up the next day. He had no children—no living children, he reminded himself—so as soon as he was declared dead the bulk of his property would go to his mother. And according to Tennessee law his father would not automatically acquire control over any of it. In the testament part of the document he stated his hope that his mother would leave the abusive sonofabitch and live in the apartment over the dojo, but that was up to her. All he could do was make the property available to her.

Ten percent of the business went to Ronnie, and the will stated Dylan's hope that his assistant would continue to teach after Dylan's passing.

His Jeep he left to Cody. To facilitate the bequeathal, and as an excuse to talk to her, he called and asked her to keep it at her house while he made a trip to Scotland.

There was a very long silence on the other end, then she said, "You're not coming back, are you, Dylan?"

He hesitated before answering, but said, "I hope not."

There was another long silence, and he realized she was crying. She said, "I'm going to miss you."

"I must do this."

"I know. You won't live to see the twenty-first century,

but I think you were never meant to. I think you always were meant to live back then. I hope you find what you're looking for."

He thanked her, but knew it was entirely possible he wouldn't find anything at all. "I'll miss you. I did in the years I was gone."

She laughed through her tears. "You've been my best friend my whole life, Dylan. I'll never forget you. Hey, try to be famous so I can read about you in a book somewhere, okay?"

He had to laugh, because talking had become impossible.

There was little to pack for the trip. Just a few days' travel clothes, a new linen sark like the one he'd worn to the Games, his leggings and dirks, a bag of cinnamon jawbreakers, and a large bottle of aspirin.

He visited his mother the day before his flight to London, while Dad was out, to tell her he was going to Scotland.

"Oh, how nice!" she enthused, and hugged him. "Have a wonderful time, dear. Take pictures, and you'll have to tell me all about it when you come back."

His heart broke. Of course he couldn't tell her he wasn't coming back. There was no way for him to tell her goodbye the way he wanted. All he could say was, "Sure."

But there was one thing he needed to address. He sat on the sofa and she sat in the Lesser Chair, though Dad's chair would have been closer. So he moved to the other end of the sofa. "Mom," he hoped this wouldn't upset her, but knew it would, "have you ever thought about leaving Dad?"

She made a noise, and he couldn't tell if it was of anger or just surprise. She looked flustered. For a long time she sat, and a crease grew in her brow. He waited. Then she said, "Dylan, I have no place to go."

"If you did, then what?"

"Your father and I have been married for a long time, Dylan."

"Mom, he beats you. He humiliates you. He deserves to . . ." Dylan never finished the sentence. He knew if he weren't leaving he would eventually kill his father, and that would be the worst of all. "Mom, just promise me you'll think about it. And if the opportunity comes to move out, take it."

"Dylan . . ."

"Do you want to be free of him?"

Her fingers twisted, and she shrugged. "I would like him to stop."

"No, Mom. Do you want to be free? Because he's never going to stop. He's going to keep it up until one of you is dead. And it'll probably be you if you don't leave. Promise me, Mom. Tell me you'll move out if you can."

There was a long silence, and he waited again for a reply. Finally, she said, "All right, but I don't see how that will ever happen."

"You never know. Sometimes things are meant to happen and they surprise us."

She sighed. "All right, dear, I promise." Dylan knew she thought she was humoring him, but he also knew she would remember the promise once she'd inherited the dojo.

"And there's one other thing." He realized this was beginning to sound like a final goodbye, but he had to say this. "You know that guy I was named after?"

"Bob Dylan?"

He chuckled. "No, the other guy. Black Dylan Matheson, the Scottish highwayman Grandfather Matheson used to talk about. What do you know about him? Where does that story come from?"

Mom thought for a moment, then said slowly, "I think . . . I think it was in World War II. When your grandfather was stationed in England. He said he met an RAF officer there with the same name as his: James Matheson. They got to know each other and were talking about the history of the clan, and the other James told your grandfather about the highwayman in his family tree."

Dylan's pulse picked up. "Was the officer a direct descendant?"

She shrugged. "I'm afraid I don't know."

He lowered his head to hide his disappointment. "Have you ever thought about finding out more about Black Dylan?"

"No, not really." There was a puzzled edge to her voice.

"I hope you will. And try looking under the Gaelic for it, *Dilean Dubh*. I mean, I'm not certain but I think you might find out some interesting stuff."

"All right. I'll do that."

When he told his mother goodbye, he knew it would be forever. He hugged her and kissed her cheek, then hugged her again. It puzzled her, he could tell, but he was then able to make his trip without looking back.

He tried to sleep on the flight over to England, but fidgeted the entire way. Some sleep was to be had on the train from London to Glasgow, but it was intermittent. After Glasgow, his pulse picked up and he had to take deep breaths.

He'd come five thousand miles in a little over a day, and knew that soon such convenient travel would be impossible for him. Not to mention instantaneous long-distance communication would end, so would shopping off the rack, fresh fruit, and sanitation. But what he was going toward made all those things unimportant.

In Glasgow he rented a car and continued his journey north. The scenery rolling past was familiar, but strange. The mountains hadn't changed, but the moors and glens had certainly. Some forests were gone, and others had popped up, the land covered with Christmas-tree-looking firs that seemed out of place. The road, which hadn't existed even as a track in his time, crossed lands he'd traversed on foot many times, then went farther north, across the Highland line.

As he approached Ft. William, tension crept up his back and he had to shrug his shoulders and stretch his neck to keep his muscles from bunching into a knot. He'd not been back this way since his escape, and just being in that part of Scotland gave him the creeps. Though the town had changed so much as to be unrecognizable on any level, he recognized the surrounding mountains and knew the road was taking him straight to the fort.

Then he spotted the low, grass-covered stone walls on his left, and realized the thing had been torn down and the road ran straight through where it had been. It was gone. The place of torture where he'd almost lost his life hundreds of years ago was truly history. Only decayed remnants were left.

In shock, he buzzed through the two roundabouts beside

the ruins, and pulled over in front of a fast-food restaurant. He sat at the side of the road and leaned forward on the steering wheel to compose himself and bring under control a sudden fit of shaking, thankful and relieved that awful place had been destroyed. Looking back over his shoulder, he saw the site was now occupied by a grocery store and a train station. He was glad.

Finally he went back through the roundabouts and headed back up the road toward Inverness, up Glen Mór, then zagged to the northwest, then northeast again to the eastern tail of Glen Ciorram, where he again turned to the west and south. But he didn't go all the way into town. He didn't want to see it as it had become. He'd passed signs indicating to tourists directions to the castle, as well as the local whiskey distillery. The road and scattered houses he saw dotting the glen floor indicated the village itself would be far more changed than he wanted to see. He passed an historical marker bearing the words, "Queen Anne Garrison, 1707" and an arrow pointing along a road that meandered to his left. He shook his head and figured that nasty little bunkhouse must have changed a lot for it to attract tourists now.

On the approach before the curve in the glen, before coming within sight of the *Tigh*, he turned off at the little black and white sign with an arrow that indicated *"Broch Sidhe."* He parked in the small lot at the mouth of the tiny glen, got out of the car, then took from his pocket his passport and wallet, which he emptied of money and credit cards then dumped on the floor of the car. With his *sgian dubh*, which was still sharpened for shaving, he put a small slit in his left forearm across the old scar, and bled for a moment on the steering wheel and seat. Closure for Mom. He didn't want her to spend the rest of her life looking for him. Then he tore a strip of cloth from his T-shirt to bandage his arm, and left the car door hanging open.

He picked up his overnight bag to follow the flagstone walk, which looked quite old. It may have been there as long as a hundred years, but it was new to him. The tower had been preserved almost exactly as he'd last seen it, though the oak tree had grown and spread till almost the entire tower floor was now in shade. The grass was neatly groomed,

mown and Weed-wacked to perfection, and the black fungus
made a delicate design in the green. Dylan poked a finger
into the sod at his feet and found the dirt below just as red
as ever. Even the fallen pieces of stone from the walls looked
the same as before, though one section of wall was now held
up by steel rods set into the ground. The parking lot had
been empty, and so was the tower. The sun was about to set,
and this time of year, this far north, it set quickly.

"Sinann." Did he expect an answer? She had to still be
alive, and still be there, simply because any other possibility
was unthinkable. "Sinann. Please don't play games. I need
you."

There was a long wait, then he said again, unsure now,
"Sinann?" He sighed in disappointment at the silence.

"So you've learned my name." Her voice made his heart
leap. He spun to find her perched on the steps just below the
oak branches. Relief washed over him.

"Sinann, I want to go home."

"You are home. For two years, all I heard was *Send me
home, I wish to go home*, and now you're home and you're
still saying it." She looked tired. There was no aging on her
body, but her eyes were weary and her shoulders sagged.
"You were right, you know. History cannae be changed.
Naught would be accomplished by going back. The English
would still own Scotland, and the clans would still become
a thing of the past—a gimmick for selling plaid undergar-
ments to gawking tourists from the colonies. The language
is dying. Scotland is slave to the English government."

"That's not true."

Her eyebrows went up, but that was all. Her reaction was
alarming for its lack of her characteristic energy whether of
agreement or disagreement. "Indeed?"

"Oh, aye. Ask any American of mixed Scottish and English descent how they identify, and they'll tell you either
English or Scottish but rarely do they say British. Ask why
many of the most courageous and loyal soldiers in the English army wear kilts and until recently wore them into battle.
Ask why the place is known as Scotland and not North Brit-
ain as it was during the Clearances when sheep became more
important to the English than people. Ask why, though the

Sassunaich tried to destroy the language after the '45, it's
still not dead and in fact is being taught in schools for the
first time in centuries. Modern books are being published in
Gaelic . . . children's books and poetry, not just the Bible.
Ask why, Sinann, after almost three hundred years, Scotland
finally has its own parliament again. It's because we who
were not part of the system fought against it as long as we
could, and they . . . our descendants . . . still fight within the
system for the right to be who we are, and distinguishable
from the English. The resistance succeeded because it prevented complete subjugation and genocide. Sinann, we did
save our people."

"If it's accomplished, then why go back?"

Dumb question. "Cait."

"You want to steal her away from her lawful husband."

"I want to rescue her from a man who despises her. And
my son. I want to be a father to my son."

Sinann leaned toward him, her hands on her knees.
"Would you like to know what happened to them?"

"No! I want to be there!" His gut knotted, and his wound
ached so he pressed his hand to his side. Breathing became
difficult. "I want to make it happen and watch it happen. I
want to raise my boy and make sure he's safe from . . ." The
horror of the persecutions during Ciaran's lifetime slammed
into him and his throat tightened. "I have to make sure he's
going to live. Just like every other Scot who fought the English and their bigotry, I have to make sure my child doesn't
suffer subjugation and . . . genocide."

What Sinann had said earlier struck him. She'd finally
admitted history couldn't be changed. If that were the case,
then she would already know whether or not he'd returned
to the past because she would remember seeing him there.
He looked around at the stone blocks that were where they'd
always been. The large one under which he'd hidden his
guineas lay exactly where he'd left it. He went behind it and
dug his fingers under the edge for purchase.

"What are you doing?"

"Just checking." He pulled hard to dislodge the stone from
its seat, then took a deep breath and lifted. His side ached,

and the pain sharpened as he strained, but slowly the stone tilted up to stand on its side.

"What's under there?"

"Something you don't know about." He dug through the muck where it had lain, and found no coins. But what he did find took him by surprise. A piece of cellophane stuck to his fingers and he pulled it from the mud. Some spit and a wipe across the grass revealed printing on the plastic. It was the wrapper from a cinnamon-flavored jawbreaker. He stood and said to Sinann, "You're going to send me back."

"How do you figure that?"

He threw his modern cash and credit cards into the mud under the rock, to add to the appearance he'd left of his murder, then went around and shoved the stone back down where it had been.

He turned toward Sinann and sat on the chunk of stone as he wiped his muddy fingers on his jeans. "You said you can't change history. You were waiting for me here, and I'll bet you knew I was coming, which you wouldn't have known if you hadn't sent me back. You didn't know about the gold pieces I left under this rock the day I was arrested. Nobody did, not even Cait." Then he held up the bit of plastic in his fingers. "This is a wrapper from a cinnamon jawbreaker, which is one of my few weaknesses, and it's been there a long time. I'm willing to bet it was left by me after my return to the past."

"You dinnae ken that."

"But you do. You know I was never meant to see the twenty-first century. You know there are no accidents, and you were meant to send that sword after me. You also know you're going to send me back, but you just want to give me grief before you do."

A tiny smile curled her mouth. "As you modern folk would say, I'm busted." Her smile left. "But what you also dinnae ken is this: you see, young Dylan, I was there the day you died for true. It was a black, terrible day, and all that heartened me was I knew I would see you once more when you would come to me now. After I send you back, I'll not be seeing you ever again." She paused and looked up to the purpling sky. Her eyes shone with grief. "I've had a long

life, and the ending of it will be lonely. The faeries left in
this world are too few, and mortals no longer ken the *Sidhe*.
I'll be missing you terribly."

A lump rose to his throat. "I hadn't realized—"

"Of course not. You humans all think the *Sidhe* have nae
feelings." Tears spilled to her face and her voice tightened.
"Go. Leave me." She raised her hand to do it.

"Wait!"

She sighed. "What is it now?!"

He began kicking off his shoes and went to dig into his
overnight bag. His jeans he shed and dropped on the ground,
then his T-shirt and jockey shorts. He strapped on his *sgian
dubh*, pulled on the sark and his baldric with the empty scabbard, then strapped his leggings on with Brigid in her accustomed place. His new rubber-soled suede boots went back
on, then he stood facing Sinann. "Ready." Then, "Oh, wait!"
He dug through the bag again and came back with the plastic
bag filled with cinnamon jawbreakers and the bottle of aspirin he'd brought, which he patted flat and secured under
the straps of his left legging. "Now."

Sinann fluttered down to him. She gazed at him a moment, and he could see her heart breaking. "You're my *Cuchulain*, Dylan Robert Matheson, my hero. I care for you
more than you can know." She laid a hand aside his cheek.
"Goodbye forever, brave one." Sinann raised her hand again,
and a tiny smile curled the corners of her mouth. "And say
hello to myself, would ye?"

"I will."

"I know." She waved her hand, and the world began to
go dark. She burst into tears, then was gone.

When the light returned, once again he found himself on
the battlefield of Sheriffmuir, standing where he'd been the
moment he was wounded. The battle raged around him, and
he picked his sword off the ground to defend himself against
an English dragoon that swept down on him. One quick parry
and thrust, and the red-coated soldier died, stabbed in the
throat. Sinann was there, gawking like she was seeing a
ghost.

"You're alive! Did I do that?" she asked, astonished.

"Nae, ye did not." Dylan, overjoyed to see her, scabbarded his sword, took her face between his hands, and kissed her forehead. Grinning, he shouted over the battle around them, "But yourself says hello." Then he took her by the waist and lifted her into the air. "Fly!" He threw her skyward and she flew. "It's not safe down here!"

Dylan drew the sword again, looked around, and realized no time had passed since his wounding. Horses screamed and wounded men cried out among the trampled heather. Blood was everywhere, and Dylan's new shoes slipped in it on the rocky, muddy ground. For one horrifying moment he realized the puddle in the stone he stood on was his own blood, but he shook that from his mind and turned to engage another dragoon who rode down on him with sword cocked for attack.

The Jacobites were still retreating, scattered hopelessly among the low hills, and Dylan fell back before the English horse, almost to the river, protecting his back but otherwise accomplishing nothing. By the time the English began to lay off, the Jacobite ranks were torn to shreds. It was plain Mar's troops were beaten.

Dylan, not recovered enough from surgery for stamina, gasped and pressed his hand to his aching side. He needed to find Mar, but couldn't see where the battle commander had gone. Then, at the top of the distant muir, Mar appeared with a large contingent of men that had been separated from the units that now had their backs to the river. The Hanoverians, when they saw the approach of Jacobites behind, were called off to face the group on the hill. The Jacobite men below waited, breathless, expecting Mar to charge so their own remnants could harass from behind, but the command never came. The Hanoverians were allowed to regroup and face the Jacobites above.

Dylan then knew this was Mar's fatal mistake. If the Earl would attack Argyll just then, he had a chance to beat the Hanoverians and gain a victory that would have galvanized the uprising. Dylan knew this, and so must have many men there that day. But there was no way for Dylan to urge the attack, even if Mar would listen. Argyll's troops stood between him and the man Dylan would need to convince in order to change the outcome of the battle. He stood and stared at the bewigged, aristocrat Mar, willing him to see his error, but knew it was no use. He couldn't change anything because even his presence wasn't change. He'd always been a part of this history.

The beaten Jacobite forces by the river lay, exhausted and bloody, while Mar's relatively fresh troops retained the hill. Dylan watched the standoff, cursing Mar under his breath. Darkness fell, swiftly as it did this time of year, and Mar quit the hill, moving off the muir, letting Argyll have the battlefield and leaving the exhausted men by the river to make their own way to safety.

The battle was over. The uprising was as good as over. Across the bloodied ground Argyll's men were plundering the dead and murdering wounded Jacobites with their bayonets. Dylan spat, frustrated and angry, and knew it was time to get the hell out and tend to his own business in Edinburgh. Many of the men around him felt the same way and began to disperse to the north, across the river. Dylan spotted a stray English cavalry horse nearby, grazing idly in the twilight, and took a run toward it. He hauled himself into the saddle in a single motion, picked up the reins, and wheeled toward the hills where Argyll's men were now going through the Highlanders' kilts and sporrans.

A shout came from the MacGregors behind him, a familiar voice. "*A Dhilein Dubh nan Chlaidheimh!*"

Dylan stopped and wheeled back. Black Dylan of the Sword. He was not surprised. He'd known sooner or later he'd be named for his coloring. He recognized the voice. "Seumas!" He peered into the thickening dusk at a figure that had just topped a low rise.

"Where are you going?" Seumas Glas was a large, dark shadow. The MacGregor reinforcements had arrived, but far too late.

"*A Chaitrionagh!*" shouted Dylan. With that, he wheeled once more and charged toward the muir which happened to stand between himself and Hanoverian-occupied Edinburgh. Hovering, Sinann zoomed up behind him and followed.

Over the next rise, he found the *Sassunaich* going through the thousands of kilts and sporrans left on the ground by the Jacobite army, and finding little more than threadbare wool and sacks of oatmeal. He reined in, and his anger surged at the sight of the English thieves rummaging for money and valuables. One Redcoat in the midst of them was removing a black sporran from a reddish-brown-and-black kilt. The belt and a length of plaid dangled from the bundle, the belt buckled into a loop. Dylan crouched over his horse's neck and urged it into a gallop, straight for the *Sassunach*, blowing past one surprised dragoon after another. In passing the man with his kilt, he reached down to yank kilt and sporran by plaid and belt from the astonished Englishman's hands.

He was almost to the muir when a shout finally went up. Gunfire popped, and musket balls whizzed past his head like bumblebees from hell. He urged his horse to greater speed, holding his kilt aloft, the end of the long plaid flapping behind him like a Highland flag, and defiant laughter burst from him. He made a level spot on a rise just below the muir, reined in, and wheeled to face the Redcoats. Holding his kilt over his head, he shouted to the English with every shred of his soul, *"Alba gu brath!"* Scotland forever! Then he threw back his head and uttered a blood-curdling Rebel Yell. As the *Sassunaich* took aim for another volley, Black Dylan wheeled again and bolted for Edinburgh and Cait.

POSTSCRIPT

The events in this story happened. Except, of course, for the bits I made up. Though many of these incidents were not uncommon in the place and period, the fictional characters are not based on actual people. Glen Ciorram does not, and never did, exist ("ciorram" means "disaster" or "maiming" in Scots Gaelic), and none of the Mathesons nor Bedfords in this story are meant to represent historical members of Clan Matheson nor the Bedford family.

However, the characters that *were* drawn from history are as true as possible to what is known about them. They are: Rob Roy MacGregor and his sons; Iain Glas Campbell of Breadalbane; Alasdair Roy; Alasdair MacGregor of Balhaldie; James Graham, fourth Marquis of Montrose; John Erskine, sixth Earl of Mar; John Campbell, second Duke of Argyll; Alexander Gordon of Auchintoul; John Dalrymple, Scotland Secretary of State; Queen Anne of England; King George I of England; King James VIII of Scotland; Cuchulain of Muirthemne; Sinann Eire, granddaughter of the sea god, Lir.

On spelling: In the early eighteenth century, spelling was a dodgy affair any way one looks at it. Standardized spelling in English didn't come along for another century at least, and for Gaelic it didn't happen until the latter part of the twentieth century. The spellings for Gaelic words in this book are from the MacLennan dictionary, which tends to the archaic and therefore lends itself to the period. All other words are either English or dialect words used by English-speaking Scots, and for the sake of internal consistency are spelled according to American usage.

Email J. Ardian Lee at ardian@sff.net, or visit the newsgroup news://news.sff.net/sff.people.ardian.